PENGUIN BOOKS

TH
CLASSIC

Julian Symons made a reputation before the Second World War as the editor of *Twentieth-Century Verse*, a magazine which published most of the young poets outside the immediate Auden circle. He has since become a celebrated writer of crime fiction and is also recognized as the greatest British expert on the genre. His history of the form, *Bloody Murder*, was called by Len Deighton 'the classic study of crime fiction', and was awarded the Mystery Writers of America Edgar Allan Poe Award in 1973. He has also written extensively about real-life crime in *A Reasonable Doubt* and *Crime and Detection from 1840*, and has written many articles on the historical background of both real and fictional crime. In 1976 he succeeded Agatha Christie as the President of the Detection Club, and was made a Grand Master of the Swedish Academy of Detection in 1977. He was created a Grand Master by the Mystery Writers of America in 1982. Mr Symons also has a separate reputation as a biographer and as a social and military historian. In 1975 he was made a Fellow of the Royal Society of Literature. His recent crime works include *Sweet Adelaide*, *The Detling Murders*, *The Tigers of Subtopia and Other Stories* and *The Name of Annabel Lee*. Several of his books are published in Penguins.

The Penguin

CLASSIC CRIME OMNIBUS

edited by
Julian Symons

PENGUIN BOOKS

Penguin Books Ltd, Harmondsworth, Middlesex, England
Penguin Books, 40 West 23rd Street, New York, New York 10010, U.S.A.
Penguin Books Australia Ltd, Ringwood, Victoria, Australia
Penguin Books Canada Ltd, 2801 John Street, Markham, Ontario, Canada L3R 1B4
Penguin Books (N.Z.) Ltd, 182–190 Wairau Road, Auckland 10, New Zealand

—

First published 1984

This collection copyright © Julian Symons, 1984
All rights reserved

—

Typeset, printed and bound in Great Britain by
Hazell Watson & Viney Limited,
Member of the BPCC Group,
Aylesbury, Bucks
Set in VIP Baskerville

Contents

Acknowledgements

Ernest Bramah: 'The Coin of Dionysius', from *Max Carrados*, published by Methuen, London.

John Dickson Carr: 'The Proverbial Murder', from *The Third Bullet*. Reproduced by kind permission of David Higham Associates Ltd.

G. K. Chesterton: 'The Wrong Shape'. Reprinted by permission of Dodd, Mead and Company Inc. from *The Innocence of Father Brown* by G. K. Chesterton. Copyright © 1911 by Dodd, Mead and Company. Copyright renewed 1938 by Frances B. Chesterton. Acknowledgement is also made to Miss D. E. Collins, Cassell Ltd and A. P. Watt Ltd.

Agatha Christie: 'The Submarine Plans', from *Hercule Poirot's Early Cases*. Reprinted by permission of Dodd, Mead and Company Inc. from *Hercule Poirot's Cases* by Agatha Christie. Copyright © 1925 by Agatha Christie. Copyright renewed 1952 by Agatha Christie Mallowan.

Edmund Crispin: 'Who Killed Baker?', from *Fen Country*. Reprinted by permission of Walker and Co. Inc., A. P. Watt Ltd, Mrs Ann Montgomery, Geoffrey Bush and Victor Gollancz Ltd.

Ursula Curtiss: 'Change of Climate'. Acknowledgement is made to the author. Copyright © 1967 by Ursula Curtiss. First published in *Ellery Queen's Mystery Magazine*. Reprinted also by permission of A. M. Heath and Co. Ltd.

Roald Dahl: 'The Landlady'. Reprinted by permission of Murray Pollinger. Copyright © 1959 by Roald Dahl. From *Kiss Kiss*, published by Michael Joseph Ltd and Penguin Books Ltd. Also reproduced by permission of Alfred A. Knopf Inc.

Stanley Ellin: 'The Question', from *The Blessington Method*. Reprinted by permission of Curtis Brown Ltd. Copyright © 1962 by Stanley Ellin.

William Faulkner: 'Smoke', from *Knight's Gambit*. Reproduced by permission of the author's literary estate, Chatto and Windus Ltd, and Alfred A. Knopf Inc.

Introduction

In her magisterial introduction to the first of three volumes called *Great Short Stories of Detection, Mystery and Horror*, Dorothy L. Sayers emphasized the unquestionable truth that the detective story began as a short tale, not as a novel. She went on to take as starting-points extracts from 'the Jewish Apocrypha, Herodotus and the Aeneid', rather over-enthusiastically because these are only puzzles or battles of wits, and not tales in which detection plays a major part. But no matter. Whether one traces the detective story's origins to the Bible, or Voltaire's *Zadig* or, as I should, to Poe, the important thing is that the short story preceded the novel.

In the latter part of the nineteenth century it developed into a tale that could be read comfortably at a sitting, a tale containing some kind of puzzle to which an investigator found the solution. The puzzle might be that of a locked room, or of a cipher to be decoded, like Poe's 'Murders in the Rue Morgue' and 'The Gold-Bug', a parody of detective work such as Wilkie Collins's 'The Biter Bit', or a tale in which the detective's personality was more important than the problems he solved, like Sherlock Holmes's adventures, but its aim was to occupy an idle hour. With the spread of railway travel, and the increasing popularity of magazines devised to make the journey pass pleasantly, the detective short story was much in demand. Queues formed at railway station bookstalls to buy the *Strand Magazine* containing the latest Holmes story. And, as Sir Hugh Greene has shown in his selections from other Victorians and Edwardians, Holmes had many rivals, although they were all his inferiors.

Any collection of classic tales must include some of these stories, which were often immensely ingenious, although their creators had no space and little inclination for subtleties of characterization. The readers of the time wanted adventure and excitement, and would have found psychological themes and speculations very much out of place. But literary forms change, especially if their popularity depends directly upon social circumstances. Just as the replacement of the three-volume novel by the single-decker meant an enlargement of and a change in the book-buying public, so the later development of the motor car and the steady decrease in rail travel spelled the decline of the short story. It remained the dominant form of crime fiction until the end of the First World War, and was then gradually replaced by the novel. The increase of leisure for housewives given by labour-saving devices in the twenties and thirties, and the spread of libraries through which fiction could be borrowed cheaply (in those days public libraries gave only a tiny part of their budget to crime fiction), meant that many of the new detective novelists were women. From hundreds of Boots' and Smith's branches throughout Britain the works of Christie, Sayers, Allingham and many others now forgotten were borrowed for twopence a week. A single long tale was preferred to a number of short ones, and by the thirties few collections of short stories were being published. The anthologies edited by Sayers, of which the first appeared in 1928, were successful because they *were* anthologies, containing the work of many writers. It became, and remains, publishing wisdom that volumes of short stories by a single writer do not sell.

In the last fifty-odd years this situation has not greatly changed: yet the short story has survived, and even flourished. It has in the hands of the best practitioners a tautness and sharpness often lacking in the full-length novel. Effects can be produced – macabre, baffling, gruesomely comic – that make similar attempts in the novel seem ponderous. The short story exploits a single theme, strikes throughout a particular note, and so possesses unity and a distinctive shape. It is not, or should not be, a novel cut down and with all characterization removed, so that only the puzzle remains. The crime short story has its own form, and when successfully realized offers a pleasure different from that given by the full-length book. Writers were drawn to it, even in the years when it was most thoroughly in the doldrums, because of the problems it posed.

Some of those problems are recent. Sayers remarked in 1928 that 'the mystery-monger's principal difficulty is that of varying his surprises', and saw signs 'that the possibilities of the formula are becoming exhausted'. It is a mark of the crime story's flexibility that although the form and the formulas have changed, there are still new ways of creating surprise, always a fresh trick to be turned. Some of these tricks are mechanical, so that where once a poisonous stamp produced a corpse, now a computer game is programmed to kill the player: but the most interesting reflect the shifts in our attitude to crime and punishment in the twentieth century, as do some of the stories in this collection.

There are three reasons for choosing the twenty-five stories printed here. The first is personal enjoyment. No anthology is worth much if it does not reflect to some degree the editor's preferences. In the crime story mine are for ingenuity and imagination, controlled always by some degree of realism. Tales of the supernatural, semi-science-fiction mysteries about the future, do nothing to quicken my pulse, and very few short spy stories seem to me successful. (The rare exceptions, like Maugham's Ashenden tales, were too long for inclusion.) Long police procedural stories seem to me much better than short ones.

I looked also for variety and novelty. When reading a collection of stories I am pleased if they vary in length and style. Accordingly there are very short stories here, like those by Graham Greene and Patricia Highsmith, and long, comparatively leisurely ones by Doyle, Faulkner and Queen. A very short story tends to be anecdotal rather than reflective, but I enjoy anecdotes although I would not want to read a book that was filled with them. The variety here extends to subjects and styles. The range is deliberately wide, including samples of American Bizarre, Domestic Documentary, Venus Flytrap and Outrageous Last Line.

And the question of novelty inevitably concerned me, in a way that it did not trouble an editor collecting stories half a century ago. Anthologies have proliferated since the Second World War, collections of 'best mysteries' of almost every conceivable kind being put between covers – best detective, best thriller, spy, psychological, locked room, gourmet, sport, tales of poisoning – the list is not exhaustive. There are stories which have appeared so often in anthologies that they are familiar to everybody who reads crime stories. Aldous Huxley's 'The Gioconda Smile' is one, Roald Dahl's 'Lamb to the Slaughter' another, John Dickson Carr's 'The Gentleman from Paris' a third. These are all excellent tales, sometimes the best things their writers have done in the crime field, and it would have been easy to make a book of them, working from other anthologies as lazy editors of poetry anthologies sometimes do. But I have looked for good things less familiar, in one case including a story never reprinted after its prize-winning appearance more than thirty years ago.

Of course, such a story is and must be a rarity. Poe and Doyle must be in a collection like this one, and everything they wrote in the criminal line is well known, but there are cases in which I have preferred freshness to fame. Are the stories included as good as those left out? Often, but not always. To take a single example, Chesterton's 'The Queer Feet' is probably the finest of all Father Brown stories, but it has been too much anthologized. The less-known 'The Wrong Shape', included here, is both ingenious and delightful. Everything has been chosen because it seems to me good of its kind, but to stick on a label like 'the best' would be both presumptuous and meaningless. What I can almost guarantee is that the most passionate addict of fictional crime and detection will find between these covers tales that are enjoyable and unfamiliar.

Julian Symons

Ambrose Bierce

A WATCHER
BY THE DEAD

Ambrose Gwinett Bierce, who was probably born in 1842 and disappeared in revolutionary Mexico in 1913, remains an underestimated writer. When his *Collected Works* were ignored or coolly received on their publication in 1912 he published a typical couplet:

> Mark how my fame rings out in every zone,
> A thousand critics shouting: 'He's unknown!'

Bierce was the Mencken of his time, a savage and sometimes crude satirical writer who scourged literary men, social aspirants and politicians equally, in weekly columns written for various papers. On one occasion, when he learned that the president of a company he was attacking also owned the paper Bierce edited, he threatened to expose the man unless he sold his shares in the paper – which, astonishingly, he did. Bierce later spent twenty years as a writer for the *Examiner*, the paper given to William Randolph Hearst by his father. In San Francisco he was called 'Almighty God Bierce' from his initials, and his journalistic power was great.

Much of Bierce's writing was topical, and has no interest today. His verses, *Black Beetles in Amber*, are no more than vigorous and competent, and although the *Devil's Dictionary* remains alive and apposite (*'impeccable* – not liable to detection, *immoral* – inexpedient, *impostor* – a rival aspirant to public honors', are three definitions taken from a single page), it is the stories he wrote at intervals throughout his life that keep his name known today. Some, like 'My Favorite Murder', told by the exultant murderer ('In point of atrocity my murder of Uncle William has seldom been excelled'), set out to shock and fully succeed, others are dramatic and melodramatic, the best macabre and wholly original. *In The Midst of Life*, the best collection, contains some masterly stories. 'A Watcher by the Dead' is one of them.

I

In an upper room of an unoccupied dwelling in that part of San Francisco known as North Beach lay the body of a man under a sheet. The hour was near nine in the evening; the room was dimly lighted by a single candle. Although the weather was warm, the two windows, contrary to the custom which gives the dead plenty of air, were closed and the blinds drawn down. The furniture of the room consisted of but three pieces – an arm-chair, a small reading-stand, supporting the candle, and a long kitchen-table, supporting the body of the man. All these, as also the corpse, would seem to have been recently brought in, for an observer, had there been one, would have seen that all were free from dust, whereas everything else in the room was pretty thickly coated with it, and there were cobwebs in the angles of the walls.

Under the sheet the outlines of the body could be traced, even the features, these having that unnaturally sharp definition which seems to belong to faces of the dead, but is really characteristic of those only that have been wasted by disease. From the silence of the room one would rightly have inferred that it was not in the front of the house, facing a street. It really faced nothing but a high breast of rock, the rear of the building being set into a hill.

As a neighbouring church clock was striking nine with an indolence which seemed to imply such an indifference to the flight of time that one could hardly help wondering why it took the trouble to strike at all, the single door of the room was opened and a man entered, advancing toward the body. As he did so the door closed, apparently of its own volition; there was a grating, as of a key turned with difficulty, and the snap of the lock bolt as it shot into its socket. A sound of retiring footsteps in the passage outside ensued, and the man was, to all appearance, a prisoner. Advancing to the table, he stood a moment looking down at the body; then, with a slight shrug of the shoulders, walked over to one of the windows and hoisted the blind. The darkness outside was absolute, the panes were covered with dust, but, by wiping this away, he could see that the window was fortified with strong iron bars crossing it within a few inches of the glass, and embedded in the masonry on each side. He examined the other window. It was the same. He manifested no great curiosity in the matter, did not even so much as raise the sash. If he was a prisoner he was apparently a tractable one. Having completed his examination of the room, he seated himself in the armchair, took a book from his pocket, drew the stand with its candle alongside and began to read.

The man was young – not more than thirty – dark in complexion, smooth-shaven, with brown hair. His face was thin and high-nosed, with a broad forehead and a 'firmness' of the chin and jaw which is said by those having it to denote resolution. The eyes were grey and steadfast, not moving except with definitive purpose. They were now for the greater part of the time fixed upon his book, but he occasionally withdrew them and turned them to the body on the table, not, apparently, from any dismal fascination which, under such circumstances, it might be supposed to exercise upon even a courageous person, nor with a conscious rebellion against the opposite influence which might dominate a timid one. He looked at it as if in his reading he had come upon something recalling him to a sense of his surroundings. Clearly this watcher by the dead was discharging his trust with intelligence and composure, as became him.

After reading for perhaps a half-hour he seemed to come to the end of a chapter and quietly laid away the book. He then rose, and, taking the reading-stand from the floor, carried it into a corner of the room near one of the windows, lifted the candle from it, and returned to the empty fireplace before which he had been sitting.

A moment later he walked over to the body on the table, lifted the sheet, and turned it back from the head, exposing a mass of dark hair and a thin face-cloth, beneath which the features showed with even sharper definition than before. Shading his eyes by interposing his free hand between them and the candle, he stood looking at his motionless companion with a serious and tranquil regard. Satisfied with his inspection, he pulled the sheet over the face again, and, returning to his chair, took some matches off the candlestick, put them in the side-pocket of his sack coat and sat down. He then lifted the candle from its socket and looked at it critically, as if calculating how long it would last. It was barely two inches long; in another hour he would be in darkness! He replaced it in the candlestick and blew it out.

II

In a physician's office in Kearny Street three men sat about a table, drinking punch and smoking. It was late in the evening, almost midnight, indeed, and there had been no lack of punch. The eldest of the three, Dr Helberson, was the host; it was in his rooms they sat. He was about thirty years of age; the others were even younger; all were physicians.

'The superstitious awe with which the living regard the dead,' said Dr Helberson, 'is hereditary and incurable. One need no more be ashamed of it than of the fact that he inherits, for example, an incapacity for mathematics, or a tendency to lie.'

The others laughed. 'Oughtn't a man to be ashamed to be a liar?' asked the youngest of the three, who was, in fact, a medical student not yet graduated.

'My dear Harper, I said nothing about that. The tendency to lie is one thing; lying is another.'

'But do you think,' said the third man, 'that this superstitious feeling, this fear of the dead, reasonless as we know it to be, is universal? I am myself not conscious of it.'

'Oh, but it is "in your system" for all that,' replied Helberson: 'it needs only the right conditions – what Shakespeare calls the "confederate season" – to manifest itself in some very disagreeable way that will open your eyes. Physicians and soldiers are, of course, more nearly free from it than others.'

'Physicians and soldiers; – why don't you add hangmen and headsmen? Let us have in all the assassin classes.'

'No, my dear Mancher; the juries will not let the public executioners acquire sufficient familiarity with death to be altogether unmoved by it.'

Young Harper, who had been helping himself to a fresh cigar at the sideboard, resumed his seat. 'What would you consider conditions under which any man of woman born would become insupportably conscious of his share of our common weakness in this regard?' he asked, rather verbosely.

'Well, I should say that if a man were locked up all night with a corpse – alone – in a dark room – of a vacant house – with no bed-covers to pull over his head – and lived through it without going altogether mad – he might justly boast himself not of woman born, nor yet, like Macduff, a product of Caesarean section.'

'I thought you never would finish piling up conditions,' said Harper; 'but I know a man who is neither a physician nor a soldier who will accept them all, for any stake you like to name.'

'Who is he?'

'His name is Jarette – a stranger in California; comes from my town in New York. I haven't any money to back him, but he will back himself with dead loads of it.'

'How do you know that?'

'He would rather bet than eat. As for fear – I dare say he thinks it some cutaneous disorder, or, possibly, a particular kind of religious heresy.'

'What does he look like?' Helberson was evidently becoming interested.

'Like Mancher, here – might be his twin brother.'

'I accept the challenge,' said Helberson, promptly.

'Awfully obliged to you for the compliment, I'm sure,' drawled Mancher, who was growing sleepy. 'Can't I get into this?'

'Not against me,' Helberson said. 'I don't want *your* money.'

'All right,' said Mancher; 'I'll be the corpse.'

The others laughed.

The outcome of this crazy conversation we have seen.

III

In extinguishing his meagre allowance of candle Mr Jarette's object was to preserve it against some unforeseen need. He may have thought, too, or half thought, that the darkness would be no worse at one time than another, and if the situation became insupportable, it would be better to have a means of relief, or even release. At any rate, it was wise to have a little reserve of light, even if only to enable him to look at his watch.

No sooner had he blown out the candle and set it on the floor at his side than he settled himself comfortably in the armchair, leaned back and closed his eyes, hoping and expecting to sleep. In this he was disappointed; he had never in his life felt less sleepy, and in a few minutes he gave up the attempt. But what could he do? He could not go groping about in the absolute darkness at the risk of bruising himself – at the risk, too, of blundering against the table and rudely disturbing the dead. We all recognize their right to lie at rest, with immunity from all that is harsh and violent. Jarette almost succeeded in making himself believe that considerations of that kind restrained him from risking the collision and fixed him to the chair.

While thinking of this matter he fancied that he heard a faint sound in the direction of the table – what kind of sound he could hardly have explained. He did not turn his head. Why should he – in the darkness? But he listened – why should he not? And listening he grew giddy and grasped the arms of the chair for support. There was a strange ringing in his ears; his head seemed bursting; his chest was oppressed by the constriction of his clothing. He wondered why it was so, and whether these were symptoms of fear. Suddenly, with a long and strong expiration, his chest appeared to collapse, and with the great gasp with which he refilled his exhausted lungs the vertigo left him, and he knew that so intently had he listened that he had held his breath almost to suffocation. The revelation was vexatious; he arose, pushed away the chair with his foot, and strode to the centre of the room. But one does not stride far in darkness; he began to grope, and, finding the wall, followed it to an angle, turned, followed it past the two windows, and there in another corner came in violent contact with the reading-stand, overturning it. It made a clatter which startled him. He was annoyed. 'How the devil could I have forgotten where it was!' he muttered, and groped his way along the third wall to the fireplace. 'I must put things to rights,' said Mr Jarette, feeling the floor for the candle.

Having recovered that, he lighted it and instantly turned his eyes to the table, where, naturally, nothing had undergone any change. The reading-stand lay unobserved upon the floor; he had forgotten to 'put it to rights'. He looked all about the room, dispersing the deeper shadows by movements of the candle in his hand, and, finally, crossing over to the door, tried it by turning and pulling the knob with all his strength. It did not yield, and this seemed to afford him a certain satisfaction; indeed, he secured it more firmly by a bolt which he had not before observed. Returning to his chair, he looked at his watch; it was half-past nine. With a start of surprise he held the watch at his ear. It had not stopped. The candle was now visibly shorter. He again extinguished it, placing it on the floor at his side as before.

Mr Jarette was not at his ease; he was distinctly dissatisfied with his surroundings, and with himself for being so. 'What have I to fear?' he thought. 'This is ridiculous and disgraceful; I will not be so great a fool.' But courage does not come of saying, 'I will be courageous', nor of recognizing its appropriateness to the occasion. The more Jarette condemned himself, the more reason he gave himself for condemnation; the greater the number of variations which he played upon the simple theme of the harmlessness of the dead, the more horrible grew the discord of his emotions. 'What!' he cried aloud in the anguish of his spirit. 'What! shall I, who have not a shade of superstition in my nature – I, who have no belief in immortality – I, who know (and never more clearly than now) that the afterlife is the dream of a desire – shall I lose at once my bet, my honour, and my self-respect, perhaps my reason, because certain savage ancestors, dwelling in caves and burrows, conceived the monstrous notion that the dead walk by night; that –' distinctly, unmistakably, Mr Jarette heard behind him a light, soft sound of footfalls, deliberate, regular, and successively nearer!

IV

Just before daybreak the next morning Dr Helberson and his young friend Harper were driving slowly through the streets of North Beach in the doctor's coupé.

'Have you still the confidence of youth in the courage or stolidity of your friend?' said the elder man. 'Do you believe that I have lost this wager?'

'I *know* you have,' replied the other, with enfeebling emphasis.

'Well, upon my soul, I hope so.'

It was spoken earnestly, almost solemnly. There was a silence for a few moments.

'Harper,' the doctor resumed, looking very serious in the shifting half-lights that entered the carriage as they passed the street-lamps, 'I don't feel altogether comfortable about this business. If your friend had not irritated me by the contemptuous manner in which he treated my doubt of his endurance – a purely physical quality – and by the cool uncivility of his suggestion that the corpse be that of a physician, I should not have gone on with it. If anything should happen, we are ruined, as I fear we deserve to be.'

'What can happen? Even if the matter should be taking a serious turn – of which I am not at all afraid – Mancher has only to resurrect himself and explain matters. With a genuine "subject" from the dissecting-room, or one of your late patients, it might be different.'

Dr Mancher, then, had been as good as his promise; he was the 'corpse'.

Dr Helberson was silent for a long time, as the carriage, at a snail's pace, crept along the same street it had travelled two or three times already. Presently he spoke: 'Well, let us hope that Mancher, if he has had to rise from the dead, has been discreet about it. A mistake in that might make matters worse instead of better.'

'Yes,' said Harper, 'Jarette would kill him. But, doctor' – looking at his watch as the carriage passed a gas-lamp – 'it is nearly four o'clock at last.'

A moment later the two had quitted the vehicle, and were walking briskly toward the long unoccupied house belonging to the doctor, in which they had immured Mr Jarette, in accordance with the terms of the mad wager. As they neared it, they met a man running. 'Can you tell me,' he cried, suddenly checking his speed, 'where I can find a physician?'

'What's the matter?' Helberson asked, non-committal.

'Go and see for yourself,' said the man, resuming his running.

They hastened on. Arrived at the house, they saw several persons entering in haste and excitement. In some of the dwellings near by and across the way, the chamber windows were thrown up, showing a protrusion of heads. All heads were asking questions, none heeding the questions of the others. A few of the windows with closed blinds were illuminated; the inmates of those rooms were dressing to come down. Exactly opposite the door of the house which they sought, a street-lamp threw a yellow, insufficient light upon the scene, seeming to say that it could disclose a good deal more if it wished. Harper, who was now deathly pale, paused at the door and laid a hand upon his companion's arm. 'It's all up with us, doctor,' he said in extreme agitation, which contrasted strangely with his free and easy words; 'the game has gone against us all. Let's not go in there; I'm for lying low.'

'I'm a physician,' said Dr Helberson, calmly; 'there may be need of one.'

They mounted the doorsteps and were about to enter. The door was open; the street-lamp opposite lighted the passage into which it opened. It was full of people. Some had ascended the stairs at the farther end, and, denied admittance above, waited for better fortune. All were talking, none listening. Suddenly, on the upper landing there was a great commotion; a man had sprung out of a door and was breaking away from those endeavouring to detain him. Down through the mass of affrighted idlers he came, pushing them aside, flattening them against the wall on one side, or compelling them to cling by the rail on the other, clutching them by the throat, striking them savagely, thrusting them back down the stairs, and walking over the fallen. His clothing was in disorder, he was without a hat. His eyes, wild and restless, had in them something more terrifying than his apparently superhuman strength. His face, smooth-shaven, was bloodless, his hair snow white.

As the crowd at the foot of the stairs, having more freedom, fell away to let him pass, Harper sprang forward. 'Jarette! Jarette!' he cried.

Dr Helberson seized Harper by the collar and dragged him back. The man looked into their faces without seeming to see them, and sprang through the door, down the steps, into the street and away. A stout policeman, who had had inferior success in conquering his way down the stairway, followed a moment later and started in pursuit, all the heads in the windows – those of women and children now – screaming in guidance.

The stairway being now partly cleared, most of the crowd having rushed down to the street to observe the flight and pursuit, Dr Helberson mounted to the landing, followed by Harper. At a door in the upper passage an officer denied them admittance. 'We are physicians,' said the doctor, and they passed in. The room was full of men, dimly seen, crowded about a table. The newcomers edged their way forward, and looked over the shoulders of those in the front rank. Upon the table, the lower limbs covered with a sheet, lay the body of a man, brilliantly illuminated by the beam of a bull's-eye lantern held by a policeman standing at the feet. The others, excepting those near the head – the officer himself – all were in darkness. The face of the body showed yellow, repulsive, horrible! The eyes were partly open and upturned, and the jaw fallen; traces of froth defiled the lips, the chin, the cheeks. A tall man, evidently a physician, bent over the body with his hand thrust under the shirt front. He withdrew it and placed two fingers in the open mouth. 'This man has been about two hours dead,' said he. 'It is a case for the coroner.'

He drew a card from his pocket, handed it to the officer, and made his way toward the door.

'Clear the room – out, all!' said the officer, sharply, and the body disappeared as if it had been snatched away, as he shifted the lantern and flashed its beam of light here and there against the faces of the crowd. The effect was amazing! The men, blinded, confused, almost terrified, made a tumultuous rush for the door, pushing, crowding, and tumbling over one another as they fled, like the hosts of Night before the shafts of Apollo. Upon the struggling, trampling mass the officer poured his light without pity and without cessation. Caught in the current, Helberson and Harper were swept out of the room and cascaded down the stairs into the street.

'Good God, doctor! did I not tell you that Jarette would kill him?' said Harper, as soon as they were clear of the crowd.

'I believe you did,' replied the other without apparent emotion.

They walked on in silence, block after block. Against the greying east the dwellings of our hill tribes showed in silhouette. The familiar milk-waggon was already astir in the streets; the baker's man would soon come upon the scene; the newspaper carrier was abroad in the land.

'It strikes me, youngster,' said Helberson, 'that you and I have been having too much of the morning air lately. It is unwholesome; we need a change. What do you say to a tour in Europe?'

'When?'

'I'm not particular. I should suppose that four o'clock this afternoon would be early enough.'

'I'll meet you at the boat,' said Harper.

V

Seven years afterward these two men sat upon a bench in Madison Square, New York, in familiar conversation. Another man, who had been observing them for some time, himself unobserved, approached and, courteously lifting his hat from locks as white as snow, said: 'I beg your pardon, gentlemen, but when you have killed a man by coming to life, it is best to change clothes with him, and at the first opportunity make a break for liberty.'

Helberson and Harper exchanged significant glances. They were apparently amused. The former then looked the stranger kindly in the eye, and replied:

'That has always been my plan. I entirely agree with you as to its advant—'

He stopped suddenly and grew deathly pale. He stared at the man, open-mouthed; he trembled visibly.

'Ah!' said the stranger, 'I see that you are indisposed, doctor. If you cannot treat yourself, Dr Harper can do something for you, I am sure.'

'Who the devil are you?' said Harper bluntly.

The stranger came nearer, and, bending toward them, said in a whisper: 'I call myself Jarette sometimes, but I don't mind telling you, for old friendship, that I am Dr William Mancher.'

The revelation brought both men to their feet. 'Mancher!' they cried in a breath; and Helberson added: 'It is true, by God!'

'Yes,' said the stranger, smiling vaguely, 'it is true enough, no doubt.'

He hesitated, and seemed to be trying to recall something, then began humming a popular air. He had apparently forgotten their presence.

'Look here, Mancher,' said the elder of the two, 'tell us just what occurred that night – to Jarette, you know.'

'Oh, yes, about Jarette,' said the other. 'It's odd I should have neglected to tell you – I tell it so often. You see I knew, by overhearing him talking to himself, that he was pretty badly frightened. So I couldn't resist the temptation to come to life and have a bit of fun out of him – I couldn't, really. That was all right, though certainly I did not think he would take it seriously; I did not, truly. And afterward – well, it was a tough job changing places with him, and then – damn you! you didn't let me out!'

Nothing could exceed the ferocity with which these last words were delivered. Both men stepped back in alarm.

'We? – why – why –,' Helberson stammered, losing his self-possession utterly, 'we had nothing to do with it.'

'Didn't I say you were Doctors Hellborn and Sharper?' inquired the lunatic, laughing.

'My name is Helberson, yes; and this gentleman is Mr Harper,' replied the former, reassured. 'But we are not physicians now; we are – well, hang it, old man, we are gamblers.'

And that was the truth.

'A very good profession – very good, indeed; and, by the way, I hope Sharper here paid over Jarette's money like an honest stakeholder. A very good and honourable profession,' he repeated, thoughtfully, moving carelessly away; 'but I stick to the old one. I am High Supreme Medical Officer of the Bloomington Asylum; it is my duty to cure the superintendent.'

Ernest Bramah

THE COIN OF DIONYSIUS

Ernest Bramah Smith (1868–1942), who wrote as Ernest Bramah, is chiefly remembered today as the author of several books about a figure named Kai Lung, written with unbearable whimsicality in a mock-Chinese manner. (Bramah had not been to China.) In spite, or perhaps because, of this whimsicality, the Kai Lung tales have devoted admirers. His stories about the blind detective Max Carrados, on the other hand, are undeservedly out of print.

In the unceasing quest during the first two decades of this century for a detective who should be as impressive as Sherlock Holmes, yet wholly different from him, Carrados was a felicitous invention. He insists that blindness is an advantage, because his other senses are so marvellously developed that he can hear sounds inaudible to other people, and has a sense of smell able to detect from a distance that a man is wearing a false moustache. He is also able to feel the aura of other people, so that he can recognize an acquaintance before he speaks. The story chosen here from *Max Carrados* (1914), the first and best of three short-story collections (there is also a poor Carrados novel), is the opening tale, in which Carrados meets again the old friend who under the name of Louis Carlyle is to become his Watson. The finest of the Carrados stories are too long for inclusion here, but this one serves well as an introduction to the blind detective and his methods.

It was eight o'clock at night and raining, scarcely a time when a business so limited in its clientele as that of a coin dealer could hope to attract any customer, but a light was still showing in the small shop that bore over its window the name of Baxter, and in the even smaller office at the back the proprietor himself sat reading the latest *Pall Mall*. His enterprise seemed to be justified, for presently the door bell gave its announcement, and throwing down his paper Mr Baxter went forward.

As a matter of fact the dealer had been expecting someone and his manner as he passed into the shop was unmistakably suggestive of a caller of importance. But at the first glance towards his visitor the excess of deference melted out of his bearing, leaving the urbane, self-possessed shopman in the presence of the casual customer.

'Mr Baxter, I think?' said the latter. He had laid aside his dripping umbrella and was unbuttoning overcoat and coat to reach an inner pocket. 'You hardly remember me, I suppose? Mr Carlyle – two years ago I took up a case for you –'

'To be sure. Mr Carlyle, the private detective –'

'Inquiry agent,' corrected Mr Carlyle precisely.

'Well,' smiled Mr Baxter, 'for that matter I am a coin dealer and not an antiquarian or a numismatist. Is there anything in that way that I can do for you?'

'Yes,' replied his visitor; 'it is my turn to consult you.' He had taken a small wash-leather bag from the inner pocket and now turned something carefully out upon the counter. 'What can you tell me about that?'

The dealer gave the coin a moment's scrutiny.

'There is no question about this,' he replied. 'It is a Sicilian tetradrachm of Dionysius.'

'Yes, I know that – I have it on the label out of the cabinet. I can tell you further that it's supposed to be one that Lord Seastoke gave two hundred and fifty pounds for at the Brice sale in '94.'

'It seems to me that you can tell me more about it than I can tell you,' remarked Mr Baxter. 'What is it that you really want to know?'

'I want to know,' replied Mr Carlyle, 'whether it is genuine or not.'

'Has any doubt been cast upon it?'

'Certain circumstances raised a suspicion – that is all.'

The dealer took another look at the tetradrachm through his magnifying glass, holding it by the edge with the careful touch of an expert. Then he shook his head slowly in a confession of ignorance.

'Of course I could make a guess –'

'No, don't,' interrupted Mr Carlyle hastily. 'An arrest hangs on it and nothing short of certainty is any good to me.'

'Is that so, Mr Carlyle?' said Mr Baxter, with increased interest. 'Well, to be quite candid, the thing is out of my line. Now if it was a rare Saxon penny or a doubtful noble I'd stake my reputation on my opinion, but I do very little in the classical series.'

Mr Carlyle did not attempt to conceal his disappointment as he returned the coin to the bag and replaced the bag in the inner pocket.

'I had been relying on you,' he grumbled reproachfully. 'Where on earth am I to go now?'

'There is always the British Museum.'

'Ah, to be sure, thanks. But will anyone who can tell me be there now?'

'Now? No fear!' replied Mr Baxter. 'Go round in the morning –'

'But I must know tonight,' explained the visitor, reduced to despair again. 'Tomorrow will be too late for the purpose.'

Mr Baxter did not hold out much encouragement in the circumstances.

'You can scarcely expect to find anyone at business now,' he remarked. 'I should have been gone these two hours myself only I happened to have an appointment with an American millionaire who fixed his own time.' Something indistinguishable from a wink slid off Mr Baxter's right eye. 'Offmunson he's called, and a bright young pedigree-hunter has traced his descent from Offa, King of Mercia. So he – quite naturally – wants a set of Offas as a sort of collateral proof.'

'Very interesting,' murmured Mr Carlyle, fidgeting with his watch. 'I should love an hour's chat with you about your millionaire customers – some other time. Just now – look here, Baxter, can't you give me a line of introduction to some dealer in this sort of thing who happens to live in town? You must know dozens of experts.'

'Why, bless my soul, Mr Carlyle, I don't know a man of them away from his business,' said Mr Baxter, staring. 'They may live in Park Lane or they may live in Petticoat Lane for all I know. Besides, there aren't so many experts as you seem to imagine. And the two best will very likely quarrel over it. You've had to do with "expert witnesses", I suppose?'

'I don't want a witness; there will be no need to give evidence. All I want is an absolutely authoritative pronouncement that I can act on. Is there no one who can really say whether the thing is genuine or not?'

Mr Baxter's meaning silence became cynical in its implication as he continued to look at his visitor across the counter. Then he relaxed.

'Stay a bit; there is a man – an amateur – I remember hearing wonderful things about some time ago. They say he really does know.'

'There you are,' exclaimed Mr Carlyle, much relieved. 'There always is someone. Who is he?'

'Funny name,' replied Baxter. 'Something Wynn or Wynn something.' He craned his neck to catch sight of an important motor car that was drawing to the kerb before his window. 'Wynn Carrados! You'll excuse me now, Mr Carlyle, won't you? This looks like Mr Offmunson.'

Mr Carlyle hastily scribbled the name down on his cuff.

'Wynn Carrados, right. Where does he live?'

'Haven't the remotest idea,' replied Baxter, referring the arrangement of his tie to the judgment of the wall mirror. 'I have never seen the man myself. Now, Mr Carlyle, I'm sorry I can't do any more for you. You won't mind, will you?'

Mr Carlyle could not pretend to misunderstand. He enjoyed the distinction of holding open the door for the transatlantic representative of the line of Offa as he went out, and then made his way through the muddy streets back to his office. There was only one way of tracing a private individual at such short notice – through the pages of the directories, and the gentleman did not flatter himself by a very high estimate of his chances.

Fortune favoured him, however. He very soon discovered a Wynn Carrados living at Richmond, and, better still, further search failed to unearth another. There was, apparently, only one householder at all events of that name in the neighbourhood of London. He jotted down the address and set out for Richmond.

The house was some distance from the station, Mr Carlyle learned. He took a taxicab and drove, dismissing the vehicle at the gate. He prided himself on his power of observation and the accuracy of the deductions which resulted from it – a detail of his business. 'It's nothing more than using one's eyes and putting two and two together,' he would modestly declare, when he wished to be deprecatory rather than impressive, and by the time he had reached the front door of 'The Turrets' he had formed some opinion of the position and tastes of the man who lived there.

A man-servant admitted Mr Carlyle and took in his card – his private card with the bare request for an interview that would not detain Mr Carrados for ten minutes. Luck still favoured him; Mr Carrados was at home and would see him at once. The servant, the hall through which they passed, and the room into which he was shown, all contributed something to the deductions which the quietly observant gentleman was half unconsciously recording.

'Mr Carlyle,' announced the servant.

The room was a library or study. The only occupant, a man of about Carlyle's own age, had been using a typewriter up to the moment of his visitor's entrance. He now turned and stood up with an expression of formal courtesy.

'It's very good of you to see me at this hour,' apologized the caller.

The conventional expression of Mr Carrados's face changed a little.

'Surely my man has got your name wrong?' he exclaimed. 'Isn't it Louis Calling?'

The visitor stopped short and his agreeable smile gave place to a sudden flash of anger or annoyance.

'No, sir,' he replied stiffly. 'My name is on the card which you have before you.'

'I beg your pardon,' said Mr Carrados, with perfect good humour. 'I hadn't seen it. But I used to know a Calling some years ago – at St Michael's.'

'St Michael's!' Mr Carlyle's features underwent another change, no less instant and sweeping than before. 'St Michael's! Wynn Carrados? Good heavens! It isn't Max Wynn – old "Winning" Wynn?'

'A little older and a little fatter – yes,' replied Carrados. 'I *have* changed my name, you see.'

'Extraordinary thing meeting like this,' said his visitor, dropping into a chair and staring hard at Mr Carrados. 'I have changed more than my name. How did you recognize me?'

'The voice,' replied Carrados. 'It took me back to that little smoke-dried attic den of yours where we –'

'My God!' exclaimed Carlyle bitterly, 'don't remind me of what we were going to do in those days.' He looked round the well-furnished, handsome room and recalled the other signs of wealth that he had noticed. 'At all events, you seem fairly comfortable, Wynn.'

'I am alternately envied and pitied,' replied Carrados, with a placid tolerance of circumstance that seemed characteristic of him. 'Still, as you say, I am fairly comfortable.'

'Envied, I can understand. But why are you pitied?'

'Because I am blind,' was the tranquil reply.

'Blind!' exclaimed Mr Carlyle, using his own eyes superlatively. 'Do you mean – literally blind?'

'Literally . . . I was riding along a bridle-path through a wood about a dozen years ago with a friend. He was in front. At one point a twig sprang back – you know how easily a thing like that happens. It just flicked my eye – nothing to think twice about.'

'And that blinded you?'

'Yes, ultimately. It's called amaurosis.'

'I can scarcely believe it. You seem so sure and self-reliant. Your eyes are full of expression – only a little quieter than they used to be. I believe you were typing when I came . . . Aren't you having me?'

'You miss the dog and the stick?' smiled Carrados. 'No; it's a fact.'

'What an awful infliction for you, Max. You were always such an impulsive, reckless sort of fellow – never quiet. You must miss such a fearful lot.'

'Has anyone else recognized you?' asked Carrados quietly.

'Ah, that was the voice, you said,' replied Carlyle.

'Yes; but other people heard the voice as well. Only I had no blundering, self-confident eyes to be hoodwinked.'

'That's a rum way of putting it,' said Carlyle. 'Are your ears never hoodwinked, may I ask?'

'Not now. Nor my fingers. Nor any of my other senses that have to look out for themselves.'

'Well, well,' murmured Mr Carlyle, cut short in his sympathetic emotions. 'I'm glad you take it so well. Of course, if you find it an advantage to be blind, old man –' He stopped and reddened. 'I beg your pardon,' he concluded stiffly.

'Not an advantage perhaps,' replied the other thoughtfully. 'Still it has compensations that one might not think of. A new world to explore, new experiences, new powers awakening; strange new perceptions; life in the fourth dimension. But why do you beg my pardon, Louis?'

'I am an ex-solicitor, struck off in connection with the falsifying of a trust account, Mr Carrados,' replied Carlyle, rising.

'Sit down, Louis,' said Carrados suavely. His face, even his incredibly living eyes, beamed placid good nature. 'The chair on which you will sit, the roof above you, all the comfortable surroundings to which you have so amiably alluded, are the direct result of falsifying a trust account. But do I call you "Mr Carlyle" in consequence? Certainly not, Louis.'

'I did not falsify the account,' cried Carlyle hotly. He sat down, however, and added more quietly: 'But why do I tell you all this? I have never spoken of it before.'

'Blindness invites confidence,' replied Carrados. 'We are out of the running – human rivalry ceases to exist. Besides, why shouldn't you? In my case the account *was* falsified.'

'Of course that's all bunkum, Max,' commented Carlyle. 'Still, I appreciate your motive.'

'Practically everything I possess was left to me by an American cousin, on the condition that I took the name of Carrados. He made his fortune by an ingenious conspiracy of doctoring the crop reports and unloading favourably in consequence. And I need hardly remind you that the receiver is equally guilty with the thief.'

'But twice as safe. I know something of that, Max . . . Have you any idea what my business is?'

'You shall tell me,' replied Carrados.

'I run a private inquiry agency. When I lost my profession I had to do something for a living. This occurred. I dropped my name, changed my appearance and opened an office. I knew the legal side down to the ground and I got a retired Scotland Yard man to organize the outside work.'

'Excellent!' cried Carrados. 'Do you unearth many murders?'

'No,' admitted Mr Carlyle; 'our business lies mostly on the conventional lines among divorce and defalcation.'

'That's a pity,' remarked Carrados. 'Do you know, Louis, I always had a secret ambition to be a detective myself. I have even thought lately that I might still be able to do something at it if the chance came my way. That makes you smile?'

'Well, certainly, the idea –'

'Yes, the idea of a blind detective – the blind tracking the alert –'

'Of course, as you say, certain faculties are no doubt quickened,' Mr Carlyle hastened to add considerately, 'but, seriously, with the exception of an artist, I don't suppose there is any man who is more utterly dependent on his eyes.'

Whatever opinion Carrados might have held privately, his genial exterior did not betray a shadow of dissent. For a minute he continued to smoke as though he derived an actual visual enjoyment from the blue sprays that travelled and dispersed across the room. He had already placed before his visitor a box containing cigars of a brand which that gentleman keenly appreciated but generally regarded as unattainable, and the matter-of-fact ease and certainty with which the blind man had brought the box and put it before him had sent a questioning flicker through Carlyle's mind.

'You used to be rather fond of art yourself, Louis,' he remarked presently. 'Give me your opinion of my latest purchase – the bronze lion on the cabinet there.' Then, as Carlyle's gaze went about the room, he added quickly: 'No, not that cabinet – the one on your left.'

Carlyle shot a sharp glance at his host as he got up, but Carrados's expression was merely benignly complacent. Then he strolled across to the figure.

'Very nice,' he admitted. 'Late Flemish, isn't it?'

'No. It is a copy of Vidal's "Roaring Lion".'

'Vidal?'

'A French artist.' The voice became indescribably flat. 'He, also, had the misfortune to be blind, by the way.'

'You old humbug, Max!' shrieked Carlyle. 'You've been thinking that out for the last five minutes.' Then the unfortunate man bit his lip and turned his back towards his host.

'Do you remember how we used to pile it up on that obtuse ass Sanders and then roast him?' asked Carrados, ignoring the half-smothered exclamation with which the other man had recalled himself.

'Yes,' replied Carlyle quietly. 'This is very good,' he continued, addressing himself to the bronze again. 'How ever did he do it?'

'With his hands.'

'Naturally. But, I mean, how did he study his model?'

'Also with his hands. He called it "seeing near".'

'Even with a lion – handled it?'

'In such cases he required the services of a keeper, who brought the animal to bay while Vidal exercised his own particular gifts . . . You don't feel inclined to put me on the track of a mystery, Louis?'

Unable to regard this request as anything but one of old Max's unquenchable pleasantries, Mr Carlyle was on the point of making a suitable reply when a sudden thought caused him to smile knowingly. Up to that point he had, indeed, completely forgotten the object of his visit. Now that he remembered the doubtful Dionysius and Mr Baxter's recommendation he immediately assumed that some mistake had been made. Either Max was not the Wynn Carrados he had been seeking or else the dealer had been misinformed; for although his host was wonderfully expert in the face of his misfortune, it was inconceivable that he could decide the genuineness of a coin without seeing it. The opportunity seemed a good one of getting even with Carrados by taking him at his word.

'Yes,' he accordingly replied, with crisp deliberation, as he recrossed the room; 'yes, I will, Max. Here is the clue to what seems to be a rather remarkable fraud.' He put the tetradrachm into his host's hand. 'What do you make of it?'

For a few seconds Carrados handled the piece with the delicate manipulation of his finger-tips while Carlyle looked on with a self-appreciative grin. Then with equal gravity the blind man weighed the coin in the balance of his hand. Finally he touched it with his tongue.

'Well?' demanded the other.

'Of course I have not much to go on, and if I was more fully in your confidence I might come to another conclusion –'

'Yes, yes,' interposed Carlyle, with amused encouragement.

'Then I should advise you to arrest the parlourmaid, Nina Brun, communicate with the police authorities of Padua for particulars of the career of Helene Brunesi, and suggest to Lord Seastoke that he should return to London to see what further depredations have been made in his cabinet.'

Mr Carlyle's groping hand sought and found a chair, on to which he dropped blankly. His eyes were unable to detach themselves for a single moment from the very ordinary spectacle of Mr Carrados's mildly benevolent face, while the sterilized ghost of his now forgotten amusement still lingered about his features.

'Good heavens!' he managed to articulate, 'how do you know?'

'Isn't that what you wanted of me?' asked Carrados suavely.

'Don't humbug, Max,' said Carlyle severely. 'This is no joke.' An undefined mistrust of his own powers suddenly possessed him in the presence of this mystery. 'How do you come to know of Nina Brun and Lord Seastoke?'

'You are a detective, Louis,' replied Carrados. 'How does one know these things? By using one's eyes and putting two and two together.'

Carlyle groaned and flung out an arm petulantly.

'Is it all bunkum, Max? Do you really see all the time – though that doesn't go very far towards explaining it.'

'Like Vidal, I see very well – at close quarters,' replied Carrados, lightly running a forefinger along the inscription on the tetradrachm. 'For longer range I keep another pair of eyes. Would you like to test them?'

Mr Carlyle's assent was not very gracious; it was, in fact, faintly sulky. He was suffering the annoyance of feeling distinctly unimpressive in his own department; but he was also curious.

'The bell is just behind you, if you don't mind,' said his host. 'Parkinson will appear. You might take note of him while he is in.'

The man who had admitted Mr Carlyle proved to be Parkinson.

'This gentleman is Mr Carlyle, Parkinson,' explained Carrados the moment the man entered. 'You will remember him for the future?'

Parkinson's apologetic eye swept the visitor from head to foot, but so lightly and swiftly that it conveyed to that gentleman the comparison of being very deftly dusted.

'I will endeavour to do so, sir,' replied Parkinson, turning again to his master.

'I shall be at home to Mr Carlyle whenever he calls. That is all.'

'Very well, sir.'

'Now, Louis,' remarked Mr Carrados briskly, when the door had closed again, 'you have had a good opportunity of studying Parkinson. What is he like?'

'In what way?'

'I mean as a matter of description. I am a blind man – I haven't seen my servant for twelve years – what idea can you give me of him? I asked you to notice.'

'I know you did, but your Parkinson is the sort of man who has very little about him to describe. He is the embodiment of the ordinary. His height is about average –'

'Five feet nine,' murmured Carrados. 'Slightly above the mean.'

'Scarcely noticeably so. Clean-shaven. Medium brown hair. No particularly marked features. Dark eyes. Good teeth.'

'False,' interposed Carrados. 'The teeth – not the statement.'

'Possibly,' admitted Mr Carlyle. 'I am not a dental expert and I had no opportunity of examining Mr Parkinson's mouth in detail. But what is the drift of all this?'

'His clothes?'

'Oh, just the ordinary evening dress of a valet. There is not much room for variety in that.'

'You noticed, in fact, nothing special by which Parkinson could be identified?'

'Well, he wore an unusually broad gold ring on the little finger of the left hand.'

'But that is removable. And yet Parkinson has an ineradicable mole – a small one, I admit – on his chin. And you a human sleuth-hound. Oh, Louis!'

'At all events,' retorted Carlyle, writhing a little under this good-humoured satire, although it was easy enough to see in it Carrados's affectionate intention – 'at all events, I dare say I can give as good a description of Parkinson as he can give of me.'

'That is what we are going to test. Ring the bell again.'

'Seriously?'

'Quite. I am trying my eyes against yours. If I can't give you fifty out of a hundred I'll renounce my private detectorial ambition for ever.'

'It isn't quite the same,' objected Carlyle, but he rang the bell.

'Come in and close the door, Parkinson,' said Carrados when the man appeared. 'Don't look at Mr Carlyle again – in fact, you had better stand with your back towards him, he won't mind. Now describe to me his appearance as you observed it.'

Parkinson tendered his respectful apologies to Mr Carlyle for the liberty he was compelled to take, by the deferential quality of his voice.

'Mr Carlyle, sir, wears patent leather boots of about size seven and very little used. There are five buttons, but on the left boot one button – the third up – is missing, leaving loose threads and not the more usual metal fastener. Mr Carlyle's trousers, sir, are of a dark material, a dark grey line of about a quarter of an inch width on a darker ground. The bottoms are turned permanently up and are, just now, a little muddy, if I may say so.'

'Very muddy,' interposed Mr Carlyle generously. 'It is a wet night, Parkinson.'

'Yes, sir; very unpleasant weather. If you will allow me, sir, I will brush you in the hall. The mud is dry now, I notice. Then, sir,' continued Parkinson, reverting to the business in hand, 'there are dark green cashmere hose. A curb-pattern key-chain passes into the left-hand trouser pocket.'

From the visitor's nether garments the photographic-eyed Parkinson proceeded to higher ground, and with increasing wonder Mr Carlyle listened to the faithful catalogue of his possessions. His fetter-and-link albert of gold and platinum was minutely described. His spotted blue ascot, with its gentlemanly pearl scarfpin, was set forth, and the fact that the buttonhole in the left lapel of his morning coat showed signs of use was duly noted. What Parkinson saw he recorded but he made no deductions. A handkerchief carried in the cuff of the right sleeve was simply that to him and not an indication that Mr Carlyle was, indeed, left-handed.

But a more delicate part of Parkinson's undertaking remained. He approached it with a double cough.

'As regards Mr Carlyle's personal appearance, sir –'

'No, enough!' cried the gentleman concerned hastily. 'I am more than satisfied. You are a keen observer, Parkinson.'

'I have trained myself to suit my master's requirements, sir,' replied the man. He looked towards Mr Carrados, received a nod and withdrew.

Mr Carlyle was the first to speak.

'That man of yours would be worth five pounds a week to me, Max,' he remarked thoughtfully. 'But, of course –'

'I don't think that he would take it,' replied Carrados, in a voice of equally detached speculation. 'He suits me very well. But you have the chance of using his services – indirectly.'

'You still mean that – seriously?'

'I notice in you a chronic disinclination to take me seriously, Louis. It is really – to an Englishman – almost painful. Is there something inherently comic about me or the atmosphere of The Turrets?'

'No, my friend,' replied Mr Carlyle, 'but there is something essentially prosperous. That is what points to the improbable. Now what is it?'

'It might be merely a whim, but it is more than that,' replied Carrados. 'It is, well, partly vanity, partly *ennui*, partly' – certainly there was something more nearly tragic in his voice than comic now – 'partly hope.'

Mr Carlyle was too tactful to pursue the subject.

'Those are three tolerable motives,' he acquiesced. 'I'll do anything you want, Max, on one condition.'

'Agreed. And it is?'

'That you tell me how you knew so much of this affair.' He tapped the silver coin which lay on the table near them. 'I am not easily flabbergasted,' he added.

'You won't believe that there is nothing to explain – that it was purely second sight?'

'No,' replied Carlyle tersely; 'I won't.'

'You are quite right. And yet the thing is very simple.'

'They always are – when you know,' soliloquized the other. 'That's what makes them so confoundedly difficult when you don't.'

'Here is this one then. In Padua, which seems to be regaining its old reputation as the birthplace of spurious antiques, by the way, there lives an ingenious craftsman named Pietro Stelli. This simple soul, who possesses a talent not inferior to that of Cavino at his best, has for many years turned his hand to the not unprofitable occupation of forging rare Greek and Roman coins. As a collector and student of certain Greek colonials and a specialist in forgeries, I have been familiar with Stelli's workmanship for years. Latterly he seems to have come under the influence of an international crook called – at the moment – Dompierre, who soon saw a way of utilizing Stelli's genius on a royal scale. Helene Brunesi, who in private life is – and really is, I believe – Madame Dompierre, readily lent her services to the enterprise.'

'Quite so,' nodded Mr Carlyle, as his host paused.

'You see the whole sequence, of course?'

'Not exactly – not in detail,' confessed Mr Carlyle.

'Dompierre's idea was to gain access to some of the most celebrated cabinets of Europe and substitute Stelli's fabrications for the genuine coins. The princely collection of rarities that he would thus amass might be difficult to dispose of safely but I have no doubt that he had matured his plans. Helene, in the person of Nina Brun, an Anglicized French parlourmaid – a part which she fills to perfection – was to obtain wax impressions of the most valuable pieces and to make the exchange when the counterfeits reached her. In this way it was obviously hoped that the fraud would not come to light until long after the real coins had been sold, and I gather that she has already done her work successfully in several houses. Then, impressed by her excellent references and capable manner, my housekeeper engaged her, and for a few weeks she went about her duties here. It was fatal to this detail of the scheme, however, that I have the misfortune to be blind. I am told that Helene has so innocently angelic a face as to disarm suspicion, but I was incapable of being impressed and that good material was thrown away. But one morning my material fingers – which, of course, knew nothing of Helene's angelic face – discovered an unfamiliar touch about the surface of my favourite Euclideas, and, although there was doubtless nothing to be seen, my critical sense of smell reported that wax had been recently pressed against it. I began to make discreet inquiries and in the meantime my cabinets went to the local bank for safety. Helene countered by receiving a telegram from Angiers, calling her to the death-bed of her aged mother. The aged mother succumbed; duty compelled Helene to remain at the side of her stricken patriarchal father, and doubtless The Turrets was written off the syndicate's operations as a bad debt.'

'Very interesting,' admitted Mr Carlyle; 'but at the risk of seeming obtuse' – his manner had become delicately chastened – 'I must say that I fail to trace the inevitable connection between Nina Brun and this particular forgery – assuming that it is a forgery.'

'Set your mind at rest about that, Louis,' replied Carrados. 'It is a forgery, and it is a forgery that none but Pietro Stelli could have achieved. That is the essential connection. Of course, there are accessories. A private detective coming urgently to see me with a notable tetradrachm in his pocket, which he announces to be the clue to a remarkable fraud – well, really, Louis, one scarcely needs to be blind to see through that.'

'And Lord Seastoke? I suppose you happened to discover that Nina Brun had gone there?'

'No, I cannot claim to have discovered that, or I should certainly have warned him at once when I found out – only recently – about the gang. As a matter of fact, the last information I had of Lord Seastoke was a line in yesterday's *Morning Post* to the effect that he was still at Cairo. But many of these pieces –' He brushed his finger almost lovingly across the vivid chariot race that embellished the reverse of the coin, and broke off to remark: 'You really ought to take up the subject, Louis. You have no idea how useful it might prove to you some day.'

'I really think I must,' replied Carlyle grimly. 'Two hundred and fifty pounds the original of this cost, I believe.'

'Cheap, too; it would make five hundred pounds in New York today. As I was saying, many are literally unique. This gem by Kimon is – here is his signature, you see; Peter is particularly good at lettering – and as I handled the genuine tetradrachm about two years ago, when Lord Seastoke exhibited it at a meeting of our society in Albemarle Street, there is nothing at all wonderful in my being able to fix the locale of your mystery. Indeed, I feel that I ought to apologize for it all being so simple.'

'I think,' remarked Mr Carlyle, critically examining the loose threads on his left boot, 'that the apology on that head would be more appropriate from me.'

John Dickson Carr

THE PROVERBIAL MURDER

John Dickson Carr (1906–77), alias Carter Dickson, might at the beginning of his literary career have had Marvell's lines in mind:

> My love is of a birth as rare
> As 'tis, for object, strange and high;
> It was begotten by despair
> Upon impossibility.

Or at least it was in impossibilities that Carr dealt from his very first book (*It Walks By Night*, 1930) onwards, and the idea of repeating them with variations in book after book would have driven any other crime novelist to despair. The impossibilities were locked room mysteries, and Carr's ingenuity in devising them was extraordinary. He produced so many that another name had to be used, another detective invented, even though Carr's Dr Gideon Fell and Carter Dickson's Sir Henry Merrivale were very similar in speech and style. The saturnine Henri Bencolin solved some of the early cases; Patrick Butler appeared in later ones.

For all who enjoy the locked room tale (some don't), Carr's work in his first twenty years of writing is outstanding. Locked room mysteries have a tendency to be disappointing in their solutions, leaving one murmuring 'Is *that* all?' or 'How implausible!' when they are explained. Carr at his best is totally convincing and almost unbelievably clever, so that our gasps are all of admiration. Which is his best book? A panel of seventeen critics were asked recently to name the ten best locked room mysteries. First place went, by an overwhelming margin, to Carr's *The Hollow Man* (1935). It received almost double the votes of any other book. In the first ten also were Carr's *The Crooked Hinge* (1938) and Carter Dickson's *The Judas Window* (1938) and *The Ten Teacups* (1937).

It is safe to say that if a similar poll were taken among short stories, Carr would again have at least four titles among the first ten. One of them might be 'The Proverbial Murder'.

The timbered cottage, which belonged to Herr Dr Ludwig Meyer and which was receiving attention from the man with the field glasses, stood some distance down in the valley.

In clear moonlight, the valley was washed clean of colour except at one point, where a light showed in a window to the right of Dr Meyer's door. It was a diamond-paned window with two leaves, now closed. The lamp-light streamed out through it, touching grass and rose beds.

At a desk beside the window Dr Meyer sat at his endless writing. *A Dissertation on the Theory of the Atom* was its official title. The white cretonne curtains of the window were not drawn. From this angle the watchers had an awkward, sideways view of him.

Some quarter of a mile away, on the edge of the hill, the man with the field glasses lay flat on his face. His back ached and his arms felt cramped. Momentarily he lowered the glasses and peered round.

'S-ss-t!' he whispered. 'What are you doing? Don't light a cigarette!'

His companion's voice sounded aggrieved. 'Why not? Nobody can see it up here.'

'It's orders, that's all.'

'And anyway,' grumbled the other, 'it's two o'clock in the morning. Our bloke's not coming tonight: that's certain. Unless he's already gone in by the back door?'

'Lewes is covering the back door and the other side. Listen!'

He held up his hand. Nothing stirred in the valley. There was no noise except, far away, the faint drag and thunder of the surf at Lynmouth.

It was mellow September weather, yet the man with the field glasses, Detective-Inspector Ballard, of the Special Branch attached to the Metropolitan Police, felt an unaccountable shiver. Lifting the glasses again, he raked the path leading up to the cottage. He looked at the lighted window. Beyond the edge of a cretonne curtain, he could just make out a part of the bony profile, the thick spectacles, the fish-like movements of the mouth, as Dr Meyer filled page after page of neat handwriting.

'If you ask me,' grumbled Sergeant Buck, 'the AC's barking up the wrong tree this time. This Meyer is a distinguished scientist – a real refugee –'

'No.'

'But where's your evidence?'

'In cases of this kind,' returned Ballard, lowering the glasses to rub his aching eyes, 'you can't afford to go by the rules of legal evidence. The AC isn't sure; but he thinks the tip-off came from Meyer's wife.'

Sergeant Buck whistled.

'A good German hausfrau tip off the English?'

'That's just it. She's not German: she's English. There are some very funny things going on in this country at the moment, my lad. If we can nab the man who's coming to see Meyer tonight, we'll catch somebody high up. We can –'

'Listen!' said Buck.

It was unnecessary to ask anyone to listen. The report of the firearm crashed and rolled in that little valley. It was an illusion, but Ballard almost imagined he could hear the wiry *whing* of the bullet.

Both men jumped to their feet. Ballard, his knee joints painful from their cramped position, whisked up the glasses again and scanned the front of the cottage. His gaze came to rest on the window.

'Poachers?' suggested Buck.

'That was no poacher,' said Inspector Ballard. 'That was an Army rifle. And it didn't miss either. Come on!'

The pygmy picture rose in his mind as he scrambled down the hill: the flutter of the cretonne curtain, the bald head fallen forward across the desk. Neither he nor Buck made any effort at concealment. The echoes hardly seemed to have settled in the valley when they arrived in front of the house. Holding his companion back, Ballard pointed.

The lighted window was not far up from the ground. First of all Ballard noticed the bullet hole in the glass, close to the lead joining of one of the diamond panes. It was a neatly drilled hole, with hardly any starring of the glass, such as is made by a smallish, high-velocity rifle bullet (say a ·256) fired from some distance away.

Then they both saw what was inside, lying limply across the desk with a mark on the left temple; and they both hurried for the front door.

The door-knocker was stiff and rusty, giving only a padded sound which Ballard had to supplement by banging his fist on the door. It seemed interminable minutes before the bar was drawn back on the inside, and the door opened.

A white-faced woman, carrying a kerosene lamp and with a dressing-gown hastily pulled round her, peered out at them. She was perhaps thirty-five, some ten or fifteen years younger than Ludwig Meyer. Though not pretty, she was attractive in a pink-and-white fashion; blue-eyed, with heavy, rich-brushed fair hair over her shoulders.

'Mrs Meyer?'

'Yes?' She moistened her lips.

'We're police officers, ma'am. I'm afraid something has happened to your husband.'

Slowly Harriet Meyer held up the lamp. Just as slowly, she turned round and looked toward the door of the room on the right of the hall. The lamp wobbled in her hand, its golden light spilling and breaking among shadows.

'I heard it,' she said, 'I wondered.'

Gritting her teeth, she turned round and walked toward the door of that room. With a word of apology Ballard brushed past her.

'Well,' said Sergeant Buck, after a pause, 'there's nothing we can do for *him*, sir.'

There was not. They stood in a long, low-ceilinged room, its walls lined with improvised bookshelves. The smell of burning oil from the lamp on the desk by the window competed with a fog of rank tobacco smoke. A long china-bowled pipe lay on the desk near the dead man's hand. The fountain pen had slipped from his fingers. His face and shoulders lay against the paper-strewn desk; but, as the creaking of their footsteps jarred the floor, he slowly slid off and fell with an unnerving thump on his side. It was a grotesque mimicry of life which made Harriet Meyer cry out.

'Steady, ma'am,' said Ballard.

Circling the body, he went to the window and tried to peer out. But in the dazzle between lamp and moonlight he could see nothing. The bullet hole in the glass, he noted, had tiny splinters – the little shell-shaped grooves on the edge of the opening – which showed that the bullet had been fired from outside.

Inspector Ballard drew a deep breath and turned round.

'Tell us about it, ma'am,' he said.

Late on the following afternoon, Colonel Penderel sat in a wicker chair on the lawn before the Red Lodge, and looked gloomily at his shoes.

Everything about Red Lodge, like Colonel Penderel himself, was of a brushed trimness. The lawn was of that smooth green which seems to have lighter stripes in it; the house, of mellow red brick under mellow September sunshine, opened friendly doors to all the world.

But Hubert Penderel, a long lean man with big shoes, and wiry wintry-looking hair like his cropped moustache, slouched down in the chair. He clenched his big-knuckled fist, stared at it, and brought it down on the arm of the chair. Then he glanced round – and stopped guiltily as he caught sight of a brown-haired girl in a sleeveless white tennis frock, who had just come round the side of the house with a tennis racket under her arm.

The girl did not hesitate. She studied him for a moment, out of blue eyes wide-spaced above a short straight nose. A coloured silk scarf was tied round her head. Then she marched across the lawn, swinging the tennis racket as though she were going to hit somebody with it.

'Daddy,' she said abruptly, 'what on earth *is* it?'

Colonel Penderel said nothing.

'There *is* something,' she insisted. 'There has been, ever since that police superintendent came here this morning. What is it? Have you been getting into trouble with your car again?'

Colonel Penderel raised his head.

'Professor Meyer's been shot,' he answered with equal abruptness. 'Somebody plugged him through the window last night with a ·303 service rifle – Nancy, how would you like to see your old man arrested for murder?'

He had tried to say the last words whimsically. But he was not a very good actor, and his conception of the whimsical was somewhat heavy-handed.

Nancy Penderel backed away.

'What on earth are you talking about?'

'Fact,' said the Colonel, giving a slight flick to his shoulders. He peered round the lawn, hunching up his shoulders. 'That superintendent (Willet, his name is) wanted to know if I owned a rifle. I said yes: the one we all used to shoot with, on our own range. He said, where was it kept? I said, in the garden shed. He said, could he see it? I said, certainly.'

Nancy was having difficulty in adjusting her wits to this.

'He said, can I borrow this?' the Colonel concluded, hunching up his shoulders still further, and avoiding her eye. 'He took it away with him. It can't be the rifle that killed Meyer. But if by any chance it should happen to be –?'

'Dr Meyer?' Nancy breathed. 'Dr Meyer *dead*?'

Colonel Penderel jumped to his feet.

'I didn't like the blighter.' His tone was querulous. 'Everybody knows it. We had a rare old row only three days ago. Not because he was a

German, mind. After all, I've got a German staying here as my guest, haven't I? But – well, there it is. And another thing. That garden shed has a Yale lock. *I've* got the only key.'

There was another wicker chair near her father's. Nancy groped across to it, and sat down.

She felt no sense of danger or tragedy. It was merely that she could not understand. It was as though, in the midst of a dinner, the cloth were suddenly twitched off and all the dishes with their contents over-turned.

It was a pleasant afternoon. She had just finished playing three sets of tennis with Carl Kuhn. There couldn't, she assured herself, be anything really wrong: nothing that could blacken the daylight or spoil her week. Yet she watched her father tramping up and down the lawn, in his old chequered brown-and-black sports coat, more disturbed than she had ever seen him.

'But it's absurd!' Nancy cried. 'We can't take it seriously. Everybody knows you. The local police know you.'

'Ah,' said Colonel Penderel. 'Yes. The local police know me. But the fellows who've taken this over aren't local. They're down here from Scotland Yard.'

'Scotland Yard?'

'Special Branch. Look here, mouse.' He approached closer, and lowered his voice. 'Keep this under your hat. Don't mention it to your mother, whatever you do. But this fellow Meyer *was* a wrong 'un. A spy.'

'Impossible! That doddery little man?'

'Fact. Willet wouldn't say much, naturally. But I did gather they've got the goods on him, and his papers prove it. Damn it, you can't trust anybody nowadays, can you?'

Colonel Penderel's face darkened. He rubbed his hands together with a dry, rustling sound.

'If that's what he was – I say, good luck to the man who plugged him! But I didn't do it. Can you imagine me sneaking up on a man (that's what worries me, mouse) and letting drive at him when he wasn't looking?'

'No, of course not.' Nancy was beginning to reflect. 'If anybody killed him, I'm betting it was that simpering blonde wife of his.'

'Harriet Meyer? Great Scott, no!'

'Why not? She's fifteen years younger than he is. And they live all alone in that house, without even a maid to help with the work.'

Colonel Penderel was honest enough not to pursue this. He shook his head.

'There are reasons why not, mouse. Which you might understand, or you might not . . .'

'Daddy, stop treating me like a child! Why couldn't she have done it?'

'First, because the bullet that killed Meyer came from outside. Second, because there were Special Branch men watching every side of the house, and nobody went out or in at any time – certainly not Harriet Meyer. Third, they made an immediate search of the house, and there was no weapon in it except an old 16-bore shotgun which couldn't possibly have fired a rifle bullet.'

'S-ss-t!' said Nancy warningly.

Colonel Penderel whirled round.

The latch of the front gate was being lifted. Detective-Inspector Ballard, nondescript and fortyish, might have been any business man; but to the two watchers he had policeman written all over him. He came up the brick path smiling pleasantly, and raised his hat.

And, at the same time, Carl Kuhn strolled out of the open front door.

Carl Kuhn, in his late twenties, was one of those Teutonic types which seem all the more Nordic for being dark instead of fair. He was a middle-sized, stockily built, amiable young man with a ruddy complexion and a vast fund of chuckles. His heavy black hair grew low on his forehead; a narrow moustache followed the line of his wide mouth. Wearing white flannels, a sports coat, and a silk scarf, he came sauntering across the lawn to put his hands on the back of Nancy's chair.

But nobody looked at him.

'Good afternoon,' Ballard said pleasantly. 'Colonel Penderel?'

'I am Colonel Penderel,' said the owner of that name, looking very hard at him. 'This is my daughter. And Mr Kuhn.'

Ballard gave them a brief glance.

'Colonel Penderel, I am a police officer investigating the murder of Dr Ludwig Meyer,' continued Ballard; and Kuhn, who had started to light a cigarette, flicked up his head and blew two jets of smoke through his nostrils like an amiable dragon. 'I wonder if I could have a word with you in private, sir?'

'Say it,' said the Colonel.

'Pardon?'

'If you've got anything to say to me,' pursued the Colonel, sitting down deliberately and taking tight hold of the arms of the chair, 'say it. Here. Now. In front of these people.'

'You're sure that's what you'd prefer, sir?'

'Yes.'

Ballard's own deliberate gaze moved round the group. He took a note-book out of his pocket.

'Well, sir, you own a rifle. This morning you loaned that rifle to Superintendent Willet.'

'Yes?'

'Certain tests,' said Ballard, 'were made with this ·303 rifle by the ballistics consultant to the Devonshire County Constabulary.' He looked at his notebook. ' "Number of grooves: five and a half. Direction of twist: right-hand. Individual markings –" Never mind the technicalities, though.' His manner remained expressionless, almost kindly. 'The fact is, sir, that the bullet which killed Dr Meyer was fired from your rifle.'

From behind the house came the drowsy whir of a lawn mower.

Not even yet had Nancy Penderel a full sense of danger or even death. The sheer incredibility of the thing flooded her mind. She thought of the garden shed by the tennis-court; and of the miniature rifle range, sandbags backed by sheet iron, which her father had constructed at the end of the meadow.

'I see,' observed Colonel Penderel. His manner was stiff and impassive. He lifted one hand as though to whack it down on the arm of the chair, but he lowered it gently instead. 'Someone stole it, then. Or – am I by any chance under arrest?'

Ballard smiled, though his eyes did not move.

'Hardly that, sir. All we know is that your rifle *was* used.'

Throughout this, Carl Kuhn had been shifting from one foot to the other as though in a hopping agony of indecision. He took short, quick puffs at his cigarette.

'You are not saying,' he exploded, in English not far from perfect, 'that this man Meyer was shot yesterday afternoon?'

Ballard glanced at him quickly.

'Yesterday afternoon? What makes you say that?'

'Because,' returned Kuhn, 'yesterday afternoon I took a walk in the direction of that house. It iss not more than a quarter of a mile from here. And I heard a rifle shot. I looked over the edge of the hill, and saw this Meyer standing in front of the house. He seemed very angry. But he wass not dead then. No, no, no!'

He illustrated this story by cupping his hands over his eyes, and other elaborate gestures. Ballard stared at him.

'But what did you do, sir! Didn't you go closer to see what had happened?'

'No.'

'Why not?'

'His blood,' said Kuhn, holding himself very stiffly, 'wass not my blood. His race wass not my race. I would have nothing to do with him. But there!' Kuhn's tension relaxed, and he smiled. 'Not to talk politics in this house we have agreed. Is it not so, Colonel Penderel?'

'Yes, it's so,' admitted the Colonel, shifting. 'I didn't care anything about the fellow's race or politics. I just didn't like him.' He eyed Ballard. 'I suppose you've heard all about that?'

Ballard was silent for a moment.

'Knowledge hereabouts is pretty general, sir. Is it true that on Tuesday you threatened to kill him?'

The Colonel went rather white.

'I threatened to wring his neck, if that's what you mean?'

'Why?'

'I didn't like his manners. He browbeat the tradespeople and threw his weight about wherever he went. He was supposed to have come out of Germany penniless, but he had everything he wanted. At a garden party here on Tuesday – when my wife was trying to conciliate him – he said calmly that the English had no taste, no education, no manners, and no knowledge of science.'

'Ach, so?' murmured Kuhn.

'I didn't say anything at the time. I just walked part of the way home with him, and told him a few things. There was a hell of a row, yes.'

'Oh, this is absurd!' Nancy protested; but Ballard very gently and persuasively silenced her.

'Dr Meyer,' Ballard said without comment, 'was shot at about two o'clock in the morning, with a rifle taken from the garden shed here . . .'

'Which was locked,' said the Colonel stonily, 'and to which I've got the only key.'

'Daddy!' cried Nancy.

'And,' persisted the Colonel, 'at two o'clock in the morning I was asleep. I don't sleep in the same room as my wife; and I can't produce an alibi. Furthermore, the rifle *was* in that shed as late as nine o'clock in the evening; I know, because I put away the garden sprinkler then. The window won't open and there's no way into the shed except by the door. Now you know everything. But I didn't kill Meyer.'

Ballard was about to speak when there was an interruption.

Round the side of the house, at a blundering and near-sighted gait, lumbered a twenty-stone man in a white linen suit. He wore eyeglasses on a broad black ribbon, carried a crutch-handled stick, and seemed to be muttering down the slope of his several chins.

Colonel Penderel jumped up.

'Fell!' he shouted. 'Gideon Fell! What in the name of sanity are you doing here?'

Dr Fell woke up. He beamed all over his face like Old King Cole. He swept off his broad-brimmed white hat and ducked them a sort of bow. Then, wheezing gently after the exertion of this, he scowled.

'I trust,' he said, 'you will forgive my informal entrance by way of the back garden. I was – ahem – examining your miniature rifle range.'

Inspector Ballard intervened quickly.

'You're acquainted with Dr Fell, Colonel?'

'Lord, yes! One of my oldest . . . Here, sit down! Have a drink. Have something. You don't happen to have heard what's going on here, do you?'

Dr Fell seemed uncomfortable.

'Not to put too fine a point on it,' he answered, 'yes. I came down here to discuss a point of practical science, the use of thermite in a safe-breaking case, with Dr Meyer. My second visit. I find him –' he spread out his hand, widening the fingers. 'Sir Herbert Armstrong wired to ask if I would – um – lend a little consulting assistance.'

'Glad of any help, sir,' smiled Ballard.

'Not as glad as I am,' said the Colonel. 'You see, Fell, they think I did it.'

'Nonsense!' roared Dr Fell.

'Well, what do *you* think?'

A mulish expression overspread Dr Fell's face.

'Proverbs,' he said. 'Proverbs! I don't know. Before I express my opinion, there are two things about which I must have some information. I must know all about the wild cat and the moss.'

They stared at him.

'The what, sir?' demanded Inspector Ballard.

'The wild cat,' said Dr Fell, 'and the moss.'

Grunting acceptance of the chair which Colonel Penderel set out for him, he lowered his vast bulk into it. He got out a red bandanna handkerchief and mopped his face.

'When I last visited Dr Meyer,' he went on, 'I noticed on the mantelpiece in his study a big figure of a stuffed wild cat.'

'That's right,' agreed the Colonel.

'But when I went there today, the wild cat was gone. I asked Mrs Meyer about this, and she informed me that three days ago he took the stuffed wild cat out into the garden and burned it.'

'Burned it? Why should he do that?'

'Precisely,' said Dr Fell, flourishing the handkerchief, 'the shrewd, crafty question I asked myself. Why? Then there is the question of the moss. Somebody has been pulling up large quantities of moss from the vicinity of that house.'

It was Nancy Penderel's first sight of the man about whom she had heard so much from her father. Her first impulse, on seeing Dr Fell, was to laugh. She looked again, and was not so sure.

'Mark you,' the doctor went on suddenly, 'it was always *dry* moss. Very dry moss. The picker would have no traffic with anything damp. Archons of Athens! If only –'

He shook his head, sunk deep in mazy meditations. Inspector Ballard hesitated.

'Are you sure either of those two things has any bearing on the matter, sir?'

'Not at all. But we must look for some clue or retire to Bedlam. My first thought, of course, was that the stuffed wild cat might have been used as a kind of safe: a receptacle for papers. Since our evidence proves that Dr Meyer was a German espionage agent . . .'

'S-ss-t!' warned Inspector Ballard.

But Dr Fell merely blinked at him.

'My good sir' – he spoke with some testiness – 'you can't keep it dark. Everybody in North Devon knows about it. At the pub, where I had the pleasure of lowering several pints before coming on here, the talk was of nothing else. Somebody has been industriously spreading it.'

'But observe! Dr Meyer burns the safe, but leaves the papers. A version (I suppose) of locking the stable door after the horse is stolen. And a rolling stone gathers no moss. And –' He blinked at Carl Kuhn. 'You, sir. You are the other German I've heard so much about?'

Kuhn had been shifting excitedly from one foot to the other. His colour was higher. His surprise seemed deep and genuine. Once he made a gesture like one who removes an invisible hat and stands to attention.

'At your service, Doctor,' he said.

Dr Fell scowled. 'You're not providing us with still another proverb, I hope?'

'Another proverb?'

'That birds of a feather flock together?'

Kuhn was very serious. 'No. I regret what has happened. I deeply regret it. But – do not judge too harshly. Such tasks are often glorious. I misjudged him.'

Colonel Penderel stared at him. So did Nancy. She had a confused idea that her ordered world was crumpling round her.

'Glorious!' she repeated. 'That little worm was a spy, doing heaven knows what, and you say "such things are often glorious"?'

Kuhn's colour was still higher.

'Perhaps I express myself badly in English.'

'No, you don't either! You've spent half your life in England. I've known you since you were ten years old. You're more English than German anyway.'

'I regret, no,' said Kuhn. 'I *am* a German.' He drew himself up, but his anxious eyes regarded first Nancy and then the Colonel. 'This does not interfere with our long friendship?'

'Hanged if I know *what* it does,' muttered Colonel Penderel, after a pause. 'It seems to me we've got a parable here instead of a proverb; but never mind. What I do know is that we're in an unholy mess.' He frowned. 'You didn't kill Meyer yourself, did you?'

'Is it likely?' Kuhn asked simply.

'Don't you think,' said Nancy, 'you've got rather a nerve?'

'Little one, you do not understand!' Kuhn seemed in agony. 'Ach, now, let us forget this! It is no business of ours. Instead they should inquire who was firing at Herr Meyer yesterday afternoon –'

Dr Fell spoke in such a sharp voice that they all swung round.

'What's that? Who was firing at him yesterday afternoon?'

Kuhn repeated his story. As he did so, Inspector Ballard's expression was one of growing suspicion; but Dr Fell, with a sort of half-witted enlightenment dawning in his eyes, merely shaded those eyes with his hand.

'How did you happen to be there, Mr Kuhn?' asked Ballard.

'I was going for a walk. That is all.'

'In the direction of Professor Meyer's house?'

'No, no, that was quite by chance. Man must go somewhere when he walks.'

'A point,' observed Dr Fell, 'which is sometimes open to dispute. And last night?'

'Now that is very odd.' Suddenly Kuhn knocked his knuckles against his forehead. 'I had forgotten. Excuse. You say that Herr Meyer was shot at two o'clock in the morning?'

'Yes.'

'Towser!' said Kuhn with powerful relief. 'The dog! He was restless! He kept barking!'

'That's true,' breathed Nancy.

'So. Listen to me. I was disturbed. I could not sleep. Finally I rise to my feet and put my head out of the window. I saw McCabe, the gardener, going along the path in his dressing-gown. I called and asked if he could quiet the dog, and he said he was going to do it. The stable clock, I heard, was just striking two.'

There was a silence. Kuhn's anxious eyes turned toward the Inspector.

'I see,' said Ballard, making a note. 'Alibi, eh?'

'If you wish to call it so, yes. The man McCabe will tell you what I say is true. It was bright moonlight: I saw him and he saw me.'

'Inspector,' remarked Dr Fell, without taking his hand away from his eyes, 'I think you'd better accept that.'

'Accept the alibi?'

'Yes,' said Dr Fell. With infinite labour he propelled himself to his feet on his crutch-handled stick. 'Because it isn't necessary. I know how Professor Meyer really died. As a matter of fact, you told me.'

'*I* told you?' repeated Ballard.

'And if you'd care to come with me to the house,' pursued Dr Fell, 'I think I can show you.' He looked curiously at Colonel Penderel. 'If I remember correctly, my lad, you used to be something of an authority on firearms. You'd better come along too.'

'Is the answer,' asked Colonel Penderel, 'as easy as that?'

'The answer,' said Dr Fell, 'is another proverb.'

In the late afternoon light, the timbered cottage in the valley stood deserted and rather sinister. The bullet hole in the diamond-paned glass looked like a scar on a body.

Repeated knockings on the door roused nobody. Dr Fell tried the knob, and found it was open. He beckoned Inspector Ballard inside for a short whispered conference, after which the Inspector disappeared. Then Dr Fell, his face very red, invited the other three in.

Colonel Penderel walked in boldly. Nancy and Carl Kuhn followed with more hesitation. The German was obviously upset, and muttered something to himself as he crossed the threshold.

In the long, low-ceilinged study there was still a smell of stale tobacco smoke. Ludwig Meyer's body had been removed. Of his murder there now remained no trace except a spot of brown, dried blood on the papers which littered his desk. They were the sheets of his latest scientific treatise, which he would not now complete.

Dr Fell, his underlip drawn up over his bandit's moustache, stood in the doorway. His eyes moved left toward the mantelpiece in the narrower wall of the oblong, and right toward the window in the wall facing it. He lumbered across to the desk, where he turned round.

'Here,' he said, tapping the desk, 'is where Meyer was sitting. Here' – he picked up a few sheets of manuscript, and dropped them – 'is Meyer's last book. Here' – he drew open a drawer of the desk – 'was the evidence which proved, so very obviously, that Meyer was an espionage agent. By thunder, but wasn't it obvious!'

He closed the drawer with a bang. Only the sun entered. The bang of the drawer shook and disturbed dust motes against the sunlight. Dr Fell reached across and fingered the cretonne curtain. It was very warm in here, so warm that Nancy Penderel's head swam.

'I have a particular question to ask,' continued Dr Fell. He looked at the Colonel. 'Why is everybody so sure that the bullet which killed Meyer was fired from your rifle?'

Colonel Penderel put a hand to his forehead.

'See here, Fell,' he began querulously, but checked himself. 'It *was* fired from my rifle, wasn't it?'

'Oh, yes. I merely ask the question. Why is everyone so sure of that?'

'Because of the distinctive marks of rifling left on the bullet,' returned the other.

'True. Palpably and painfully true. Harrumph. Now, then: you've built a miniature rifle range in the meadow behind your house, haven't you?'

'You ought to know,' retorted the Colonel, regarding him with some exasperation. 'You said you'd been looking at it.'

'And what do you use to catch the bullets there?'

'Soft sand.'

'So that,' said Dr Fell, 'the many rounds fired into that sand would be lying about all over the place?'

'Yes.'

'Yes. And each bullet, though keeping exactly its original shape, would bear the distinctive marking of your rifle. Wouldn't it?'

The door of the study banged open, making them all jump. Inspector Ballard entered and gave Dr Fell a significant glance, and nodded.

Dr Fell drew a deep breath, shutting his eyes for a moment before he went on.

'You see,' he said, 'this crime is very much more ingenious than it looks.

A certain person who is listening to me now has created something of an artistic masterpiece.

'Those bullets, for instance. A bullet, selected for its most distinctive markings, could be fished out of that soft sand. It could easily be fitted into a loaded cartridge case and fired again. Couldn't it?'

'Not without . . .' Colonel Penderel began, but Dr Fell stopped him.

'Then there is this question of the window curtain.' The doctor leaned across and flicked it with his thumb and forefinger. But he was not looking at it; he was looking at Inspector Ballard.

'You, Inspector, were watching this house last night with a pair of field glasses. On the second the shot was fired, you jumped up and focused your glasses on this window. At least, so you told me this morning?'

'Yes, sir. That's right.'

'And, when the shot was fired, you saw this curtain flutter. Is that correct too?'

In Ballard's mind the picture returned with sharp clearness of light and shadow. He nodded.

'It is a flat impossibility,' said Dr Fell, 'for any shot fired from some distance away outside a closed window to agitate a curtain *inside* that window. There is only one thing which could have caused it; the expansion of gases from the muzzle of a firearm when the shot was fired in this room.'

Supporting himself on his stick, he lumbered across to the door, which was an inch or two open. He opened it fully into the little hall.

Just outside, her fingers pressed to her cheeks, stood Harriet Meyer. Her startled expression, with the upper lip slightly lifted to expose the teeth, was caught as though by a camera.

'Come in, Mrs Meyer,' said Dr Fell. 'Will you tell us how you killed your husband, or shall I?'

She struck out at him with a slap like a cat's. When he tried to catch her arm, she backed away swiftly to the other side of the room. There she stood against the bookshelves: her blue eyes as shallow as a doll's, but her breast rising and falling heavily.

Again Dr Fell drew a weary breath.

'Colonel Penderel,' he continued, 'will tell you that a ·303 bullet can be fired from a 16-bore shotgun, such as the one in this house. When you say it "can't possibly" be done, you don't really mean that. What you mean is that it can't be fired without leaving traces, and it can't be fired with accuracy.

'But accuracy, at more or less point-blank range, isn't necessary. And there is one way of firing it, out of a smooth-barrelled shotgun, so that it leaves no traces. You'll find that method fully outlined in Gross's *Criminal Investigation*.'

Colonel Penderel's eyes opened wide, and then narrowed.

'Moss!' he said. 'By the Lord Harry, dry moss! I must have been half-witted. Wrap the bullet in dry moss. It doesn't touch the inside of the gun, and no marks are left. The combustion ignites and destroys the moss: so that there's nothing left except a fouled barrel. When I was musketry instructor . . .'

Nancy was pointing wordlessly to the window.

Dr Fell nodded again.

'Oh, yes,' he agreed, contemplating the bullet hole. 'Made yesterday afternoon, as you've guessed. Made by a bullet out of a real rifle, probably a ·256. Made, of course, to set the stage.

'While her husband was occupied elsewhere, this lady calculated all angles, stood back some distance, and fired a clean hole through the window – lodging the bullet in a stuffed wild cat on the mantelpiece. If you will just note the line of fire, here, you'll see what happened.

'She could explain to Professor Meyer that she had been practising, and made a wild shot. We can't blame him for being "enraged". But it was an accident. Later she could burn the stuffed figure and hide the rifle outside the house. Then she was ready for real business that night.

'She and her husband lived alone here. There was nobody to notice that inconspicuous hole in the window – until the time came for it to be noticed. There would be (as she had arranged) police officers round the house, to trap a mythical spy-head who was supposed to be calling on Dr Meyer. They would not come close until they heard a shot. But when they heard a shot, it would be too late.'

Still Harriet Meyer had not spoken. Her eyes, with the poised look of one who cannot decide whether to fight or run, moved round the room.

'She had only,' said Dr Fell, 'to walk in here. Meyer would turn round (you note the position of the door) so that his left temple would be exposed. Any aftersmell of smokeless powder, which is very slight, would go unnoticed in the fog of rank tobacco smoke.

'The crime was all outlined for her, of course. In any good German scientist's house you are likely to find a copy of Hans Gross's *System der Kriminalistik*. There's one, I think, in the shelf just over her head now.'

They heard Harriet Meyer's fingernails scratch against the books. Two voices spoke almost together.

'Frau Meyer –' began Kuhn.

'But she's English!' cried Nancy.

'Of course she is,' said Dr Fell, and rapped the ferrule of his stick sharply against the floor. 'Confound it, don't you realize that's what makes her so dangerous?'

Harriet Meyer threw back her head and laughed.

'Don't you see,' thundered Dr Fell, 'that poor old Meyer, objectionable as he was, wasn't a spy at all? That he was just what he pretended to be? That this charming lady here, a convert to what some call the modern ideology, was the real spy?

'The Special Branch thought they were hot on Meyer's track because all trails led to his house. They were getting too close. So she had to sacrifice him. She tipped off the police and planned Meyer's murder, leaving incriminating evidence which was far too incriminating to be true, and bringing the police themselves as witnesses to her innocence. By thunder, I rather admire her!'

Harriet Meyer was still laughing. But it was a choked, vicious sort of laughter which turned her listeners cold. And it stopped, with a whistling inhalation of breath, as Inspector Ballard walked slowly across toward her.

Her eyes searched him. Then she seemed to make up her mind. She straightened up, heels together. Her hand flashed outwards, palm upper-most, in salute. Then, striking at him with the same hand, she lowered her head and ran for the door.

Dr Fell seized Ballard's arm.

'Let her go,' he said quietly. 'The house is surrounded. She won't get far. You have that shotgun safely locked up?'

'Yes; but –'

'The traces of burned moss in the barrel should be good enough. These clever people usually overlook something.'

The room was very hot. Again Dr Fell got out his bandanna handkerchief and mopped his face. Carl Kuhn hurried across to the window and peeped out.

'You would not,' said Dr Fell softly, 'you would not like her to get away?'

'I cannot say,' said Kuhn, whose face had lost its colour. 'I do not know. She is a compatriot of yours, not mine. It is none of my affair.'

Dr Fell stowed away his handkerchief.

'Sir,' he said gravely, 'I know nothing against you. I believe you to be an honest man.'

Kuhn ducked his head, and his heels came together.

'Even if you were not, you fly your own colours and present yourself for what you are. But there' – he pointed his stick in the direction Harriet Meyer had taken – 'there goes a portent and a warning. The alien we can deal with. But the hypnotized zealot among ourselves, the bat and the owl and the mole who would ruin us with the best intentions, is another thing. It has happened before. It may happen again. It is what we have to fear; and, by the grace of God, *all* we have to fear!'

In silence he put on his broad-brimmed white hat.

'And now you must excuse me,' he added, 'I have no relish for cases such as this.'

'I said it was Harriet,' Nancy told him, in a voice hardly above a whisper. 'I always thought she was queerer than he was. And yet, you know, I didn't *really* think so either. What did you mean when you told us the answer to this whole business was a proverb?'

Dr Fell made a hideous face.

'Oh, that?' he said. 'I wondered if she might be our quarry when I heard about her denouncing her husband to the police. Haven't I heard somewhere that people who live in glass houses shouldn't throw stones?'

G. K. Chesterton

THE WRONG SHAPE

A good deal of G. K. Chesterton's writing points up the difficulty of defining the crime story's limits. His fine early novel *The Man Who Was Thursday* (1908) can reasonably be called a mystery, yet Chesterton's concern here is only nominally with the revolutionary anarchists who are named for the days of the week, and in reality with the nature of religion and the idea that some truths cannot be apprehended through reason. Yet if we say that this book is not truly within the genre, there can be no doubt that Chesterton was fascinated by the possibilities of the crime short story as literary form. He deprecated those who thought that speaking of a good detective story was 'like speaking of a good devil', and asserted that this was the only form of popular literature that 'expressed some sense of the poetry of modern life'.

This is in part special pleading for his own short detective stories, which are contained in the five Father Brown collections (available in a single Penguin volume), and in *The Club of Queer Trades, The Poet and the Lunatics, Four Faultless Felons, The Man Who Knew Too Much* and *The Paradoxes of Mr Pond*. All of them contain clever stories, insistently poetic about the colour and quality of life; many approach through ingenious paradoxes what their creator felt to be unacknowledged truths about nature, society or religion. The best of them, by general consent, are the Father Brown tales, especially those in the first two collections. The twists and turns on almost every page, the language rich as whipped cream, the apparent incredibilities explained at the end with a whisk of the conjurer's cloak to reveal the missing rabbit, make the tales too heady a diet for continuous consumption. No more than two or three should be read at a time. Read more and you may find yourself picking holes, asking tediously rational questions. Chesterton's stories ask to be wondered at, not textually examined.

'The Wrong Shape' comes from the first collection, *The Innocence of Father Brown*, published in 1911. It has a nice period feeling in the setting, the Ninetyish poet Leonard Quinton who 'indulged his lust for colour somewhat to the neglect of form – even of good form' seems just right, and the puzzle enchants the sensibility even though it may not permanently convince the logical mind.

Gilbert Keith Chesterton (1874–1936) was a journalist, essayist, poet and novelist, and possessed so many talents that none of them was ever fully exploited. He was, as his works show, a convinced Christian throughout his life, and was converted to Roman Catholicism in 1922. He was the first President of England's Detection Club from its foundation in 1930 until his death.

Certain of the great roads going north out of London continue far into the country a sort of attenuated and interrupted spectre of a street, with great gaps in the building, but preserving the line. Here will be a group of shops, followed by a fenced field or paddock, and then a famous public house, and then perhaps a market garden or a nursery garden, and then one large private house, and then another field and another inn, and so on. If anyone walks along one of these roads he will pass a house which will probably catch his eye, though he may not be able to explain its attraction. It is a long, low house, running parallel with the road, painted mostly white and pale green, with a veranda and sun-blinds, and porches capped with those quaint sort of cupolas like wooden umbrellas that one sees in some old-fashioned houses. In fact, it is an old-fashioned house, very English and very suburban in the good old wealthy Clapham sense. And yet the house has a look of having been built chiefly for the hot weather. Looking at its white paint and sun-blinds one thinks vaguely of puggarees and even of palm trees. I cannot trace the feeling to its root; perhaps the place was built by an Anglo-Indian.

Anyone passing this house, I say, would be namelessly fascinated by it; would feel that it was a place about which some story was to be told. And he would have been right, as you shall shortly hear. For this is the story – the story of the strange things that did really happen in it in the Whitsuntide of the year 18—.

Anyone passing the house on the Thursday before Whit Sunday at about half-past four p.m. would have seen the front door open, and Father Brown, of the small church of St Mungo, come out smoking a large pipe in company with a very tall French friend of his called Flambeau, who was smoking a very small cigarette. These persons may or may not be of interest to the reader, but the truth is that they were not the only interesting things that were displayed when the front door of the white-and-green house was opened. There are further peculiarities about this house, which must be described to start with, not only that the reader may understand this tragic tale, but also that he may realize what it was that the opening of the door revealed.

The whole house was built upon the plan of a T, but a T with a very long cross piece and a very short tail piece. The long cross piece was the frontage that ran along in face of the street, with the front door in the middle; it was two stories high, and contained nearly all the important rooms. The short tail piece, which ran out at the back immediately opposite the front door, was one storey high, and consisted only of two long rooms, the one leading into the other. The first of these two rooms was the study in which the celebrated Mr Quinton wrote his wild Oriental poems and romances. The farther room was a glass conservatory full of tropical blossoms of quite unique and almost monstrous beauty, and on such afternoons as these was glowing with gorgeous sunlight. Thus when the hall door was open, many a passer-by literally stopped to stare and gasp; for he looked down a perspective of rich apartments to something really like a transformation scene in a fairy play: purple clouds and golden suns and crimson stars that were at once scorchingly vivid and yet transparent and far away.

Leonard Quinton, the poet, had himself most carefully arranged this effect; and it is doubtful whether he so perfectly expressed his personality in any of his poems. For he was a man who drank and bathed in colours, who indulged his lust for colour somewhat to the neglect of form – even of good form. This it was that had turned his genius so wholly to eastern art and imagery; to those bewildering carpets or blinding embroideries in which all the colours seem fallen into a fortunate chaos, having nothing to typify or to teach. He had attempted, not perhaps with complete artistic success, but with acknowledged imagination and invention, to compose epics and love stories reflecting the riot of violent and even cruel colour; tales of tropical heavens of burning gold or blood-red copper; of eastern heroes who rode with twelve-turbaned mitres upon elephants painted purple or peacock green; of gigantic jewels that a hundred negroes could not carry, but which burned with ancient and strange-hued fires.

In short (to put the matter from the more common point of view), he dealt much in eastern heavens rather worse than most western hells; in eastern monarchs, whom we might possibly call maniacs; and in eastern jewels which a Bond Street jeweller (if the hundred staggering negroes brought them into his shop) might possibly not regard as genuine. Quinton was a genius, if a morbid one; and even his morbidity appeared more in his life than in his work. In temperament he was weak and waspish, and his health had suffered heavily from Oriental experiments with opium. His wife – a handsome, hard-working, and, indeed, over-worked woman – objected to the opium, but objected much more to a live Indian hermit in white and yellow robes, whom her husband had insisted on entertaining for months together, a Virgil to guide his spirit through the heavens and the hells of the east.

It was out of this artistic household that Father Brown and his friend stepped on to the doorstep; and to judge from their faces they stepped out of it with much relief. Flambeau had known Quinton in wild student days in Paris, and they had renewed the acquaintance for a weekend; but apart from Flambeau's more responsible developments of late, he did not get on well with the poet now. Choking oneself with opium and writing little erotic verses on vellum was not his notion of how a gentleman should go to the devil. As the two paused on the doorstep, before taking a turn in the garden, the front garden gate was thrown open with violence, and a young man with a billycock hat on the back of his head tumbled up the steps in his eagerness. He was a dissipated-looking youth with a gorgeous red necktie all awry, as if he had slept in it, and he kept fidgeting and lashing about with one of those little jointed canes.

'I say,' he said breathlessly, 'I want to see old Quinton. I must see him. Has he gone?'

'Mr Quinton is in, I believe,' said Father Brown, cleaning his pipe, 'but I do not know if you can see him. The doctor is with him at present.'

The young man, who seemed not to be perfectly sober, stumbled into the hall; and at the same moment the doctor came out of Quinton's study, shutting the door and beginning to put on his gloves.

'See Mr Quinton?' said the doctor coolly. 'No, I'm afraid you can't. In fact, you mustn't on any account. Nobody must see him; I've just given him his sleeping draught.'

'No, but look here, old chap,' said the youth in the red tie, trying affectionately to capture the doctor by the lapels of his coat. 'Look here. I'm simply sewn up, I tell you. I – '

'It's no good, Mr Atkinson,' said the doctor, forcing him to fall back; 'when you can alter the effects of a drug I'll alter my decision,' and, settling on his hat, he stepped out into the sunlight with the other two. He was a bull-necked, good-tempered little man with a small moustache, inexpressibly ordinary, yet giving an impression of capability.

The young man in the billycock, who did not seem to be gifted with any tact in dealing with people beyond the general idea of clutching hold of their coats, stood outside the door, as dazed as if he had been thrown out bodily, and silently watched the other three walk away together through the garden.

'That was a sound, spanking lie I told just now,' remarked the medical man, laughing. 'In point of fact, poor Quinton doesn't have his sleeping draught for nearly half an hour. But I'm not going to have him bothered with that little beast, who only wants to borrow money that he wouldn't pay back if he could. He's a dirty little scamp, though he is Mrs Quinton's brother, and she's as fine a woman as ever walked.'

'Yes,' said Father Brown. 'She's a good woman.'

'So I propose to hang about the garden till the creature has cleared off,' went on the doctor, 'and then I'll go in to Quinton with the medicine. Atkinson can't get in, because I locked the door.'

'In that case, Dr Harris,' said Flambeau, 'we might as well walk round at the back by the end of the conservatory. There's no entrance to it that way but it's worth seeing, even from the outside.'

'Yes, and I might get a squint at my patient,' laughed the doctor, 'for he prefers to lie on an ottoman right at the end of the conservatory amid all those blood-red poinsettias; it would give me the creeps. But what are you doing?'

Father Brown had stopped for a moment, and picked up out of the long grass, where it had almost been wholly hidden, a queer, crooked Oriental knife, inlaid exquisitely in coloured stones and metals.

'What is this?' asked Father Brown, regarding it with some disfavour.

'Oh, Quinton's, I suppose,' said Dr Harris carelessly; 'he has all sorts of Chinese knick-knacks about the place. Or perhaps it belongs to the mild Hindu of his whom he keeps on a string.'

'What Hindu?' asked Father Brown, still staring at the dagger in his hand.

'Oh, some Indian conjurer,' said the doctor lightly; 'a fraud, of course.'

'You don't believe in magic?' asked Father Brown without looking up.

'Oh crikey! Magic!' said the doctor.

'It's very beautiful,' said the priest in a low, dreaming voice; 'the colours are very beautiful. But it's the wrong shape.'

'What for?' asked Flambeau, staring.

'For anything. It's the wrong shape in the abstract. Don't you ever feel that about Eastern art? The colours are intoxicatingly lovely; but the shapes are mean and bad – deliberately mean and bad. I have seen wicked things in a Turkey carpet.'

'*Mon Dieu!*' cried Flambeau, laughing.

'They are letters and symbols in a language I don't know; but I know they stand for evil words,' went on the priest, his voice growing lower and lower. 'The lines go wrong on purpose – like serpents doubling to escape.'

'What the devil are you talking about?' said the doctor with a loud laugh.

Flambeau spoke quietly to him in answer. 'The Father sometimes gets this mystic's cloud on him,' he said; 'but I give you fair warning that I have never known him have it except when there was some evil quite near.'

'Oh, rats!' said the scientist.

'Why, look at it,' cried Father Brown, holding out the crooked knife at arm's length, as if it were some glittering snake. 'Don't you see it is the wrong shape? Don't you see that it has no hearty and plain purpose? It does not point like a spear. It does not sweep like a scythe. It does not *look* like a weapon. It looks like an instrument of torture.'

'Well, as you don't seem to like it,' said the jolly Harris, 'it had better be taken back to its owner. Haven't we come to the end of this confounded conservatory yet? This house is the wrong shape, if you like.'

'You don't understand,' said Father Brown, shaking his head. 'The shape of this house is quaint – it is even laughable. But there is nothing *wrong* about it.'

As they spoke they came round the curve of glass that ended the conservatory, an uninterrupted curve, for there was neither door nor window by which to enter at that end. The glass, however, was clear, and the sun still bright, though beginning to set; and they could see not only the flamboyant blossoms inside, but the frail figure of the poet in a brown velvet coat lying languidly on the sofa, having, apparently, fallen half asleep over a book. He was a pale, slight man, with loose, chestnut hair and a fringe of beard that was the paradox of his face, for the beard made him look less manly. These traits were well known to all three of them; but even had it not been so, it may be doubted whether they would have looked at Quinton just then. Their eyes were riveted on another object.

Exactly in their path, immediately outside the round end of the glass building, was standing a tall man, whose drapery fell to his feet in faultless white, and whose bare, brown skull, face, and neck gleamed in the setting sun like a splendid bronze. He was looking through the glass at the sleeper, and he was more motionless than a mountain.

'Who is that?' cried Father Brown, stepping back with a hissing intake of his breath.

'Oh, it's only that Hindu humbug,' growled Harris; 'but I don't know what the deuce he's doing here.'

'It looks like hypnotism,' said Flambeau, biting his black moustache.

'Why are you unmedical fellows always talking bosh about hypnotism?' cried the doctor. 'It looks a deal more like burglary.'

'Well, we will speak to it, at any rate,' said Flambeau, who was always for action. One long stride took him to the place where the Indian stood. Bowing from his great height, which overtopped even the Oriental's, he said with placid impudence:

'Good evening, sir. Do you want anything?'

Quite slowly, like a great ship turning into a harbour, the great yellow face turned, and looked at last over its white shoulder. They were startled to see that its yellow eyelids were quite sealed, as in sleep. 'Thank you,' said the face in excellent English. 'I want nothing.' Then, half opening the lids, so as to show a slit of opalescent eyeball, he repeated, 'I want nothing.' Then he opened his eyes wide with a startling stare, said, 'I want nothing,' and went rustling away into the rapidly darkening garden.

'The Christian is more modest,' muttered Father Brown; 'he wants something.'

'What on earth was he doing?' asked Flambeau, knitting his black brows and lowering his voice.

'I should like to talk to you later,' said Father Brown.

The sunlight was still a reality, but it was the red light of evening, and the bulk of the garden trees and bushes grew blacker and blacker against it. They turned round the end of the conservatory, and walked in silence down the other side to get round to the front door. As they went they seemed to wake something, as one startles a bird, in the deeper corner between the study and the main building; and again they saw the white-robed fakir slide out of the shadow, and slip round towards the front door. To their surprise, however, he had not been alone. They found themselves abruptly pulled up and forced to banish their bewilderment by the appearance of Mrs Quinton, with her heavy golden hair and square pale face, advancing on them out of the twilight. She looked a little stern, but was entirely courteous.

'Good evening, Dr Harris,' was all she said.

'Good evening, Mrs Quinton,' said the little doctor heartily. 'I am just going to give your husband his sleeping draught.'

'Yes,' she said in a clear voice. 'I think it is quite time.' And she smiled at them, and went sweeping into the house.

'That woman's over-driven,' said Father Brown; 'that's the kind of woman that does her duty for twenty years, and then does something dreadful.'

The little doctor looked at him for the first time with an eye of interest. 'Did you ever study medicine?' he asked.

'You have to know something of the mind as well as the body,' answered the priest; 'we have to know something of the body as well as the mind.'

'Well,' said the doctor, 'I think I'll go and give Quinton his stuff.'

They had turned the corner of the front façade, and were approaching the front doorway. As they turned into it they saw the man in the white robe for the third time. He came so straight towards the front door that it seemed quite incredible that he had not just come out of the study opposite to it. Yet they knew that the study door was locked.

Father Brown and Flambeau, however, kept this weird contradiction to themselves, and Dr Harris was not a man to waste his thoughts on the impossible. He permitted the omnipresent Asiatic to make his exit, and then stepped briskly into the hall. There he found a figure which he had already forgotten. The inane Atkinson was still hanging about, humming and poking things with his knobby cane. The doctor's face had a spasm of disgust and decision, and he whispered rapidly to his companion: 'I must lock the door again, or this rat will get in. But I shall be out again in two minutes.'

He rapidly unlocked the door and locked it again behind him, just balking a blundering charge from the young man in the billycock. The young man threw himself impatiently on a hall chair. Flambeau looked at a Persian illumination on the wall; Father Brown, who seemed in a sort of daze, dully eyed the door. In about four minutes the door was opened again. Atkinson was quicker this time. He sprang forward, held the door open for an instant, and called out: 'Oh, I say, Quinton, I want –'

From the other end of the study came the clear voice of Quinton, in something between a yawn and a yell of weary laughter.

'Oh, I know what you want. Take it, and leave me in peace. I'm writing a song about peacocks.'

Before the door closed half a sovereign came flying through the aperture; and Atkinson, stumbling forward, caught it with singular dexterity.

'So that's settled,' said the doctor, and, locking the door savagely, he led the way out into the garden.

'Poor Leonard can get a little peace now,' he added to Father Brown; 'he's locked in all by himself for an hour or two.'

'Yes,' answered the priest; 'and his voice sounded jolly enough when we left him.' Then he looked gravely round the garden, and saw the loose figure of Atkinson standing and jingling the half-sovereign in his pocket, and beyond, in the purple twilight, the figure of the Indian sitting bolt upright upon a bank of grass with his face turned towards the setting sun. Then he said abruptly: 'Where is Mrs Quinton?'

'She has gone up to her room,' said the doctor. 'That is her shadow on the blind.'

Father Brown looked up, and frowningly scrutinized a dark outline at the gas-lit window.

'Yes,' he said, 'that is her shadow,' and he walked a yard or two and threw himself upon a garden seat.

Flambeau sat down beside him; but the doctor was one of those energetic people who live naturally on their legs. He walked away, smoking, into the twilight, and the two friends were left together.

'My father,' said Flambeau in French, 'what is the matter with you?'

Father Brown was silent and motionless for half a minute, then he said: 'Superstition is irreligious, but there is something in the air of this place. I think it's that Indian – at least, partly.'

He sank into silence, and watched the distant outline of the Indian, who still sat rigid as if in prayer. At first sight he seemed motionless, but as Father Brown watched him he saw that the man swayed ever so slightly with a rhythmic movement, just as the dark tree-tops swayed ever so slightly in the little wind that was creeping up the dim garden paths and shuffling the fallen leaves a little.

The landscape was growing rapidly dark, as if for a storm, but they could still see all the figures in their various places. Atkinson was leaning against a tree, with a listless face; Quinton's wife was still at her window; the doctor had gone strolling round the end of the conservatory; they could see his cigar like a will-o'-the-wisp; and the fakir still sat rigid and yet rocking, while the trees above him began to rock and almost to roar. A storm was certainly coming.

'When that Indian spoke to us,' went on Brown in a conversational undertone, 'I had a sort of vision, a vision of him and all his universe. Yet he only said the same thing three times. When first he said, "I want nothing", it meant only that he was impenetrable, that Asia does not give itself away. Then he said again, "I want nothing", and I knew that he meant that he was sufficient to himself, like a cosmos, that he needed no God, neither admitted any sins. And when he said the third time, "I want nothing", he said it with blazing eyes. And I knew that he meant literally what he said; that nothing was his desire and his home; that he was weary for nothing as for wine; that annihilation, the mere destruction of everything or anything –'

Two drops of rain fell; and for some reason Flambeau started and looked up, as if they had stung him. And the same instant the doctor down by the end of the conservatory began running towards them, calling out something as he ran.

As he came among them like a bombshell the restless Atkinson happened to be taking a turn nearer to the house front; and the doctor clutched him by the collar in a convulsive grip. 'Foul play!' he cried; 'what have you been doing to him, you dog?'

The priest had sprung erect, and had the voice of steel of a soldier in command.

'No fighting,' he cried coolly; 'we are enough to hold anyone we want to. What is the matter, doctor?'

'Things are not right with Quinton,' said the doctor, quite white. 'I could just see him through the glass, and I don't like the way he's lying. It's not as I left him, anyhow.'

'Let us go in to him,' said Father Brown shortly. 'You can leave Mr Atkinson alone. I have had him in sight since we heard Quinton's voice.'

'I will stop here and watch him,' said Flambeau hurriedly. 'You go in and see.'

The doctor and the priest flew to the study door, unlocked it, and fell into the room. In doing so they nearly fell over the large mahogany table in the centre at which the poet usually wrote; for the place was lit only by a small fire kept for the invalid. In the middle of this table lay a single sheet of paper, evidently left there on purpose. The doctor snatched it up, glanced at it, handed it to Father Brown, and crying, 'Good God, look at that!' plunged towards the glass room beyond, where the terrible tropic flowers seemed to keep a crimson memory of the sunset.

Father Brown read the words three times before he put down the paper. The words were: 'I die by my own hand; yet I die murdered!' They were in the quite inimitable, not to say illegible, handwriting of Leonard Quinton.

Then Father Brown, still keeping the paper in his hand, strode towards the conservatory, only to meet his medical friend coming back with a face of assurance and collapse. 'He's done it,' said Harris.

They went together through the gorgeous unnatural beauty of cactus and azalea and found Leonard Quinton, poet and romancer, with his head hanging downward off his ottoman and his red curls sweeping the ground. Inside his left side was thrust the queer dagger that they had picked up in the garden, and his limp hand still rested on the hilt.

Outside, the storm had come at one stride, like the night in Coleridge, and garden and glass roof were darkening with driving rain. Father Brown seemed to be studying the paper more than the corpse; he held it close to his eyes; and seemed trying to read it in the twilight. Then he held it up against the faint light, and, as he did so, lightning stared at them for an instant so white that the paper looked black against it.

Darkness full of thunder followed, and after the thunder Father Brown's voice said out of the dark: 'Doctor, this paper is the wrong shape.'

'What do you mean?' asked Dr Harris, with a frowning stare.

'It isn't square,' answered Brown. 'It has a sort of edge snipped off at the corner. What does it mean?'

'How the deuce should I know?' growled the doctor. 'Shall we move this poor chap, do you think? He's quite dead.'

'No,' answered the priest; 'we must leave him as he lies and send for the police.' But he was still scrutinizing the paper.

As they went back through the study he stopped by the table and picked up a small pair of nail scissors. 'Ah,' he said with a sort of relief; 'this is what he did it with. But yet –' And he knitted his brows.

'Oh, stop fooling with that scrap of paper,' said the doctor emphatically. 'It was a fad of his. He had hundreds of them. He cut all his paper like that,' as he pointed to a stack of sermon paper still unused on another and smaller table. Father Brown went up to it and held up a sheet. It was the same irregular shape.

'Quite so,' he said. 'And here I see the corners that were snipped off.' And to the indignation of his colleague he began to count them.

'That's all right,' he said, with an apologetic smile. 'Twenty-three sheets cut and twenty-two corners cut off them. And as I see you are impatient we will rejoin the others.'

'Who is to tell his wife?' asked Dr Harris. 'Will you go and tell her now, while I send a servant for the police?'

'As you will,' said Father Brown indifferently. And he went out to the hall door.

Here also he found a drama, though of a more grotesque sort. It showed nothing less than his big friend Flambeau in an attitude to which he had long been unaccustomed, while upon the pathway at the bottom of the steps was sprawling with his boots in the air the amiable Atkinson, his billycock hat and walking-cane sent flying in opposite directions along the path. Atkinson had at length wearied of Flambeau's almost paternal custody, and had endeavoured to knock him down, which was by no means a smooth game to play with the Roi des Apaches, even after that monarch's abdication.

Flambeau was about to leap upon his enemy and secure him once more, when the priest patted him easily on the shoulder.

'Make it up with Mr Atkinson, my friend,' he said. 'Beg a mutual pardon and say "Good night". We need not detain him any longer.' Then, as Atkinson rose somewhat doubtfully and gathered his hat and stick and went towards the garden gate, Father Brown said in a more serious voice: 'Where is that Indian?'

They all three (for the doctor had joined them) turned involuntarily towards the dim grassy bank amid the tossing trees, purple with twilight, where they had last seen the brown man swaying in his strange prayers. The Indian was gone.

'Confound him,' said the doctor, stamping furiously. 'Now I know that it was that nigger that did it.'

'I thought you didn't believe in magic,' said Father Brown quietly.

'No more I did,' said the doctor, rolling his eyes. 'I only know that I loathed that yellow devil when I thought he was a sham wizard. And I shall loathe him more if I come to think he was a real one.'

'Well, his having escaped is nothing,' said Flambeau. 'For we could have proved nothing and done nothing against him. One hardly goes to the parish constable with a story of suicide imposed by witchcraft or auto-suggestion.'

Meanwhile Father Brown had made his way into the house, and now went to break the news to the wife of the dead man.

When he came out again he looked a little pale and tragic; but what passed between them in that interview was never known, even when all was known.

Flambeau, who was talking quietly with the doctor, was surprised to see his friend reappear so soon at his elbow; but Brown took no notice, and merely drew the doctor apart. 'You have sent for the police, haven't you?' he asked.

'Yes,' answered Harris. 'They ought to be here in ten minutes.'

'Will you do me a favour?' said the priest quietly. 'The truth is, I make a collection of these curious stories, which often contain, as in the case of our Hindu friend, elements which can hardly be put into a police report. Now, I want you to write out a report of this case for my private use. Yours is a clever trade,' he said, looking the doctor gravely and steadily in the face. 'I sometimes think that you know some details of this matter which you have not thought fit to mention. Mine is a confidential trade like yours, and I will treat anything you write for me in strict confidence. But write the whole.'

The doctor, who had been listening thoughtfully with his head a little on one side, looked the priest in the face for an instant, and said: 'All right,' and went into the study, closing the door behind him.

'Flambeau,' said Father Brown, 'there is a long seat there under the veranda, where we can smoke, out of the rain. You are my only friend in the world, and I want to talk to you. Or, perhaps, be silent with you.'

They established themselves comfortably in the veranda seat; Father Brown, against his common habit, accepted a good cigar and smoked it steadily in silence, while the rain shrieked and rattled on the roof of the veranda.

'My friend,' he said at length, 'this is a very queer case. A very queer case.'

'I should think it was,' said Flambeau, with something like a shudder.

'You call it queer, and I call it queer,' said the other, 'and yet we mean quite opposite things. The modern mind always mixes up two different ideas: mystery in the sense of what is marvellous, and mystery in the sense of what is complicated. That is half its difficulty about miracles. A miracle is startling; but it is simple. It is simple because it *is* a miracle. It is power coming directly from God (or the devil) instead of indirectly through nature or human wills. Now you mean that this business is marvellous because it is miraculous, because it is witchcraft worked by a wicked Indian. Understand, I do not say that it was not spiritual or diabolic. Heaven and hell only know by what surrounding influences strange sins come into the lives of men. But for the present my point is this: If it was pure magic, as you think, then it is marvellous; but it is not mysterious — that is, it is not complicated. The quality of a miracle is mysterious, but its manner is simple. Now, the manner of this business has been the reverse of simple.'

The storm that had slackened for a little seemed to be swelling again, and there came heavy movements as of faint thunder. Father Brown let fall the ash of his cigar and went on:

'There has been in this incident,' he said, 'a twisted, ugly, complex quality that does not belong to the straight bolts either of heaven or hell. As one knows the crooked track of a snail, I know the crooked track of a man.'

The white lightning opened its enormous eye in one wink, the sky shut up again, and the priest went on:

'Of all these crooked things, the crookedest was the shape of that piece of paper. It was crookeder than the dagger that killed him.'

'You mean the paper on which Quinton confessed his suicide,' said Flambeau.

'I mean the paper on which Quinton wrote, "I die by my own hand",' answered Father Brown. 'The shape of that paper, my friend, was the wrong shape; the wrong shape, if ever I have seen it in this wicked world.'

'It only had a corner snipped off,' said Flambeau, 'and I understand that all Quinton's paper was cut that way.'

'It was a very odd way,' said the other, 'and a very bad way, to my taste and fancy. Look here, Flambeau, this Quinton – God receive his soul! – was perhaps a bit of a cur in some ways, but he really was an artist, with the pencil as well as the pen. His handwriting, though hard to read, was bold and beautiful. I can't prove what I say; I can't prove anything. But I tell you with the full force of conviction that he could never have cut that mean little piece off a sheet of paper. If he had wanted to cut down paper for some purpose of fitting in, or binding up, or what not, he would have made quite a different slash with the scissors. Do you remember the shape? It was a mean shape. It was a wrong shape. Like this. Don't you remember?'

And he waved his burning cigar before him in the darkness, making irregular squares so rapidly that Flambeau really seemed to see them as fiery hieroglyphics upon the darkness – hieroglyphics such as his friend had spoken of, which are undecipherable, yet can have no good meaning.

'But,' said Flambeau, as the priest put his cigar in his mouth again and leaned back, staring at the roof. 'Suppose somebody else did use the scissors. Why should somebody else, cutting pieces off his sermon paper, make Quinton commit suicide?'

Father Brown was still leaning back and staring at the roof, but he took his cigar out of his mouth and said: 'Quinton never did commit suicide.'

Flambeau stared at him. 'Why, confound it all,' he cried; 'then why did he confess to suicide?'

The priest leaned forward again, settled his elbows on his knees, looked at the ground, and said in a low distinct voice: 'He never did confess to suicide.'

Flambeau laid his cigar down. 'You mean,' he said, 'that the writing was forged?'

'No,' said Father Brown; 'Quinton wrote it all right.'

'Well, there you are,' said the aggravated Flambeau; 'Quinton wrote: "I die by my own hand", with his own hand on a plain piece of paper.'

'Of the wrong shape,' said the priest calmly.

'Oh, the shape be damned!' cried Flambeau. 'What has the shape to do with it?'

'There were twenty-three snipped papers,' resumed Brown unmoved, 'and only twenty-two pieces snipped off. Therefore one of the pieces had been destroyed, probably that from the written paper. Does that suggest anything to you?'

A light dawned on Flambeau's face, and he said: 'There was something else written by Quinton, some other words. "They will tell you I die by my own hand", or "Do not believe that —" '

'Hotter, as the children say,' said his friend. 'But the piece was hardly half an inch across; there was no room for one word let alone five. Can you think of anything hardly bigger than a comma which the man with hell in his heart had to tear away as a testimony against him?'

'I can think of nothing,' said Flambeau at last.

'What about quotation marks?' said the priest, and flung his cigar far into the darkness like a shooting star.

All words had left the other man's mouth, and Father Brown said, like one going back to fundamentals:

'Leonard Quinton was a romancer, and was writing an Oriental romance about wizardry and hypnotism. He —'

At this moment the door opened briskly behind them and the doctor came out with his hat on. He put a long envelope into the priest's hands.

'That's the document you wanted,' he said, 'and I must be getting home. Good night.'

'Good night,' said Father Brown, as the doctor walked briskly to the gate. He had left the front door open, so that a shaft of gaslight fell upon them. In the light of this Brown opened the envelope and read the following words:

Dear Father Brown, – *Vicisti, Galilaee!* Otherwise, damn your eyes, which are very penetrating ones. Can it be possible that there is something in all that stuff of yours after all?

I am a man who has ever since boyhood believed in Nature and in all natural functions and instincts, whether men called them moral or immoral. Long before I became a doctor, when I was a schoolboy keeping mice and spiders, I believed that to be a good animal is the best thing in the world. But just now I am shaken; I have believed in Nature; but it seems as if Nature could betray a man. Can there be anything in your bosh? I am really getting morbid.

I loved Quinton's wife. What was there wrong in that? Nature told me to, and it's love that makes the world go round. I also thought, quite sincerely, that she would be happier with a clean animal like me than with that tormenting little lunatic. What was there wrong with that? I was only facing facts, like a man of science. She would have been happier.

According to my own creed I was quite free to kill Quinton, which was the best thing for everybody, even himself. But as a healthy animal I had no notion of killing myself. I resolved, therefore, that I would never do it until I saw a chance that would leave me scot free. I saw that chance this morning.

I have been three times, all told, into Quinton's study today. The first time I went in he would talk about nothing but the weird tale, called 'The Curse of a Saint', which he was writing, which was all about how some Indian hermit made an English colonel kill himself by thinking about him. He showed me the last sheets, and even read me the last paragraph, which was something like this: 'The conqueror of the Punjab, a mere yellow skeleton, but still gigantic, managed to lift himself on his elbow and gasp in his nephew's ear: "I die by my own hand, yet I die murdered!" ' It so happened, by one chance out of a hundred, that those last words were written at the top of a new sheet of paper. I left the room, and went out into the garden intoxicated with a frightful opportunity.

We walked round the house, and two more things happened in my favour. You suspected an Indian, and you found a dagger which the Indian might most probably use. Taking the opportunity to stuff it in my pocket I went back to Quinton's study, locked the door, and gave him his sleeping draught. He was against answering Atkinson at all, but I urged him to call out and quiet the fellow, because I wanted a clear proof that Quinton was alive when I left the room for the second time. Quinton lay down in the conservatory, and I came through the study. I am a quick man with my hands, and in a minute and a half I had done what I wanted to do. I had emptied all the first part of Quinton's romance into the fireplace, where it burnt to ashes. Then I saw that the quotation marks wouldn't do, so I snipped them off, and to make it seem likelier, snipped the whole quire to match. Then I came out with the knowledge that Quinton's confession of suicide lay on the front table, while Quinton lay alive, but asleep, in the conservatory beyond.

The last act was a desperate one; you can guess it: I pretended to have seen Quinton dead and rushed to his room. I delayed you with the paper; and, being a quick man with my hands, killed Quinton while you were looking at his confession of suicide. He was half-asleep, being drugged, and I put his own hand on the knife and drove it into his body. The knife was of so queer a shape that no one but an operator could have calculated the angle that would reach his heart. I wonder if you noticed this.

When I had done it the extraordinary thing happened. Nature deserted me. I felt ill. I felt just as if I had done something wrong. I think my brain is breaking up; I feel some sort of desperate pleasure in thinking I have told the thing to somebody; that I shall not have to be alone with it if I marry and have children. What is the matter with me? . . . Madness . . . or can one have remorse, just as if one were in Byron's poems! I cannot write any more. – JAMES ERSKINE HARRIS.

Father Brown carefully folded up the letter and put it in his breast pocket just as there came a loud peal at the gate bell, and the wet waterproofs of several policemen gleamed in the road outside.

Agatha Christie

THE SUBMARINE
PLANS

The fame and popularity of Agatha Mary Clarissa Christie (1890–1976) has survived her death, fuelled in part by the lushly expensive, properly artificial production of several books as films: one with Albert Finney as a masterly Poirot, others with Peter Ustinov demonstrably Peter Ustinov. But this is only part of the story. The enduring success of her books springs also from the extraordinary ingenuity of the problems conceived and solved in the never-never land of her imagination where it seems always to be tea-time in some Edwardian year. The colonels, doctors, lawyers and others who inhabit this world are no more real than Cluedo figures, but there was no end to the infinite variety of murder methods, particularly those connected with poison, conceived by this Cleopatra of old Thames.

The Christie short stories are more sketchy and less ingenious than the novels, yet a collection like this would be incomplete without her name in the contents list. So here is 'The Submarine Plans', one of Poirot's early cases, involving in a good pre-First-World-War manner the plans of the new Z type submarine, a bluff sailor who is First Sea Lord and a Minister of Defence who will become Prime Minister. Ah, happy simplicities of the days before le Carré and Deighton!

A note had been brought by special messenger. Poirot read it, and a gleam of excitement and interest came into his eyes as he did so. He dismissed the man with a few curt words and then turned to me.

'Pack a bag with all haste, my friend. We're going down to Sharples.'

I started at the mention of the famous country place of Lord Alloway. Head of the newly formed Ministry of Defence, Lord Alloway was a prominent member of the Cabinet. As Sir Ralph Curtis, head of a great engineering firm, he had made his mark in the House of Commons, and he was now freely spoken of as *the* coming man, and the one most likely to be asked to form a ministry should the rumours as to Mr David MacAdam's health prove well founded.

A big Rolls-Royce car was waiting for us below, and as we glided off into the darkness, I plied Poirot with questions.

'What on earth can they want us for at this time of night?' I demanded. It was past eleven.

Poirot shook his head. 'Something of the most urgent, without doubt.'

'I remember,' I said, 'that some years ago there was some rather ugly scandal about Ralph Curtis, as he then was – some jugglery with shares, I believe. In the end, he was completely exonerated; but perhaps something of the kind has arisen again?'

'It would hardly be necessary for him to send for me in the middle of the night, my friend.'

I was forced to agree, and the remainder of the journey was passed in silence. Once out of London, the powerful car forged rapidly ahead, and we arrived at Sharples in a little under the hour.

A pontifical butler conducted us at once to a small study where Lord Alloway was awaiting us. He sprang up to greet us – a tall, spare man who seemed actually to radiate power and vitality.

'M. Poirot, I am delighted to see you. It is the second time the Government has demanded your services. I remember only too well what you did for us during the war, when the Prime Minister was kidnapped in that astounding fashion. Your masterly deductions – and may I add, your discretion? – saved the situation.'

Poirot's eyes twinkled a little.

'Do I gather then, milor', that this is another case for – discretion?'

'Most emphatically. Sir Harry and I – oh, let me introduce you – Admiral Sir Harry Weardale, our First Sea Lord – M. Poirot and – let me see, Captain –'

'Hastings,' I supplied.

'I've often heard of you, M. Poirot,' said Sir Harry, shaking hands. 'This is a most unaccountable business, and if you can solve it, we'll be extremely grateful to you.'

I liked the First Sea Lord immediately, a square, bluff sailor of the good old-fashioned type.

Poirot looked inquiringly at them both, and Alloway took up the tale.

'Of course, you understand that all this is in confidence, M. Poirot. We have had a most serious loss. The plans of the new Z type of submarine have been stolen.'

'When was that?'

'Tonight – less than three hours ago. You can appreciate perhaps, M. Poirot, the magnitude of the disaster. It is essential that the loss should not be made public. I will give you the facts as briefly as possible. My guests over the weekend were the Admiral, here, his wife and son, and a Mrs Conrad, a lady well known in London society. The ladies retired to bed early – about ten o'clock; so did Mr Leonard Weardale. Sir Harry is down here partly for the purpose of discussing the construction of this new type of submarine with me. Accordingly, I asked Mr Fitzroy, my secretary, to get out the plans from the safe in the corner there, and to arrange them ready for me, as well as various other documents that bore upon the subject in hand. While he was doing this, the Admiral and I strolled up and down the terrace, smoking cigars and enjoying the warm June air. We finished our smoke and our chat, and decided to get down to business. Just as we turned at the far end of the terrace, I fancied I saw a shadow slip out of the french window here, cross the terrace, and disappear. I paid very little attention, however. I knew Fitzroy to be in this room, and it never entered my head that anything might be amiss. There, of course, I am to blame. Well, we retraced our steps along the terrace and entered this room by the window just as Fitzroy entered it from the hall.

' "Got everything out we are likely to need, Fitzroy?" I asked.

' "I think so, Lord Alloway. The papers are all on your desk," he answered. And then he wished us both goodnight.

' "Just wait a minute," I said, going to the desk. "I may want something I haven't mentioned."

'I looked quickly through the papers that were lying there.

' "You've forgotten the most important of the lot, Fitzroy," I said. "The actual plans of the submarine!"

' "The plans are right on top, Lord Alloway."

' "Oh no, they're not," I said, turning over the papers.

' "But I put them there not a minute ago!"

' "Well, they're not here now," I said.

'Fitzroy advanced with a bewildered expression on his face. The thing seemed incredible. We turned over the papers on the desk; we hunted through the safe; but at last we had to make up our minds to it that the papers were gone – and gone within the short space of about three minutes while Fitzroy was absent from the room.'

'Why did he leave the room?' asked Poirot quickly.

'Just what I asked him,' exclaimed Sir Harry.

'It appears,' said Lord Alloway, 'that just when he had finished arranging the papers on my desk, he was startled by hearing a woman scream. He dashed out into the hall. On the stairs he discovered Mrs Conrad's French maid. The girl looked very white and upset, and declared that she had seen a ghost – a tall figure dressed all in white that moved without a sound. Fitzroy laughed at her fears and told her, in more or less polite language, not to be a fool. Then he returned to this room just as we entered from the window.'

'It all seems very clear,' said Poirot thoughtfully. 'The only question is, was the maid an accomplice? Did she scream by arrangement with her confederate lurking outside, or was he merely waiting there in the hope of an opportunity presenting itself? It was a man, I suppose – not a woman you saw?'

'I can't tell you, M. Poirot. It was just a – shadow.'

The Admiral gave such a peculiar snort that it could not fail to attract attention.

'M. l'Amiral has something to say, I think,' said Poirot quietly, with a slight smile. 'You saw this shadow, Sir Harry?'

'No, I didn't,' returned the other. 'And neither did Alloway. The branch of a tree flapped, or something, and then afterwards, when we discovered the theft, he leaped to the conclusion that he had seen someone pass across the terrace. His imagination played a trick on him; that's all.'

'I am not usually credited with having much imagination,' said Lord Alloway with a slight smile.

'Nonsense, we've all got imagination. We can all work ourselves up to believe that we've seen more than we have. I've had a lifetime of experience at sea, and I'll back my eyes against those of any landsman. I was looking right down the terrace, and I'd have seen the same if there was anything to see.'

He was quite excited over the matter. Poirot rose and stepped quickly to the window.

'You permit?' he asked. 'We must settle this point if possible.'

He went out upon the terrace, and we followed him. He had taken an electric torch from his pocket, and was playing the light along the edge of the grass that bordered the terrace.

'Where did he cross the terrace, milor'?' he asked.

'About opposite the window, I should say.'

Poirot continued to play the torch for some minutes longer, walking the entire length of the terrace and back. Then he shut it off and straightened himself up.

'Sir Harry is right – and you are wrong, milor',' he said quietly. 'It rained heavily earlier this evening. Anyone who passed over that grass could not avoid leaving footmarks. But there are none – none at all.'

His eyes went from one man's face to the other's. Lord Alloway looked bewildered and unconvinced; the Admiral expressed a noisy gratification.

'Knew I couldn't be wrong,' he declared. 'Trust my eyes anywhere.'

He was such a picture of an honest old sea-dog that I could not help smiling.

'So that brings us to the people in the house,' said Poirot smoothly. 'Let us come inside again. Now, milor', while Mr Fitzroy was speaking to the maid on the stairs, could anyone have seized the opportunity to enter the study from the hall?'

Lord Alloway shook his head.

'Quite impossible – they would have had to pass him in order to do so.'

'And Mr Fitzroy himself – you are sure of him, eh?'

Lord Alloway flushed.

'Absolutely, M. Poirot. I will answer confidently for my secretary. It is quite impossible that he should be concerned in the matter in any way.'

'Everything seems to be impossible,' remarked Poirot rather drily. 'Possibly the plans attached to themselves a little pair of wings, and flew away – comme ça!' He blew his lips out like a comical cherub.

The whole thing is impossible,' declared Lord Alloway impatiently. 'But I beg, M. Poirot, that you will not dream of suspecting Fitzroy. Consider for one moment – had he wished to take the plans, what could have been easier for him than to take a tracing of them without going to the trouble of stealing them?'

'There, milor',' said Poirot with approval, 'you make a remark *bien juste* – I see that you have a mind orderly and methodical. *L'Angleterre* is happy in possessing you.'

Lord Alloway looked rather embarrassed by this sudden burst of praise. Poirot returned to the matter in hand.

'The room in which you had been sitting all the evening –'

'The drawing-room? Yes?'

'That also has a window on the terrace, since I remember your saying you went out that way. Would it not be possible for someone to come out by the drawing-room window and in by this one while Mr Fitzroy was out of the room, and return the same way?'

'But we'd have seen them,' objected the Admiral.

'Not if you had your backs turned, walking the other way.'

'Fitzroy was only out of the room a few minutes, the time it would take us to walk to the end and back.'

'No matter – it is a possibility – in fact, the only one as things stand.'

'But there was no one in the drawing-room when we went out,' said the Admiral.

'They may have come there afterwards.'

'You mean,' said Lord Alloway slowly, 'that when Fitzroy heard the maid scream and went out, someone was already concealed in the drawing-room, and that they darted in and out through the windows, and only left the drawing-room when Fitzroy had returned to this room?'

'The methodical mind again,' said Poirot, bowing. 'You express the matter perfectly.'

'One of the servants, perhaps?'

'Or a guest. It was Mrs Conrad's maid who screamed. What exactly can you tell me of Mrs Conrad?'

Lord Alloway considered for a minute.

'I told you that she is a lady well known in society. That is true in the sense that she gives large parties, and goes everywhere. But very little is known as to where she really comes from, and what her past life has been. She is a lady who frequents diplomatic and Foreign Office circles as much as possible. The Secret Service is inclined to ask – why?'

'I see,' said Poirot. 'And she was asked here this weekend –'

'So that – shall we say? – we might observe her at close quarters.'

'*Parfaitement!* It is possible that she has turned the tables on you rather neatly.'

Lord Alloway looked discomfited, and Poirot continued: 'Tell me, milor', was any reference made in her hearing to the subjects you and the Admiral were going to discuss together?'

'Yes,' admitted the other. 'Sir Harry said: "And now for our submarine! To work!" or something of that sort. The others had left the room, but she had come back for a book.'

'I see,' said Poirot thoughtfully. 'Milor', it is very late – but this is an urgent affair. I would like to question the members of this house-party at once if it is possible.'

'It can be managed, of course,' said Lord Alloway. 'The awkward thing is, we don't want to let it get about more than can be helped. Of course, Lady Juliet Weardale and young Leonard are all right – but Mrs Conrad, if she is not guilty, is rather a different proposition. Perhaps you could just state that an important paper is missing, without specifying what it is, or going into any of the circumstances of the disappearance?'

'Exactly what I was about to propose myself,' said Poirot, beaming. 'In fact, in all three cases. Monsieur the Admiral will pardon me, but even the best of wives –'

'No offence,' said Sir Harry. 'All women talk, bless 'em! I wish Juliet would talk a little more and play bridge a little less. But women are like that nowadays, never happy unless they're dancing or gambling. I'll get Juliet and Leonard up, shall I, Alloway?'

'Thank you. I'll call the French maid. M. Poirot will want to see her, and she can rouse her mistress. I'll attend to it now. In the meantime, I'll send Fitzroy along.'

Mr Fitzroy was a pale, thin young man with pince-nez and a frigid expression. His statement was practically word for word what Lord Alloway had already told us.

'What is your own theory, Mr Fitzroy?'

Mr Fitzroy shrugged his shoulders.

'Undoubtedly someone who knew the hang of things was waiting his chance outside. He could see what went on through the window, and he slipped in when I left the room. It's a pity Lord Alloway didn't give chase then and there when he saw the fellow leave.'

Poirot did not undeceive him. Instead he asked: 'Do you believe the story of the French maid – that she had seen a ghost?'

'Well, hardly, M. Poirot!'

'I mean – that she really thought so?'

'Oh, as to that, I can't say. She certainly seemed rather upset. She had her hands to her head.'

'Aha!' cried Poirot with the air of one who has made a discovery. 'Is that so indeed – and she was without doubt a pretty girl?'

'I didn't notice particularly,' said Mr Fitzroy in a repressive voice.

'You did not see her mistress, I suppose?'

'As a matter of fact, I did. She was in the gallery at the top of the steps and was calling her – "Léonie!" Then she saw me – and of course retired.'

'Upstairs,' said Poirot, frowning.

'Of course, I realize that all this is very unpleasant for me – or rather would have been, if Lord Alloway had not chanced to see the man actually leaving. In any case, I should be glad if you would make a point of searching my room – and myself.'

'You really wish that?'

'Certainly I do.'

What Poirot would have replied I do not know, but at that moment Lord Alloway reappeared and informed us that the two ladies and Mr Leonard Weardale were in the drawing-room.

The women were in becoming négligés. Mrs Conrad was a beautiful woman of thirty-five, with golden hair and a slight tendency to *embonpoint*. Lady Juliet Weardale must have been forty, tall and dark, very thin, still beautiful, with exquisite hands and feet, and a restless, haggard manner. Her son was rather an effeminate-looking young man, as great a contrast to his bluff, hearty father as could well be imagined.

Poirot gave forth the little rigmarole we had agreed upon, and then explained that he was anxious to know if anyone had heard or seen anything that night which might assist us.

Turning to Mrs Conrad first, he asked her if she would be so kind as to inform him exactly what her movements had been.

'Let me see . . . I went upstairs. I rang for my maid. Then, as she did not put in an appearance, I came out and called her. I could hear her talking on the stairs. After she had brushed my hair, I sent her away – she was in a very curious nervous state. I read awhile and then went to bed.'

'And you, Lady Juliet?'

'I went straight upstairs and to bed. I was very tired.'

'What about your book, dear?' asked Mrs Conrad with a sweet smile.

'My book?' Lady Juliet flushed.

'Yes, you know, when I sent Léonie away, you were coming up the stairs. You had been down to the drawing-room for a book, you said.'

'Oh yes, I did go down. I – I forgot.'

Lady Juliet clasped her hands nervously together.

'Did you hear Mrs Conrad's maid scream, milady?'

'No – no, I didn't.'

'How curious – because you must have been in the drawing-room at the time.'

'I heard nothing,' said Lady Juliet in a firmer voice.

Poirot turned to young Leonard.

'Monsieur?'

'Nothing doing. I went straight upstairs and turned in.'

Poirot stroked his chin.

'Alas, I fear there is nothing to help me here. Mesdames and monsieur, I regret – I regret infinitely to have deranged you from your slumbers for so little. Accept my apologies, I pray of you.'

Gesticulating and apologizing, he marshalled them out. He returned with the French maid, a pretty, impudent-looking girl. Alloway and Weardale had gone out with the ladies.

'Now, mademoiselle,' said Poirot in a brisk tone, 'let us have the truth. Recount to me no histories. Why did you scream on the stairs?'

'Ah, monsieur, I saw a tall figure – all in white –'

Poirot arrested her with an energetic shake of his forefinger.

'Did I not say, recount to me no histories? I will make a guess. He kissed you, did he not? M. Leonard Weardale, I mean?'

'*Eh bien, monsieur*, and after all, what is a kiss?'

'Under the circumstances, it is most natural,' replied Poirot gallantly. 'I myself, or Hastings here – but tell me just what occurred.'

'He came up behind me, and caught me. I was startled, and I screamed. If I had known, I would not have screamed – but he came upon me like a cat. Then came *M. le secrétaire*. M. Leonard flew up the stairs. And what could I say? Especially to a *jeune homme comme ça – tellement comme il faut? Ma foi*, I invent a ghost.'

'And all is explained,' cried Poirot genially. 'You then mounted to the chamber of Madame your mistress. Which is her room, by the way?'

'It is at the end, monsieur. That way.'

'Directly over the study, then. *Bien*, mademoiselle, I will detain you no longer. And *la prochaine fois*, do not scream.'

Handing her out, he came back to me with a smile.

'An interesting case, is it not, Hastings? I begin to have a few little ideas. *Et vous?*'

'What was Leonard Weardale doing on the stairs? I don't like that young man, Poirot. He's a thorough young rake, I should say.'

'I agree with you, *mon ami*.'

'Fitzroy seems an honest fellow.'

'Lord Alloway is certainly insistent on that point.'

'And yet there is something in his manner –'

'That is almost too good to be true? I felt it myself. On the other hand, our friend Mrs Conrad is certainly not good at all.'

'And her room is over the study,' I said musingly, and keeping a sharp eye on Poirot.

He shook his head with a slight smile.

'No, *mon ami*, I cannot bring myself seriously to believe that that immaculate lady swarmed down the chimney, or let herself down from the balcony.'

As he spoke, the door opened, and to my great surprise, Lady Juliet Weardale flitted in.

'M. Poirot,' she said somewhat breathlessly, 'can I speak to you alone?'

'Milady, Captain Hastings is as my other self. You can speak before him as though he were a thing of no account, not there at all. Be seated, I pray you.'

She sat down, still keeping her eyes fixed on Poirot.

'What I have to say is – rather difficult. You are in charge of this case. If the – papers were to be returned, would that end the matter? I mean, could it be done without questions being asked?'

Poirot stared hard at her.

'Let me understand you, madame. They are to be placed in my hand – is that right? And I am to return them to Lord Alloway on the condition that he asks no questions as to where I got them?'

She bowed her head. 'That is what I mean. But I must be sure there will be no – publicity.'

'I do not think Lord Alloway is particularly anxious for publicity,' said Poirot grimly.

'You accept then?' she cried eagerly in response.

'A little moment, milady. It depends on how soon you can place those papers in my hands.'

'Almost immediately.'

Poirot glanced up at the clock.

'How soon, exactly?'

'Say – ten minutes,' she whispered.

'I accept, milady.'

She hurried from the room. I pursed my mouth up for a whistle.

'Can you sum up the situation for me, Hastings?'

'Bridge,' I replied succinctly.

'Ah, you remember the careless words of Monsieur the Admiral! What a memory! I felicitate you, Hastings.'

We said no more, for Lord Alloway came in, and looked inquiringly at Poirot.

'Have you any further ideas, M. Poirot? I am afraid the answers to your questions have been rather disappointing.'

'Not at all, milor'. They have been quite sufficiently illuminating. It will be unnecessary for me to stay here any longer, and so, with your permission, I return at once to London.'

Lord Alloway seemed dumbfounded.

'But – but what have you discovered? Do you know who took the plans?'

'Yes, milor', I do. Tell me – in the case of the papers being returned to you anonymously, you would prosecute no further inquiry?'

Lord Alloway stared at him.

'Do you mean on payment of a sum of money?'

'No, milor', returned unconditionally.'

'Of course, the recovery of the plans is the great thing,' said Lord Alloway slowly. He still looked puzzled and uncomprehending.

'Then I should seriously recommend you to adopt that course. Only you, the Admiral and your secretary know of the loss. Only they need know of the restitution. And you may count on me to support you in every way – lay the mystery on my shoulders. You asked me to restore the papers – I have done so. You know no more.' He rose and held out his hand. 'Milor', I am glad to have met you. I have faith in you – and your devotion to England. You will guide her destinies with a strong, sure hand.'

'M. Poirot – I swear to you that I will do my best. It may be a fault, or it may be a virtue – but I believe in myself.'

'So does every great man. Me, I am the same!' said Poirot grandiloquently.

The car came round to the door in a few minutes, and Lord Alloway bade us farewell on the steps with renewed cordiality.

'That is a great man, Hastings,' said Poirot as we drove off. 'He has brains, resource, power. He is the strong man that England needs to guide her through these difficult days of reconstruction.'

'I'm quite ready to agree with all you say, Poirot – but what about Lady Juliet? Is she to return the papers straight to Alloway? What will she think when she finds you have gone off without a word?'

'Hastings, I will ask you a little question. Why, when she was talking with me, did she not hand me the plans then and there?'

'She hadn't got them with her.'

'Perfectly. How long would it take her to fetch them from her room? Or from any hiding-place in the house? You need not answer. I will tell you. Probably about two minutes and a half! Yet she asks for ten minutes. Why? Clearly she has to obtain them from some other person, and to reason or argue with that person before they give them up. Now, what person could that be? Not Mrs Conrad, clearly, but a member of her own family, her husband or son. Which is it likely to be? Leonard Weardale said he went straight to bed. We know that to be untrue. Supposing his mother went to his room and found it empty; supposing she came down filled with a nameless dread – he is no beauty that son of hers! She does not find him, but later she hears him deny that he ever left his room. She leaps to the conclusion that he is the thief. Hence her interview with me.

'But, *mon ami*, we know something that Lady Juliet does not. We know that her son could not have been in the study, because he was on the stairs, making love to the pretty French maid. Although she does not know it, Leonard Weardale has an alibi.'

'Well, then, who did steal the papers? We seem to have eliminated everybody – Lady Juliet, her son, Mrs Conrad, the French maid –'

'Exactly. Use your little grey cells, my friend. The solution stares you in the face.'

I shook my head blankly.

'But yes! If you would only persevere! See, then, Fitzroy goes out of the study; he leaves the papers on the desk. A few minutes later Lord Alloway enters the room, goes to the desk, and the papers are gone. Only two things are possible: either Fitzroy did *not* leave the papers on the desk, but put them in his pocket – and that is not reasonable, because as Alloway pointed out, he could have taken a tracing at his own convenience any time – or else the papers were still on the desk when Lord Alloway went to it – in which case they went into *his* pocket.'

'Lord Alloway the thief,' I said, dumbfounded. 'But why? Why?'

'Did you not tell me of some scandal in the past? He was exonerated, you said. But suppose, after all, it had been true? In English public life there must be no scandal. If this were raked up and proved against him now – goodbye to his political career. We will suppose that he was being blackmailed, and the price asked was the submarine plans.'

'But the man's a black traitor!' I cried.

'Oh no, he is not. He is clever and resourceful. Supposing, my friend, that he copied those plans, making – for he is a clever engineer – a slight alteration in each part which will render them quite impracticable. He hands the faked plans to the enemy's agent – Mrs Conrad, I fancy; but in order that no suspicion of their genuineness may arise, the plans must seem to be stolen. He does his best to throw no suspicion on anyone in the house, by pretending to see a man leaving the window. But there he ran up against the obstinacy of the Admiral. So his next anxiety is that no suspicion shall fall on Fitzroy.'

'This is all guesswork on your part, Poirot,' I objected.

'It is psychology, *mon ami*. A man who had handed over the real plans would not be overscrupulous as to who was likely to fall under suspicion. And why was he so anxious that no details of the robbery should be given to Mrs Conrad? Because he had handed over the faked plans earlier in the evening, and did not want her to know that the theft could only have taken place later.'

'I wonder if you are right,' I said.

'Of course I am right. I spoke to Alloway as one great man to another – and he understood perfectly. You will see.'

One thing is quite certain. On the day when Lord Alloway became Prime Minister, a cheque and a signed photograph arrived; on the photograph were the words: '*To my discreet friend, Hercule Poirot – from Alloway.*'

I believe that the Z type of submarine is causing great exultation in naval circles. They say it will revolutionize modern naval warfare. I have heard that a certain foreign power essayed to construct something of the same kind and the result was a dismal failure. But I still consider that Poirot was guessing. He will do it once too often one of these days.

Edmund Crispin
and Geoffrey Bush

WHO KILLED
BAKER?

Edmund Crispin (1921–78), born Robert Bruce Montgomery, was always known to his friends as Bruce. The course of his career was unusual. Most crime writers come to the form after attempting some other kind of literature, or as a sideline occupation from an office job. Crispin's first book, *The Case of the Gilded Fly*, appeared when he was just down from Oxford, in his early twenties. His friends there included Kingsley Amis, Philip Larkin and Alan Ross, and Ross has said how immensely knowledgeable and sophisticated he seemed as an undergraduate, somebody who had always read the latest novel and knew the latest literary theory.

Crispin went on producing a book a year for eight years, and then gave up to write film music (he wrote music for thirty-eight films in all), perhaps promising himself that he would return to the crime form in a year or two. In fact he wrote only one more crime story, the disappointing *The Glimpses of the Moon* (1977).

The other eight novels reflect the exuberance and light-hearted charm of Crispin's personality. The American critic Anthony Boucher called him a blend of John Dickson Carr, Michael Innes, M. R. James and the Marx Brothers, and that seems a fair enough description. He took immense pains over the construction of his early books, but still did not take himself, his crime stories, or anything else quite seriously. The result is books which are tremendous fun to read. The best are *The Moving Toyshop* and *Love Lies Bleeding*, but all are expressions of his belief that 'crime stories in general and detective stories in particular should be essentially imaginative and artificial in order to make their best effect'.

He gave to short stories the same care in construction that were applied to his novels, with similar results. 'Who Killed Baker?', co-written with Geoffrey Bush, comes from one of two collections of short stories, *Beware of the Trains* and *Fen Country*, both of which are strongly recommended. The perfectly fair but absolutely outrageous trick in 'Who Killed Baker?' is one that delighted its author.

Wakefield was attending a series of philosophy lectures at London University, and for the past ten minutes his fellow-guests at Haldane's had been mutely enduring a précis of the lecturer's main contentions.

'What it amounts to, then,' said Wakefield, towards what they hoped was the close of what they hoped was his peroration, 'is that philosophy deals not so much with the answers to questions about Man and the Universe as with the problem of *what questions may properly be asked*. Improper questions' – here a little man named Fielding, whom no one knew very well, choked suddenly over his port and had to be led out – 'improper questions can only confuse the issue. And it's this aspect of philosophy which in my opinion defines its superiority to other studies, such as – such as' – Wakefield's eye lighted on Gervase Fen, who was stolidly cracking walnuts opposite – 'such as, well, criminology, for instance.'

Fen roused himself.

'Improper questions,' he said reflectively. 'I remember a case which illustrates very clearly how –'

'Defines,' Wakefield repeated at a higher pitch, 'its superiority to –'

But at this point, Haldane, perceiving that much more of Wakefield on epistemology would certainly bring the party to a premature end, contrived adroitly to upset his port into Wakefield's lap, and in the mêlée which ensued it proved possible to detach the conversational initiative from Wakefield and confer it on Fen.

'*Who killed Baker?*' With this rather abrupt query Fen established a foothold while Wakefield was still scrubbing ineffectually at his damp trousers with a handkerchief. 'The situation which resulted in Baker's death wasn't in itself specially complicated or obscure, and in consequence the case was solved readily enough.'

'Yes, it would be, of course,' said Wakefield sourly, 'if you were solving it.'

'Oh, but I wasn't.' Fen shook his head decisively, and Wakefield, shifting about uncomfortably in the effort to remove wet barathea from contact with his skin, glowered at him. 'The case was solved by a very able Detective-Inspector of the County CID, by name Casby, and it was from him that I heard of it, quite recently, while we were investigating the death of that Swiss schoolmaster at Cotten Abbas. As nearly as I can, I'll tell it to you the way he told me. And I ought to warn you in advance that it's a case in which the mode of telling is important – as important, probably, as the thing told . . .

'At the time of his death Baker was about forty-five, a self-important little man with very black, heavily brilliantined hair, an incipient paunch, dandified clothes, and a twisted bruiser's nose which was the consequence not of pugnacity but of a fall from a bicycle in youth. He was not, one gathers, at all a pleasing personality, and he had crowned his dislikeable qualities by marrying, and subsequently bullying, a wife very much younger and more attractive than himself. For a reason which the sequel will make obvious, there's not much evidence as to the form this bullying took, but it was real enough – no question about that – and three years of it drove the wretched woman, more for consolation than for passion, into the arms of the chauffeur, a gloomy, sallow young man named Arnold Snow. Since Snow had never read D. H. Lawrence, his chief emotion in the face of Mary Baker's advances was simple surprise, and to do him justice, he seems never to have made the smallest attempt to capitalize his position in any of the obvious ways. But, of course, the neighbours talked; there are precedents enough for such a relationship's ending in disaster.'

Haldane nodded. 'Rattenbury,' he suggested, 'and Stoner.'

'That sort of thing, yes. It wasn't a very sensible course for Mary Baker to adopt, the more so as for religious reasons she had a real horror of divorce. But she was one of those warm, good-natured, muddle-headed women – not, in temperament, unlike Mrs Rattenbury – to whom a man's affection is overwhelmingly necessary, as much for emotional as for physical reasons; and three years of Baker had starved that side of her so effectively that when she did break out, she broke out with a vengeance. I've seen a photograph of her, and can tell you that she was rather a big woman (though not fat), as dark as her husband or her lover, with a large mouth and eyes, and a Rubensish figure. Why she married Baker in the first place I really can't make out. He was well-to-do – or anyway seemed so – but Mary was the sort of woman to whom money quite genuinely means nothing; and oddly enough, Snow seems to have been as indifferent to it as she.

'Baker was a manufacturer. His factory just outside Twelford made expensive model toys – ships, aeroplanes, cars, and so forth. The demand for such things is strictly limited – people who know the value of money very properly hesitate before spending fifteen guineas on a toy which their issue are liable to sit on, or drop into a pond, an hour later – and when Philip Eckerson built a factory in Ruislip for producing the same sort of thing, only more cheaply, Baker's profits dropped with some abruptness to rather less than half what they'd been before. So for five years there was a price-war – a price-war beneficial to the country's nurseries, but ruinous to Baker and Eckerson alike. When eventually they met, to arrange a merger, both of them were close to bankruptcy.

'It was on March 10th of this year that they met – not on neutral territory, but in Baker's house at Twelford, where Eckerson was to stay the night. Eckerson was an albino, which is uncommon, but apart from that the only remarkable thing about him was obstinacy, and since he confined this trait to business, the impression he made on Mary Baker during his visit to her house was in every respect colourless. She was aware, in a vague, general way, that he was her husband's business rival, but she bore him not the least malice on that account; and as to Snow, the mysteries of finance were beyond him, and from first to last he never understood how close to the rocks his employer's affairs had drifted. In any case, neither he nor Mary Baker had much attention to spare for Eckerson, because an hour or two before Eckerson arrived Baker summoned the pair of them to his study, informed them that he knew of their liaison, and stated that he would take steps immediately to obtain a divorce.

'It's doubtful, I think, if he really intended to do anything of the kind. He didn't sack Snow, he didn't order his wife out of the house, and apparently he had no intention of leaving the house himself – all of which would amount, in law, to condoning his wife's adultery and nullifying the suit. No, he was playing cat-and-mouse, that was all; he knew his wife's horror of divorce, and wished quite simply to make her miserable for as long as the pretence of proceedings could be kept up; but neither Mary nor Snow had the wit to see that he was duping them for his own pleasure, and they assumed in consequence that he meant every word he said. Mary became hysterical – in which condition she confided her obsession about divorce to Snow. And Snow, a remarkably naïve and impressionable young man, took it all *au grand sérieux*. He had not, up to now, displayed any notable animus against Baker, but Mary's terror and wretchedness fanned hidden fires, and from then on he was implacable. They were a rather pitiful pair, these two young people cornered by an essentially rather trivial issue, but their very ignorance made them dangerous, and if

Baker had had more sense he'd never have played such an imbecile trick on them. Psychologically, he was certainly in a morbid condition, for apparently he was prepared to let the relationship go on, provided he could indulge his sadistic instincts in this weird and preposterous fashion. What the end of it all would have been, if death hadn't intervened, one doesn't, of course, know.

'Well, in due course Eckerson arrived, and Mary entertained him as well as her emotional condition would allow, and he sat up with Baker till the small hours, talking business. The two men antagonized one another from the start; and the more they talked, the more remote did the prospect of a merger become, until in the latter stages all hope of it vanished, and they went to their beds on the very worst of terms, with nothing better to look forward to than an extension of their present cut-throat competition, and eventual ruin. You'd imagine that self-interest would be strong enough, in a case like that, to compel them to some sort of agreement, but it wasn't – and of course the truth of the matter is that each was hoping that, if competition continued, the other would crack first, leaving a clear field. So they parted on the landing with mutual, and barely concealed, ill-will; and the house slept.

'The body was discovered shortly after nine next morning, and the discoverer was Mrs Blaine, the cook. Unlike Snow, who lived in, Mrs Blaine had a bed-sitting-room in the town; and it was as she was making her way round to the back door of Baker's house, to embark on the day's duties, that she glanced in at the drawing-room window and saw the gruesome object which lay in shadow on the hearth-rug. Incidentally, you mustn't waste any of your energy suspecting Mrs Blaine of the murder; I can assure you she had nothing to do with it, and I can assure you, too, that her evidence, for what little it was worth, was the truth, the whole truth, and nothing but the truth . . .

'Mrs Blaine looked in at the window, and her first thought, to use her own words, "was that 'e'd fainted". But the streaks of blood on the corpse's hair disabused her of this notion without much delay, and she hurried indoors to rouse the household. Well, in due course Inspector Casby arrived, and in due course assembled such evidence as there was. The body lay prone on a rug soaked with dark venous blood, and the savage cut which had severed the internal jugular vein had obviously come from behind, and been wholly unexpected. Nearby, and innocent of fingerprints, lay the sharp kitchen knife which had done the job. Apart from these things, there was no clue.

'No clue, that is, of a positive sort. But there *had* been an amateurish attempt to make the death look like a consequence of burglary – or rather, to be more accurate, of housebreaking. The pane of a window had been broken, with the assistance of flypaper to prevent the fragments from scattering, and a number of valuables were missing. But the breakfast period is not a time usually favoured by thieves, there were no footprints or marks of any kind on the damp lawn and flower bed beneath the broken window (which was not, by the way, the window through which Mrs Blaine had looked, but another, at right angles to it, on a different side of the house), and finally – and in Inspector Casby's opinion, most conclusive of all – one of the objects missing was a tiny but very valuable bird-study by the Chinese emperor Hui Tsung, which Baker, no connoisseur or collector of such things, had inherited from a great-uncle. The ordinary thief, Casby argued, would scarcely give a Chinese miniature a second glance, let alone remove it. No, the burglary was bogus; and unless you postulated an implausibly sophisticated double-bluff, then the murder had been done by one of the three people sleeping in the house. As to motive – well, you know all about that already; and one way and another it didn't take Inspector Casby more than twenty-four hours to make his arrest.'

Somewhat grudgingly, Fen relinquished the walnuts and applied himself to stuffed dates instead. His mouth full, he looked at the company expectantly; and with equal expectancy the company looked back at him. It was Wakefield who broke the silence.

'But that can't be *all*,' he protested.

'Certainly it's all,' said Fen. 'I've told you the story as Inspector Casby told it to me, and I now repeat the question he asked me at the end of it – and which I was able to answer, by the way: *Who killed Baker?*'

Wakefield stared mistrustfully. 'You've left something out.'

'Nothing, I assure you. If anything, I've been rather more generous with clues than Inspector Casby was. But if you still have no idea who killed Baker, I'll give you another hint: he died at 9 a.m. Does that help?'

They thought about this. Apparently it didn't help in the least.

'All right,' Wakefield said sulkily at last. 'We give up. Who killed Baker?'

And Fen replied blandly, 'The public executioner killed him – after he had been tried and convicted for the murder of Eckerson.'

For a moment Wakefield sat like one stupefied; then he emitted a howl of rage. 'Unfair!' he shouted, banging on the table. 'Trickery!'

'Not at all.' Fen was unperturbed. 'It's a trick story, admittedly, but you were given ample warning of that. It arose out of a discussion about the propriety of asking certain questions; and there was only one question –

Who killed Baker? – which I asked. What's more, I emphasized at the outset that the mode of telling was as important as the thing told.

'But quite apart from all that, you had your clue. Mrs Blaine, looking in through a window at a figure lying in shadow, concluded that violence had been done for the reason that she saw blood on the hair. Now that blood, as I mentioned, was dark venous blood; and I mentioned also that Baker had black, heavily brilliantined hair. Is it conceivable that dark blood would be *visible* on such hair – visible, that is, when the body was in shadow and the observer outside the window of the room in which it lay? Of course not. Therefore, the body was not Baker's. But it couldn't have been Mary Baker's, or Snow's, since they too were black-haired – and that leaves only Eckerson. Eckerson was an albino, which means that his hair was white; and splotches of blood would show up on white hair all right – even though it was in shadow, and Mrs Blaine some distance away. Who, then, would want to kill Eckerson? Baker, obviously, and Baker alone – I emphasized that both Snow and Mary were quite indifferent to the visitor. And who, after the arrest, would be likely to kill (notice, please, that I never at any time said "murder") Baker? There's only one possible answer to that . . .'

'And what happened to the wife?' Haldane asked. 'Did she marry Snow?'

'No. He melted,' said Fen complacently, 'away. She married someone else, though, and according to Inspector Casby is very happy now. Baker's and Eckerson's businesses both collapsed under heavy debts, and no longer exist.'

There was a pause; then: 'The nature of existence,' said Wakefield suddenly, 'has troubled philosophers in all ages. What are the sensory and mental processes which cause us to assert that this table, for instance, is *real?* The answer given by the subjective idealists –'

'Will have to wait,' said Haldane firmly, 'till we meet again.' He pushed back his chair. 'Let's go and see what the women are up to, shall we?'

Ursula Curtiss

CHANGE OF
CLIMATE

Ursula Curtiss (1923–) was born into an American family of literary crime. Her mother, Helen Reilly, wrote some forty crime stories, and her elder sister Mary McMullen is also a detective story writer. Helen Reilly was an early writer of the police procedural story, but Ursula Curtiss specializes in women's novels, a vague but meaningful term which in her case implies suspense achieved through a tale about young women or girls in danger, either because of some special knowledge they possess or through something accidentally seen without its meaning being understood. This is not my favourite kind of crime fiction, but Curtiss turns it to varied use in books like *The Noonday Devil* (1951) and *Letter of Intent* (1971).

Her short stories are another matter. They are subtler than the novels, and more directly concerned with human relationships. I am not sure that I understand all the implications of 'Change of Climate' after several readings, but I am in no doubt about its being a story of unusual distinction in the genre.

'One lam chop,' wrote Chloe Carpenter in her diary on an evening in late June – at nine years of age she had, and would have all her life, a natural talent for misspelling – 'one baked potatoe, some string beans, a pice of apple pie.' She studied the last item and then, because caret marks were still in her future and this was to be a very exact account, she crossed it out and wrote, 'a small pice of apple pie'.

Hester Carpenter had no idea that her daughter was keeping this meticulous record of Hester's food intake – fortunately; it would have made her self-conscious to the point of being unable to eat at all. But Tom Carpenter knew about it, and was both touched and approving. It seemed to him the day-by-day log of a miracle, although that was the very word he was supposed to avoid.

'Oh, she'll do better in the Southwest, no doubt about it,' the doctor had said two months ago in Massachusetts. 'In fact, to put it baldly, I doubt very seriously if she'd survive another winter here. But I have to warn you, Tom – after the first dramatic improvement there still may be difficulties. Chances are she'll acquire new allergies, and then there's always the existing damage. You mustn't expect a miracle.'

Hester had never been really strong – it was her look of almost luminous fragility which had first caught Tom's eye; but she had not developed asthma until a year after their marriage. Or perhaps it had been there for some time, masquerading as frequent attacks of bronchitis and a faint but noticeable shortness of breath after activities like climbing stairs. In any case, the asthma had become sharply worse after Chloe's birth. At first there were seasons of the year when Hester was entirely free of it; gradually these periods shortened, and pneumonia began to make its appearance.

They saw a parade of specialists – bald and conservative, young and daring, whose advice, with minor differences, came to much the same thing in the end: avoid the known allergens – among them, cat dander; pursue a dust-free routine in the house; and 'learn to live with your illness'.

Surprisingly enough, until Chloe was seven years old, they managed the last instruction almost as easily as the first two. Hester was determined not to become a professional invalid, or to make a martyr of her husband and a slave of her small daughter; and for a long time she succeeded. She hoarded her strength in unobtrusive ways; on bad days, when the sound of her breathing was like a loud and steady filing, she retired to piled pillows behind her bedroom door.

She had grown up in the small town of Falcon, Massachusetts, and Tom did not have to worry about her being lonely while he was at his office and Chloe at school. Girls she had known since high school dropped in, and neighbors made morning visits for coffee, usually bringing along a sumptuous homemade pastry at which Hester could only nibble. Chloe, arriving home at three o'clock, leaped enthusiastically into her role of 'house-woman' – 'Housewife, do you suppose she means?' Hester asked Tom, laughing – and polished everything that could possibly be polished: vases, candlesticks, tabletops.

As a result, the little house glowed more than the prescribed dust-free routine demanded; it held a concert of personalities as undivided as a clover. Hale and hearty visitors went away with an illogical feeling of envy; they said, 'There's nothing like trouble to bind a family together,' but they knew it was more than that.

When Chloe was almost eight, Hester had her first bad attack of pneumonia. Six months later she had another and worse one, shrouded in an oxygen tent while Tom spent two tormented nights at her bedside and the nurses smiled at him with terrifying cheerfulness.

He made the decision then, knowing that it meant giving up the well-paid job which had enabled him to meet the medical bills; giving up their home and their friends. Although it was not really a decision at all in the sense of choosing between alternatives, because it was clear now that there was no alternative. While Hester convalesced, much more slowly than ever before, he quietly organized the move to the Southwest.

June turned and became July. Hester had gained six pounds, and her pearly skin was acquiring a faint tan. The one unfortunate side effect from the change of climate – sinus trouble, which the doctor assured them could be alleviated by drops – seemed a small price to pay.

Chloe had been her mother's anxious companion for too long to let go all at once, but little by little, as Hester grew stronger, Chloe explored a world strange to eastern eyes – a world with fleet little blue lizards, roadrunners, and even, in their landlord's back field, an aristocratic but friendly horse that came promptly up to the fence for the carrot or apple she brought. In spite of the wanderings which seemed to her boundless, but were actually contained in less than a half acre, Chloe was always in the driveway to greet Tom when he got home from work.

She was there on a late afternoon in mid-July, wiry, sunburnt, and clearly bursting with something. When Tom asked his ritual, 'What did you do today?' she said excitedly, 'Oh, Daddy, I helped Mrs Whitman tear up all her flowers. Look!'

Tom did not merely look; he gaped, appalled. Mrs Whitman was the other tenant of the duplex apartment, a pleasant gray-haired woman whose chief preoccupation seemed to be the deep brilliant border that edged her little lawn on three sides. The border was now bare drying earth, the flowers themselves a heap of ruffled and shriveling color piled up outside the gate.

To Tom, for just a flash, the child looking up at him seemed to have the wanton triumph of a small boy standing with his slingshot near a shattered greenhouse – and then Chloe was saying defensively, 'The flowers, I don't know which ones, made Mother sneeze and her eyes puff up, so Mrs Whitman *said* to.'

Hester was tranquilly regretful. 'It's too bad about Mrs Whitman's garden, isn't it? I felt awful, telling her about the doctor's orders – you know, to sit out in the sun for a little while every day – but she understood perfectly; in fact, she couldn't have been nicer. I came right in and baked her a batch of brownies.'

Tom, remembering the weeks of Mrs Whitman's assiduous weeding, cultivating, watering, sent a look of wonderment at his wife's back. Did Hester possibly think that a confection hastily whipped up in the kitchen –? No, of course she didn't; she had simply made a small token apology in the only way she could on the spur of the moment.

. . . But, he thought later that night while Hester slept, her breath quiet and even, she had been mistaken in thinking that Mrs Whitman had 'understood perfectly'. That brutal heap of uprooted flowers, piled there openly by someone who loved them, was a statement of cold anger only emphasized by the invitation to the complainant's child to come and help with the carnage.

It was too bad in every sense, because Tom had hoped that Hester, so used to the daily companionship of other women, would start making friends in the neighborhood. His last waking reflection, still troubled, was that it might not be a bad idea to have Chloe, an avid car washer, surprise Mrs Whitman tomorrow or the next day by scrubbing her little cherry-red Volkswagen . . .

*

When Tom hinted worriedly to Hester about her possible loneliness, she denied it cheerfully. Her friends back East had been marvelous, and of course she missed them; but it was a positive luxury now to be able to do, unassisted, so many of the domestic things they had helped her with before. And of course – here she glanced around vaguely – she had Chloe for company.

But this, although it was not borne in on Tom immediately, was less and less the case . . .

The doctor was enormously pleased with Hester's progress, and she apparently took this as *carte blanche* because, by the time August had arrived, she was seldom still. Wearing Bermuda shorts, a thing she could not have done before because of the sticklike thinness of her legs, Hester took down and washed and rehung the venetian blinds; she carried out the scatter rugs to air. She also washed the windows, inside and out, scoured the oven, and began on the paintwork. If the apartment did not have the warm glow of the little house back East, it was at least very shiny.

Tom did not find it surprising, in view of Hester's steady gain, that Chloe had stopped keeping her diary; the last entry, for July 26th, was: 'Steak, asparagis, mashed potatoes, vinila ice cream.' He now had a small but annoying problem of his own: his sinuses had evidently become affected by the dry heat and at night, frequently, his forehead felt bound with iron. Hester's wonder-working nose drops, trickling bitterly down the back of his throat no matter how carefully he administered them, did not seem to help.

One night in mid-August, when he was cautiously congratulating himself on feeling fine, a tense pain came creeping back at the dinner table. Maybe a storm approaching, thought Tom; the sky looked thunderous and he had sensed electricity in the air ever since his return home from work. Well, they needed the rain –

'Eat your dinner!' said Hester in a voice that made Tom's fork jump in his hand. He glanced at her astoundedly – she had delivered the words like a cuff; but her attention was on Chloe, fair head bent, hands in her lap although they were having roast chicken, which she loved.

'Eat your dinner,' repeated Hester more quietly and perhaps more dangerously. The storm which Tom had thought so innocently to be in the upper elements was closer, and he was so bewildered that he could only stare.

'I'm not hungry,' said Chloe, the corners of her mouth beginning to waver helplessly, 'I feel sick.'

'Very well, then, you're excused,' said Hester evenly, and held herself remorselessly still and attentive while the child pushed back her chair, dropped her napkin, bumped her head on the table in the course of retrieving it, and then fled.

The door of her bedroom closed. Hester sprinkled salt and said calmly to Tom, 'You look tired – was it a rough day?'

'Not bad,' said Tom distractedly, putting down his own napkin and starting to rise. This was like a dream, in which elk went by in Easter bonnets and nobody thought it odd at all. 'I'll go see what's the matter with –'

'Chloe is sulking because that foolish horse is gone,' said Hester casually, and proceeded to tell him.

Tom had been aware of the affection between Chloe and the horse in the next field, and knew that the landlord let her mount occasionally and go for blissful ambles. As the horse was trained to halt the instant the weight in the saddle began to slip, it had seemed the most innocent of diversions. What Tom hadn't known – 'I hate being such a constant nuisance to everybody' – was that Hester reacted badly to close contact with horses, and had begun to wheeze when Chloe came in from her rides.

She had, she said, forbidden Chloe to ride the horse, but at every opportunity the child had slipped over to the fence to caress the white-blazed face and brush the dark-gold mane dedicatedly. '– which came to pretty much the same thing,' said Hester ruefully. 'Mr Lacey saw the problem right away, and said his son would be delighted to keep the horse at his place – it doesn't get enough exercise here anyway. Somehow, I expected Chloe to understand.'

Or understand *perfectly*, like Mrs Whitman with her flowers? Tom was shocked at this disloyal thought – they were here after all for Hester's health, and allergies were not to be played around with; but his forehead now felt sealed with pain. When he had eaten what he could of his dinner he picked up Chloe's untouched plate. 'I think I'll bring this in to her now.'

Hester's eyebrows rose, but all she said was, 'If you think it's wise.'

Chloe got over the horse, as Hester had sensibly predicted she would, and settled herself to the serious business of making friends in the neighborhood before the opening of school. This was not the automatic process of a child who had been constantly with other children, but an almost adult approach. As a result, she was home at noontime for a sandwich and milk, usually with a standoffish and staring little girl in tow.

Tom took his headaches to a doctor, was informed that his sinuses were as clear as a bell, and, although he kept it from Hester so that she would not worry, he began to take the tranquilizers the doctor prescribed.

Hester bloomed, even in the scorching heat. Her delicate tan had turned brown, and she was strong and rangy. She was busy making new curtains, busy registering Chloe for school, busy waxing the floors, relining the kitchen shelves, taking down and washing the ceiling light fixtures. She had grown used to, as Tom and Chloe had, her own newly nasal voice, although she would say irritably now and then, 'I sound exactly like a duck.'

Although it was only the end of August, the annual weather prophets were out in force. Tom and Hester, who could seldom find any news of Massachusetts in the local papers, nevertheless learned with guilty pleasure that an early and very hard winter was predicted for the East.

(But how warm and snug the little house in Massachusetts had been, with Hester on the couch in a pretty housecoat, Chloe bustling importantly in the kitchen, Tom peacefully reading the evening paper while the wind raged outside and the fire simmered and snapped on the hearth. Lamplight over everything, and a perfect security that had nothing to do with locks or bolts or storm windows.)

We are all happy, Tom informed himself, swallowing his white pill; the pity is that we didn't do this sooner.

School was to begin on August 29th. On the 27th, coming home with the commissioned notebooks and pencils and lunch box, Tom saw that Chloe had washed Mrs Whitman's car again; the little red Volkswagen was dripping and flashing in the sun. And there was, mystifyingly, a cat fight in progress somewhere close by. Of all the things Hester couldn't have near her . . . How could a cat have gotten –?

He was alarmedly out of his car and inside the gate when the menacing shrills became distinguishable words instead of rising and falling howls. '– *so* nice of you to be sweet and considerate with the neighbors,' shrieked the cat voice. 'Never mind me, *I* don't count. But how many times have I told you about those filthy sneakers? And look at those shorts. You've been in the wading pool with those dreadful children, haven't you, Miss? I said, *Haven't you, Miss?*'

There was an odd sound then, not a response from Chloe but still a sound. Tom's stupefied eye caught a lunge past the screen door; his ear heard a panting, 'There you stay!' and then a sharp bang.

The bang seemed to split the frontal bones of his head. Standing paralyzed on the path, at once incredulous and certain, he realized that this strident plunging creature in Bermuda shorts was his gentle luminous Hester, this contemptible 'Miss' his skinny worshipful child.

He made himself go in. Hester was washing lettuce at the sink, her hands unsteady. There was no sign of Chloe. Tom said with a weariness he did not know he had accumulated, 'What's the matter?' and Hester whirled.

'You'll have to talk to that child, Tom.' *That child.* 'She's always been spoiled, but now she's completely out of hand.'

Spoiled. The nine-year-old who by now was an expert at doing dishes, ironing her own clothes, compiling bizarrely spelled shopping lists, and trudging faithfully around supermarkets . . . 'What's she done?'

'Disobeyed me, deliberately. There are some very dubious-looking children up the street who have a wading pool, and I told Chloe that she was not to go there.'

'Hester, this was a hot afternoon –'

'That's not the point. The point is that I told her not to,' said Hester, spacing the last five words almost softly. By contrast, pots and their lids leaped into a clattering frenzy under her hands when she turned to the stove, and the glance she flung at Tom was razorish with – was it anger? Or some perverse excitement? Something, at any rate, that changed her into the kind of woman you saw dragging a small sobbing child ruthlessly by the hand, jerking all the harder when the child stumbled.

'I think we'd better get it clear here and now that I won't stand for this kind of behaviour,' the stranger at the stove was saying in her nasal and driving voice. 'If you don't punish her, I will.'

There were still a few shafts of late sunlight in Chloe's prim little room. She lay on her bed with her back to the door, not so much crying as shuddering, taking convulsive breaths which she buried fiercely in the pillow. Tom sat down on the bed and turned her gently to face him; he had to glance away quickly for a moment, feeling his own throat prickle at the dull red mark on her cheek.

That was the curious sound he had heard. From outside.

He had meant to tell Chloe quietly and reasonably that she could not disobey her mother, making it – because he realized suddenly that in the past week or so they had understood each other very well indeed – more of a father-to-daughter warning than a parental thunderbolt. But the reasonable words would not come; so he simply sat there, stroking the tumbled hair away from her forehead and talking about small detached things until she was able to heave a very deep breath with only the barest tremor.

She said, 'Mother doesn't like being better, does she.'

It was neither a question nor an accusation. It was an observation delivered with adult despair, and it encompassed much more than a hard humiliating slap. It took in the last – three weeks, four? Tom could not be sure, in his shock at the nakedness of the words, any more than a man could be sure when, after living with an obscure pain that frightened him, he was asked by the doctor who put an exact finger on the source, 'How long have you had this?'

He didn't – at the moment he couldn't – answer his child. He gave her forehead a final pat and walked to the window, where he gazed out blindly into the coming dusk.

Was it possible? Could Hester have acquired the last allergy of all, and be no more able to assimilate health than cat dander? Were there personalities who could not thrive, or thrive sanely, on physical well-being?

It was appalling to think so, but it was less spine-touching than the notion that this personality had dwelt inside Hester all along, and had simply never been well enough to come out before. How, in that case, it must have raged and struggled against the tranquility and binding love in the little Massachusetts house . . .

Tom's shoulder muscles gave a quick cold ripple as he shook that off and went back to the first possibility. If their past happiness even in the face of illness had been so present in his mind, how much more so must it have been in Hester's? Certainly she had never consciously liked being a semi-invalid, but – the stream of solicitous friends dropping in, the cheerful little gifts of a crocheted bed jacket or a homemade coffee cake, the momentous gaining or losing of half a pound – and, yes, the attention.

Chloe had been her devoted shadow, but now, like any other healthy nine-year-old, Chloe roamed and played. And Hester had flung herself into frenetic activity, perhaps battling unconsciously with this terrible new allergy before it began to win.

Tom had never asked, but he was coldly sure now that Chloe had admired and helped in Mrs Whitman's garden. She had worshipped the friendly horse. She had set about making friends, to prepare herself for entering a strange school, and been invited to wade in a backyard pool. The sacrifices to Hester had not been voluntary, or even appeasing, but they had certainly been made.

And yet . . . Hester will be as upset as I am, said Tom to himself.

Hester was not. Told falsely that Chloe was asleep, she said with an edge, 'Funny how easily she falls asleep on nights when we have meat loaf,' and attacked her own dinner with zest. It was very good meat loaf, and a few small bites of it settled in Tom's stomach like the best cement; Chloe's vacant place at the table, and the silence from her room, pressed upward against his ribs.

Although Hester said nothing further about punishing Chloe, her face was curiously set, and when she asked Tom after the dishes were done, 'Aren't you going to take your usual walk?' he manufactured a yawn and said, 'Too tired.'

He was, of course, not worried about any small personal action which might be taken in his absence down the long driveway. Certainly not. He was simply – tired.

He lay awake all night – not like someone with merely restless intervals, but literally all night. Once he got up quietly to look in at and cover Chloe; for the rest, he listened to his wife's deep untroubled breathing and studied a number of scenes which unwound like tape against the black ceiling.

In the morning he said cheerfully to Chloe, 'Come on, I'll buy you a new dress for school,' and to Hester, 'They're having some kind of executive session at the office and I don't have to be in until eleven.'

Surely Hester did not look somehow impotent as they left?

'Daddy,' said Chloe hesitantly in the car – she was pleating the fabric of her skirt incessantly, a new and disturbing habit – 'won't Mother be mad because she didn't come too?'

'She's got a million things to do,' Tom said airily, and bore her off to the back-to-school department of a downtown store. He found a reliable-looking saleswoman to whom he gave vague suggestions about a dress, and told Chloe firmly to wait for him there.

There were public phone booths on the first floor, and from one of these Tom sent himself an urgent telegram signed with the name of his former employer in Massachusetts; he would be home to open it when it arrived, so that no question would be raised as to its place of origin. To make doubly sure, he instructed the operator to have the message delivered; there would be no one at that telephone all day, he said.

From the phone booth, because it was somehow of immense importance that Chloe should not even uncomprehendingly hear what he was going to say, he proceeded to the railroad station. Judging by a few banners strung about it was 'Sunshine Appreciation Week', which was just chasing out 'Eat More Cottage Cheese Week'. When he asked the pretty clerk at a ticket window for two and a half fares to Falcon, Massachusetts, she said with arch reproachfulness, 'Oh, surely that's a round trip, sir?'

The buoyancy assumed for Chloe's sake had left him. Perhaps as a result of his sleepless night his ears resounded queerly with the doctor's voice. 'To put it baldly, I doubt very seriously . . .' and the prediction of the weather prophets.

There was nothing momentous in the glance he sent through the ticket window. To the pretty clerk, who remembered him for approximately a minute afterward, he was just an ordinary, pleasant-looking man; fair, thirty-fivish, rather tired, with lines around his mouth. There was certainly no special inflection in his voice when he said, as though arousing himself from a dream, 'No – that will be one way.'

Roald Dahl

THE LANDLADY

Like Stanley Ellin, Roald Dahl (1916–) is known, at least among addicts of crime, particularly for one story, 'Lamb to the Slaughter', with its masterly means of disposal for the murder weapon. Unlike Ellin, however, Dahl would probably not regard himself as a crime writer. Yet although it is true that such mesmerically powerful tales as 'Skin' and 'Taste' do not involve an actual crime, their ambience is both criminal and creepy. Roald Dahl knows just how far to push the reader, just how much his imagination will accept and even enjoy, before the moment when fascinated horror changes to distaste, the moment of rejection. For almost every reader there will be some Dahl stories he dislikes too much to want to read them again. Many of the tales are implicitly (hardly ever explicitly) about sex, expressed as a struggle for supremacy or for money, often powered by emotional cruelty.

'The Landlady' is a comparatively quiet Dahl tale, but it carries his unmistakable *frisson* of sexual feeling in the landlady's appreciation of Billy Weaver's beautiful teeth, and of her former lodger's skin which was 'just like a baby's'. And it is typical of his tact that in this genuinely horrific story nothing other than commonplace words are said.

Billy Weaver had travelled down from London on the slow afternoon train, with a change at Swindon on the way, and by the time he got to Bath it was about nine o'clock in the evening and the moon was coming up out of a clear starry sky over the houses opposite the station entrance. But the air was deadly cold and the wind was like a flat blade of ice on his cheeks.

'Excuse me,' he said, 'but is there a fairly cheap hotel not too far away from here?'

'Try The Bell and Dragon,' the porter answered, pointing down the road. 'They might take you in. It's about a quarter of a mile along on the other side.'

Billy thanked him and picked up his suitcase and set out to walk the quarter-mile to The Bell and Dragon. He had never been to Bath before. He didn't know anyone who lived there. But Mr Greenslade at the Head Office in London had told him it was a splendid city. 'Find your own lodgings,' he had said, 'and then go along and report to the Branch Manager as soon as you've got yourself settled.'

Billy was seventeen years old. He was wearing a new navy-blue overcoat, a new brown trilby hat, and a new brown suit, and he was feeling fine. He walked briskly down the street. He was trying to do everything briskly these days. Briskness, he had decided, was *the* one common characteristic of all successful businessmen. The big shots up at Head Office were absolutely fantastically brisk all the time. They were amazing.

There were no shops on this wide street that he was walking along, only a line of tall houses on each side, all of them identical. They had porches and pillars and four or five steps going up to their front doors, and it was obvious that once upon a time they had been very swanky residences. But now, even in the darkness, he could see that the paint was peeling from the woodwork on their doors and windows, and that the handsome white façades were cracked and blotchy from neglect.

Suddenly, in a downstairs window that was brilliantly illuminated by a street-lamp not six yards away, Billy caught sight of a printed notice propped up against the glass in one of the upper panes. It said BED AND

BREAKFAST. There was a vase of pussy-willows, tall and beautiful, standing just underneath the notice.

He stopped walking. He moved a bit closer. Green curtains (some sort of velvety material) were hanging down on either side of the window. The pussy-willows looked wonderful beside them. He went right up and peered through the glass into the room, and the first thing he saw was a bright fire burning in the hearth. On the carpet in front of the fire, a pretty little dachshund was curled up asleep with its nose tucked into its belly. The room itself, so far as he could see in the half-darkness, was filled with pleasant furniture. There was a baby-grand piano and a big sofa and several plump armchairs; and in one corner he spotted a large parrot in a cage. Animals were usually a good sign in a place like this, Billy told himself; and all in all, it looked to him as though it would be a pretty decent house to stay in. Certainly it would be more comfortable than The Bell and Dragon.

On the other hand, a pub would be more congenial than a boarding-house. There would be beer and darts in the evenings, and lots of people to talk to, and it would probably be a good bit cheaper, too. He had stayed a couple of nights in a pub once before and he had liked it. He had never stayed in any boarding-houses, and, to be perfectly honest, he was a tiny bit frightened of them. The name itself conjured up images of watery cabbage, rapacious landladies, and a powerful smell of kippers in the living-room.

After dithering about like this in the cold for two or three minutes, Billy decided that he would walk on and take a look at The Bell and Dragon before making up his mind. He turned to go.

And now a queer thing happened to him. He was in the act of stepping back and turning away from the window when all at once his eye was caught and held in the most peculiar manner by the small notice that was there. BED AND BREAKFAST, it said. BED AND BREAKFAST, BED AND BREAKFAST, BED AND BREAKFAST. Each word was like a large black eye staring at him through the glass, holding him, compelling him, forcing him to stay where he was and not to walk away from that house, and the next thing he knew, he was actually moving across from the window to the front door of the house, climbing the steps that led up to it, and reaching for the bell.

He pressed the bell. Far away in a back room he heard it ringing, and then *at once* – it must have been at once because he hadn't even had time to take his finger from the bell-button – the door swung open and a woman was standing there.

Normally you ring the bell and you have at least a half-minute's wait before the door opens. But this dame was like a jack-in-the-box. He pressed the bell – and out she popped! It made him jump.

She was about forty-five or fifty years old, and the moment she saw him, she gave him a warm welcoming smile.

'*Please* come in,' she said pleasantly. She stepped aside, holding the door wide open, and Billy found himself automatically starting forward into the house. The compulsion or, more accurately, the desire to follow after her into that house was extraordinarily strong.

'I saw the notice in the window,' he said, holding himself back.

'Yes, I know.'

'I was wondering about a room.'

'It's *all* ready for you, my dear,' she said. She had a round pink face and very gentle blue eyes.

'I was on my way to The Bell and Dragon,' Billy told her. 'But the notice in your window just happened to catch my eye.'

'My dear boy,' she said, 'why don't you come in out of the cold?'

'How much do you charge?'

'Five and sixpence a night, including breakfast.'

It was fantastically cheap. It was less than half of what he had been willing to pay.

'If that is too much,' she added, 'then perhaps I can reduce it just a tiny bit. Do you desire an egg for breakfast? Eggs are expensive at the moment. It would be sixpence less without the egg.'

'Five and sixpence is fine,' he answered. 'I should like very much to stay here.'

'I knew you would. Do come in.'

She seemed terribly nice. She looked exactly like the mother of one's best school-friend welcoming one into the house to stay for the Christmas holidays. Billy took off his hat, and stepped over the threshold.

'Just hang it there,' she said, 'and let me help you with your coat.'

There were no other hats or coats in the hall. There were no umbrellas, no walking-sticks – nothing.

'We have it *all* to ourselves,' she said, smiling at him over her shoulder as she led the way upstairs. 'You see, it isn't very often I have the pleasure of taking a visitor into my little nest.'

The old girl is slightly dotty, Billy told himself. But at five and sixpence a night, who gives a damn about that? 'I should've thought you'd be simply swamped with applicants,' he said politely.

'Oh, I am, my dear, I am, of course I am. But the trouble is that I'm inclined to be just a teeny weeny bit choosy and particular – if you see what I mean.'

'Ah, yes.'

'But I'm always ready. Everything is always ready day and night in this house just on the off-chance that an acceptable young gentleman will come along. And it is such a pleasure, my dear, such a very great pleasure when now and again I open the door and I see someone standing there who is just *exactly* right.' She was half-way up the stairs, and she paused with one hand on the stair-rail, turning her head and smiling down at him with pale lips. 'Like you,' she added, and her blue eyes travelled slowly all the way down the length of Billy's body, to his feet, and then up again.

On the first-floor landing she said to him, 'This floor is mine.'

They climbed up a second flight. 'And this one is *all* yours,' she said. 'Here's your room. I do hope you'll like it.' She took him into a small but charming front bedroom, switching on the light as she went in.

'The morning sun comes right in the window, Mr Perkins. It *is* Mr Perkins, isn't it?'

'No,' he said. 'It's Weaver.'

'Mr Weaver. How nice. I've put a water-bottle between the sheets to air them out, Mr Weaver. It's such a comfort to have a hot water-bottle in a strange bed with clean sheets, don't you agree? And you may light the gas fire at any time if you feel chilly.'

'Thank you,' Billy said. 'Thank you ever so much.' He noticed that the bedspread had been taken off the bed, and that the bedclothes had been neatly turned back on one side, all ready for someone to get in.

'I'm so glad you appeared,' she said, looking earnestly into his face. 'I was beginning to get worried.'

'That's all right,' Billy answered brightly. 'You mustn't worry about me.' He put his suitcase on the chair and started to open it.

'And what about supper, my dear? Did you manage to get anything to eat before you came here?'

'I'm not a bit hungry, thank you,' he said. 'I think I'll just go to bed as soon as possible because tomorrow I've got to get up rather early and report to the office.'

'Very well, then. I'll leave you now so that you can unpack. But before you go to bed, would you be kind enough to pop into the sitting-room on the ground floor and sign the book? Everyone has to do that because it's the law of the land, and we don't want to go breaking any laws at *this* stage of the proceedings, do we?' She gave him a little wave of the hand and went quickly out of the room and closed the door.

Now, the fact that his landlady appeared to be slightly off her rocker didn't worry Billy in the least. After all, she was not only harmless – there was no question about that – but she was also quite obviously a kind and generous soul. He guessed that she had probably lost a son in the war, or something like that, and had never got over it.

So a few minutes later, after unpacking his suitcase and washing his hands, he trotted downstairs to the ground floor and entered the living-room. His landlady wasn't there, but the fire was glowing in the hearth, and the little dachshund was still sleeping in front of it. The room was wonderfully warm and cosy. I'm a lucky fellow, he thought, rubbing his hands. This is a bit of all right.

He found the guest-book lying open on the piano, so he took out his pen and wrote down his name and address. There were only two other entries above his on the page, and, as one always does with guest-books, he started to read them. One was a Christopher Mulholland from Cardiff. The other was Gregory W. Temple from Bristol.

That's funny, he thought suddenly. Christopher Mulholland. It rings a bell.

Now where on earth had he heard that rather unusual name before?

Was he a boy at school? No. Was it one of his sister's numerous young men, perhaps, or a friend of his father's? No, no, it wasn't any of those. He glanced down again at the book.

Christopher Mulholland   *231 Cathedral Road, Cardiff*
Gregory W. Temple   *27 Sycamore Drive, Bristol*

As a matter of fact, now he came to think of it, he wasn't at all sure that the second name didn't have almost as much of a familiar ring about it as the first.

'Gregory Temple?' he said aloud, searching his memory. 'Christopher Mulholland? . . .'

'Such charming boys,' a voice behind him answered, and he turned and saw his landlady sailing into the room with a large silver tea-tray in her hands. She was holding it well out in front of her, and rather high up, as though the tray were a pair of reins on a frisky horse.

'They sound somehow familiar,' he said.

'They do? How interesting.'

'I'm almost positive I've heard those names before somewhere. Isn't that queer? Maybe it was in the newspapers. They weren't famous in any way, were they? I mean famous cricketers or footballers or something like that?'

'Famous,' she said, setting the tea-tray down on the low table in front of the sofa. 'Oh no, I don't think they were famous. But they were extra-ordinarily handsome, both of them, I can promise you that. They were tall and young and handsome, my dear, just exactly like you.'

Once more, Billy glanced down at the book. 'Look here,' he said, noticing the dates. 'This last entry is over two years old.'

'It is?'

'Yes, indeed. And Christopher Mulholland's is nearly a year before that – more than *three years* ago.'

'Dear me,' she said, shaking her head and heaving a dainty little sigh. 'I would never have thought it. How time does fly away from us all, doesn't it, Mr Wilkins?'

'It's Weaver,' Billy said. 'W-e-a-v-e-r.'

'Oh, of course it is!' she cried, sitting down on the sofa. 'How silly of me. I do apologize. In one ear and out the other, that's me, Mr Weaver.'

'You know something?' Billy said. 'Something that's really quite extraordinary about all this?'

'No, dear, I don't.'

'Well, you see – both of these names, Mulholland and Temple, I not only seem to remember each one of them separately, so to speak, but somehow or other, in some peculiar way, they both appear to be sort of connected together as well. As though they were both famous for the same sort of thing, if you see what I mean – like . . . well . . . like Dempsey and Tunney, for example, or Churchill and Roosevelt.'

'How amusing,' she said. 'But come over here now, dear, and sit down beside me on the sofa and I'll give you a nice cup of tea and a ginger biscuit before you go to bed.'

'You really shouldn't bother,' Billy said. 'I didn't mean you to do anything like that.' He stood by the piano, watching her as she fussed about with the cups and saucers. He noticed that she had small, white, quickly moving hands, and red finger-nails.

'I'm almost positive it was in the newspapers I saw them,' Billy said. 'I'll think of it in a second. I'm sure I will.'

There is nothing more tantalizing than a thing like this which lingers just outside the borders of one's memory. He hated to give up.

'Now wait a minute,' he said. 'Wait just a minute. Mulholland . . . Christopher Mulholland . . . wasn't *that* the name of the Eton schoolboy who was on a walking-tour through the West Country, and then all of a sudden . . .'

'Milk?' she said. 'And sugar?'

'Yes, please. And then all of a sudden . . .'

'Eton schoolboy?' she said. 'Oh no, my dear, that can't possibly be right because *my* Mr Mulholland was certainly not an Eton schoolboy when he came to me. He was a Cambridge undergraduate. Come over here now and sit next to me and warm yourself in front of this lovely fire. Come on. Your tea's all ready for you.' She patted the empty place beside her on the sofa, and she sat there smiling at Billy and waiting for him to come over.

He crossed the room slowly, and sat down on the edge of the sofa. She placed his teacup on the table in front of him.

'*There* we are,' she said. 'How nice and cosy this is, isn't it?'

Billy started sipping his tea. She did the same. For half a minute or so, neither of them spoke. But Billy knew that she was looking at him. Her body was half-turned towards him, and he could feel her eyes resting on his face, watching him over the rim of her teacup. Now and again, he caught a whiff of a peculiar smell that seemed to emanate directly from her person. It was not in the least unpleasant, and it reminded him – well, he wasn't quite sure what it reminded him of. Pickled walnuts? New leather? Or was it the corridors of a hospital?

'Mr Mulholland was a great one for his tea,' she said at length. 'Never in my life have I seen anyone drink as much tea as dear, sweet Mr Mulholland.'

'I suppose he left fairly recently,' Billy said. He was still puzzling his head about the two names. He was positive now that he had seen them in the newspapers – in the headlines.

'Left?' she said, arching her brows. 'But my dear boy, he never left. He's still here. Mr Temple is also here. They're on the third floor, both of them together.'

Billy set down his cup slowly on the table, and stared at his landlady. She smiled back at him, and then she put out one of her white hands and patted him comfortingly on the knee. 'How old are you, my dear?' she asked.

'Seventeen.'

'Seventeen!' she cried. 'Oh, it's the perfect age! Mr Mulholland was also seventeen. But I think he was a trifle shorter than you are, in fact I'm sure he was, and his teeth weren't *quite* so white. You have the most beautiful teeth, Mr Weaver, did you know that?'

'They're not as good as they look,' Billy said. 'They've got simply masses of fillings in them at the back.'

'Mr Temple, of course, was a little older,' she said, ignoring his remark.

'He was actually twenty-eight. And yet I never would have guessed it if he hadn't told me, never in my whole life. There wasn't a *blemish* on his body.'

'A what?' Billy said.

'His skin was *just* like a baby's.'

There was a pause. Billy picked up his teacup and took another sip of his tea, then he set it down again gently in its saucer. He waited for her to say something else, but she seemed to have lapsed into another of her silences. He sat there staring straight ahead of him into the far corner of the room, biting his lower lip.

'That parrot,' he said at last. 'You know something? It had me completely fooled when I first saw it through the window from the street. I could have sworn it was alive.'

'Alas, no longer.'

'It's most terribly clever the way it's been done,' he said. 'It doesn't look in the least bit dead. Who did it?'

'I did.'

'*You* did?'

'Of course,' she said. 'And you have met my little Basil as well?' She nodded towards the dachshund curled up so comfortably in front of the fire. Billy looked at it. And suddenly, he realized that this animal had all the time been just as silent and motionless as the parrot. He put out a hand and touched it gently on the top of its back. The back was hard and cold, and when he pushed the hair to one side with his fingers, he could see the skin underneath, greyish-black and dry and perfectly preserved.

'Good gracious me,' he said. 'How absolutely fascinating.' He turned away from the dog and stared with deep admiration at the little woman beside him on the sofa. 'It must be most awfully difficult to do a thing like that.'

'Not in the least,' she said. 'I stuff *all* my little pets myself when they pass away. Will you have another cup of tea?'

'No, thank you,' Billy said. The tea tasted faintly of bitter almonds, and he didn't much care for it.

'You did sign the book, didn't you?'

'Oh, yes.'

'That's good. Because later on, if I happen to forget what you were called, then I can always come down here and look it up. I still do that almost every day with Mr Mulholland and Mr . . . Mr . . .'

'Temple,' Billy said. 'Gregory Temple. Excuse my asking, but haven't there been *any* other guests here except them in the last two or three years?'

Holding her teacup high in one hand, inclining her head slightly to the left, she looked up at him out of the corners of her eyes and gave him another gentle little smile.

'No, my dear,' she said. 'Only you.'

Arthur Conan Doyle

THE COPPER BEECHES

The first two Sherlock Holmes adventures were novels, but it was not until a short story, 'A Scandal in Bohemia', appeared in the *Strand Magazine* of July 1891 that Arthur Conan Doyle, the young doctor who had given up general practice and was vainly struggling to make a living as an eye specialist, found the perfect form for his Great Detective.

That form was the short story, which allowed Conan Doyle to pose and solve a puzzle without the need to invent a book-length plot, yet still gave room for the creation of the uneasy emotional atmosphere that touches much of his best writing. The pattern that suited him was a Holmes–Watson opening which, perhaps through the arrival of a client, enabled Holmes to show his deductive skill; then the propounding of the puzzle; a visit to the scene of the crime, or suspected crime; clues spotted there by Holmes which remained unnoticed by others; and finally, the solution. This pattern is followed in most of the first and probably finest collection, the *Adventures*, and by the last tale in that volume, 'The Copper Beeches'.

A dozen or more Holmes stories have their particular felicities of deductive skill, or special phrases that stamp Conan Doyle's mark upon them. 'The Copper Beeches' demonstrates particularly the macabre side of the author's imagination. The 'dear little romper' whose particular pleasure is to kill cockroaches with a slipper, the odd demand that Violet Hunter should cut her hair short, her employer's insistence that she shall wear a special dress – well, sophisticated readers today realize at once that Miss Hunter is being used as part of some physical deception. The things that really chill one, however, are that the colour of the dress is electric blue, and the chopped-off hair 'luxuriant, and of a rather peculiar tint of chestnut'. There is something perverse and frightening about the story. Like a number of others it gives the reader a puzzle to solve, but also sets the nerves tingling, and leaves scenes that stay in the imagination.

Sir Arthur Conan Doyle (1860–1930) was a Victorian man of action and public affairs, and also a writer who found his style and subjects generally restricted by the age in which he grew up. In the best of the Sherlock Holmes tales, as in a few other short stories (but none of the novels), his interest in the dark corners of the imagination ran free.

'To the man who loves art for its own sake,' remarked Sherlock Holmes, tossing aside the advertisement sheet of the *Daily Telegraph*, 'it is frequently in its least important and lowliest manifestations that the keenest pleasure is to be derived. It is pleasant to me to observe, Watson, that you have so far grasped this truth that in these little records of our cases which you have been good enough to draw up, and, I am bound to say, occasionally to embellish, you have given prominence not so much to the many *causes célèbres* and sensational trials in which I have figured, but rather to those incidents which may have been trivial in themselves, but which have given room for those faculties of deduction and of logical synthesis which I have made my special province.'

'And yet,' said I, smiling, 'I cannot quite hold myself absolved from the charge of sensationalism which has been urged against my records.'

'You have erred, perhaps,' he observed, taking up a glowing cinder with the tongs, and lighting with it the long cherrywood pipe which was wont to replace his clay when he was in a disputatious rather than a meditative mood – 'you have erred, perhaps, in attempting to put colour and life into each of your statements, instead of confining yourself to the task of placing upon record that severe reasoning from cause to effect which is really the only notable feature about the thing.'

'It seems to me that I have done you full justice in the matter,' I remarked with some coldness, for I was repelled by the egotism which I had more than once observed to be a strong factor in my friend's singular character.

'No, it is not selfishness or conceit,' said he, answering, as was his wont, my thoughts rather than my words. 'If I claim full justice for my art, it is because it is an impersonal thing – a thing beyond myself. Crime is common. Logic is rare. Therefore it is upon the logic rather than upon the crime that you should dwell. You have degraded what should have been a course of lectures into a series of tales.'

It was a cold morning of the early spring, and we sat after breakfast on either side of a cheery fire in the old room in Baker Street. A thick fog rolled down between the lines of dun-coloured houses, and the opposing windows loomed like dark, shapeless blurs, through the heavy yellow wreaths. Our gas was lit, and shone on the white cloth, and glimmer of china and metal, for the table had not been cleared yet. Sherlock Holmes had been silent all the morning, dipping continuously into the advertisement columns of a succession of papers, until at last, having apparently given up his search, he had emerged in no very sweet temper to lecture me upon my literary shortcomings.

'At the same time,' he remarked, after a pause, during which he had sat puffing at his long pipe and gazing down into the fire, 'you can hardly be open to a charge of sensationalism, for out of these cases which you have been so kind as to interest yourself in, a fair proportion do not treat of crime, in its legal sense, at all. The small matter in which I endeavoured to help the King of Bohemia, the singular experience of Miss Mary Sutherland, the problem connected with the man with the twisted lip, and the incident of the noble bachelor, were all matters which are outside the pale of the law. But in avoiding the sensational, I fear that you may have bordered on the trivial.'

'The end may have been so,' I answered, 'but the methods I hold to have been novel and of interest.'

'Pshaw, my dear fellow, what do the public, the great unobservant public, who could hardly tell a weaver by his tooth or a compositor by his left thumb, care about the finer shades of analysis and deduction! But, indeed, if you are trivial, I cannot blame you, for the days of the great cases are past. Man, or at least criminal man, has lost all enterprise and originality. As to my own little practice, it seems to be degenerating into an agency for recovering lost lead pencils and giving advice to young ladies from boarding-schools. I think that I have touched bottom at last, however. This note I had this morning marks my zero point, I fancy. Read it!' He tossed a crumpled letter across to me.

It was dated from Montague Place upon the preceding evening, and ran thus:

Dear Mr Holmes – I am very anxious to consult you as to whether I should or should not accept a situation which has been offered to me as governess. I shall call at half-past ten tomorrow, if I do not inconvenience you – Yours faithfully,
Violet Hunter.

'Do you know the young lady?' I asked.
'Not I.'
'It is half-past ten now.'

'Yes, and I have no doubt that is her ring.'

'It may turn out to be of more interest than you think. You remember that the affair of the blue carbuncle, which appeared to be a mere whim at first, developed into a serious investigation. It may be so in this case also.'

'Well, let us hope so! But our doubts will very soon be solved, for here, unless I am much mistaken, is the person in question.'

As he spoke the door opened, and a young lady entered the room. She was plainly but neatly dressed, with a bright, quick face, freckled like a plover's egg, and with the brisk manner of a woman who has had her own way to make in the world.

'You will excuse my troubling you, I am sure,' said she, as my companion rose to greet her; 'but I have had a very strange experience, and as I have no parents or relations of any sort from whom I could ask advice, I thought that perhaps you would be kind enough to tell me what I should do.'

'Pray take a seat, Miss Hunter. I shall be happy to do anything that I can to serve you.'

I could see that Holmes was favourably impressed by the manner and speech of his new client. He looked her over in his searching fashion, and then composed himself with his lids drooping and his fingertips together to listen to her story.

'I have been a governess for five years,' said she, 'in the family of Colonel Spence Munro, but two months ago the Colonel received an appointment at Halifax, in Nova Scotia, and took his children over to America with him, so that I found myself without a situation. I advertised and I answered advertisements, but without success. At last the little money which I had saved began to run short, and I was at my wits' end as to what I should do.

'There is a well-known agency for governesses in the West End called Westaway's, and there I used to call about once a week in order to see whether anything had turned up which might suit me. Westaway was the name of the founder of the business, but it is really managed by Miss Stoper. She sits in her own little office, and the ladies who are seeking employment wait in an ante-room, and are then shown in one by one, when she consults her ledgers, and sees whether she has anything which would suit them.

'Well, when I called last week I was shown into the little office as usual, but I found that Miss Stoper was not alone. A prodigiously stout man with a very smiling face, and a great heavy chin which rolled down in fold upon fold over his throat, sat at her elbow with a pair of glasses on his nose, looking very earnestly at the ladies who entered. As I came in he gave quite a jump in his chair, and turned quickly to Miss Stoper:

' "That will do," said he; "I could not ask for anything better. Capital! Capital!" He seemed quite enthusiastic and rubbed his hands together in the most genial fashion. He was such a comfortable-looking man that it was quite a pleasure to look at him.

' "You are looking for a situation, miss?" he asked.

' "Yes, sir."

' "As governess?"

' "Yes, sir."

' "And what salary do you ask?"

' "I had four pounds a month in my last place with Colonel Spence Munro."

' "Oh, tut, tut! sweating – rank sweating!" he cried, throwing his fat hands out into the air like a man who is in a boiling passion. "How could anyone offer so pitiful a sum to a lady with such attractions and accomplishments?"

' "My accomplishments, sir, may be less than you imagine," said I. "A little French, a little German, music and drawing –"

' "Tut, tut!" he cried. "This is all quite beside the question. The point is, have you or have you not the bearing and deportment of a lady? There it is in a nutshell. If you have not, you are not fitted for the rearing of a child who may some day play a considerable part in the history of the country. But if you have, why, then how could any gentleman ask you to condescend to accept anything under the three figures? Your salary with me, madam, would commence at a hundred pounds a year."

'You may imagine, Mr Holmes, that to me, destitute as I was, such an offer seemed almost too good to be true. The gentleman, however, seeing perhaps the look of incredulity upon my face, opened a pocket-book and took out a note.

' "It is also my custom," said he, smiling in the most pleasant fashion until his eyes were just two shining slits, amid the white creases of his face, "to advance to my young ladies half their salary beforehand, so that they may meet any little expenses of their journey and their wardrobe."

'It seemed to me that I had never met so fascinating and so thoughtful a man. As I was already in debt to my tradesmen, the advance was a great convenience, and yet there was something unnatural about the whole transaction which made me wish to know a little more before I quite committed myself.

' "May I ask where you live, sir?" said I.

' "Hampshire. Charming rural place. The Copper Beeches, five miles on the far side of Winchester. It is the most lovely country, my dear young lady, and the dearest old country house."

' "And my duties, sir? I should be glad to know what they would be."

' "One child – one dear little romper just six years old. Oh, if you could see him killing cockroaches with a slipper! Smack! smack! smack! Three gone before you could wink!" He leaned back in his chair and laughed his eyes into his head again.

'I was a little startled at the nature of the child's amusement, but the father's laughter made me think that perhaps he was joking.

' "My sole duties, then," I asked, "are to take charge of a single child?"

' "No, no, not the sole, not the sole, my dear young lady," he cried. "Your duty would be, as I am sure your good sense would suggest, to obey any little commands which my wife might give, provided always that they were such commands as a lady might with propriety obey. You see no difficulty, heh?"

' "I should be happy to make myself useful."

' "Quite so. In dress now, for example! We are faddy people, you know – faddy, but kind-hearted. If you were asked to wear any dress which we might give you, you would not object to our little whim. Heh?"

' "No," said I, considerably astonished at his words.

' "Or to sit here, or sit there, that would not be offensive to you?"

' "Oh, no."

' "Or, to cut your hair quite short before you come to us?"

'I could hardly believe my ears. As you may observe, Mr Holmes, my hair is somewhat luxuriant, and of a rather peculiar tint of chestnut. It has been considered artistic. I could not dream of sacrificing it in this offhand fashion.

' "I am afraid that that is quite impossible," said I. He had been watching me eagerly out of his small eyes, and I could see a shadow pass over his face as I spoke.

' "I am afraid that it is quite essential," said he. "It is a little fancy of my wife's, and ladies' fancies, you know, madam, ladies' fancies must be consulted. And so you won't cut your hair?"

' "No, sir, I really could not," I answered firmly.

' "Ah, very well; then that quite settles the matter. It is a pity, because in other respects you would really have done very nicely. In that case, Miss Stoper, I had best inspect a few more of your young ladies."

'The manageress had sat all this while busy with her papers without a word to either of us, but she glanced at me now with so much annoyance upon her face that I could not help suspecting that she had lost a handsome commission through my refusal.

' "Do you desire your name to be kept upon the books?" she asked.

' "If you please, Miss Stoper."

' "Well, really, it seems rather useless, since you refuse the most excellent offers in this fashion," said she sharply. "You can hardly expect us to exert ourselves to find another such opening for you. Good day to you, Miss Hunter." She struck a gong upon the table, and I was shown out by the page.

'Well, Mr Holmes, when I got back to my lodgings and found little enough in the cupboard, and two or three bills upon the table, I began to ask myself whether I had not done a very foolish thing. After all, if these people had strange fads, and expected obedience on the most extraordinary matters, they were at least ready to pay for their eccentricity. Very few governesses in England are getting a hundred a year. Besides, what use was my hair to me? Many people are improved by wearing it short, and perhaps I should be among the number. Next day I was inclined to think that I had made a mistake, and by the day after I was sure of it. I had almost overcome my pride, so far as to go back to the agency and inquire whether the place was still open, when I received this letter from the gentleman himself. I have it here, and I will read it to you:

THE COPPER BEECHES, NEAR WINCHESTER.

Dear Miss Hunter – Miss Stoper has very kindly given me your address, and I write from here to ask you whether you have reconsidered your decision. My wife is very anxious that you should come, for she has been much attracted by my description of you. We are willing to give thirty pounds a quarter, or £120 a year, so as to recompense you for any little inconvenience which our fads may cause you. They are not very exacting after all. My wife is fond of a particular shade of electric blue, and would like you to wear such a dress indoors in the morning. You need not, however, go to the expense of purchasing one, as we have one belonging to my dear daughter Alice (now in Philadelphia) which would, I should think, fit you very well. Then, as to sitting here or there, or amusing yourself in any manner indicated, that need cause you no inconvenience. As regards your hair, it is no doubt a pity, especially as I could not help remarking its beauty during our short interview, but I am afraid that I must remain firm upon this point, and I only hope that the increased salary may recompense you for the loss. Your duties, as far as the child is concerned, are very light. Now do try to come, and I shall meet you with the dog-cart at Winchester. Let me know your train – Yours faithfully,

Jephro Rucastle.

'That is the letter which I have just received, Mr Holmes, and my mind is made up that I will accept it. I thought, however, that before taking the final step, I should like to submit the whole matter to your consideration.'

'Well, Miss Hunter, if your mind is made up, that settles the question,' said Holmes, smiling.

'But you would not advise me to refuse?'

'I confess that it is not the situation which I should like to see a sister of mine apply for.'

'What is the meaning of it all, Mr Holmes?'

'Ah, I have no data. I cannot tell. Perhaps you have yourself formed some opinion?'

'Well, there seems to me to be only one possible solution. Mr Rucastle seemed to be a very kind, good-natured man. Is it not possible that his wife is a lunatic, that he desires to keep the matter quiet for fear she should be taken to an asylum, and that he humours her fancies in every way in order to prevent an outbreak.'

'That is a possible solution – in fact, as matters stand, it is the most probable one. But in any case it does not seem to be a nice household for a young lady.'

'But the money, Mr Holmes, the money!'

'Well, yes, of course, the pay is good – too good. That is what makes me uneasy. Why should they give you £120 a year, when they could have the pick for £40? There must be some strong reason behind.'

'I thought that if I told you the circumstances you would understand afterwards if I wanted your help. I should feel so much stronger if I felt that you were at the back of me.'

'Oh, you may carry that feeling away with you. I assure you that your little problem promises to be the most interesting which has come my way for some months. There is something distinctly novel about some of the features. If you should find yourself in doubt or in danger –'

'Danger! What danger do you foresee?'

Holmes shook his head gravely. 'It would cease to be a danger if we could define it,' said he. 'But at any time, day or night, a telegram would bring me down to your help.'

'That is enough.' She rose briskly from her chair with the anxiety all swept from her face. 'I shall go down to Hampshire quite easy in my mind now. I shall write to Mr Rucastle at once, sacrifice my poor hair tonight, and start for Winchester tomorrow.' With a few grateful words to Holmes she bade us both good-night, and bustled off upon her way.

'At least,' said I, as we heard her quick, firm step descending the stairs, 'she seems to be a young lady who is very well able to take care of herself.'

'And she would need to be,' said Holmes gravely; 'I am much mistaken if we do not hear from her before many days are past.'

It was not very long before my friend's prediction was fulfilled. A fortnight went by, during which I frequently found my thoughts turning in her direction, and wondering what strange side alley of human experience this lonely woman had strayed into. The unusual salary, the curious conditions, the light duties, all pointed to something abnormal, though whether a fad or a plot, or whether the man were a philanthropist or a villain, it was quite beyond my powers to determine. As to Holmes, I observed that he sat frequently for half an hour on end, with knitted brows and an abstracted air, but he swept the matter away with a wave of his hand when I mentioned it. 'Data! data! data!' he cried impatiently. 'I can't make bricks without clay.' And yet he would always wind up by muttering that no sister of his should ever have accepted such a situation.

The telegram which we eventually received came late one night, just as I was thinking of turning in, and Holmes was settling down to one of those all-night researches which he frequently indulged in, when I would leave him stooping over a retort and a test-tube at night, and find him in the same position when I came down to breakfast in the morning. He opened the yellow envelope, and then, glancing at the message, threw it across to me.

'Just look up the trains in Bradshaw,' said he, and turned back to his chemical studies.

The summons was a brief and urgent one.

Please be at the Black Swan Hotel at Winchester at midday tomorrow (it said). Do come! I am at my wits' end.

Hunter.

'Will you come with me?' asked Holmes, glancing up.

'I should wish to.'

'Just look it up, then.'

'There is a train at half-past nine,' said I, glancing over my Bradshaw. 'It is due at Winchester at 11.30.'

'That will do very nicely. Then perhaps I had better postpone my analysis of the acetones, as we may need to be at our best in the morning.'

By eleven o'clock the next day we were well upon our way to the old English capital. Holmes had been buried in the morning papers all the way down, but after we had passed the Hampshire border he threw them down, and began to admire the scenery. It was an ideal spring day, a light blue sky, flecked with little fleecy white clouds drifting across from west to east. The sun was shining very brightly, and yet there was an exhilarating nip in the air, which set an edge to a man's energy. All over the countryside, away to the rolling hills around Aldershot, the little red and grey roofs of the farm-steadings peeped out from amidst the light green of the new foliage.

'Are they not fresh and beautiful?' I cried, with all the enthusiasm of a man fresh from the fogs of Baker Street.

But Holmes shook his head gravely.

'Do you know, Watson,' said he, 'that it is one of the curses of a mind with a turn like mine that I must look at everything with reference to my own special subject. You look at these scattered houses, and you are impressed by their beauty. I look at them, and the only thought which comes to me is a feeling of their isolation, and of the impunity with which crime may be committed there.'

'Good heavens!' I cried. 'Who would associate crime with these dear old homesteads?'

'They always fill me with a certain horror. It is my belief, Watson, founded upon my experience, that the lowest and vilest alleys in London do not present a more dreadful record of sin than does the smiling and beautiful countryside.'

'You horrify me!'

'But the reason is very obvious. The pressure of public opinion can do in the town what the law cannot accomplish. There is no lane so vile that the scream of a tortured child, or the thud of a drunkard's blow, does not beget sympathy and indignation among the neighbours, and then the whole machinery of justice is ever so close that a word of complaint can set it going, and there is but a step between the crime and the dock. But look at these lonely houses, each in its own fields, filled for the most part with poor ignorant folk who know little of the law. Think of the deeds of hellish cruelty, the hidden wickedness which may go on, year in, year out, in such places, and none the wiser. Had this lady who appeals to us for help gone to live in Winchester, I should never have had a fear for her. It is the five miles of country which makes the danger. Still, it is clear that she is not personally threatened.'

'No. If she can come to Winchester to meet us she can get away.'

'Quite so. She has her freedom.'

'What *can* be the matter, then? Can you suggest no explanation?'

'I have devised seven separate explanations, each of which would cover the facts as far as we know them. But which of these is correct can only be determined by the fresh information which we shall no doubt find waiting for us. Well, there is the tower of the Cathedral, and we shall soon learn all that Miss Hunter has to tell.'

The 'Black Swan' is an inn of repute in the High Street, at no distance from the station, and there we found the young lady waiting for us. She had engaged a sitting-room, and our lunch awaited us upon the table.

'I am so delighted that you have come,' she said earnestly, 'it is so kind of you both; but indeed I do not know what I should do. Your advice will be altogether invaluable to me.'

'Pray tell us what has happened to you.'

'I will do so, and I must be quick, for I have promised Mr Rucastle to be back before three. I got his leave to come into town this morning, though he little knew for what purpose.'

'Let us have everything in its due order.' Holmes thrust his long thin legs out towards the fire, and composed himself to listen.

'In the first place, I may say that I have met, on the whole, with no actual ill-treatment from Mr and Mrs Rucastle. It is only fair to them to say that. But I cannot understand them, and I am not easy in my mind about them.'

'What can you not understand?'

'Their reasons for their conduct. But you shall have it all just as it occurred. When I came down Mr Rucastle met me here, and drove me in his dog-cart to Copper Beeches. It is, as he said, beautifully situated, but it is not beautiful in itself, for it is a large square block of a house, whitewashed, but all stained and streaked with damp and bad weather. There are grounds round it, woods on three sides, and on the fourth a field which slopes down to the Southampton high-road, which curves past about a hundred yards from the front door. This ground in front belongs to the house, but the woods all round are part of Lord Southerton's preserves. A clump of copper beeches immediately in front of the hall door has given its name to the place.

'I was driven over by my employer, who was as amiable as ever, and was introduced by him that evening to his wife and the child. There was no truth, Mr Holmes, in the conjecture which seemed to us to be probable in your rooms at Baker Street. Mrs Rucastle is not mad. I found her to be a silent, pale-faced woman, much younger than her husband, not more than thirty, I should think, while he can hardly be less than forty-five. From their conversation I have gathered that they have been married about seven years, that he was a widower, and that his only child by the first wife was the daughter who has gone to Philadelphia. Mr Rucastle told me in private that the reason why she had left them was that she had an unreasoning aversion to her stepmother. As the daughter could not have been less than twenty, I can quite imagine that her position must have been uncomfortable with her father's young wife.

'Mrs Rucastle seemed to me to be colourless in mind as well as in feature. She impressed me neither favourably nor the reverse. She was a nonentity. It was easy to see that she was passionately devoted both to her husband and to her little son. Her light grey eyes wandered continually from one to the other, noting every little want and forestalling it if possible. He was kind to her also in his bluff, boisterous fashion, and on the whole they seemed to be a happy couple. And yet she had some secret sorrow, this woman. She would often be lost in deep thought, with the saddest look upon her face. More than once I have surprised her in tears. I have thought sometimes that it was the disposition of her child which weighed upon her mind, for I have never met so utterly spoilt and so ill-natured a little creature. He is small for his age, with a head which is quite disproportionately large. His whole life appears to be spent in an alternation between savage fits of passion and gloomy intervals of sulking. Giving pain to any creature weaker than himself seems to be his one idea of amusement, and he shows quite remarkable talent in planning the capture of mice, little birds, and insects. But I would rather not talk about the creature, Mr Holmes, and, indeed, he has little to do with my story.'

'I am glad of all details,' remarked my friend, 'whether they seem to you to be relevant or not.'

'I shall try not to miss anything of importance. The one unpleasant thing about the house, which struck me at once, was the appearance and conduct of the servants. There are only two, a man and his wife. Toller, for that's his name, is a rough, uncouth man, with grizzled hair and whiskers, and a perpetual smell of drink. Twice since I have been with them he has been quite drunk, and yet Mr Rucastle seemed to take no notice of it. His wife is a very tall and strong woman with a sour face, as silent as Mrs Rucastle, and much less amiable. They are a most unpleasant couple, but fortunately I spend most of my time in the nursery and my own room, which are next to each other in one corner of the building.

'For two days after my arrival at the Copper Beeches my life was very quiet; on the third, Mrs Rucastle came down just after breakfast and whispered something to her husband.

' "Oh yes," said he, turning to me, "we are very much obliged to you, Miss Hunter, for falling in with our whims so far as to cut your hair. I assure you that it has not detracted in the tiniest iota from your appearance. We shall now see how the electric blue dress will become you. You will find it laid out upon the bed in your room, and if you would be so good as to put it on we should both be extremely obliged."

'The dress which I found waiting for me was of a peculiar shade of blue. It was of excellent material, a sort of beige, but it bore unmistakable signs of having been worn before. It could not have been a better fit if I had been measured for it. Both Mr and Mrs Rucastle expressed a delight at the look of it which seemed quite exaggerated in its vehemence. They were waiting for me in the drawing-room, which is a very large room, stretching along the entire front of the house, with three long windows reaching down to the floor. A chair had been placed close to the central window, with its back turned towards it. In this I was asked to sit, and then Mr Rucastle, walking up and down on the other side of the room, began to tell me a series of the funniest stories that I have ever listened to. You cannot imagine how comical he was, and I laughed until I was quite weary. Mrs Rucastle, however, who has evidently no sense of humour, never so much as smiled, but sat with her hands in her lap, and a sad, anxious look upon her face. After an hour or so, Mr Rucastle suddenly remarked that it was time to commence the duties of the day, and that I might change my dress, and go to little Edward in the nursery.

'Two days later this same performance was gone through under exactly similar circumstances. Again I changed my dress, again I sat in the window, and again I laughed very heartily at the funny stories of which my employer had an immense repertoire, and which he told inimitably. Then he handed me a yellow-backed novel, and, moving my chair a little sideways, that my own shadow might not fall upon the page, he begged me to read aloud to him. I read for about ten minutes, beginning in the heart of a chapter, and then suddenly, in the middle of a sentence, he ordered me to cease and change my dress.

'You can easily imagine, Mr Holmes, how curious I became as to what the meaning of this extraordinary performance could possibly be. They were always very careful, I observed, to turn my face away from the window, so that I became consumed with the desire to see what was going on behind my back. At first it seemed to be impossible, but I soon devised a means. My hand mirror had been broken, so a happy thought seized me, and I concealed a little of the glass in my handkerchief. On the next occasion, in the midst of my laughter, I put my handkerchief up to my eyes, and was able with a little management to see all that there was behind me. I confess that I was disappointed. There was nothing.

'At least, that was my first impression. At the second glance, however, I perceived that there was a man standing in the Southampton road, a small bearded man in a grey suit, who seemed to be looking in my direction. The road is an important highway, and there are usually people there. This man, however, was leaning against the railings which bordered our field, and was looking earnestly. I lowered my handkerchief, and glanced at Mrs Rucastle to find her eyes fixed upon me with a most searching gaze. She said nothing, but I am convinced that she had divined that I had a mirror in my hand, and had seen what was behind me. She rose at once.

' "Jephro," said she, "there is an impertinent fellow upon the road there who stares up at Miss Hunter."

' "No friend of yours, Miss Hunter?" he asked.

' "No; I know no one in these parts."

' "Dear me! How very impertinent! Kindly turn round, and motion him to go away."

' "Surely it would be better to take no notice?"

' "No, no, we should have him loitering here always. Kindly turn round, and wave him away like that."

'I did as I was told, and at the same instant Mrs Rucastle drew down the blind. That was a week ago, and from that time I have not sat again in the window, nor have I worn the blue dress, nor seen the man in the road.'

'Pray continue,' said Holmes. 'Your narrative promises to be a most interesting one.'

'You will find it rather disconnected, I fear, and there may prove to be little relation between the different incidents of which I speak. On the very first day that I was at Copper Beeches, Mr Rucastle took me to a small outhouse which stands near the kitchen door. As we approached it I heard the sharp rattling of a chain, and the sound as of a large animal moving about.

' "Look in here!" said Mr Rucastle, showing me a slit between two planks. "Is he not a beauty?"

'I looked through, and was conscious of two glowing eyes, and of a vague figure huddled up in the darkness.

' "Don't be frightened," said my employer, laughing at the start which I had given. "It's only Carlo, my mastiff. I call him mine, but really old Toller, my groom, is the only man who can do anything with him. We feed him once a day, and not too much then, so that he is always as keen as mustard. Toller lets him loose every night, and God help the trespasser whom he lays his fangs upon. For goodness' sake don't you ever on any pretext set your foot over the threshold at night, for it is as much as your life is worth."

'The warning was no idle one, for two nights later I happened to look out of my bedroom window about two o'clock in the morning. It was a beautiful moonlight night, and the lawn in front of the house was silvered over and almost as bright as day. I was standing wrapped in the peaceful beauty of the scene, when I was aware that something was moving under the shadow of the copper beeches. As it emerged into the moonshine I saw what it was. It was a giant dog, as large as a calf, tawny-tinted, with hanging jowl, black muzzle, and huge projecting bones. It walked slowly across the lawn and vanished into the shadow upon the other side. That dreadful silent sentinel sent a chill to my heart, which I do not think that any burglar could have done.

'And now I have a very strange experience to tell you. I had, as you know, cut off my hair in London, and I had placed it in a great coil at the bottom of my trunk. One evening, after the child was in bed, I began to amuse myself by examining the furniture of my room, and by rearranging my own little things. There was an old chest of drawers in the room, the two upper ones empty and open, the lower one locked. I had filled the two first with my linen, and as I had still much to pack away, I was naturally annoyed at not having the use of the third drawer. It struck me that it might have been fastened by a mere oversight, so I took out my bunch of keys and tried to open it. The very first key fitted to perfection, and I drew the drawer open. There was only one thing in it, but I am sure that you would never guess what it was. It was my coil of hair.

'I took it up and examined it. It was of the same peculiar tint, and the same thickness. But then the impossibility of the thing obtruded itself upon me. How *could* my hair have been locked in the drawer? With trembling hands I undid my trunk, turned out the contents, and drew from the bottom my own hair. I laid the two tresses together, and I assure you they were identical. Was it not extraordinary? Puzzle as I would I could make nothing at all of what it meant. I returned the strange hair to the drawer, and I said nothing of the matter to the Rucastles, as I felt that I had put myself in the wrong by opening a drawer which they had locked.

'I am naturally observant as you may have remarked, Mr Holmes, and I soon had a pretty good plan of the whole house in my head. There was one wing, however, which appeared not to be inhabited at all. A door which faced that which led into the quarters of the Tollers opened into this suite, but it was invariably locked. One day, however, as I ascended the stair, I met Mr Rucastle coming out through this door, his keys in his hand, and a look on his face which made him a very different person to the round jovial man to whom I was accustomed. His cheeks were red, his brow was all crinkled with anger, and the veins stood out at his temples with passion. He locked the door, and hurried past me without a word or a look.

'This aroused my curiosity; so when I went out for a walk in the grounds with my charge, I strolled round to the side from which I could see the windows of this part of the house. There were four of them in a row, three of which were simply dirty, while the fourth was shuttered up. They were evidently all deserted. As I strolled up and down, glancing at them occasionally, Mr Rucastle came out to me, looking as merry and jovial as ever.

' "Ah!" said he, "you must not think me rude if I passed you without a word, my dear young lady. I was preoccupied with business matters."

'I assured him that I was not offended. "By the way," said I, "you seem to have quite a suite of spare rooms up there, and one of them has the shutters up."

' "Photography is one of my hobbies," said he. "I have made my dark-room up there. But, dear me! what an observant young lady we have come upon. Who would have believed it? Who would have ever believed it?" He spoke in a jesting tone, but there was no jest in his eyes as he looked at me. I read suspicion there, and annoyance, but no jest.

'Well, Mr Holmes, from the moment that I understood that there was something about that suite of rooms which I was not to know, I was all on fire to go over them. It was not mere curiosity, though I have my share of that. It was more a feeling of duty – a feeling that some good might come from my penetrating to this place. They talk of woman's instinct; perhaps it was woman's instinct which gave me that feeling. At any rate, it was there; and I was keenly on the look-out for any chance to pass the forbidden door.

'It was only yesterday that the chance came. I may tell you that, besides Mr Rucastle, both Toller and his wife find something to do in these deserted rooms, and I once saw him carrying a large black linen bag with him through the door. Recently he has been drinking hard, and yesterday evening he was very drunk; and, when I came upstairs, there was the key in the door. I have no doubt at all that he had left it there. Mr and Mrs Rucastle were both downstairs, and the child was with them, so that I had an admirable opportunity. I turned the key gently in the lock, opened the door, and slipped through.

'There was a little passage in front of me, unpapered and uncarpeted, which turned at a right angle at the farther end. Round this corner were three doors in a line, the first and third of which were open. They each led into an empty room, dusty and cheerless, with two windows in the one, and one in the other, so thick with dirt that the evening light glimmered dimly through them. The centre door was closed, and across the outside of it had been fastened one of the broad bars of an iron bed, padlocked at one end to a ring in the wall, and fastened at the other with stout cord. The door itself was locked as well, and the key was not there. This barricaded door corresponded clearly with the shuttered window outside, and yet I could see by the glimmer from beneath it that the room was not in darkness. Evidently there was a skylight which let in light from above. As I stood in the passage gazing at this sinister door, and wondering what secret it might veil, I suddenly heard the sound of steps within the room, and saw a shadow pass backwards and forwards against the little slit of dim light which shone out from under the door. A mad, unreasoning terror rose up in me at the sight, Mr Holmes. My overstrung nerves failed me suddenly, and I turned and ran – ran as though some dreadful hand were behind me, clutching at the skirt of my dress. I rushed down the passage, through the door, and straight into the arms of Mr Rucastle, who was waiting outside.

' "So," said he, smiling, "it was you, then. I thought it must be when I saw the door open."

' "Oh, I am so frightened!" I panted.

' "My dear young lady! my dear young lady!" – you cannot think how caressing and soothing his manner was – "and what has frightened you, my dear young lady?"

'But his voice was just a little too coaxing. He overdid it. I was keenly on my guard against him.

' "I was foolish enough to go into the empty wing," I answered. "But it is so lonely and eerie in this dim light that I was frightened and ran out again. Oh, it is so dreafully still in there!"

' "Only that?" said he, looking at me keenly.

' "Why, what do you think?" I asked.

' "Why do you think that I lock this door?"

' "I am sure that I do not know."

' "It is to keep people out who have no business there. Do you see?" He was still smiling in the most amiable manner.

' "I am sure if I had known –"

' "Well, then, you know now. And if you ever put your foot over that threshold again –" here in an instant the smile hardened into a grin of rage, and he glared down at me with the face of a demon, "I'll throw you to the mastiff."

'I was so terrified that I do not know what I did. I suppose that I must have rushed past him into my room. I remember nothing until I found myself lying on my bed trembling all over. Then I thought of you, Mr Holmes. I could not live there longer without some advice. I was frightened of the house, of the man, of the woman, of the servants, even of the child. They were all horrible to me. If I could only bring you down all would be well. Of course I might have fled from the house, but my curiosity was almost as strong as my fears. My mind was soon made up. I would send you a wire. I put on my hat and cloak, went down to the office, which is about half a mile from the house, and then returned, feeling very much easier. A horrible doubt came into my mind as I approached the door lest the dog might be loose, but I remembered that Toller had drunk himself into a state of insensibility that evening, and I knew that he was the only one in the household who had any influence with the savage creature, or who would venture to set him free. I slipped in in safety, and lay awake half the night in my joy at the thought of seeing you. I had no difficulty in getting leave to come into Winchester this morning, but I must be back before three o'clock, for Mr and Mrs Rucastle are going on a visit, and will be away all the evening, so that I must look after the child. Now I have told you all my adventures, Mr Holmes, and I should be very glad if you could tell me what it all means, and, above all, what I should do.'

Holmes and I had listened spellbound to this extraordinary story. My friend rose now, and paced up and down the room, his hands in his pockets, and an expression of the most profound gravity upon his face.

'Is Toller still drunk?' he asked.

'Yes. I heard his wife tell Mrs Rucastle that she could do nothing with him.'

'That is well. And the Rucastles go out tonight?'

'Yes.'

'Is there a cellar with a good strong lock?'

'Yes, the wine cellar.'

'You seem to me to have acted all through this matter like a brave and sensible girl, Miss Hunter. Do you think that you could perform one more feat? I should not ask it of you if I did not think you a quite exceptional woman.'

'I will try. What is it?'

'We shall be at the Copper Beeches by seven o'clock, my friend and I.

The Rucastles will be gone by that time, and Toller will, we hope, be incapable. There only remains Mrs Toller, who might give the alarm. If you could send her into the cellar, on some errand, and then turn the key upon her, you would facilitate matters immensely.'

'I will do it.'

'Excellent! We shall then look thoroughly into the affair. Of course there is only one feasible explanation. You have been brought there to personate someone, and the real person is imprisoned in this chamber. That is obvious. As to who this prisoner is, I have no doubt that it is the daughter, Miss Alice Rucastle, if I remember right, who was said to have gone to America. You were chosen, doubtless, as resembling her in height, figure, and the colour of your hair. Hers had been cut off, very possibly in some illness through which she has passed, and so, of course, yours had to be sacrificed also. By a curious chance you came upon her tresses. The man in the road was, undoubtedly, some friend of hers – possibly her fiancé – and no doubt as you wore the girl's dress, and were so like her, he was convinced from your laughter, whenever he saw you, and afterwards from your gesture, that Miss Rucastle was perfectly happy, and that she no longer desired his attentions. The dog is let loose at night to prevent him from endeavouring to communicate with her. So much is fairly clear. The most serious point in the case is the disposition of the child.'

'What on earth has that to do with it?' I ejaculated.

'My dear Watson, you as a medical man are continually gaining light as to the tendencies of a child by the study of the parents. Don't you see that the converse is equally valid? I have frequently gained my first real insight into the character of parents by studying their children. This child's disposition is abnormally cruel, merely for cruelty's sake, and whether he derives this from his smiling father, as I should suspect, or from his mother, it bodes evil for the poor girl who is in their power.'

'I am sure that you are right, Mr Holmes,' cried our client. 'A thousand things come back to me which make me certain that you have hit it. Oh, let us lose not an instant in bringing help to this poor creature.'

'We must be circumspect, for we are dealing with a very cunning man. We can do nothing until seven o'clock. At that hour we shall be with you, and it will not be long before we solve the mystery.'

We were as good as our word, for it was just seven when we reached the Copper Beeches, having put up our trap at a wayside public-house. The group of trees, with their dark leaves shining like burnished metal in the light of the setting sun, were sufficient to mark the house even had Miss Hunter not been standing smiling on the doorstep.

'Have you managed it?' asked Holmes.

A loud thudding noise came from somewhere downstairs. 'That is Mrs Toller in the cellar,' said she. 'Her husband lies snoring on the kitchen rug. Here are his keys which are the duplicates of Mr Rucastle's.'

'You have done well indeed!' cried Holmes, with enthusiasm. 'Now lead the way, and we shall soon see the end of this black business.'

We passed up the stair, unlocked the door, followed on down a passage, and found ourselves in front of the barricade which Miss Hunter had described. Holmes cut the cord and removed the transverse bar. Then he tried the various keys in the lock, but without success. No sound came from within, and at the silence Holmes' face clouded over.

'I trust that we are not too late,' said he. 'I think, Miss Hunter, that we had better go in without you. Now, Watson, put your shoulder to it, and we shall see whether we cannot make our way in.'

It was an old rickety door and gave at once before our united strength. Together we rushed into the room. It was empty. There was no furniture save a little pallet bed, a small table, and a basketful of linen. The skylight above was open, and the prisoner gone.

'There has been some villainy here,' said Holmes; 'this beauty has guessed Miss Hunter's intentions, and has carried his victim off.'

'But how?'

'Through the skylight. We shall soon see how he managed it.' He swung himself up on to the roof. 'Ah, yes,' he cried, 'here's the end of a long light ladder against the eaves. That is how he did it.'

'But it is impossible,' said Miss Hunter, 'the ladder was not there when the Rucastles went away.'

'He has come back and done it. I tell you that he is a clever and dangerous man. I should not be very much surprised if this were he whose step I hear now upon the stair. I think, Watson, that it would be as well for you to have your pistol ready.'

The words were hardly out of his mouth before a man appeared at the door of the room, a very fat and burly man, with a heavy stick in his hand. Miss Hunter screamed and shrunk against the wall at the sight of him, but Sherlock Holmes sprang forward and confronted him.

'You villain,' said he, 'where's your daughter?'

The fat man cast his eyes round, and then up at the open skylight.

'It is for me to ask you that,' he shrieked, 'you thieves! Spies and thieves! I have caught you, have I! You are in my power. I'll serve you!' He turned and clattered down the stairs as hard as he could go.

'He's gone for the dog!' cried Miss Hunter.

'I have my revolver,' said I.

'Better close the front door,' cried Holmes, and we all rushed down the stairs together. We had hardly reached the hall when we heard the baying of a hound, and then a scream of agony, with a horrible worrying sound which it was dreadful to listen to. An elderly man with a red face and shaking limbs came staggering out at a side-door.

'My God!' he cried. 'Someone has loosed the dog. It's not been fed for two days. Quick, quick, or it'll be too late!'

Holmes and I rushed out, and round the angle of the house, with Toller hurrying behind us. There was the huge famished brute, its black muzzle buried in Rucastle's throat, while he writhed and screamed upon the ground. Running up, I blew its brains out, and it fell over with its keen white teeth still meeting in the great creases of his neck. With much labour we separated them, and carried him, living but horribly mangled, into the house. We laid him upon the drawing-room sofa, and having despatched the sobered Toller to bear the news to his wife, I did what I could to relieve his pain. We were all assembled round him when the door opened, and a tall, gaunt woman entered the room.

'Mrs Toller!' cried Miss Hunter.

'Yes, miss. Mr Rucastle let me out when he came back before he went up to you. Ah, miss, it is a pity you didn't let me know what you were planning, for I would have told you that your pains were wasted.'

'Ha!' said Holmes, looking keenly at her. 'It is clear that Mrs Toller knows more about this matter than anyone else.'

'Yes, sir, I do, and I am ready enough to tell what I know.'

'Then pray sit down, and let us hear it, for there are several points on which I must confess that I am still in the dark.'

'I will soon make it clear to you,' said she; 'and I'd have done so before now if I could ha' got out from the cellar. If there's police-court business over this, you'll remember that I was the one that stood your friend, and that I was Miss Alice's friend too.

'She was never happy at home, Miss Alice wasn't, from the time that her father married again. She was slighted like, and had no say in anything; but it never really became bad for her until after she met Mr Fowler at a friend's house. As well as I could learn, Miss Alice had rights of her own by will, but she was so quiet and patient, she was, that she never said a word about them, but just left everything in Mr Rucastle's hands. He knew he was safe with her; but when there was a chance of a husband coming forward, who would ask for all that the law could give him, then her father thought it time to put a stop on it. He wanted her to sign a paper so that whether she married or not, he could use her money. When she wouldn't do it, he kept on worrying her until she got brain fever, and for six weeks was at death's door. Then she got better at last, all worn to a shadow, and with her beautiful hair cut off; but that didn't make no change in her young man, and he stuck to her as true as man could be.'

'Ah,' said Holmes, 'I think that what you have been good enough to tell us makes the matter fairly clear, and that I can deduce all that remains. Mr Rucastle, then, I presume, took to this system of imprisonment?'

'Yes, sir.'

'And brought Miss Hunter down from London in order to get rid of the disagreeable persistence of Mr Fowler.'

'That was it, sir.'

'But Mr Fowler, being a persevering man, as a good seaman should be, blockaded the house, and, having met you, succeeded by certain arguments, metallic or otherwise, in convincing you that your interests were the same as his.'

'Mr Fowler was a very kind-spoken, free-handed gentleman,' said Mrs Toller serenely.

'And in this way he managed that your good man should have no want of drink, and that a ladder should be ready at the moment when your master had gone.'

'You have it, sir, just as it happened.'

'I am sure we owe you an apology, Mrs Toller,' said Holmes, 'for you have certainly cleared up everything which puzzled us. And here comes the country surgeon and Mrs Rucastle, so I think, Watson, that we had best escort Miss Hunter back to Winchester, as it seems to me that our *locus standi* now is rather a questionable one.'

And thus was solved the mystery of the sinister house with the copper beeches in front of the door. Mr Rucastle survived, but was always a broken man, kept alive solely through the care of his devoted wife. They still live with their old servants, who probably know so much of Rucastle's past life that he finds it difficult to part from them. Mr Fowler and Miss Rucastle were married, by special licence, in Southampton the day after their flight, and he is now the holder of a Government appointment in the Island of Mauritius. As to Miss Violet Hunter, my friend Holmes, rather to my disappointment, manifested no further interest in her when once she had ceased to be the centre of one of his problems, and she is now the head of a private school at Walsall, where I believe that she has met with considerable success.

Stanley Ellin

THE QUESTION

Ellery Queen, or the half of him that was Frederic Dannay, has told the tale of how Stanley Ellin's first short story, 'The Specialty of the House', was submitted out of the blue to *Ellery Queen's Mystery Magazine*, accepted, entered in the magazine's annual prize contest and received an award as Best First Story. And of how critics then complained, saying that it should have received the major award as Best Story of the Year, and in the words of one critic was 'worth all the rest of the Queen's Awards together'.

Stanley Ellin was born in 1916. 'The Specialty of the House', which is the delicious Lamb Amirstan served on special occasions at Sbirro's, remains his most famous short story, a fact which might draw a wry smile from this tough, witty New Yorker who looks like a medium-sized friendly bear. For although he is an extremely slow writer Ellin has written many other short stories of varied excellence – tragic, ironic, comic, but most of them saying something about the dark side of our civilization. There are surprise endings but no puzzles in his tales, and the great quality he has revived in a period when many mechanically perfect but basically uninteresting short stories are written is that of imagination. He is a novelist also, and *The Eighth Circle* (1958) and *Mirror, Mirror on the Wall* (1972) in particular are books of quality, but they don't compare with the short stories, which may be found in two collections, *Mystery Stories* (1956) and *The Blessington Method* (1964).

After ruling out 'The Specialty of the House' because of its familiarity, I brooded on half a dozen stories. They included 'The Cat's Paw', 'The Best of Everything' (which made a fine film), and 'You Can't Be a Little Girl All Your Life'. In the end I chose 'The Question', which like the others gives the essential Ellin flavour.

I am an electrocutioner . . . I prefer this word to executioner; I think words make a difference. When I was a boy, people who buried the dead were undertakers, and then somewhere along the way they became morticians and are better off for it.

Take the one who used to be the undertaker in my town. He was a decent, respectable man, very friendly if you'd let him be, but hardly anybody would let him be. Today, his son – who now runs the business – is not an undertaker but a mortician, and is welcome everywhere. As a matter of fact, he's an officer in my Lodge and is one of the most popular members we have. And all it took to do that was changing one word to another. The job's the same but the word is different, and people somehow will always go by words rather than meanings.

So, as I said, I am an electrocutioner – which is the proper professional word for it in my state where the electric chair is the means of execution.

Not that this is my profession. Actually, it's a sideline, as it is for most of us who perform executions. My real business is running an electrical supply and repair shop just as my father did before me. When he died I inherited not only the business from him, but also the position of state's electrocutioner.

We established a tradition, my father and I. He was running the shop profitably even before the turn of the century when electricity was a comparatively new thing, and he was the first man to perform a successful electrocution for the state. It was not the state's first electrocution, however. That one was an experiment and was badly bungled by the engineer who installed the chair in the state prison. My father, who had helped install the chair, was the assistant at the electrocution, and he told me that everything that could go wrong that day did go wrong. The current was eccentric, his boss froze on the switch, and the man in the chair was alive and kicking at the same time he was being burned to a crisp. The next time, my father offered to do the job himself, rewired the chair, and handled the switch so well that he was offered the job of official electrocutioner.

I followed in his footsteps, which is how a tradition is made, but I am afraid this one ends with me. I have a son, and what I said to him and what he said to me is the crux of the matter. He asked me a question – well, in my opinion, it was the kind of question that's at the bottom of most of the world's troubles today. There are some sleeping dogs that should be left to lie; there are some questions that should not be asked.

To understand all this, I think you have to understand me, and nothing could be easier. I'm sixty, just beginning to look my age, a little overweight, suffer sometimes from arthritis when the weather is damp. I'm a good citizen, complain about my taxes but pay them on schedule, vote for the right party, and run my business well enough to make a comfortable living from it.

I've been married thirty-five years and never looked at another woman in all that time. Well, looked maybe, but no more than that. I have a married daughter and a grand-daughter almost a year old, and the prettiest, smilingest baby in town. I spoil her and don't apologize for it, because in my opinion that is what grandfathers were made for – to spoil their grandchildren. Let mama and papa attend to the business; grandpa is there for the fun.

And beyond all that I have a son who asks questions. The kind that shouldn't be asked.

Put the picture together, and what you get is someone like yourself. I might be your next-door neighbor, I might be your old friend, I might be the uncle you meet whenever the family gets together at a wedding or a funeral. I'm like you.

Naturally, we all look different on the outside but we can still recognize each other on sight as the same kind of people. Deep down inside where it matters we have the same feelings, and we know that without any questions being asked about them.

'But,' you might say, 'there is a difference between us. You're the one who performs the executions, and I'm the one who reads about them in the papers, and that's a big difference, no matter how you look at it.'

Is it? Well, look at it without prejudice, look at it with absolute honesty, and you'll have to admit that you're being unfair.

Let's face the facts, we're all in this together. If an old friend of yours happens to serve on a jury that finds a murderer guilty, you don't lock the door against him, do you? More than that: if you could get an introduction to the judge who sentences that murderer to the electric chair, you'd be proud of it, wouldn't you? You'd be honored to have him sit at your table, and you'd be quick enough to let the world know about it.

And since you're so willing to be friendly with the jury that convicts and the judge that sentences, what about the man who has to pull the switch? He's finished the job you wanted done, he's made the world a better place for it. Why must he go hide away in a dark corner until the next time he's needed?

There's no use denying that nearly everybody feels he should, and there's less use denying that it's a cruel thing for anyone in my position to face. If you don't mind some strong language, it's a damned outrage to hire a man for an unpleasant job, and then despise him for it. Sometimes it's hard to abide such righteousness.

How do I get along in the face of it? The only way possible – by keeping my secret locked up tight and never being tempted to give it away. I don't like it that way, but I'm no fool about it.

The trouble is that I'm naturally easygoing and friendly. I'm the sociable kind. I like people, and I want them to like me. At Lodge meetings or in the clubhouse down at the golf course I'm always the center of the crowd. And I know what would happen if at any such time I ever opened my mouth and let that secret out. A five-minute sensation, and after that the slow chill setting in. It would mean the end of my whole life then and there, the kind of life I want to live, and no man in his right mind throws away sixty years of his life for a five-minute sensation.

You can see I've given the matter a lot of thought. More than that, it hasn't been idle thought. I don't pretend to be an educated man, but I'm willing to read books on any subject that interests me, and execution has been one of my main interests ever since I got into the line. I have the books sent to the shop where nobody takes notice of another piece of mail, and I keep them locked in a bin in my office so that I can read them in private.

There's a nasty smell about having to do it this way – at my age you hate to feel like a kid hiding himself away to read a dirty magazine – but I have no choice. There isn't a soul on earth outside of the warden at state's prison and a couple of picked guards there who know I'm the one pulling the switch at an execution, and I intend it to remain that way.

Oh, yes, my son knows now. Well, he's difficult in some ways, but he's no fool. If I wasn't sure he would keep his mouth shut about what I told him, I wouldn't have told it to him in the first place.

Have I learned anything from those books? At least enough to take a pride in what I'm doing for the state and the way I do it. As far back in history as you want to go there have always been executioners. The day that men first made laws to help keep peace among themselves was the day the first executioner was born. There have always been law-breakers; there must always be a way of punishing them. It's as simple as that.

The trouble is that nowadays there are too many people who don't want it to be as simple as that. I'm no hypocrite, I'm not one of those narrow-minded fools who thinks that every time a man comes up with a generous impulse he's some kind of crackpot. But he can be mistaken. I'd put most of the people who are against capital punishment in that class. They are fine, highminded citizens who've never in their lives been close enough to a murderer or rapist to smell the evil in him. In fact, they're so fine and highminded that they can't imagine anyone in the world not being like themselves. In that case, they say anybody who commits murder or rape is just a plain, ordinary human being who's had a bad spell. He's no criminal, they say, he's just sick. He doesn't need the electric chair; all he needs is a kindly old doctor to examine his head and straighten out the kinks in his brain.

In fact, they say there is no such thing as a criminal at all. There are only well people and sick people, and the ones who deserve all your worry and consideration are the sick ones. If they happen to murder or rape a few of the well ones now and then, why, just run for the doctor.

This is the argument from beginning to end, and I'd be the last one to deny that it's built on honest charity and good intentions. But it's a mistaken argument. It omits the one fact that matters. When anyone commits murder or rape he is no longer in the human race. A man has a human brain and a God-given soul to control his animal nature. When the animal in him takes control he's not a human being any more. Then he has to be exterminated the way any animal must be if it goes wild in the middle of helpless people. And my duty is to be the exterminator.

It could be that people just don't understand the meaning of the word *duty* any more. I don't want to sound old-fashioned, God forbid, but when I was a boy things were more straightforward and clear-cut. You learned to tell right from wrong, you learned to do what had to be done, and you didn't ask questions every step of the way. Or if you had to ask any questions, the ones that mattered were *how* and *when*.

Then along came psychology, along came the professors, and the main question was always *why*. Ask yourself *why, why, why* about everything you do, and you'll end up doing nothing. Let a couple of generations go along that way, and you'll finally have a breed of people who sit around in trees like monkeys, scratching their heads.

Does this sound far-fetched? Well, it isn't. Life is a complicated thing to live. All his life a man finds himself facing one situation after another, and the way to handle them is to live by the rules. Ask yourself *why* once too often, and you can find yourself so tangled up that you go under. The show must go on. Why? Women and children first. Why? My country, right or wrong. Why? Never mind your duty. Just keep asking *why* until it's too late to do anything about it.

Around the time I first started going to school my father gave me a dog, a collie pup named Rex. A few years after Rex suddenly became unfriendly, the way a dog will sometimes, and then vicious, and then one day he bit my mother when she reached down to pat him.

The day after that I saw my father leaving the house with his hunting rifle under his arm and with Rex on a leash. It wasn't the hunting season, so I knew what was going to happen to Rex and I knew why. But it's forgivable in a boy to ask things that a man should be smart enough not to ask.

'Where are you taking Rex?' I asked my father. 'What are you going to do with him?'

'I'm taking him out back of town,' my father said. 'I'm going to shoot him.'

'But why?' I said, and that was when my father let me see that there is only one answer to such a question.

'Because it has to be done,' he said.

I never forgot that lesson. It came hard; for a while I hated my father for it, but as I grew up I came to see how right he was. We both knew why the dog had to be killed. Beyond that, all questions would lead nowhere. Why the dog had become vicious, why God had put a dog on earth to be killed this way – these are the questions that you can talk out to the end of time, and while you're talking about them you still have a vicious dog on your hands.

It is strange to look back and realize now that when the business of the dog happened, and long before it and long after it, my father was an electrocutioner, and I never knew it. Nobody knew it, not even my mother. A few times a year my father would pack his bag and a few tools and go away for a couple of days, but that was all any of us knew. If you asked him where he was going he would simply say he had a job to do out of town. He was not a man you'd ever suspect of philandering or going off on a solitary drunk, so nobody gave it a second thought.

It worked the same way in my case. I found out how well it worked when I finally told my son what I had been doing on those jobs out of town, and that I had gotten the warden's permission to take him on as an assistant and train him to handle the chair himself when I retired. I could tell from the way he took it that he was as thunderstruck at this as I had been thirty years before when my father had taken me into his confidence.

'Electrocutioner?' said my son. 'An *electrocutioner?*'

'Well, there's no disgrace to it,' I said. 'And since it's got to be done, and somebody has to do it, why not keep it in the family? If you knew anything about it, you'd know it's a profession that's often passed down in a family from generation to generation. What's wrong with a good, sound tradition? If more people believed in tradition you wouldn't have so many troubles in the world today.'

It was the kind of argument that would have been more than enough to convince me when I was his age. What I hadn't taken into account was that my son wasn't like me, much as I wanted him to be. He was a grown man in his own right, but a grown man who had never settled down to his responsibilities. I had always kept closing my eyes to that. I had always seen him the way I wanted to and not the way he was.

When he left college after a year, I said, all right, there are some people who aren't made for college, I never went there, so what difference does it make. When he went out with one girl after another and could never make up his mind to marrying any of them, I said, well, he's young, he's sowing his wild oats, the time will come soon enough when he's ready to take care of a home and family. When he sat day-dreaming in the shop instead of tending to business I never made a fuss about it. I knew when he put his mind to it he was as good an electrician as you could ask for, and in these soft times people are allowed to do a lot more dreaming and a lot less working than they used to.

The truth was that the only thing that mattered to me was being his friend. For all his faults he was a fine-looking boy with a good mind. He wasn't much for mixing with people, but if he wanted to he could win anyone over. And in the back of my mind all the while he was growing up was the thought that he was the only one who would learn my secret some day, and would share it with me, and make it easier to bear. I'm not secretive by nature. A man like me needs a thought like that to sustain him.

So when the time came to tell him he shook his head and said no. I felt that my legs had been kicked out from under me. I argued with him and he still said no, and I lost my temper.

'Are you against capital punishment?' I asked him. 'You don't have to apologize if you are. I'd think all the more of you, if that's your only reason.'

'I don't know if it is,' he said.

'Well, you ought to make up your mind one way or the other,' I told him. 'I'd hate to think you were like every other hypocrite around who says it's all right to condemn a man to the electric chair and all wrong to pull the switch.'

'Do I have to be the one to pull it?' he said. 'Do you?'

'Somebody has to do it. Somebody always has to do the dirty work for the rest of us. It's not like the Old Testament days when everybody did it for himself. Do you know how they executed a man in those days? They laid him on the ground tied hand and foot, and everybody around had to heave rocks on him until he was crushed to death. They didn't invite anybody to stand around and watch. You wouldn't have had much choice then, would you?'

'I don't know,' he said. And then because he was as smart as they come and knew how to turn your words against you, he said, 'After all, I'm not without sin.'

'Don't talk like a child,' I said. 'You're without the sin of murder on you or any kind of sin that calls for execution. And if you're so sure the Bible has all the answers, you might remember that you're supposed to render unto Caesar the things that are Caesar's.'

'Well,' he said, 'in this case I'll let you do the rendering.'

I knew then and there from the way he said it and the way he looked at me that it was no use trying to argue with him. The worst of it was knowing that we had somehow moved far apart from each other and would never really be close again. I should have had sense enough to let it go at that. I should have just told him to forget the whole thing and keep his mouth shut about it.

Maybe if I had ever considered the possibility of his saying no, I would have done it. But because I hadn't considered any such possibility I was caught off balance. I was too much upset to think straight. I will admit it now. It was my own fault that I made an issue of things and led him to ask the one question he should never have asked.

'I see,' I told him. 'It's the same old story, isn't it? Let somebody else do it. But if they pull your number out of a hat and you have to serve on a jury and send a man to the chair, that's all right with you. At least, it's all right as long as there's somebody else to do the job that you and the judge and every decent citizen wants done. Let's face the facts, boy, you don't have the guts. I'd hate to think of you even walking by the death house. The shop is where you belong. You can be nice and cozy there, wiring up fixtures and ringing the cash register. I can handle my duties without your help.'

It hurt me to say it. I had never talked like that to him before, and it hurt. The strange thing was that he didn't seem angry about it; he only looked at me puzzled.

'Is that all it is to you?' he said. 'A duty?'

'Yes.'

'But you get paid for it, don't you?'

'I get paid little enough for it.'

He kept looking at me that way. 'Only a duty?' he said, and never took his eyes off me. 'But you enjoy it, don't you?'

That was the question he asked.

You enjoy it, don't you? You stand there looking through a peephole in the wall at the chair. In thirty years I have stood there more than a hundred times looking at that chair. The guards bring somebody in. Usually he is in a daze; sometimes he screams, throws himself around and fights. Sometimes it is a woman, and a woman can be as hard to handle as a man when she is led to the chair. Sooner or later, whoever it is is strapped down and the black hood is dropped over his head. Now your hand is on the switch.

The warden signals, and you pull the switch. The current hits the body like a tremendous rush of air suddenly filling it. The body leaps out of the chair with only the straps holding it back. The head jerks, and a curl of smoke comes from it. You release the switch and the body falls back again.

You do it once more, do it a third time to make sure. And whenever your hand presses the switch you can see in your mind what the current is doing to that body and what the face under the hood must look like.

Enjoy it?

That was the question my son asked me. That was what he said to me, as if I didn't have the same feelings deep down in me that we all have.

Enjoy it?

But, my God, how could anyone *not* enjoy it!

William Faulkner

SMOKE

One novel and one book of short stories in the large output of William Faulkner (1897–1962) may truly be put into the crime genre. These are the melodramatic tale of sexual violence *Sanctuary* (1931), which Faulkner later said he wrote in three weeks as a deliberate potboiler, and *Knight's Gambit* (1949). Other books which contain some ingredients of crime fiction are *Light in August, Absalom, Absalom* (which contains some detective devices) and *Intruder in the Dust*. In 1950 Faulkner was awarded the Nobel Prize.

He was an avid reader of detective stories with a true interest in the form, and the six stories in *Knight's Gambit* involve genuine detection. Gavin Stevens, attorney of Yoknapatawpha County, shows similarities to Uncle Abner, the creation of Melville Davisson Post, but is still a distinctive character. 'Smoke' gives a good impression of Stevens's homespun shrewdness, and the fact that the Watson is his unsophisticated nephew adds depth and plausibility to this and the other tales. With the publication of *Intruder in the Dust* in 1948, where Stevens was involved in showing that a negro had been framed for murder, and the collection of the short stories as a volume in the following year, Faulkner seems to have felt that he had no further use for the formulas and devices of the detective story.

Anselm Holland came to Jefferson many years ago. Where from, no one knew. But he was young then and a man of parts, or of presence at least, because within three years he had married the only daughter of a man who owned two thousand acres of some of the best land in the county, and he went to live in his father-in-law's house, where two years later his wife bore him twin sons and where a few years later still the father-in-law died and left Holland in full possession of the property, which was now in his wife's name. But even before that event, we in Jefferson had already listened to him talking a trifle more than loudly of 'my land, my crops'; and those of us whose fathers and grandfathers had been bred here looked upon him a little coldly and a little askance for a ruthless man and (from tales told about him by both white and negro tenants and by others with whom he had dealings) for a violent one. But out of consideration for his wife and respect for his father-in-law, we treated him with courtesy if not with regard. So when his wife, too, died while the twin sons were still children, we believed that he was responsible, that her life had been worn out by the crass violence of an underbred outlander. And when his sons reached maturity and first one and then the other left home for good and all, we were not surprised. And when one day six months ago he was found dead, his foot fast in the stirrup of the saddled horse which he rode, and his body pretty badly broken where the horse had apparently dragged him through a rail fence (there still showed at the time on the horse's back and flanks the marks of the blows which he had dealt it in one of his fits of rage), there was none of us who was sorry, because a short time before that he had committed what to men of our town and time and thinking was the unpardonable outrage. On the day he died it was learned that he had been digging up the graves in the family cemetery where his wife's people rested, among them the grave in which his wife had lain for thirty years. So the crazed, hate-ridden old man was buried among the graves which he had attempted to violate, and in the proper time his will was offered for probate. And we learned the substance of the will without surprise. We were not surprised to learn that even from beyond the grave he had struck one final blow at those alone whom he could now injure or outrage: his remaining flesh and blood.

At the time of their father's death the twin sons were forty. The younger one, Anselm, Junior, was said to have been the mother's favourite – perhaps because he was the one who was most like his father. Anyway, from the time of her death, while the boys were still children almost, we would hear of trouble between Old Anse and Young Anse, with Virginius, the other twin, acting as mediator and being cursed for his pains by both father and brother; he was that sort, Virginius was. And Young Anse was his sort too; in his late teens he ran away from home and was gone ten years. When he returned he and his brother were of age, and Anselm made formal demand upon his father that the land which we now learned was held by Old Anse only in trust be divided and he – Young Anse – be given his share. Old Anse refused violently. Doubtless the request had been as violently made, because the two of them, Old Anse and Young Anse, were so much alike. And we heard that, strange to say, Virginius had taken his father's side. We heard that, that is. Because the land remained intact, and we heard how, in the midst of a scene of unparalleled violence even for them – a scene of such violence that the negro servants all fled the house and scattered for the night – Young Anse departed, taking with him the team of mules which he did own; and from that day until his father's death, even after Virginius also had been forced to leave home, Anselm never spoke to his father and brother again. He did not leave the county this time, however. He just moved back into the hills ('where he can watch what the old man and Virginius are doing,' some of us said and all of us thought); and for the next fifteen years he lived alone in a dirt-floored, two-room cabin, like a hermit, doing his own cooking, coming into town behind his two mules not four times a year. Some time earlier he had been arrested and tried for making whisky. He made no defence, refusing to plead either way, was fined both on the charge and for contempt of court, and flew into a rage exactly like his father when his brother Virginius offered to pay the fine. He tried to assault Virginius in the courtroom and went to the penitentiary at his own demand and was pardoned eight months later for good behaviour and returned to his cabin – a dark, silent, aquiline-faced man whom both neighbours and strangers let severely alone.

The other twin, Virginius, stayed on, farming the land which his father had never done justice to even while he was alive. (They said of Old Anse, 'wherever he came from and whatever he was bred to be, it was not a farmer.' And so we said among ourselves, taking it to be true, 'That's the trouble between him and Young Anse: watching his father mistreat the land which his mother aimed for him and Virginius to have.') But Virginius stayed on. It could not have been much fun for him, and we said later that Virginius should have known that such an arrangement could not last. And then later than that we said, 'Maybe he did know.' Because that was Virginius. You didn't know what he was thinking at the time, any time. Old Anse and Young Anse were like water. Dark water, maybe; but men could see what they were about. But no man ever knew what Virginius was thinking or doing until afterward. We didn't even know what happened that time when Virginius, who had stuck it out alone for ten years while Young Anse was away, was driven away at last; he didn't tell it, not even to Granby Dodge, probably. But we knew Old Anse and we knew Virginius, and we could imagine it, about like this:

We watched Old Anse smouldering for about a year after Young Anse took his mules and went back into the hills. Then one day he broke out; maybe like this, 'You think that, now your brother is gone, you can just hang around and get it all, don't you?'

'I don't want it all,' Virginius said. 'I just want my share.'

'Ah,' Old Anse said. 'You'd like to have it parcelled out right now too, would you? Claim like him it should have been divided up when you and him came of age.'

'I'd rather take a little of it and farm it right than to see it all in the shape it's in now,' Virginius said, still just, still mild – no man in the county ever saw Virginius lose his temper or even get ruffled, not even when Anselm tried to fight him in the courtroom about that fine.

'You would, would you?' Old Anse said. 'And me that's kept it working at all, paying the taxes on it, while you and your brother have been putting money by every year, tax-free.'

'You know Anse never saved a nickel in his life,' Virginius said. 'Say what you want to about him, but don't accuse him of being forehanded.'

'Yes, by heaven! He was man enough to come out and claim what he thought was his and get out when he never got it. But you. You'll just hang around, waiting for me to go, with that damned meal mouth of yours. Pay me the taxes on your half back to the day your mother died, and take it.'

'No,' Virginius said. 'I won't do it.'

'No,' Old Anse said. 'No. Oh, no. Why spend your money for half of it when you can set down and get all of it some day without putting out a cent.' Then we imagined Old Anse (we thought of them as sitting down until now, talking like two civilized men) rising, with his shaggy head and his heavy eyebrows. 'Get out of my house!' he said. But Virginius didn't move, didn't get up, watching his father. Old Anse came toward him, his hand raised. 'Get. Get out of my house. By heaven, I'll . . .'

Virginius went, then. He didn't hurry, didn't run. He packed up his belongings (he would have more than Anse; quite a few little things) and went four or five miles to live with a cousin, the son of a remote kinsman of his mother. The cousin lived alone, on a good farm too, though now eaten up with mortgages, since the cousin was no farmer either, being half a stock-trader and half a lay preacher – a small, sandy, nondescript man whom you would not remember a minute after you looked at his face and then away – and probably no better at either of these than at farming. Without haste Virginius left, with none of his brother's foolish and violent finality; for which, strange to say, we thought none the less of Young Anse for showing, possessing. In fact, we always looked at Virginius a little askance too; he was a little too much master of himself. For it is human nature to trust quickest those who cannot depend on themselves. We called Virginius a deep one; we were not surprised when we learned how he had used his savings to disencumber the cousin's farm. And neither were we surprised when a year later we learned how Old Anse had refused to pay the taxes on his land and how, two days before the place would have gone delinquent, the sheriff received anonymously in the mail cash to the exact penny of the Holland assessment. 'Trust Virginius,' we said, since we believed we knew that the money needed no name to it. The sheriff had notified Old Anse.

'Put it up for sale and be damned,' Old Anse said. 'If they think that all they have to do is set there waiting, the whole brood and biling of them . . .'

The sheriff sent Young Anse word. 'It's not my land,' Young Anse sent back.

The sheriff notified Virginius. Virginius came to town and looked at the tax books himself. 'I got all I can carry myself, now,' he said. 'Of course, if he lets it go, I hope I can get it. But I don't know. A good farm like that won't last long or go cheap.' And that was all. No anger, no astonishment, no regret. But he was a deep one; we were not surprised when we learned how the sheriff had received that package of money, with the unsigned note: *Tax money for Anselm Holland farm. Send receipt to Anselm Holland, Senior.* 'Trust Virginius,' we said. We thought about Virginius quite a lot during the next year, out there in a strange house, farming strange land, watching the farm and the house where he was born and that was rightfully his going to ruin. For the old man was letting it go completely now: year by year the good broad fields were going back to jungle and gully, though still each January the sheriff received that anonymous money in the mail and sent the receipt to Old Anse, because the old man had stopped coming to town altogether now, and the very house was falling down about his head, and nobody save Virginius ever stopped there. Five or six times a year he would ride up to the front porch, and the old man would come out and bellow at him in savage and violent vituperation, Virginius taking it quietly, talking to the few remaining negroes once he had seen with his own eyes that his father was all right, then riding away again. But nobody else ever stopped there, though now and then from a distance someone would see the old man going about the mournful and shaggy fields on the old white horse which was to kill him.

Then last summer we learned that he was digging up the graves in the cedar grove where five generations of his wife's people rested. A negro reported it, and the county health officer went out there and found the white horse tied in the grove, and the old man himself came out of the grove with a shotgun. The health officer returned, and two days later a deputy went out there and found the old man lying beside the horse, his foot fast in the stirrup, and on the horse's rump the savage marks of the stick – not a switch: a stick – where it had been struck again and again and again.

So they buried him, among the graves which he had violated. Virginius and the cousin came to the funeral. They were the funeral, in fact. For Anse, Junior, didn't come. Nor did he come near the place later, though Virginius stayed long enough to lock the house and pay the negroes off. But he too went back to the cousin's, and in due time Old Anse's will was offered for probate to Judge Dukinfield. The substance of the will was no secret; we all learned of it. Regular it was, and we were surprised neither at its regularity nor at its substance nor its wording: *. . . with the exception of these two bequests, I give and bequeath . . . my property to my elder son Virginius, provided it be proved to the satisfaction of the . . . Chancellor that it was the said Virginius who has been paying the taxes on my land, the . . . Chancellor to be the sole and unchallenged judge of the proof.*

The other two bequests were:

To my younger son Anselm, I give . . . two full sets of mule harness, with the condition that this . . . harness be used by . . . Anselm to make one visit to my grave. Otherwise this . . . harness to become and remain part . . . of my property as described above.

To my cousin-in-law Granby Dodge I give . . . one dollar in cash, to be used by him for the purchase of a hymn book or hymn books, as a token of my gratitude for his having fed and lodged my son Virginius since . . . Virginius quitted my roof.

That was the will. And we watched and listened to hear or see what

Young Anse would say or do. And we heard and saw nothing. And we watched to see what Virginius would do. And he did nothing. Or we didn't know what he was doing, what he was thinking. But that was Virginius. Because it was all finished then, anyway. All he had to do was to wait until Judge Dukinfield validated the will, then Virginius could give Anse his half – if he intended to do this. We were divided there. 'He and Anse never had any trouble,' some said. 'Virginius never had any trouble with anybody,' others said. 'If you go by that token, he will have to divide that farm with the whole county.' 'But it was Virginius that tried to pay Anse's fine that time,' the first ones said. 'And it was Virginius that sided with his father when Young Anse wanted to divide the land, too,' the second ones said.

So we waited and we watched. We were watching Judge Dukinfield now; it was suddenly as if the whole thing had shifted into his hands; as though he sat godlike above the vindictive and jeering laughter of that old man who even underground would not die, and above these two irreconcilable brothers who for fifteen years had been the same as dead to each other. But we thought that in his last coup, Old Anse had overreached himself; that in choosing Judge Dukinfield, the old man's own fury had checkmated him; because in Judge Dukinfield we believed that Old Anse had chosen the one man among us with sufficient probity and honour and good sense – that sort of probity and honour which has never had time to become confused and self-doubting with too much learning in the law. The very fact that the validating of what was a simple enough document appeared to be taking him an overlong time, was to us but fresh proof that Judge Dukinfield was the one man among us who believed that justice is fifty per cent legal knowledge and fifty per cent unhaste and confidence in himself and in God.

So as the expiration of the legal period drew near, we watched Judge Dukinfield as he went daily between his home and his office in the courthouse yard. Deliberate and unhurried he moved – a widower of sixty and more, portly, white-headed, with an erect and dignified carriage which the negroes called 'rear-backted.' He had been appointed Chancellor seventeen years ago; he possessed little knowledge of the law and a great deal of hard common sense; and for thirteen years now no man had opposed him for re-election, and even those who would be most enraged by his air of bland and affable condescension voted for him on occasion with a kind of childlike confidence and trust. So we watched him without impatience, knowing that what he finally did would be right, not because he did it, but because he would not permit himself or anyone else to do anything until it was right. So each morning we would see him cross the Square at exactly ten minutes past eight o'clock and go on to the courthouse, where the negro janitor had preceded him by exactly ten minutes, with the clocklike precision with which the block signal presages the arrival of the train, to open the office for the day. The Judge would enter the office, and the negro would take his position in a wire-mended splint chair in the flagged passage which separated the office from the courthouse proper where he would sit all day long and doze, as he had done for seventeen years. Then at five in the afternoon the negro would wake and enter the office and perhaps wake the Judge too, who had lived long enough to have learned that the onus of any business is usually in the hasty minds of those theoreticians who have no business of their own; and then we would watch them cross the Square again in single file and go on up the street toward home, the two of them, eyes front and about fifteen feet apart, walking so erect that the two frock coats made by the same tailor and to the Judge's measure fell from the two pairs of shoulders in single boardlike planes, without intimation of waist or of hips.

Then one afternoon, a little after five o'clock, men began to run suddenly across the Square, toward the courthouse. Other men saw them and ran too, their feet heavy on the paving, among the wagons and the cars, their voices tense, urgent, 'What? What is it?' 'Judge Dukinfield,' the word went; and they ran on and entered the flagged passage between the courthouse and the office, where the old negro in his cast-off frock coat stood beating his hands on the air. They passed him and ran into the office. Behind the table the Judge sat, leaning a little back in his chair, quite comfortable. His eyes were open, and he had been shot neatly once through the bridge of the nose, so that he appeared to have three eyes in a row. It was a bullet, yet no man about the Square that day, or the old negro who had sat all day long in the chair in the passage, had heard any sound.

It took Gavin Stevens a long time, that day – he and the little brass box. Because the Grand Jury could not tell at first what he was getting at – if any man in that room that day, the jury, the two brothers, the cousin, the old negro, could tell. So at last the Foreman asked him point blank:

'Is it your contention, Gavin, that there is a connection between Mr Holland's will and Judge Dukinfield's murder?'

'Yes,' the county attorney said. 'And I'm going to contend more than that.'

They watched him: the jury, the two brothers. The old negro and the cousin alone were not looking at him. In the last week the negro had apparently aged fifty years. He had assumed public office concurrently with the Judge; indeed, because of that fact, since he had served the Judge's family for longer than some of us could remember. He was older than the Judge, though until that afternoon a week ago he had looked forty years younger – a wizened figure, shapeless in the voluminous frock coat, who reached the office ten minutes ahead of the Judge and opened it and swept it and dusted the table without disturbing an object upon it, all with a skilful slovenliness that was fruit of seventeen years of practice, and then repaired to the wire-bound chair in the passage to sleep. He seemed to sleep, that is. (The only other way to reach the office was by means of the narrow private stair which led down from the courtroom, used only by the presiding judge during court term, who even then had to cross the passage and pass within eight feet of the negro's chair unless he followed the passage to where it made an L beneath the single window in the office, and climbed through that window.) For no man or woman had ever passed that chair without seeing the wrinkled eyelids of its occupant open instantaneously upon the brown, irisless eyes of extreme age. Now and then we would stop and talk to him, to hear his voice roll in rich mispronunciation of the orotund and meaningless legal phraseology which he had picked up unawares, as he might have disease germs, and which he reproduced with an *ex-cathedra* profundity that caused more than one of us to listen to the Judge himself with affectionate amusement. But for all that he was old; he forgot our names at times and confused us with one another; and, confusing our faces and our generations too, he waked sometimes from his light slumber to challenge callers who were not there, who had been dead for many years. But no one had ever been known to pass him unawares.

But the others in the room watched Stevens – the jury about the table, the two brothers sitting at opposite ends of the bench, with their dark, identical, aquiline faces, their arms folded in identical attitudes. 'Are you contending that Judge Dukinfield's slayer is in this room?' the Foreman asked.

The county attorney looked at them, at the faces watching him. 'I'm going to contend more than that,' he said.

'Contend?' Anselm, the younger twin, said. He sat alone at his end of the bench, with the whole span of bench between him and the brother to whom he had not spoken in fifteen years, watching Stevens with a hard, furious, unwinking glare.

'Yes,' Stevens said. He stood at the end of the table. He began to speak,

looking at no one in particular, speaking in an easy, anecdotal tone, telling
what we already knew, referring now and then to the other twin, Virginius,
for corroboration. He told about Young Anse and his father. His tone was
fair, pleasant. He seemed to be making a case for the living, telling about
how Young Anse left home in anger, in natural anger at the manner in
which his father was treating that land which had been his mother's and
half of which was at the time rightfully his. His tone was quite just,
specious, frank; if anything, a little partial to Anselm, Junior. That was it.
Because of that seeming partiality, that seeming glozing, there began to
emerge a picture of Young Anse that was damning him to something
which we did not then know, damned him because of that very desire for
justice and affection for his dead mother, warped by the violence which he
had inherited from the very man who had wronged him. And the two
brothers sitting there, with that space of friction-smooth plank between
them, the younger watching Stevens with that leashed, violent glare, the
elder as intently, but with a face unfathomable. Stevens now told how
Young Anse left in anger, and how a year later Virginius, the quieter one,
the calmer one, who had tried more than once to keep peace between
them, was driven away in turn. And again he drew a specious, frank
picture: of the brothers separated, not by the living father, but by what
each had inherited from him; and drawn together, bred together, by that
land which was not only rightfully theirs, but in which their mother's
bones lay.

'So there they were, watching from a distance that good land going to
ruin, the house in which they were born and their mother was born falling
to pieces because of a crazed old man who attempted at the last, when he
had driven them away and couldn't do anything else to them, to deprive
them of it for good and all by letting it be sold for non-payment of taxes.
But somebody foiled him there, someone with foresight enough and self-
control enough to keep his own counsel about what wasn't anybody else's
business anyway so long as the taxes were paid. So then all they had to do
was to wait until the old man died. He was old anyway and, even if he had
been young, the waiting would not have been very hard for a self-controlled
man, even if he did not know the contents of the old man's will. Though
that waiting wouldn't have been so easy for a quick, violent man, especially
if the violent man happened to know or suspect the substance of the will
and was satisfied and, further, knew himself to have been irrevocably
wronged; to have had citizenship and good name robbed through the
agency of a man who had already despoiled him and had driven him out
of the best years of his life among men, to live like a hermit in a hill cabin.

A man like that would have neither the time nor the inclination to bother much with either waiting for something or not waiting for it.'

They stared at him, the two brothers. They might have been carved in stone, save for Anselm's eyes. Stevens talked quietly, not looking at anyone in particular. He had been county attorney for almost as long as Judge Dukinfield had been chancellor. He was a Harvard graduate: a loose-jointed man with a mop of untidy iron-grey hair, who could discuss Einstein with college professors and who spent whole afternoons among the squatting men against the walls of country stores, talking to them in their idiom. He called these his vacations.

'Then in time the father died, as any man who possessed self-control and foresight would have known. And his will was submitted for probate; and even folks way back in the hills heard what was in it, heard how at last that mistreated land would belong to its rightful owner. Or owners, since Anse Holland knows as well as we do that Virge would no more take more than his rightful half, will or no will, now than he would have when his father gave him the chance. Anse knows that because he knows that he would do the same thing – give Virge his half – if he were Virge. Because they were both born to Anselm Holland, but they were born to Cornelia Mardis too. But even if Anse didn't know, believe, that, he would know that the land which had been his mother's and in which her bones now lie would now be treated right. So maybe that night when he heard that his father was dead, maybe for the first time since Anse was a child, since before his mother died maybe and she would come upstairs at night and look into the room where he was asleep and go away; maybe for the first time since then, Anse slept. Because it was all vindicated then, you see: the outrage, the injustice, the lost good name, and the penitentiary stain – all gone now like a dream. To be forgotten now, because it was all right. By that time, you see, he had got used to being a hermit, to being alone; he could not have changed after that long. He was happier where he was, alone back there. And now to know that it was all past like a bad dream, and that the land, his mother's land, her heritage and her mausoleum, was now in the hands of the one man whom he could and would trust, even though they did not speak to each other. Don't you see?'

We watched him as we sat about the table which had not been disturbed since the day Judge Dukinfield died, upon which lay still the objects which had been, next to the pistol muzzle, his last sight on earth, and with which we were all familiar for years – the papers, the foul inkwell, the stubby pen to which the Judge clung, the small brass box which had been his superfluous paperweight. At their opposite ends of the wooden bench, the twin brothers watched Stevens, motionless, intent.

'No, we don't see,' the Foreman said. 'What are you getting at? What is the connection between all this and Judge Dukinfield's murder?'

'Here it is,' Stevens said. 'Judge Dukinfield was validating that will when he was killed. It was a queer will; but we all expected that of Mr Holland. But it was all regular, the beneficiaries are all satisfied; we all know that half of that land is Anse's the minute he wants it. So the will is all right. Its probation should have been just a formality. Yet Judge Dukinfield had had it in abeyance for over two weeks when he died. And so that man who thought that all he had to do was to wait –'

'What man?' the Foreman said.

'Wait,' Stevens said. 'All that man had to do was to wait. But it wasn't the waiting that worried him, who had already waited fifteen years. That wasn't it. It was something else, which he learned (or remembered) when it was too late, which he should not have forgotten; because he is a shrewd man, a man of self-control and foresight; self-control enough to wait fifteen years for his chance, and foresight enough to have prepared for all the incalculables except one: his own memory. And when it was too late, he remembered that there was another man who would also know what he had forgotten about. And that other man who would know it was Judge Dukinfield. And that thing which he would also know was that that horse could not have killed Mr Holland.'

When his voice ceased there was no sound in the room. The jury sat quietly about the table, looking at Stevens. Anselm turned his leashed, furious face and looked once at his brother, then he looked at Stevens again, leaning a little forward now. Virginius had not moved; there was no change in his grave, intent expression. Between him and the wall the cousin sat. His hands lay on his lap and his head was bowed a little, as though he were in church. We knew of him only that he was some kind of an itinerant preacher, and that now and then he gathered up strings of scrubby horses and mules and took them somewhere and swapped or sold them. Because he was a man of infrequent speech who in his dealings with men betrayed such an excruciating shyness and lack of confidence that we pitied him, with that kind of pitying disgust you feel for a crippled worm, dreading even to put him to the agony of saying 'yes' or 'no' to a question. But we heard how on Sundays, in the pulpits of country churches, he became a different man, changed; his voice then timbrous and moving and assured out of all proportion to his nature and his size.

'Now, imagine the waiting,' Stevens said, 'with that man knowing what was going to happen before it had happened, knowing at last that the reason why nothing was happening, why that will had apparently gone into Judge Dukinfield's office and then dropped out of the world, out of the knowledge of man, was because he had forgotten something which he should not have forgotten. And that was that Judge Dukinfield also knew that Mr Holland was not the man who beat that horse. He knew that Judge Dukinfield knew that the man who struck that horse with that stick so as to leave marks on its back was the man who killed Mr Holland first and then hooked his foot in that stirrup and struck that horse with a stick to make it bolt. But the horse didn't bolt. The man knew beforehand that it would not; he had known for years that it would not, but he had forgotten that. Because while it was still a colt it had been beaten so severely once that ever since, even at the sight of a switch in the rider's hand, it would lie down on the ground, as Mr Holland knew, and as all who were close to Mr Holland's family knew. So it just lay down on top of Mr Holland's body. But that was all right too, at first; that was just as well. That's what that man thought for the next week or so, lying in his bed at night and waiting, who had already waited fifteen years. Because even then, when it was too late and he realized that he had made a mistake, he had not even then remembered all that he should never have forgotten. Then he remembered that too, when it was too late, after the body had been found and the marks of the stick on the horse seen and remarked and it was too late to remove them. They were probably gone from the horse by then, anyway. But there was only one tool he could use to remove them from men's minds. Imagine him then, his terror, his outrage, his feeling of having been tricked by something beyond retaliation: that furious desire to turn time back for just one minute, to undo or to complete when it is too late. Because the last thing which he remembered when it was too late was that Mr Holland had bought that horse from Judge Dukinfield, the man who was sitting here at this table, passing on the validity of a will giving away two thousand acres of some of the best land in the county. And he waited, since he had but one tool that would remove those stick marks, and nothing happened. And nothing happened, and he knew why. And he waited as long as he dared, until he believed that there was more at stake than a few roods and squares of earth. So what else could he do but what he did?'

His voice had hardly ceased before Anselm was speaking. His voice was harsh, abrupt. 'You're wrong,' he said.

As one, we looked at him where he sat forward on the bench, in his muddy boots and worn overalls, glaring at Stevens; even Virginius turned and looked at him for an instant. The cousin and the old negro alone had not moved. They did not seem to be listening. 'Where am I wrong?' Stevens said.

But Anselm did not answer. He glared at Stevens. 'Will Virginius get the place in spite of . . . of . . .'

'In spite of what?' Stevens said.

'Whether he . . . that . . .'

'You mean your father? Whether he died or was murdered?'

'Yes,' Anselm said.

'Yes. You and Virge get the land whether the will stands up or not, provided, of course, that Virge divides with you if it does. But the man that killed your father wasn't certain of that and he didn't dare to ask. Because he didn't want that. He wanted Virge to have it all. That's why he wants that will to stand.'

'You're wrong,' Anselm said, in that harsh, sudden tone. 'I killed him. But it wasn't because of that damned farm. Now bring on your sheriff.'

And now it was Stevens who, gazing steadily at Anselm's furious face, said quietly: 'And I say that you are wrong, Anse.'

For some time after that we who watched and listened dwelt in anticlimax, in a dreamlike state in which we seemed to know beforehand what was going to happen, aware at the same time that it didn't matter because we should soon wake. It was as though we were outside of time, watching events from outside; still outside of and beyond time since that first instant when we looked again at Anselm as though we had never seen him before. There was a sound, a slow, sighing sound, not loud; maybe of relief – something. Perhaps we were all thinking how Anse's nightmare must be really over at last; it was as though we too had rushed suddenly back to where he lay as a child in his bed and the mother who they said was partial to him, whose heritage had been lost to him, and even the very resting place of her tragic and long quiet dust outraged, coming in to look at him for a moment before going away again. Far back down time that was, straight though it be. And straight though that corridor was, the boy who had lain unawares in that bed had got lost in it, as we all do, must, ever shall; that boy was as dead as any other of his blood in that violated cedar grove, and the man at whom we looked, we looked at across the irrevocable chasm, with pity perhaps, but not with mercy. So it took the sense of Stevens' words about as long to penetrate to us as it did to Anse; he had to repeat himself, 'Now I say that you are wrong, Anse.'

'What?' Anse said. Then he moved. He did not get up, yet somehow he seemed to lunge suddenly, violently. 'You're a liar. You –'

'You're wrong, Anse. You didn't kill your father. The man who killed your father was the man who could plan and conceive to kill that old man who sat here behind this table every day, day after day, until an old negro would come in and wake him and tell him it was time to go home – a man who never did man, woman, or child aught but good as he believed that he and God saw it. It wasn't you that killed your father. You demanded of him what you believed was yours, and when he refused to give it, you left, went away, never spoke to him again. You heard how he was mistreating the place but you held your peace, because the land was just "that damned farm". You held your peace until you heard how a crazy man was digging up the graves where your mother's flesh and blood and your own was buried. Then, and then only, you came to him, to remonstrate. But you were never a man to remonstrate, and he was never a man to listen to it. So you found him there, in the grove, with the shotgun. I don't even expect you paid much attention to the shotgun. I reckon you just took it away from him and whipped him with your bare hands and left him there beside the horse; maybe you thought that he was dead. Then somebody happened to pass there after you were gone and found him; maybe that someone had been there all the time, watching. Somebody that wanted him dead too; not in anger and outrage, but by calculation. For profit, by a will, maybe. So he came there and he found what you had left and he finished it: hooked your father's foot in that stirrup and tried to beat that horse into bolting to make it look well, forgetting in his haste what he should not have forgot. But it wasn't you. Because you went back home, and when you heard what had been found, you said nothing. Because you thought something at the time which you did not even say to yourself. And when you heard what was in the will you believed that you knew. And you were glad then. Because you had lived alone until youth and wanting things were gone out of you; you just wanted to be quiet as you wanted your mother's dust to be quiet. And besides, what could land and position among men be to a man without citizenship, with a blemished name?'

We listened quietly while Stevens' voice died in that little room in which no air ever stirred, no draught ever blew because of its position, its natural lee beneath the courthouse wall.

'It wasn't you that killed your father or Judge Dukinfield either, Anse. Because if that man who killed your father had remembered in time that

Judge Dukinfield once owned that horse, Judge Dukinfield would be alive today.'

We breathed quietly, sitting about the table behind which Judge Dukinfield had been sitting when he looked up into the pistol. The table had not been disturbed. Upon it still lay the papers, the pens, the inkwell, the small, curiously chased brass box which his daughter had fetched him from Europe twelve years ago – for what purpose neither she nor the Judge knew, since it would have been suitable only for bath salts or tobacco, neither of which the Judge used – and which he had kept for a paperweight, that, too, superfluous where no draught ever blew. But he kept it there on the table, and all of us knew it, had watched him toy with it while he talked, opening the spring lid and watching it snap viciously shut at the slightest touch.

When I look back on it now, I can see that the rest of it should not have taken as long as it did. It seems to me now that we must have known all the time; I still seem to feel that kind of disgust without mercy which after all does the office of pity, as when you watch a soft worm impaled on a pin, when you feel that retching revulsion – would even use your naked palm in place of nothing at all, thinking, 'Go on. Mash it. Smear it. Get it over with.' But that was not Stevens' plan. Because he had a plan, and we realized afterward that, since he could not convict the man, the man himself would have to. And it was unfair, the way he did it; later we told him so. ('Ah,' he said. 'But isn't justice always unfair? Isn't it always composed of injustice and luck and platitude in unequal parts?')

But anyway we could not see yet what he was getting at as he began to speak again in that tone – easy, anecdotal, his hand resting now on the brass box. But men are moved so much by preconceptions. It is not realities, circumstances, that astonish us; it is the concussion of what we should have known, if we had only not been so busy believing what we discover later we had taken for the truth for no other reason than that we happened to be believing it at the moment. He was talking about smoking again, about how a man never really enjoys tobacco until he begins to believe that it is harmful to him, and how non-smokers miss one of the greatest pleasures in life for a man of sensibility: the knowledge that he is succumbing to a vice which can injure himself alone.

'Do you smoke, Anse?' he said.

'No,' Anse said.

'You don't either, do you, Virge?'

'No,' Virginius said. 'None of us ever did – father or Anse or me. We heired it, I reckon.'

'A family trait,' Stevens said. 'Is it in your mother's family too? Is it in your branch, Granby?'

The cousin looked at Stevens, for less than a moment. Without moving he appeared to writhe slowly within his neat, shoddy suit. 'No sir. I never used it.'

'Maybe because you are a preacher,' Stevens said. The cousin didn't answer. He looked at Stevens again with his mild, still, hopelessly abashed face. 'I've always smoked,' Stevens said. 'Ever since I finally recovered from being sick at it at the age of fourteen. That's a long time, long enough to have become finicky about tobacco. But most smokers are, despite the psychologists and the standardized tobacco. Or maybe it's just cigarettes that are standardized. Or maybe they are just standardized to laymen, non-smokers. Because I have noticed how non-smokers are apt to go off half cocked about tobacco, the same as the rest of us go off half cocked about what we do not ourselves use, are not familiar with, since man is led by his pre- (or mis-) conceptions. Because you take a man who sells tobacco even though he does not use it himself, who watches customer after customer tear open the pack and light the cigarette just across the counter from him. You ask him if all tobacco smells alike, if he cannot distinguish one kind from another by the smell. Or maybe it's the shape and colour of the package it comes in; because even the psychologists have not yet told us just where seeing stops and smelling begins, or hearing stops and seeing begins. Any lawyer can tell you that.'

Again the Foreman checked him. We had listened quietly enough, but I think we all felt that to keep the murderer confused was one thing, but that we, the jury, were another. 'You should have done all this investigating before you called us together,' the Foreman said. 'Even if this be evidence, what good will it do without the body of the murderer be apprehended? Conjecture is all well enough –'

'All right,' Stevens said. 'Let me conjecture a little more, and if I don't seem to progress any, you tell me so, and I'll stop my way and do yours. And I expect that at first you are going to call this taking a right smart of liberty even with conjecture. But we found Judge Dukinfield dead, shot between the eyes, in this chair behind this table. That's not conjecture. And Uncle Job was sitting all day long in that chair in the passage, where anyone who entered this room (unless he came down the private stair from the courtroom and climbed through the window) would have to pass within three feet of him. And no man that we know of has passed Uncle Job in that chair in seventeen years. That's not conjecture.'

'Then what is your conjecture?'

But Stevens was talking about tobacco again, about smoking. 'I stopped in West's drug store last week for some tobacco, and he told me about a man who was particular about his smoking also. While he was getting my tobacco from the case, he reached out a box of cigarettes and handed it to me. It was dusty, faded, like he had had it a long time, and he told me how a drummer had left two of them with him years ago. "Ever smoke them?" he said. "No," I said. "They must be city cigarettes." Then he told me how he had sold the other package just that day. He said he was behind the counter, with the newspaper spread on it, sort of half reading the paper and half keeping the store while the clerk was gone to dinner. And he said he never heard or saw the man at all until he looked up and the man was just across the counter, so close that it made him jump. A smallish man in city clothes, West said, wanting a kind of cigarette that West had never heard of. "I haven't got that kind," West said. "I don't carry them." "Why don't you carry them?" the man said. "I have no sale for them," West said. And he told about the man in his city clothes, with a face like a shaved wax doll, and eyes with a still way of looking and a voice with a still way of talking. Then West said he saw the man's eyes and he looked at his nostrils, and then he knew what was wrong. Because the man was full of dope right then. "I don't have any calls for them," West said. "What am I trying to do now?" the man said. "Trying to sell you flypaper?" Then the man bought the other package of cigarettes and went out. And West said that he was mad and he was sweating too, like he wanted to vomit, he said. He said to me, "If I had some devilment I was scared to do myself, you know what I'd do? I'd give that fellow about ten dollars and I'd tell him where the devilment was and tell him not to never speak to me again. When he went out, I felt just exactly like that. Like I was going to be sick." '

Stevens looked about at us; he paused for a moment. We watched him: 'He came here from somewhere in a car, a big roadster, that city man did. That city man that ran out of his own kind of tobacco.' He paused again, and then he turned his head slowly and he looked at Virginius Holland. It seemed like a full minute that we watched them looking steadily at one another. 'And a nigger told me that that big car was parked in Virginius Holland's barn the night before Judge Dukinfield was killed.' And for another time we watched the two of them looking steadily at each other, with no change of expression on either face. Stevens spoke in a tone quiet, speculative, almost musing. 'Someone tried to keep him from coming out here in that car, that big car that anyone who saw it once would remember and recognize. Maybe that someone wanted to forbid him to come in it, threaten him. Only the man that Doctor West sold those cigarettes to wouldn't have stood for very much threatening.'

'Meaning me, by "someone",' Virginius said. He did not move or turn away his steady stare from Stevens' face. But Anselm moved. He turned his head and he looked at his brother, once. It was quite quiet, yet when the cousin spoke we could not hear or understand him at once; he had spoken but one time since we entered the room and Stevens locked the door. His voice was faint; again and without moving he appeared to writhe faintly beneath his clothes. He spoke with that abashed faintness, that excruciating desire for effacement with which we were all familiar.

'That fellow you're speaking of, he come to see me,' Dodge said. 'Stopped to see me. He stopped at the house about dark that night and said he was hunting to buy up little-built horses to use for this – this game –'

'Polo?' Stevens said. The cousin had not looked at anyone while he spoke; it was as though he were speaking to his slowly moving hands upon his lap.

'Yes, sir. Virginius was there. We talked about horses. Then the next morning he took his car and went on. I never had anything that suited him. I don't know where he come from nor where he went.'

'Or who else he came to see,' Stevens said. 'Or what else he came to do. You can't say that.'

Dodge didn't answer. It was not necessary, and again he had fled behind the shape of his effacement like a small and weak wild creature into a hole.

'That's my conjecture,' Stevens said.

And then we should have known. It was there to be seen, bald as a naked hand. We should have felt it – the someone in that room who felt what Stevens had called that horror, that outrage, that furious desire to turn time back for a second, to unsay, to undo. But maybe the someone had not felt it yet, had not yet felt the blow, the impact, as for a second or two a man may be unaware that he has been shot. Because now it was Virge that spoke, abruptly, harshly, 'How are you going to prove that?'

'Prove what, Virge?' Stevens said. Again they looked at each other, quiet, hard, like two boxers. Not swordsmen, but boxers; or at least with pistols. 'Who it was who hired that gorilla, that thug, down here from Memphis? I don't have to prove that. He told that. On the way back to Memphis he ran down a child at Battenburg (he was still full of dope; likely he had taken another shot of it when he finished his job here), and they caught him and locked him up and when the dope began to wear off he told where he had been, whom he had been to see, sitting in the cell in the jail there, jerking and snarling, after they had taken the pistol with the silencer on it away from him.'

'Ah,' Virginius said. 'That's nice. So all you've got to do is to prove that he was in this room that day. And how will you do that? Give that old nigger another dollar and let him remember again?'

But Stevens did not appear to be listening. He stood at the end of the table, between the two groups, and while he talked now he held the brass box in his hand, turning it, looking at it, talking in that easy, musing tone. 'You all know the peculiar attribute which this room has. How no draught ever blows in it. How when there has been smoking here on a Saturday, say, the smoke will still be here on Monday morning when Uncle Job opens the door, lying against the baseboard there like a dog asleep, kind of. You've all seen that.'

We were sitting a little forward now, like Anse, watching Stevens.

'Yes,' the Foreman said. 'We've seen that.'

'Yes,' Stevens said, still as though he were not listening, turning the closed box this way and that in his hand. 'You asked me for my conjecture. Here it is. But it will take a conjecturing man to do it – a man who could walk up to a merchant standing behind his counter, reading a newspaper with one eye and the other eye on the door for customers, before the merchant knew he was there. A city man, who insisted on city cigarettes. So this man left that store and crossed to the courthouse and entered and went on upstairs, as anyone might have done. Perhaps a dozen men saw him; perhaps twice that many did not look at him at all, since there are two places where a man does not look at faces: in the sanctuaries of civil law, and in public lavatories. So he entered the courtroom and came down the private stairs and into the passage, and saw Uncle Job asleep in his chair. So maybe he followed the passage, and climbed through the window behind Judge Dukinfield's back. Or maybe he walked right past Uncle Job, coming up from behind, you see. And to pass within eight feet of a man asleep in a chair would not be very hard for a man who could walk up to a merchant leaning on the counter of his own store. Perhaps he even lighted the cigarette from the pack that West had sold him before even Judge Dukinfield knew that he was in the room. Or perhaps the Judge was aleep in his chair, as he sometimes was. So perhaps the man stood there and finished the cigarette and watched the smoke pour slowly across the table and bank up against the wall, thinking about the easy money, the easy hicks, before he even drew the pistol. And it made less noise than the striking of the match which lighted the cigarette, since he had guarded so against noise that he forgot about silence. And then he went back as he came, and the dozen men and the two dozen saw him and did not see him, and at five that afternoon Uncle Job came in to wake the Judge and tell him it was time to go home. Isn't that right, Uncle Job?'

The old negro looked up. 'I looked after him, like I promised Mistis,' he said. 'And I worried with him, like I promised Mistis I would. And I come in here and I thought at first he was asleep, like he sometimes –'

'Wait,' Stevens said. 'You came in and you saw him in the chair, as always, and you noticed the smoke against the wall behind the table as you crossed the floor. Wasn't that what you told me?'

Sitting in his mended chair, the old negro began to cry. He looked like an old monkey, weakly crying black tears, brushing at his face with the back of a gnarled hand that shook with age, with something. 'I come in here many's the time in the morning, to clean up. It would be laying there, that smoke, and him that never smoked a lick in his life coming in and sniffing with that high nose of hisn and saying, "Well, Job, we sholy smoked out that corpus juris coon last night." '

'No,' Stevens said. 'Tell about how the smoke was there behind that table that afternoon when you came to wake him to go home, when there hadn't anybody passed you all that day except Mr Virge Holland yonder. And Mr Virge don't smoke, and the Judge didn't smoke. But that smoke was there. Tell what you told me.'

'It was there. And I thought that he was asleep like always, and I went to wake him up –'

'And this little box was sitting on the edge of the table where he had been handling it while he talked to Mr Virge, and when you reached your hand to wake him –'

'Yes, sir. It jumped off the table and I thought he was asleep –'

'The box jumped off the table. And it made a noise and you wondered why that didn't wake the Judge, and you looked down at where the box was lying on the floor in the smoke, with the lid open, and you thought that it was broken. And so you reached your hand down to see, because the Judge liked it because Miss Emma had brought it back to him from across the water, even if he didn't need it for a paperweight in his office. So you closed the lid and set it on the table again. And then you found that the Judge was more than asleep.'

He ceased. We breathed quietly, hearing ourselves breathe. Stevens seemed to watch his hand as it turned the box slowly this way and that. He had turned a little from the table in talking with the old negro, so that now he faced the bench rather than the jury, the table. 'Uncle Job calls this a gold box. Which is as good a name as any. Better than most. Because all metal is about the same; it just happens that some folks want one kind more than another. But it all has certain general attributes, likenesses. One of them is, that whatever is shut up in a metal box will stay in it unchanged for a longer time than in a wooden or paper box. You can shut up smoke, for instance, in a metal box with a tight lid like this one, and even a week later it will still be there. And not only that, a chemist or a smoker or tobacco seller like Doctor West can tell what made the smoke, what kind of tobacco, particularly if it happens to be a strange brand, a kind not sold in Jefferson, and of which he just happened to have two packs and remembered who he sold one of them to.'

We did not move. We just sat there and heard the man's urgent stumbling feet on the floor, then we saw him strike the box from Stevens' hand. But we were not particularly watching him, even then. Like him, we watched the box bounce into two pieces as the lid snapped off, and emit a fading vapour which dissolved sluggishly away. As one we leaned across the table and looked down upon the sandy and hopeless mediocrity of Granby Dodge's head as he knelt on the floor and flapped at the fading smoke with his hands.

'But I still don't . . .' Virginius said. We were outside now, in the courthouse yard, the five of us, blinking a little at one another as though we had just come out of a cave.

'You've got a will, haven't you?' Stevens said. Then Virginius stopped perfectly still, looking at Stevens.

'Oh,' he said at last.

'One of those natural mutual deed-of-trust wills that any two business partners might execute,' Stevens said. 'You and Granby each the other's beneficiary and executor, for mutual protection of mutual holdings. That's natural. Like Granby was the one who suggested it first, by telling you how he had made you his heir. So you'd better tear it up, yours, your copy. Make Anse your heir, if you have to have a will.'

'He won't need to wait for that,' Virginius said. 'Half of that land is his.'

'You just treat it right, as he knows you will,' Stevens said. 'Anse don't need any land.'

'Yes,' Virginius said. He looked away. 'But I wish . . .'

'You just treat it right. He knows you'll do that.'

'Yes,' Virginius said. He looked at Stevens again. 'Well, I reckon I . . . we both owe you . . .'

'More than you think,' Stevens said. He spoke quite soberly. 'Or to that horse. A week after your father died, Granby bought enough rat poison to kill three elephants, West told me. But after he remembered what he had forgotten about that horse, he was afraid to kill his rats before that will was settled. Because he is a man both shrewd and ignorant at the same time: a dangerous combination. Ignorant enough to believe that the law is something like dynamite: the slave of whoever puts his hand to it first, and even then a dangerous slave; and just shrewd enough to believe that people avail themselves of it, resort to it, only for personal ends. I found that out when he sent a negro to see me one day last summer, to find out if the way in which a man died could affect the probation of his will. And I knew who had sent the negro to me, and I knew that whatever information the negro took back to the man who sent him, that man had already made up his mind to disbelieve it, since I was a servant of the slave, the dynamite. So if that had been a normal horse, or Granby had remembered in time, you would be underground now. Granby might not be any better off than he is, but you would be dead.'

'Oh,' Virginius said, quietly, soberly. 'I reckon I'm obliged.'

'Yes,' Stevens said. 'You've incurred a right smart of obligation. You owe Granby something.' Virginius looked at him. 'You owe him for those taxes he has been paying every year now for fifteen years.'

'Oh,' Virginius said. 'Yes. I thought that father . . . Every November, about, Granby would borrow money from me, not much, and not ever the same amount. To buy stocks with, he said. He paid some of it back. But he still owes me . . . no. I owe him now.' He was quite grave, quite sober. 'When a man starts doing wrong, it's not what he does; it's what he leaves.'

'But it's what he does that people will have to hurt him for, the outsiders. Because the folks that'll be hurt by what he leaves won't hurt him. So it's a good thing for the rest of us that what he does takes him out of their hands. I have taken him out of your hands now, Virge, blood or no blood. Do you understand?'

'I understand,' Virginius said. 'I wouldn't anyway . . .' Then suddenly he looked at Stevens. 'Gavin,' he said.

'What?' Stevens said.

Virginius watched him. 'You talked a right smart in yonder about chemistry and such, about that smoke. I reckon I believed some of it and I reckon I didn't believe some of it. And I reckon if I told you which I believed and didn't believe, you'd laugh at me.' His face was quite sober. Stevens' face was quite grave too. Yet there was something in Stevens' eyes, his glance; something quick and eager; not ridiculing, either. 'That was a week ago. If you had opened that box to see if that smoke was still in there, it would have got out. And if there hadn't been any smoke in that box, Granby wouldn't have given himself away. And that was a week ago. How did you know there was going to be any smoke in that box?'

'I didn't,' Stevens said. He said it quickly, brightly, cheerfully, almost happily, almost beaming. 'I didn't. I waited as long as I could before I put the smoke in there. Just before you all came into the room, I filled that box full of pipe smoke and shut it up. But I didn't know. I was a lot scareder than Granby Dodge. But it was all right. That smoke stayed in that box almost an hour.'

Jacques Futrelle

THE PHANTOM MOTOR

Jacques Futrelle was a short-story writer of extraordinary cleverness. He wrote some crime and mystery novels deservedly forgotten, but the stories about Professor Augustus S.F.X. Van Dusen, known as the Thinking Machine, are as ingenious as the later locked room deceptions of John Dickson Carr. The Professor is a logician contemptuous of all emotion, and beneath his size-eight hat is a brain so formidable that he is able to defeat the world chess champion after taking a few lessons. Does the Professor sound absurd? So he is, but he is oddly impressive too.

The most famous Thinking Machine story is 'The Problem of Cell 13', in which he 'applies his brain and ingenuity' to getting out of a prison cell, and Futrelle shows in detail how he does it. We may not exactly believe the procedure, but are bound to be impressed by it. Several of the other cases in which he has the reporter Hutchinson Hatch for assistant have the same Alice-in-Wonderland cleverness. The solution to 'The Phantom Motor' has the true Futrelle touch that leaves one gasping in admiring fury. It also has the pleasure of a genuine period piece.

Futrelle, in spite of his name, was an American, born in 1875 in Georgia. He worked for the *Boston American* where several Thinking Machine stories first appeared. He was a passenger on the *Titanic* in 1912, and went down with the ship.

I

Two dazzling white eyes bulged through the night as an automobile swept suddenly around a curve in the wide road and laid a smooth, glaring pathway ahead. Even at the distance the rhythmical crackling-chug informed Special Constable Baker that it was a gasoline car, and the headlong swoop of the unblinking lights toward him made him instantly aware of the fact that the speed ordinance of Yarborough County was being a little more than broken – it was being obliterated.

Now the County of Yarborough was a wide expanse of summer estates and superbly kept roads, level as a floor and offered distracting temptations to the dangerous pastime of speeding. But against this was the fact that the county was particular about its speed laws, so particular in fact that it had stationed half a hundred men upon its highways to abate the nuisance. Incidentally it had found that keeping record of the infractions of the law was an excellent source of income.

'Forty miles an hour if an inch,' remarked Baker to himself.

He arose from a camp-stool where he was wont to make himself comfortable from six o'clock until midnight on watch, picked up his lantern, turned up the light and stepped down to the edge of the road. He always remained on watch at the same place – at one end of a long stretch which autoists had unanimously dubbed The Trap. The Trap was singularly tempting – perfectly macadamized road bed lying between two tall stone walls with only enough of a sinuous twist in it to make each end invisible from the other. Another man, Special Constable Bowman, was stationed at the other end of The Trap and there was telephonic communication between the points, enabling the men to check each other and incidentally, if one failed to stop a car or get its number, the other would. That at least was the theory.

So now, with the utmost confidence, Baker waited beside the road. The approaching lights were only a couple of hundred yards away. At the proper instant he would raise his lantern, the car would stop, its occupants would protest and then the county would add a mite to its general fund for making the roads even better and tempting autoists still more. Or sometimes the cars didn't stop. In that event it was part of the Special Constables' duties to get the number as it flew past, and reference to the monthly automobile register would give the name of the owner. An extra fine was always imposed in such cases.

Without the slightest diminution of speed the car came hurtling on toward him and swung wide so as to take the straight path of The Trap at full speed. At the psychological instant Baker stepped out into the road and waved his lantern.

'Stop!' he commanded.

The crackling-chug came on, heedless of the cry. The auto was almost upon him before he leaped out of the road – a feat at which he was particularly expert – then it flashed by and plunged into The Trap. Baker was, at the instant, so busily engaged in getting out of the way that he couldn't read the number, but he was not disconcerted because he knew there was no escape from The Trap. On the one side a solid stone wall eight feet high marked the eastern boundary of the John Phelps Stocker country estate, and on the other side a stone fence nine feet high marked the western boundary of the Thomas Q. Rogers country estate. There was no turnout, no place, no possible way for an auto to get out of The Trap except at one of the two ends guarded by the special constables. So Baker, perfectly confident of results, seized the phone.

'Car coming through sixty miles an hour,' he bawled. 'It won't stop. I missed the number. Look out.'

'All right,' answered Special Constable Bowman.

For ten, fifteen, twenty minutes Baker waited expecting a call from Bowman at the other end. It didn't come and finally he picked up the phone again. No answer. He rang several times, battered the box and did some tricks with the receiver. Still no answer. Finally he began to feel worried. He remembered that at that same post one Special Constable had been badly hurt by a reckless chauffeur who refused to stop or turn his car when the officer stepped out into the road. In his mind's eye he saw Bowman now lying helpless, perhaps badly injured. If the car held the pace at which it passed him it would be certain death to whoever might be unlucky enough to get in its path.

With these thoughts running through his head and with genuine solicitude for Bowman, Baker at last walked on along the road of The Trap toward the other end. The feeble rays of the lantern showed the unbroken line of the cold, stone walls on each side. There was no shrubbery of any sort, only a narrow strip of grass close to the wall. The more Baker considered the matter the more anxious he became and he increased his pace a little. As he turned a gentle curve he saw a lantern in the distance coming slowly toward him. It was evidently being carried by someone who was looking carefully along each side of the road.

'Hello!' called Baker, when the lantern came within distance. 'That you, Bowman?'

'Yes,' came the hallooed response.

The lanterns moved on and met. Baker's solicitude for the other constable was quickly changed to curiosity.

'What're you looking for?' he asked.

'That auto,' replied Bowman. 'It didn't come through my end and I thought perhaps there had been an accident so I walked along looking for it. Haven't seen anything.'

'Didn't come through your end?' repeated Baker in amazement. 'Why it must have. It didn't come back my way and I haven't passed it so it must have gone through.'

'Well, it didn't,' declared Bowman conclusively. 'I was on the lookout for it, too, standing beside the road. There hasn't been a car through my end in an hour.'

Special Constable Baker raised his lantern until the rays fell full upon the face of Special Constable Bowman and for an instant they stared each at the other. Suspicion glowed from the keen, avaricious eyes of Baker.

'How much did they give you to let em' by?' he asked.

'Give me?' exclaimed Bowman, in righteous indignation. 'Give me nothing. I haven't seen a car.'

A slight sneer curled the lips of Special Constable Baker.

'Of course that's all right to report at headquarters,' he said, 'but I happen to know that the auto came in here, that it didn't go back my way, that it couldn't get out except at the ends, therefore it went your way.' He was silent for a moment. 'And whatever you got, Jim, seems to me I ought to get half.'

Then the worm – i.e., Bowman – turned. A polite curl appeared about his lips and was permitted to show through the grizzled mustache.

'I guess,' he said deliberately, 'you think because you do that, everybody else does. I haven't seen any autos.'

'Don't I always give you half, Jim?' Baker demanded, almost pleadingly.

'Well I haven't seen any car and that's all there is to it. If it didn't go back your way there wasn't any car.' There was a pause; Bowman was framing up something particularly unpleasant. 'You're seeing things, that's what's the matter.'

So was sown discord between two officers of the County of Yarborough. After awhile they separated with mutual sneers and open derision and went back to their respective posts. Each was thoughtful in his own way. At five minutes of midnight when they went off duty Baker called Bowman on the phone again.

'I've been thinking this thing over, Jim, and I guess it would be just as well if we didn't report it or say anything about it when we go in,' said Baker slowly. 'It seems foolish and if we did say anything about it it would give the boys the laugh on us.'

'Just as you say,' responded Bowman.

Relations between Special Constable Baker and Special Constable Bowman were strained on the morrow. But they walked along side by side to their respective posts. Baker stopped at his end of The Trap; Bowman didn't even look around.

'You'd better keep your eyes open tonight, Jim,' Baker called as a last word.

'I had 'em open last night,' was the disgusted retort.

Seven, eight, nine o'clock passed. Two or three cars had gone through The Trap at moderate speed and one had been warned by Baker. At a few minutes past nine he was staring down the road which led into The Trap when he saw something that brought him quickly to his feet. It was a pair of dazzling white eyes, far away. He recognized them – the mysterious car of the night before.

'I'll get it this time,' he muttered grimly, between closed teeth.

Then when the onrushing car was a full two hundred yards away Baker planted himself in the middle of the road and began to swing the lantern. The auto seemed, if anything, to be traveling even faster than on the previous night. At a hundred yards Baker began to shout. Still the car didn't lessen speed, merely rushed on. Again at the psychological instant Baker jumped. The auto whisked by as the chauffeur gave it a dextrous twist to prevent running down the Special Constable.

Safely out of its way Baker turned and stared after it, trying to read the number. He could see there was a number because a white board swung from the tail axle, but he could not make out the figures. Dust and a swaying car conspired to defeat him. But he did see that there were four persons in the car dimly silhouetted against the light reflected from the road. It was useless, of course, to conjecture as to sex for even as he looked, the fast receding car swerved around the turn and was lost to sight.

Again he rushed to the telephone; Bowman responded promptly.

'That car's gone in again,' Baker called. 'Ninety miles an hour. Look out!'

'I'm looking,' responded Bowman.

'Let me know what happens,' Baker shouted.

With the receiver to his ear he stood for ten or fifteen minutes, then Bowman hallooed from the other end.

'Well?' Baker responded. 'Get 'em?'

'No car passed through and there's none in sight,' said Bowman.

'But it went in,' insisted Baker.

'Well it didn't come out here,' declared Bowman. 'Walk along the road till I meet you and look out for it.'

Then was repeated the search of the night before. When the two men met in the middle of The Trap their faces were blank – blank as the high stone walls which stared at them from each side.

'Nothing!' said Bowman.

'Nothing!' echoed Baker.

Special Constable Bowman perched his head on one side and scratched his grizzly chin.

'You're not trying to put up a job on me?' he inquired coldly. 'You did see a car?'

'I certainly did,' declared Baker, and a belligerent tone underlay his manner. 'I certainly saw it, Jim, and if it didn't come out your end, why – why –'

He paused and glanced quickly behind him. The action inspired a sudden similar caution on Bowman's part.

'Maybe – maybe –' said Bowman after a minute, 'maybe it's a – a spook auto?'

'Well it must be,' mused Baker. 'You know as well as I do that no car can get out of this trap except at the ends. That car came in here, it isn't here now and it didn't go out your end. Now where is it?'

Bowman stared at him a minute, picked up his lantern, shook his head solemnly and wandered along the road back to his post. On his way he glanced around quickly, apprehensively, three times – Baker did the same thing four times.

On the third night the phantom car appeared and disappeared precisely as it had done previously. Again Baker and Bowman met half way between posts and talked it over.

'I'll tell you what, Baker,' said Bowman in conclusion, 'maybe you're just imagining that you see a car. Maybe if I was at your end I couldn't see it.'

Special Constable Baker was distinctly hurt at the insinuation.

'All right, Jim,' he said at last, 'if you think that way about it we'll swap posts tomorrow night. We won't have to say anything about it when we report.'

'Now that's the talk,' exclaimed Bowman with an air approaching enthusiasm. 'I'll bet I don't see it.'

On the following night Special Constable Bowman made himself comfortable on Special Constable Baker's camp-stool. And *he* saw the phantom auto. It came upon him with a rush and a crackling-chug of engine and then sped on leaving him nerveless. He called Baker over the wire and Baker watched half an hour for the phantom. It didn't appear.

Ultimately all things reach the newspapers. So with the story of the phantom auto. Hutchinson Hatch, reporter, smiled incredulously when his City Editor laid aside an inevitable cigar and tersely stated the known facts. The known facts in this instance were meager almost to the disappearing point. They consisted merely of a corroborated statement that an automobile, solid and tangible enough to all appearances, rushed into The Trap each night and totally disappeared.

But there was enough of the bizarre about it to pique the curiosity, to make one wonder, so Hatch journeyed down to Yarborough County, an hour's ride from the city, met and talked to Baker and Bowman and then, in broad daylight strolled along The Trap twice. It was a leisurely, thorough investigation with the end in view of finding out how an automobile once inside might get out again without going out either end.

On the first trip through Hatch paid particular attention to the Thomas Q. Rogers side of the road. The wall, nine feet high, was an unbroken line of stone with not the slightest indication of a secret wagon-way through it anywhere. Secret wagon-way! Hatch smiled at the phrase. But when he reached the other end – Bowman's end – of The Trap he was perfectly convinced of one thing – that no automobile had left the hard, macadam-ized road to go over, under or through the Thomas Q. Rogers wall. Returning, still leisurely, he paid strict attention to the John Phelps Stocker side, and when he reached the other end – Baker's end – he was convinced of another thing – that no automobile had left the road to go over, under or through the John Phelps Stocker wall. The only opening of any sort was a narrow footpath, not more than 16 inches wide.

Hatch saw no shrubbery along the road, nothing but a strip of scrupulously cared for grass, therefore the phantom auto could not be hidden any time, night or day. Hatch failed, too, to find any holes in the road so the automobile didn't go down through the earth. At this point he involuntarily glanced up at the blue sky above. Perhaps, he thought whimsically, the automobile was a strange sort of bird, or – or – and he stopped suddenly.

'By George!' he exclaimed. 'I wonder if –'

And the remainder of the afternoon he spent systematically making inquiries. He went from house to house, the Stocker house, the Rogers house, both of which were at the time unoccupied, then to cottage, cabin and hut in turn. But he didn't seem overladen with information when he joined Special Constable Baker at his end of The Trap that evening about seven o'clock.

Together they rehearsed the strange points of the mystery as the shadows grew about them until finally the darkness was so dense that Baker's lantern was the only bright spot in sight. As the chill of the evening closed in a certain awed tone crept into their voices. Occasionally an auto bowled along and each time as it hove in sight Hatch glanced at Baker questioningly. And each time Baker shook his head. And each time, too, he called Bowman, in this manner accounting for every car that went into The Trap.

'It'll come all right,' said Baker after a long silence, 'and I'll know it the minute it rounds the curve coming toward us. I'd know its two lights in a thousand.'

They sat still and smoked. After awhile two dazzling white lights burst into view far down the road and Baker, in excitement, dropped his pipe.

'That's her,' he declared. 'Look at her coming!'

And Hatch did look at her coming. The speed of the mysterious car was such as to make one look. Like the eyes of a giant the two lights came on toward them, and Baker perfunctorily went through the motions of attempting to stop it. The car fairly whizzed past them and the rush of air which tugged at their coats was convincing enough proof of its solidity. Hatch strained his eyes to read the number as the auto flashed past. But it was hopeless. The tail of the car was lost in an eddying whirl of dust.

'She certainly does travel,' commented Baker, softly.

'She does,' Hatch assented.

Then, for the benefit of the newspaper man, Baker called Bowman on the wire.

'Car's coming again,' he shouted. 'Look out and let me know!'

Bowman, at his end, waited twenty minutes, then made the usual report – the car had not passed. Hutchinson Hatch was a calm, cold, dispassionate young man but now a queer, creepy sensation stole along his spinal column. He lighted a cigarette and pulled himself together with a jerk.

'There's one way to find out where it goes,' he declared at last, emphatically, 'and that's to place a man in the middle just beyond the bend of The Trap and let him wait and see. If the car goes up, down, or evaporates he'll see and can tell us.'

Baker looked at him curiously.

'I'd hate to be the man in the middle,' he declared. There was something of uneasiness in his manner.

'I rather think I would, too,' responded Hatch.

On the following evening, consequent upon the appearance of the story of the phantom auto in Hatch's paper, there were twelve other reporters on hand. Most of them were openly, flagrantly sceptical; they even insinuated that no one had seen an auto. Hatch smiled wisely.

'Wait!' he advised with deep conviction.

So when the darkness fell that evening the newspaper men of a great city had entered into a conspiracy to capture the phantom auto. Thirteen of them, making a total of fifteen men with Baker and Bowman, were on hand and they agreed to a suggestion for all to take positions along the road of The Trap from Baker's post to Bowman's, watch for the auto, see what happened to it and compare notes afterwards. So they scattered themselves along a few hundred feet apart and waited. That night the phantom auto didn't appear at all and twelve reporters jeered at Hutchinson Hatch and told him to light his pipe with the story. And next night when Hatch and Baker and Bowman alone were watching the phantom auto reappeared.

II

Like a child with a troublesome problem, Hatch took the entire matter and laid it before Professor Augustus S. F. X. Van Dusen, the master brain. The Thinking Machine, with squint eyes turned steadily upward and long, slender fingers pressed tip to tip, listened to the end.

'Now I know of course that automobiles don't fly,' Hatch burst out savagely in conclusion, 'and if this one doesn't fly, there is no earthly way for it to get out of The Trap, as they call it. I went over the thing carefully – I even went so far as to examine the ground and the tops of the walls to see if a runway had been let down for the auto to go over.'

The Thinking Machine squinted at him inquiringly.

'Are you sure you saw an automobile?' he demanded irritably.

'Certainly I saw it,' blurted the reporter. 'I not only saw it – I smelled it. Just to convince myself that it was real I tossed my cane in front of the thing and it smashed it to toothpicks.'

'Perhaps, then, if everything is as you say, the auto actually *does* fly,' remarked the scientist.

The reporter stared into the calm, inscrutable face of The Thinking Machine, fearing first that he had not heard aright. Then he concluded that he had.

'You mean,' he inquired eagerly, 'that the phantom may be an auto-aeroplane affair, and that it actually does fly?'

'It's not at all impossible,' commented the scientist.

'I had an idea something like that myself,' Hatch explained, 'and questioned every soul within a mile or so but I didn't get anything.'

'The perfect stretch of road there might be the very place for some daring experimenter to get up sufficient speed to soar a short distance in a light machine,' continued the scientist.

'Light machine?' Hatch repeated. 'Did I tell you that this car had four people in it?'

'Four people!' exclaimed the scientist. 'Dear me! Dear me! That makes it very different. Of course four people would be too great a lift for an –'

For ten minutes he sat silent, and tiny, cobwebby lines appeared in his dome-like brow. Then he arose and passed into the adjoining room. After a moment Hatch heard the telephone bell jingle. Five minutes later The Thinking Machine appeared, and scowled upon him unpleasantly.

'I suppose what you really want to learn is if the car is a – a material one, and to whom it belongs?' he queried.

'That's it,' agreed the reporter, 'and of course, why it does what it does, and how it gets out of The Trap.'

'Do you happen to know a fast, long-distance bicycle rider?' demanded the scientist abruptly.

'A dozen of them,' replied the reporter promptly. 'I think I see the idea, but –'

'You haven't the faintest inkling of the idea,' declared The Thinking Machine positively. 'If you can arrange with a fast rider who can go a distance – it might be thirty, forty, fifty miles – we may end this little affair without difficulty.'

Under these circumstances Professor Augustus S. F. X. Van Dusen, Ph.D., LL.D., F.R.S., M.D., etc., etc., scientist and logician, met the famous Jimmie Thalhauer, the world's champion long distance bicyclist. He held every record from five miles up to and including six hours, had twice won the six-day race and was, altogether, a master in his field. He came in chewing a toothpick. There were introductions.

'You ride the bicycle?' inquired the crusty little scientist.

'Well, *some*,' confessed the champion modestly with a wink at Hatch.

'Can you keep up with an automobile for a distance of, say, thirty or forty miles?'

'I can keep up with anything that ain't got wings,' was the response.

'Well, to tell you the truth,' volunteered The Thinking Machine, 'there is a growing belief that this particular automobile has wings. However, if you can keep up with it –'

'Ah, quit your kiddin',' said the champion, easily. 'I can ride rings around anything on wheels. I'll start behind it and beat it where it's going.'

The Thinking Machine examined the champion, Jimmie Thalhauer, as a curiosity. In the seclusion of his laboratory he had never had an opportunity of meeting just such another worldly young person.

'How fast *can* you ride, Mr Thalhauer?' he asked at last.

'I'm ashamed to tell you,' confided the champion in a hushed voice. 'I can ride so fast that I scare myself.' He paused a moment. 'But it seems to me,' he said, 'if there's thirty or forty miles to do I ought to do it on a motorcycle.'

'Now that's just the point,' explained The Thinking Machine. 'A motorcycle makes noise and if it could have been used we would have hired a fast automobile. This proposition briefly is: I want you to ride without lights behind an automobile which may also run without lights and find out where it goes. No occupant of the car must suspect that it is followed.'

'Without lights?' repeated the champion. 'Gee! Rubber shoe, eh?'

The Thinking Machine looked his bewilderment.

'Yes, that's it,' Hatch answered for him.

'I guess it's good for a four column head? Hunh?' inquired the champion. 'Special pictures posed by the champion? Hunh?'

'Yes,' Hatch replied.

' "Tracked on a Bicycle" sounds good to me. Hunh?'

Hatch nodded.

So arrangements were concluded and then and there The Thinking Machine gave definite and conclusive instructions to the champion. While these apparently bore broadly on the problem in hand they conveyed absolutely no inkling of his plan to the reporter. At the end the champion arose to go.

'You're a most extraordinary young man, Mr Thalhauer,' commented The Thinking Machine, not without admiration for the sturdy, powerful figure.

And as Hatch accompanied the champion out the door and down the steps Jimmie smiled with easy grace.

'Nutty old guy, ain't he? Hunh?'

Night! Utter blackness, relieved only by a white, ribbon-like road which winds away mistily under a starless sky. Shadowy hedges line either side and occasionally a tree thrusts itself upward out of the sombreness. The murmur of human voices in the shadows, then the crackling-chug of an engine and an automobile moves slowly, without lights, into the road. There is the sudden clatter of an engine at high speed and the car rushes away.

From the hedge comes the faint rustle of leaves as of wind stirring, then a figure moves impalpably. A moment and it becomes a separate entity; a quick movement and the creak of a leather bicycle saddle. Silently the single figure, bent low over the handlebars, moves after the car with ever increasing momentum.

Then a long, desperate race. For mile after mile, mile after mile the auto goes on. The silent cyclist has crept up almost to the rear axle and hangs there doggedly as a racer to his pace. On and on they rush together through the darkness, the chauffeur moving with a perfect knowledge of his road, the single rider behind clinging on grimly with set teeth. The powerful, piston-like legs move up and down to the beat of the engine.

At last, with dust-dry throat and stinging, aching eyes the cyclist feels the pace slacken and instantly he drops back out of sight. It is only by sound that he follows now. The car stops; the cyclist is lost in the shadows.

For two or three hours the auto stands deserted and silent. At last the voices are heard again, the car stirs, moves away and the cyclist drops in behind. Another race which leads off in another direction. Finally, from a knoll, the lights of a city are seen. Ten minutes elapse, the auto stops, the headlights flare up and more leisurely it proceeds on its way.

On the following evening The Thinking Machine and Hutchinson Hatch called upon Fielding Stanwood, President of the Fordyce National Bank. Mr Stanwood looked at them with interrogative eyes.

'We called to inform you, Mr Stanwood,' explained The Thinking Machine, 'that a box of securities, probably United States bonds, is missing from your bank.'

'What?' exclaimed Mr Stanwood, and his face paled. 'Robbery?'

'I only know the bonds were taken out of the vault tonight by Joseph Marsh, your assistant cashier,' said the scientist, 'and that he, together with three other men, left the bank with the box and are now at – a place I can name.'

Mr Stanwood was staring at him in amazement.

'You know where they are?' he demanded.

'I said I did,' replied the scientist, shortly.

'Then we must inform the police at once, and –'

'I don't know that there has been an actual crime,' interrupted the scientist. 'I do know that every night for a week these bonds have been taken out through the connivance of your watchman and in each instance have been returned, intact, before morning. They will be returned tonight. Therefore I would advise, if you act, not to do so until the four men return with the bonds.'

It was a singular party which met in the private office of President Stanwood at the bank just after midnight. Marsh and three companions, formally under arrest, were present as were President Stanwood, The Thinking Machine and Hatch, besides detectives. Marsh had the bonds under his arms when he was taken. He talked freely when questioned.

'I will admit,' he said without hesitating, 'that I have acted beyond my rights in removing the bonds from the vault here, but there is no ground for prosecution. I am a responsible officer of this bank and have violated no trust. Nothing is missing, nothing is stolen. Every bond that went out of the bank is here.'

'But why – why did you take the bonds?' demanded Mr Stanwood.

Marsh shrugged his shoulders.

'It's what has been called a get-rich-quick scheme,' said The Thinking Machine. 'Mr Hatch and I made some investigations today. Mr Marsh and these other three are interested in a business venture which is ethically dishonest but which is within the law. They have sought backing for the scheme amounting to about a million dollars. Those four or five men of means with whom they have discussed the matter have called each night for a week at Marsh's country place. It was necessary to make them believe that there was already a million or so in the scheme, so these bonds were borrowed and represented to be owned by themselves. They were taken to and fro between the bank and his home in a kind of an automobile. This is really what happened, based on knowledge which Mr Hatch has gathered and what I myself developed by the use of a little logic.'

And his statement of the affair proved to be correct. Marsh and the others admitted the statement to be true. It was while The Thinking Machine was homeward bound that he explained the phantom auto affair to Hatch.

'The phantom auto, as you call it,' he said, 'is the vehicle in which the bonds were moved about. The phantom idea came merely by chance. On the night the vehicle was first noticed it was rushing along – we'll say to reach Marsh's house in time for an appointment. A road map will show you that the most direct line from the bank to Marsh's was through The Trap. If an automobile should go half way through there, then out across the Stocker estate to the other road, distance would be lessened by a good five miles. This saving at first was of course valuable, so the car in which they rushed into The Trap was merely taken across the Stocker estate to the road in front.'

'But how?' demanded Hatch. 'There's no road there.'

'I learned by phone from Mr Stocker that there is a narrow walk from a very narrow foot-gate in Stocker's wall on The Trap leading through the grounds to the other road. The phantom auto wasn't really an auto at all – it was merely two motor cycles arranged with seats and a steering apparatus. The French Army has been experimenting with them. The motor cycles are, of course, separate machines and as such it was easy to trundle them through a narrow gate and across to the other road. The seats are light; they can be carried under the arm.'

'Oh!' exclaimed Hatch suddenly, then after a minute: 'But what did Jimmie Thalhauer do for you?'

'He waited in the road at the other end of the foot-path from The Trap,' the scientist explained. 'When the auto was brought through and put together he followed it to Marsh's home and from there to the bank. The rest of it you and I worked out today. It's merely logic, Mr Hatch, logic.'

There was a pause.

'That Mr Thalhauer is really a marvelous young man, Mr Hatch, don't you think?'

Michael Gilbert

COUNTERPLOT

Michael Gilbert (1912–   ) has for many years written novels, short stories and plays in whatever spare time has remained from a busy life as a solicitor. He has said many times that all of his books are written on the rail journey between London and his home in Kent, which seems to suggest that he travels either on a very slow or a preternaturally steady train. His first full-length crime story, *Close Quarters*, appeared in 1947, but his first book was written when he was eighteen years old. Commenting on a remark of mine that he puts little of himself into his work and is concerned only to entertain, he said: 'I find the whole thing puzzling. What is a writer to do if he is not allowed to entertain?' But of course the implication was that a crime writer could entertain and do something more as well, by way of expressing an attitude towards the world he lives in. Gilbert always works with professional skill, but except in one or two books, including *The Night of the Twelfth* and *Death of a Favourite Girl*, rarely at full stretch.

He has written several hundred short stories, many of which have been collected between covers. Some, involving Mr Calder and Mr Behrens, are set in the world of espionage, and perhaps reveal more of their writer's essential conservatism than his other books. Others make use of his immense experience as a solicitor, and in the best of these the central figure is Patrick Petrella, who joined the Metropolitan Police at twenty-one, and has risen to become a Detective Chief Inspector in South London. 'Counterplot' is a Petrella story, light-hearted, with an ingenious turn or two in its few pages, a tale that is still teasing us slightly at the end. Entertaining, in fact.

Mrs Prior had had her eye on the grey-haired woman ever since she came into the shop. Not that there was anything obviously suspicious about her. Fiftyish, Mrs Prior guessed. Quite expensively dressed, carrying an oversized shopping bag. It was something about her manner. The unobtrusive way she sidled into the shop; the quick look which she cast around, a look which was not directed at the merchandise on the counters, but at the people.

Melluish & Sons was the most expensive of the three shops that Mrs Prior had to watch, and the most difficult to guard, dealing as it did in smallish luxury goods for women. They had lost a lot of stuff in the past twelve months and were beginning to talk about closed-circuit television.

Was that woman hanging about unnecessarily near the handbag counter? The attendant had turned her back to deal with another customer. A gloved hand flashed out. Mrs Prior was too far off to see exactly what happened, but the grey-haired woman was making for the door. It was the moment of decision.

As the woman was stepping out on to the pavement Mrs Prior intercepted her. 'Excuse me, madam,' she said. 'I wonder if you'd mind showing me what you have in that bag?'

The standard reactions. Shock, anxiety, an assumed bewilderment. 'Oh! Who are you? Why should I?'

'I am a member of the shop security staff,' said Mrs Prior. 'If I have made a mistake, I am quite prepared to apologize.'

But no apology was going to be needed. She was sure of that.

Which brought Detective Chief Inspector Petrella into the story. He listened to what Mrs Prior had to say, and to the comments of Mr Jacklin, managing director of Melluishes, and to the few incoherent remarks of the grey-haired woman.

'We can't force you to identify yourself,' said Petrella. 'But you realize that if you refuse to give us your name and address we shall have to detain you until someone does identify you.'

'Detain me? In prison?'

'You will be placed in charge of a woman police officer.'

'Oh!'

Petrella said, in his kindest voice, 'This isn't doing you any good, madam. Sooner or later we shall have to know who you are. Someone will miss you, and come along to make inquiries.' He tried a long shot. 'When your husband gets home from work —'

The word husband seemed to be the key. The woman broke down into a fit of gulping sobs. When she could speak, she said, 'I'm Mrs Kent-Smith. I live at Mapledurham Mansions.'

'Mrs Kent-Smith, eh?' said Sergeant Blencowe when she had been charged and sent home in a police car, the driver having instructions to bring her straight back if there was any doubt about her being who she said she was or living where she said she did. 'Her old man's not going to like this. He's in business. House property and things like that.'

Mr Kent-Smith arrived just when Petrella was thinking of going out to lunch. He was a man in his middle fifties, a little paunchy, but alert enough and with a useful pair of shoulders on him. Petrella had been making inquiries, and knew that he had to deal with a formidable man. Rumour said that he had been a sergeant-major in the RASC. In the years since the war he had prospered. Starting with a bombed site at the Elephant and Castle and some luck with a war damage claim he had built up a chain of shops and offices and flats, held in a honeycomb of interlocking companies which he controlled.

'I'd like to know what all this is about,' he said. 'I couldn't get much out of the wife.'

The sergeant-major was buried, deep down under layers of the self-made tycoon. But he was still there, thought Petrella.

He said, picking his words carefully, 'A woman, who identified herself as your wife, was detected leaving Melluish & Sons this morning with one of their crocodile-skin handbags —' Petrella unlocked the drawer of his desk and took it out '— which there was no record of her having paid for. Her explanation was that she had put it into her shopping bag, meaning to pay for it, and had forgotten about it.'

Mr Kent-Smith had picked up the handbag. He said, 'Silly thing to do. She could easily have bought it if she'd wanted it.' The price tag was still on it. 'Eighteen pounds. I understand from Jacklin that if I pay for it, he's prepared to call it a day.'

'If he'd said that before she was charged,' said Petrella, 'it might have saved us all a lot of trouble.'

'Can't you withdraw the charge?'

'We could decide not to proceed with it. But we'd only do that if there was insufficient evidence. That's not the case here. Far from it.'

'Who decides on these matters?'

'In this case, I do.'

'I see.'

Mr Kent-Smith was weighing him up in the thoughtful way a boxer might weigh up his adversary in the ring. He said, 'I'd better explain why this means so much to me. In the ordinary way I think I'd let it go. It's a first offence, so I assume it'd be a fine and bound over. Which would teach my wife a lesson. But I can't chance it. Not at this moment. I don't know if you follow the financial Press, Inspector?'

'I don't have much time for that sort of thing.'

'Well, I'm on the point of my first public flotation. You'll see the advertisement in the papers next week. Or you would have done.'

'You mean this will stop it.'

'It'll kill it. Stone dead. The whole thing depends on my good name. It's me they're buying. If my wife's up on a charge of shop-lifting, I might just as well call the whole thing off.'

Petrella started to say something, but Mr Kent-Smith raised his hand to stop him. He said, 'Let me finish. Shares in my holding company stand right now at a nominal one pound each. They're mostly held by me and my friends. When we get a quotation they'll go to three pounds. I can let you have five thousand shares at par. There's nothing illegal about it. That's the price at the moment. You could borrow the money from your bank.'

'I've been offered bribes before,' said Petrella to his wife that evening. 'All policemen are. But I've never been offered ten thousand pounds.'

'What did you say?'

'I said "no".'

'Quite right,' said his wife firmly.

'I'm trying hard to think so. Actually, I'm much sorrier for his wife than I am for him. I don't believe this is going to stop him. He might have to put off this flotation, or whatever it is, for six months. It'll be a nuisance, and it'll cost him more than the ten thousand he offered me. But he'll take it out on her. She's an odd woman. She came to see me before I left the station this evening. Do you know why?'

'To beg herself off the charge.'

'On the contrary. She came to apologize.'

'Apologize? For what?'

'For giving us all such a lot of trouble. She said she knew how overworked the police were.'

'It's not true!'

'Then we had a long talk about it and about her husband. How he's so busy with his work he never gets in until ten o'clock at night and goes off first thing in the morning and she never really sees him.'

'This is the first evening *you've* been in before nine this week,' said his wife pointedly.

'And how he seems to be growing away from her.'

'What were you supposed to do about it? You're a policeman, not a psychiatrist.'

'And how sorry she is she never had any children. She blames herself for it.'

His wife thought about the scrap asleep in his cot upstairs who was the centre of their existence. She had nothing to say to that.

It was on the following morning that a very worried Mr Jacklin arrived at Patton Street Police Station. The managing director of Melluish & Sons had another man with him. He said, 'Yesterday evening I thought I'd make a check of our stock of handbags. I was afraid we might have lost more than one.'

'And had you?'

'No, we hadn't.'

'That's all right then, isn't it?'

'I mean,' said Mr Jacklin slowly, 'that we hadn't even lost one.'

Petrella stared at him.

'Stock purchased, stock sold, stock remaining. The items balance exactly. That's when I began to wonder. Do you mind if I look at that handbag again?'

Petrella unlocked the drawer of his desk and got it out. Mr Jacklin took out a magnifying glass, opened the handbag, turned back the silk lining, and peered into it. He said, 'Just what I thought. This isn't one of ours. We mark them with a very small symbol. It's really just a few pinpricks.' He said to the other man, 'It's what we thought, Sam. This is one of yours, isn't it?'

The other man took over the glass and made a brief examination. 'That's right,' he said. 'That's our shop mark. Carson & Begg. Mr Jacklin thought it might be us. We're the only store in the district which handles this sort of line.'

'And have you lost one?'

'Not that I know of,' said the man. 'But I can tell you who had that one. I sold it myself three days ago. To Mrs Kent-Smith. She buys a lot of stuff from us from time to time.'

"And she paid for it.'

'Naturally.'

'Then I suppose she'd better have it back,' said Petrella weakly.

'And it won't be necessary to go on with the charge against her now,' said Mr Jacklin. 'I'm glad about that. Mr Kent-Smith's an important man in these parts, you understand.'

Petrella said he understood perfectly.

'So,' said Mr Kent-Smith. 'The whole thing was a bloody box-up. My wife gets charged with stealing something which is her own property. She's dragged round to the police station like a common criminal. *And* taken home in a police car, so that all the neighbours can get an eyeful of it.'

'If she'd given her name and some evidence of identity, none of that need have happened,' said Petrella.

'Why should she? She hadn't done anything.'

'If she hadn't done anything,' said Petrella, 'why did she tell us that story about putting the handbag into her shopping bag and forgetting about it?'

'There's no mystery about that. She said it because she was scared. And who's going to blame her? Being dragged along to the police station and bullied by a crowd of louts who call themselves policemen and don't even take the trouble to check up whether something they say has been stolen has really been stolen or not before bringing charges. And if you think you've heard the end of this, Mr Chief Inspector bloody Petrella, you can bloody well think again. I'm going straight round to my solicitor.'

'I seem to be in trouble with the law again,' said Petrella sadly. 'Last month it was libel, now it's false imprisonment.'

'Never rains but it pours,' said Chief Superintendent Watterson. 'I've been accused of a lot of things myself in my time, arson, fraud, perjury. I don't know that it ever ran to libel. You'd better warn our legal chaps.'

'What I really dislike about these law suits,' said Petrella, 'is the way they go on for months and months.'

Here, however, he was wrong. It was on the following morning that Mrs Kent-Smith called in to see him. She seemed to be in excellent spirits. She said, 'I've good news for you, Inspector. My husband is dropping his complaint against you.'

'That's certainly good news,' said Petrella. 'I wonder what made him change his mind.'

'I did.'

Petrella knew that this was the point at which he ought to stop asking questions, but the temptation was too great. He said, 'I wonder if you'll mind me asking you. How did you do it?'

Mrs Kent-Smith giggled. She said, 'I told him that if he didn't, I'd confess to three other cases of shop-lifting. I gave him all the details. And showed him the things.'

She sounded as proud as a child displaying her birthday presents.

'There was a little scarf from Simpsons. A pretty thing in pink and green. A powder compact from Greenways. Not expensive, and not in very good taste. And a cookery book from Simmonds.'

'And *had* she stolen those things?' said his wife.

'I'm afraid,' said Petrella, 'that at that point I lost my nerve. *I simply daredn't ask her.* Luckily she changed the subject. She wanted my advice about some new curtains she had bought. She had the patterns with her. I'm not very clever about colours, so I just said I thought they were a little bright. She said she thought so too. She was going to change them.'

'I see,' said his wife.

'I don't know what you mean by that,' said Petrella. 'But if you mean that you can make some sense out of it, you're a lot cleverer than I am. Why on earth should she go through all the rigmarole of buying a handbag in one shop and pretending to steal it in another?'

'Simple. She wanted her husband to pay some attention to her.'

Petrella thought about it and said, 'It's plausible.'

'It's obvious. Don't you remember that woman who set her house on fire because her husband didn't take enough notice of her?'

'If that's right,' said Petrella, 'why didn't she let him get on with his complaint against me?'

'That's easy too,' said his wife. 'You're the son she never had.'

'Good God!' said Chief Inspector Petrella.

Graham Greene

THE CASE FOR
THE DEFENCE

Graham Greene (1904–) has been concerned with crime, the psychology of the criminal, and the relationship between hunter and hunted from very early in his career. *Stamboul Train*, *England Made Me*, *A Gun For Sale*, *Brighton Rock*, *The Confidential Agent* – these books of the thirties are not exactly fitted by any label, but they are all tales of violence, pursuit and terror. And among later works *The Third Man*, *Our Man in Havana*, *The Quiet American*, *The Honorary Consul*, *The Human Factor*, all touch on themes which, in less sensitive hands, would have been straightforward tales of adventure, kidnapping, spying. Of course *Brighton Rock* is not 'about' murder, and *The Honorary Consul* is not 'about' kidnapping, yet without those central poles of narrative the books would be something other than they are. Greene's relationship with the thriller has always been a little ambiguous. He is interested in it, likes it, enjoys especially the sinister or exciting effects that can be obtained through it, yet he seems always to be using it a little less than wholeheartedly, as if afraid that too close an involvement might be infectious. This is true even of an 'entertainment' that is almost entirely a thriller, *The Ministry of Fear*.

These remarks have little application to the short stories, although a few, like 'The Basement Room', explore with beautiful delicacy childish fears of the uncertain and the unexplained. 'The Case for the Defence' is a short, clever story about, among other things, the fallibility of witnesses, and it has a characteristically disturbing question at the end.

It was the strangest murder trial I ever attended. They named it the Peckham murder in the headlines, though Northwood Street, where the old woman was found battered to death, was not strictly speaking in Peckham. This was not one of those cases of circumstantial evidence, in which you feel the jurymen's anxiety – because mistakes *have* been made – like domes of silence muting the court. No, this murderer was all but found with the body; no one present when the Crown counsel outlined his case believed that the man in the dock stood any chance at all.

He was a heavy stout man with bulging bloodshot eyes. All his muscles seemed to be in his thighs. Yes, an ugly customer, one you wouldn't forget in a hurry – and that was an important point because the Crown proposed to call four witnesses who hadn't forgotten him, who had seen him hurrying away from the little red villa in Northwood Street. The clock had just struck two in the morning.

Mrs Salmon in 15 Northwood Street had been unable to sleep; she heard a door click shut and thought it was her own gate. So she went to the window and saw Adams (that was his name) on the steps of Mrs Parker's house. He had just come out and he was wearing gloves. He had a hammer in his hand and she saw him drop it into the laurel bushes by the front gate. But before he moved away, he had looked up – at her window. The fatal instinct that tells a man when he is watched exposed him in the light of a street-lamp to her gaze – his eyes suffused with horrifying and brutal fear, like an animal's when you raise a whip. I talked afterwards to Mrs Salmon, who naturally after the astonishing verdict went in fear herself. As I imagine did all the witnesses – Henry MacDougall, who had been driving home from Benfleet late and nearly ran Adams down at the corner of Northwood Street. Adams was walking in the middle of the road looking dazed. And old Mr Wheeler, who lived next door to Mrs Parker, at No. 12, and was wakened by a noise – like a chair falling – through the thin-as-paper villa wall, and got up and looked out of the window, just as Mrs Salmon had done, saw Adams's back and, as he turned, those bulging eyes. In Laurel

Avenue he had been seen by yet another witness – his luck was badly out; he might as well have committed the crime in broad daylight.

'I understand,' counsel said, 'that the defence proposes to plead mistaken identity. Adams's wife will tell you that he was with her at two in the morning on February 14, but after you have heard the witnesses for the Crown and examined carefully the features of the prisoner, I do not think you will be prepared to admit the possibility of a mistake.'

It was all over, you would have said, but the hanging.

After the formal evidence had been given by the policeman who had found the body and the surgeon who examined it, Mrs Salmon was called. She was the ideal witness, with her slight Scotch accent and her expression of honesty, care and kindness.

The counsel for the Crown brought the story gently out. She spoke very firmly. There was no malice in her, and no sense of importance at standing there in the Central Criminal Court with a judge in scarlet hanging on her words and the reporters writing them down. Yes, she said, and then she had gone downstairs and rung up the police station.

'And do you see the man here in court?'

She looked straight across at the big man in the dock, who stared hard at her with his pekingese eyes without emotion.

'Yes,' she said, 'there he is.'

'You are quite certain?'

She said simply, 'I couldn't be mistaken, sir.'

It was all as easy as that.

'Thank you, Mrs Salmon.'

Counsel for the defence rose to cross-examine. If you had reported as many murder trials as I have, you would have known beforehand what line he would take. And I was right, up to a point.

'Now, Mrs Salmon, you must remember that a man's life may depend on your evidence.'

'I do remember it, sir.'

'Is your eyesight good?'

'I have never had to wear spectacles, sir.'

'You are a woman of fifty-five?'

'Fifty-six, sir.'

'And the man you saw was on the other side of the road?'

'Yes, sir.'

'And it was two o'clock in the morning. You must have remarkable eyes, Mrs Salmon?'

'No, sir. There was moonlight, and when the man looked up, he had the lamplight on his face.'

'And you have no doubt whatever that the man you saw is the prisoner?'

I couldn't make out what he was at. He couldn't have expected any other answer than the one he got.

'None whatever, sir. It isn't a face one forgets.'

Counsel took a look round the court for a moment. Then he said: 'Do you mind, Mrs Salmon, examining again the people in court? No, not the prisoner. Stand up, please, Mr Adams,' and there at the back of the court, with thick stout body and muscular legs and a pair of bulging eyes, was the exact image of the man in the dock. He was even dressed the same – tight blue suit and striped tie.

'Now think very carefully, Mrs Salmon. Can you still swear that the man you saw drop the hammer in Mrs Parker's garden was the prisoner – and not this man, who is his twin brother?'

Of course she couldn't. She looked from one to the other and didn't say a word.

There the big brute sat in the dock with his legs crossed and there he stood too at the back of the court and they both stared at Mrs Salmon. She shook her head.

What we saw then was the end of the case. There wasn't a witness prepared to swear that it was the prisoner he'd seen. And the brother? He had his alibi, too; he was with his wife.

And so the man was acquitted for lack of evidence. But whether – if he did the murder and not his brother – he was punished or not, I don't know. That extraordinary day had an extraordinary end. I followed Mrs Salmon out of court and we got wedged in the crowd who were waiting, of course, for the twins. The police tried to drive the crowd away, but all they could do was keep the roadway clear for traffic. I learned later that they tried to get the twins to leave by a back way, but they wouldn't. One of them – no one knew which – said, 'I've been acquitted, haven't I?' and they walked bang out of the front entrance. Then it happened. I don't know how; though I was only six feet away. The crowd moved and somehow one of the twins got pushed on to the road right in front of a bus.

He gave a squeal like a rabbit and that was all; he was dead, his skull smashed just as Mrs Parker's had been. Divine vengeance? I wish I knew. There was the other Adams getting on his feet from beside the body and looking straight over at Mrs Salmon. He was crying, but whether he was the murderer or the innocent man, nobody will ever be able to tell. But if you were Mrs Salmon, could you sleep at night?

Patricia Highsmith

THE MOBILE
BED-OBJECT

Patricia Highsmith (1921–) is an American much more famous in Europe than in her own country. In several European countries she is regarded as a novelist equal at her best to anybody now writing, her particular characteristic being an intensity of feeling generated between two characters, one of whom has committed or is contemplating a crime. Her books are not directly concerned with radical politics, but suggest nevertheless that in a world where most people are imprisoned by possessions, business routine or family habit, the criminal is potentially free.

Highsmith's short stories are often macabre. 'She is a writer who has created a world of her own – a world claustrophobic and irrational which we enter each time with a sense of personal danger, with the head half turned over the shoulder, even with a certain reluctance, for these are cruel pleasures we are going to experience', Graham Greene wrote when introducing a collection of her stories. Cruel indeed: in *The Animal-Lover's Book of Beastly Murder*, animals take appalling revenges on vicious human beings, and *Little Tales of Misogyny*, from which 'The Mobile Bed-Object' is taken, offers brief unsentimental accounts of women as predators and victims. Mildred is one of the victims, her story not unusual. It is the clipped voice in which her destruction is recounted that makes the little tale memorable.

There are lots of girls like Mildred, homeless, yet never without a roof –
most of the time the ceiling of a hotel room, sometimes that of bachelor
digs, of a yacht's cabin if they're lucky, a tent, or a caravan. Such girls are
bed-objects, the kind of thing one acquires like a hot-water bottle, a
travelling iron, an electric shoe-shiner, any little luxury of life. It is an
advantage to them if they can cook a bit, but they certainly don't have to
talk, in any language. Also they are interchangeable, like unblocked
currency or international postal reply coupons. Their value can go up or
down, depending on their age and the man currently in possession.

Mildred considered it not a bad life, and if interviewed would have
said in her earnest way, 'It's *interesting.*' Mildred never laughed, and
smiled only when she thought she should be polite. She was five feet
seven, blondish, rather slender, with a pleasant, blank face and large
blue eyes which she held wide open. She slunk rather than walked, her
shoulders hunched, hips thrust a bit forward – the way the best models
walked, she had read somewhere. This gave her a languid, pacific air.
Ambulant, she looked as if she were walking in her sleep. She was a
little more lively in bed, and this fact travelled by word of mouth, or
among men who might not speak the same tongue, by nods or small
smiles. Mildred knew her job, and it must be said for her that she
applied herself diligently to it.

She had floundered around in school till fourteen, when everyone
including her parents had deemed it senseless for her to continue. She
would marry early, her parents thought. Instead, Mildred ran away from
home, or rather was taken away by a car salesman when she was barely
fifteen. Under the salesman's direction, she wrote reassuring letters home,
saying she had a job in a nearby town as a waitress and was living in a flat
with two other girls.

By the time she was eighteen, Mildred had been to Capri, Mexico City,
Paris, even Japan, and to Brazil several times, where men usually dumped
her, since they were often on the run from something. She had been a
second prize, as it were, for one American President-elect the night of his

victory. She had been lent for two days to a sheikh in London, who had rewarded her with a rather kinky gold goblet which she had subsequently lost – not that she liked the goblet, but it must have been worth a fortune, and she often thought of its loss with regret. If she ever wished to change her man, she would simply visit an expensive bar in Rio or anywhere, on her own, and pick up another man who would be pleased to add her to his expense account, and back she would go to America or Germany or Sweden. Mildred couldn't have cared less what country she was in.

Once she was forgotten at a restaurant table, as a cigarette lighter might be left behind. Mildred noticed, but Herb didn't for some thirty minutes which were mildly worrying for Mildred, though Mildred never got really distressed about anything. She did turn to the man sitting next to her – it was a business lunch, four men, four girls – and she said, 'I thought Herb had just gone to the loo –'

'What?' The heavy-set man next to her was an American. 'Oh. He'll be back. We had some unpleasant business to talk over today, you know. Herb's upset.' The American smiled understandingly. He had his girl friend by his side, one he'd picked up last night. The girls hadn't opened their mouths, except to eat.

Herb came back and got Mildred, and they went to their hotel room, Herb in utmost gloom, because he'd come out badly in the business deal. Mildred's embraces that afternoon failed to lift Herb's spirits or his ego, and that evening Mildred was traded in. Her new guardian was Stanley, about thirty-five, pudgy, like Herb. The trade took place at cocktail time, while Mildred sipped her usual Alexander through a straw. Herb got Stanley's girl, a dumb blonde with artificially curled hair. The blondness was artificial too, though a good job, Mildred observed, make-up and hair-do being matters Mildred was an expert in. Mildred returned to the hotel briefly to pack her suitcase, then she spent the evening and night with Stanley. He hardly talked to her, but he smiled a lot, and made a lot of telephone calls. This was in Des Moines.

With Stanley, Mildred went to Chicago, where Stanley had a small flat of his own, plus a wife in a house somewhere, he said. Mildred wasn't worried about the wife. Only once in her life had she had to deal with a difficult wife who crashed into a flat. Mildred had brandished a carving knife, and the wife had fled. Usually a wife just looked dumbfounded, then sneered and walked off, obviously intending to avenge herself on her husband. Stanley was away all day ar.d didn't give her much money, which was annoying. Mildred wasn't going to stay long with Stanley, if she could help it. She'd started a savings account in a bank somewhere once, but she'd lost her pass-book and forgotten the name of the town where the bank was.

But before Mildred could make a wise move away from Stanley, she found herself given away. This was a shock. An economist would have drawn a conclusion about currency that was given away, and so did Mildred. She realized that Stanley came out a bit better in the deal he had made with the man called Louis, to whom he gave Mildred, but still –

And she was only twenty-three. But Mildred knew that was the danger age, and that she'd better play her cards carefully from now on. Eighteen was the peak, and she was five years past it, and what had she to show for it? A diamond bracelet that men eyed with greed, and that she'd twice had to get out of hock with the aid of some new bastard. A mink coat – same story. A suitcase with a couple of good-looking dresses. What did she want? Well, she wanted to continue the same life but with a sense of greater security. What would she do if her back was really to the wall? If she, kicked out maybe, not even given away, had to go to a bar and even then couldn't pick up more than a one-night stand. Well, she had some addresses of past men friends, and she could always write them and threaten to put them in her memoirs, which she could say a publisher was paying her to write. But Mildred had talked with girls twenty-five and older who'd threatened memoirs, if they weren't pensioned off for life, and she'd heard of only one who had succeeded. More often, the girls said, it was a laugh they got, or a 'Go ahead and write it' rather than any money.

So Mildred made the best of it for a few days with fat old Louis. He had a nice tabby cat, of which Mildred grew fond, but the most boring thing was that his apartment was a one-room kitchenette and dreary. Louis was good-natured but tight-fisted. Also it was embarrassing for Mildred to be sneaked out when she and Louis went out for dinner (not usually, because Louis expected her to cook and to do a little cleaning too), and when Louis had people in to talk business, to be asked to hide in the kitchenette and not to make a sound. Louis sold pianos wholesale. Mildred rehearsed the speech she was going to make soon. 'I hope you realize you haven't any hold over me, Louis . . . I'm a girl who's not used to working, not even in bed . . .'

But before she had a chance to make her speech, which would mainly have been a demand for more money, because she knew Louis had plenty tucked away, she was given away to a young salesman one night. Louis simply said, after they'd all finished dinner in a roadside café, 'Dave, why don't you take Mildred to your place for a nightcap? I've got to turn in early.' With a wink.

Dave beamed. He was nice looking, but he lived in a caravan, good

God! Mildred had no intention of becoming a *gypsy*, taking sponge baths, enduring portable loos. She was used to grand hotels with room service day and night. Dave might be young and ardent, but Mildred didn't give a damn about that. Men said women were all alike, but in her opinion it was even truer that men were all alike. All they wanted was one thing. Women at least wanted fur coats, good perfume, a holiday in the Bahamas, a cruise somewhere, jewellery – in fact, quite a number of things.

One evening when she was with Dave at a business dinner (he was a piano distributor and order-taker, though Mildred never saw a piano around the caravan), Mildred made the acquaintance of a Mr Zupp, called Sam, who had invited Dave to dine in a fancy restaurant. Inspired by three Alexanders, Mildred flirted madly with Sam, who was not unresponsive under the table, and Mildred simply announced that she was going home with Sam. Dave's mouth fell open, and he started to make a fuss, but Sam – an older, more self-assured man – most diplomatically implied that he would make a scene if it came to a fistfight, so Dave backed down.

This was a big improvement. Sam and Mildred flew at once to Paris, then to Hamburg. Mildred got new clothes. The hotel rooms were great. Mildred never knew from one day to the next what town they would be in. Now here was a man whose memoirs would be worth something, if she could only find out what he did. But when he spoke on the telephone, it was either in code, or in Yiddish, or Russian, or Arabic. Mildred had never heard such baffling languages in her life, and she was never able to find out just what he was selling. People had to sell something, didn't they? Or buy something, and if they bought something, there had to be a source of money, didn't there? So what was even the source of money? Something told Mildred that it would soon be time for her to retire. Sam Zupp seemed to have been sent by Providence. She worked on him, trying to be subtle.

'I wouldn't mind settling down,' she said.

'I'm not the marrying kind,' he retorted with a smile.

That wasn't what she meant. She meant a nest egg, and then he could say good-bye, if he wanted to. But wouldn't it take a few nest eggs to make a big nest egg? Would she have to go through all this again with future Sam Zupps? Mildred's mind staggered with the effort to see far into the future, but there seemed no doubt that she should take advantage of Mr Zupp, at least, while she had him. These ideas, or plans, frail as damaged spider webs, were swept away by the events of the days after the above conversation.

Sam Zupp was suddenly on the run. For a few days, it was aeroplanes with separate seats, because he and Mildred were not supposed to be travelling together. Once police sirens were behind them, as Sam's hired driver zoomed and careered over an alpine road, bound for Geneva. Or maybe Zurich. Mildred was in her element, ministering to Sam with handkerchiefs moistened in eau de cologne, producing a *sandwich de jambon* out of her handbag in case he was hungry, or a flask of brandy if he felt his heart fluttering. Mildred fancied herself one of the heroines she had seen in films – good films – about men and their girl friends fleeing from the awful and so unfairly well-armed police.

Her daydreams of glamour were brief. It must have been in Holland – Mildred didn't know where she was half the time – when the chauffeur-driven car suddenly screeched to a halt, just like in the films, and Mildred was bundled by both chauffeur and Sam into a mummylike casing of stiff, heavy tarpaulin, and then ropes were tied around her. She was dumped into a canal and drowned.

No one ever heard of Mildred. No one ever found her. If she had been found, there would have been no immediate means of identification, because Sam had her passport, and her handbag was in the car. She had been thrown away, as one might throw away a cricket lighter when it is used up, like a paperback one has read and which has become excess baggage. Mildred's absence was never taken seriously by anyone. The score or so people who knew and remembered her, themselves scattered about the world, simply thought she was living in some other country or city. One day, they supposed, she'd turn up again in some bar, in some hotel lobby. Soon they forgot her.

Edward D. Hoch

THE MOST
DANGEROUS MAN

'Writing a novel has always been, to me, a task to be finished as quickly as possible. Writing a short story is a pleasure one can linger over.' So Edward D. (for Dentinger) Hoch (1930–), one of the minority of modern crime writers to be essentially a short-story writer. The level of his four-hundred-odd short stories written under several names varies greatly, but the best are imaginative and highly ingenious. One would not look to him for characterization or for the development of narrative, but for the construction and solution of an apparently insoluble puzzle. He has played more variations than John Dickson Carr on the theme of the impossible crime.

No impossibilities are involved in the story printed here, however. Hoch can also be very funny, and 'The Most Dangerous Man' is a joke story. You should catch the drift quickly, indeed in the opening paragraph, but even though you do, some of the implications may be surprising. The last line is a knock-out, perfect of its kind.

The professor glanced up from the desk where a new treatise on the binomial theorem lay open before him. His ears had detected a noise upon the landing – not loud, but enough to sharpen his senses. When it was repeated, he rose from the chair and walked across the room to the bolted door.

'Who is it?' he asked.

'Dwiggins, Professor! Open the door!'

The bolt was pulled back and the professor turned up the gas-flame a bit higher. 'You arrived sooner than I had expected. Did all go well?'

Dwiggins was a slender man with black bushy hair and side-whiskers. His special value was his innate ability to assume the guise of a bumbling tradesman. The professor had known and used him many times in the past, always with success.

'It was perfect, Professor,' reported Dwiggins. 'I arranged a meeting with Archibald Andrews and told him of my needs. He agreed quite readily when I revealed the sum of money I was willing to pay.'

'Capital, Dwiggins!' The professor drew a small note-book from his pocket and made a check mark. Then, with the tip of the pencil running down a list of names, he said, 'We will have a final meeting tomorrow evening. Make certain everyone is in attendance.'

'Right you are, Professor!'

When he was alone once more, the tall pale man hurried to the window and watched the progress of Dwiggins along the opposite curb. His deeply sunken eyes scanned the alleyways, searching for a police-agent who might be following the bushy-haired man, but he saw no one. Thus far, nothing had happened to endanger his master plan.

The flickering gas-flames cast an uncertain glow over the five men who gathered in the professor's quarters the following evening. They were a mixed lot, drawn from various walks of life, but each had been chosen carefully for his special skills and accomplishments. Seated next to

Dwiggins was Coxe, the notorious bank robber, and by his side was Quinn, an expert with a knife who proudly boasted of having been a police suspect in their search for Jack the Ripper only two years earlier. Moran, the former army colonel, was present too, along with Jenkins, a street ruffian especially adept in the handling of horses.

'Now, now,' said the professor, peering and blinking at the men before him. 'We must get to the business at hand.'

'Will it be tomorrow?' asked Coxe.

The professor nodded. 'Tomorrow, the twenty-third of January, the City and Suburban Bank will make its regular Friday morning delivery of money to its branches. A two-horse van will enter the alleyway off Farringdon Street shortly after nine o'clock tomorrow morning, and proceed to the rear entrance of the bank. The flat of one Archibald Andrews overlooks this alley, and our Mr Dwiggins has been most successful in luring said Andrews away from his flat for the entire morning. Tell us how it was accomplished, Dwiggins.'

The bushy-haired man was quick to oblige. 'I approached Andrews yesterday afternoon. Knowing him to be temporarily unemployed, I presented myself as a spice merchant with expectations of setting up a small shop in Oxford Street. I offered to pay him ten pounds if he would spend Friday morning visiting a list of shops and noting the prices charged for a variety of spices. He is to begin at Covent Garden Market promptly at eight, which should keep him far enough from his rooms in Farringdon Street.'

'Tut, tut!' said the professor, shaking his head sadly. 'I fear that Archibald Andrews will learn more about the price of spices than he really needs to know. Coxe, you should have no trouble with the door to his lodgings. You and Quinn will enter the rooms at precisely half-past eight, and station yourselves at the windows overlooking the alley. When the two-horse van arrives for the money, you will open the windows and prepare to jump. As I explained earlier, there is no manner in which the robbery can be executed while the money is being loaded. The armed guards will be on the alert for trouble. And once it leaves the alley to move through the crowded London streets it will once again be safe from our hands. The one weak link in the chain occurs at the precise instant the van is locked and starts out of the alley. The armed guards will have entered a carriage to travel ahead of the van, and the van itself will be travelling so slowly that you two can easily drop onto it from Mr Andrews's second-storey windows.'

'Excuse me, Professor,' said Coxe. 'I understand all that, but what will the two guards in the carriage do when they realize we have intercepted the van?'

The professor merely smiled, blinking his puckered eyes. 'Everything is attended to. Jenkins here will be near at hand, in the guise of a hansom driver. At the proper moment his horse will appear to go out of control, and will carry the hansom cab between the guards' carriage and the van. Quinn will kill the driver of the van, and you will turn it in the opposite direction on Farringdon Street, away from the carriage. If the guards are able to get clear of the hansom and pursue you, Moran will be waiting with his air-gun.'

'Where will you be?' asked Quinn.

'Dwiggins and I will be waiting close by. Once you are on your way, we will follow.' He turned and took a cut-glass decanter from the sideboard. 'Now, gentlemen, I suggest a bit of wine to toast the success of our endeavour on the morrow.'

When Archibald Andrews left the doorway of his lodgings just before eight o'clock the following morning, Dwiggins and the professor were watching from across the street. It was a raw, blustery January morning, and the professor had turned up the collar of his greatcoat against the sharpness of the wind.

'Running like clockwork,' Dwiggins commented as he watched Andrews go off down the street.

'Good, good!' The professor slipped a watch from his inner pocket and snapped open the lid. 'Coxe and Quinn should be starting out now.'

They waited, watching the movement of shop-girls and clerks along the busy street. Then, at half-past the hour, the professor saw his two confederates enter the street door to Archibald Andrews's lodgings. Dwiggins returned from his rounds to report. 'Coxe and Quinn are in the flat, Professor. I saw them by the windows.'

'And Moran?'

'He has just arrived and stationed himself across the street from the alley. The air-gun is hidden in his walking-stick.'

'Jenkins?'

'His hansom is parked near by.'

The professor nodded. All was well.

At six minutes after nine o'clock, the two-horse van appeared and turned into the alley. A carriage drew up behind it and discharged two uniformed guards. The professor's face was oscillating slowly from side to side, in a curiously reptilian fashion, as he watched.

They waited while the minutes ticked by and the professor's sharp eyes scanned the passers-by for any sign of trouble. There seemed nothing unusual until –

'Dwiggins!'

'What is it, Professor?'

'That man hurrying through the crowd across the street – is it Archibald Andrews, returning so soon to his lodgings?'

'Bloody right it is!'

'Come on, we must stop him.'

They crossed the street quickly, and Dwiggins called out, 'Here now! I hired you to do a job for me!'

Archibald Andrews stopped in his tracks, looking from one to the other. 'I – I –'

'Speak up, man!' urged Dwiggins. 'This is my partner in the spice shop. Do you have the prices for us?'

'No, sir,' muttered Andrews. 'That is, you see, it seemed like a great deal of money for you to pay. I mentioned it to a friend of mine last evening – a physician who rooms with a consulting detective of sorts. He suggested something odd might be afoot.'

'Quickly,' snarled the professor. 'If he comes here –'

But already there was movement in the alley. The guards' carriage had moved away, and the two-horse van was starting out with its precious cargo. As the professor watched, he saw Coxe and Quinn throw back the shutters and drop through the windows onto the roof of the van.

In the same instant there came the sound of police whistles, and suddenly the van seemed alive with uniformed bobbies. Coxe and Quinn were seized by a dozen strong arms.

'Quickly!' the professor told Dwiggins. 'We must make our escape!'

'What about the others?'

But it was too late for them. Jenkins, abandoning his hansom for flight on foot, was in the clasp of a tall, sharp-featured man whose long white fingers seemed to clutch like steel.

'It is too late for them,' the professor decided. 'We can only hope that Moran was able to make good his escape.'

'How did the police discover our plans so quickly?'

'That man is a devil! – that tall one who had Jenkins in his grip! As soon as he discovered that Andrews's lodgings overlooked the alley by the bank, he must have known we were luring the man away for a number of hours while we used his flat to reach the money-van.'

'All that because I offered Andrews ten pounds?' Dwiggins followed the professor down a side street, away from the bustle of the crowds. 'Who is this man that outwitted us?'

'His name is Sherlock Holmes,' answered Professor Moriarty. 'He is the most dangerous man in London.'

P. D. James

THE VICTIM

P. D. (Phyllis Dorothy) James was born in 1920, and spent much of her working life as an administrator of the North West Regional Hospital Board, then as an adviser to the Home Office in relation to the criminal department. Her first crime story, *Cover Her Face*, appeared in 1962, and at that time she thought that the form, 'though interesting, would be too restrictive really for a serious novelist'. Later she realized that the restriction helped by imposing a discipline, and she began, at first perhaps not altogether deliberately, to write books that would avoid the standard formulas of detective fiction.

A detective, Adam Dalgleish, appears in most of them, but without being eccentric he is unusual. 'I didn't want to over-romanticize him, I didn't want him to be too much the upper-crust, splendidly mannered, rather snobbish detective very much in the English tradition.' And Dalgleish, a poet and a cool, slightly aloof personality, is both sympathetic and unconventional. The settings are also often unusual, like the home for incurables in *The Black Tower*. Furniture and fittings are described in detail, the hospital in *Shroud for a Nightingale* is entirely convincing, the opening death gruesomely realistic. The best of her books, which include the two just mentioned and *Death of an Expert Witness*, are among the most successful crime stories of recent years. The ambitious *Innocent Blood*, which abandons what she calls the 'formula' completely, shows sign of strain and artificiality.

She has written few short stories, but the best of them are marked by the realistic characterization and interest in human motives that are strong in the novels. 'The Victim' has these qualities, and without any attempt at trickiness (which is not in her line) provides a surprising ending.

You know Princess Ilsa Mancelli, of course. I mean by that that you must have seen her on the cinema screen; on television; pictured in newspapers arriving at airports with her latest husband; relaxing on their yacht; bejewelled at first nights, gala nights, at any night and in any place where it is obligatory for the rich and successful to show themselves. Even if, like me, you have nothing but bored contempt for what I believe is called an international jet set, you can hardly live in the modern world and not know Ilsa Mancelli. And you can't fail to have picked up some scraps about her past. The brief and not particularly successful screen career, when even her heart-stopping beauty couldn't quite compensate for the paucity of talent; the succession of marriages, first to the producer who made her first film and who broke a twenty-year-old marriage to get her; then to a Texan millionaire; lastly to a prince. About two months ago I saw a nauseatingly sentimental picture of her with her two-day-old son in a Rome nursing home. So it looks as if this marriage, sanctified as it is by wealth, a title and maternity, may be intended as her final adventure.

The husband before the film producer is, I notice, no longer mentioned. Perhaps her publicity agent fears that a violent death in the family, particularly an unsolved violent death, might tarnish her bright image. Blood and beauty. In the early stages of her career they hadn't been able to resist that cheap, vicarious thrill. But not now. Nowadays her early history, before she married the film producer, has become a little obscure, although there is a suggestion of poor but decent parentage and early struggles suitably rewarded. I am the most obscure part of that obscurity. Whatever you know, or think you know, of Ilsa Mancelli, you won't have heard about me. The publicity machine has decreed that I be nameless, faceless, unremembered, that I no longer exist. Ironically, the machine is right; in any real sense, I don't.

I married her when she was Elsie Bowman aged seventeen. I was Assistant Librarian at our local branch library and fifteen years older, a thirty-two-year-old virgin, a scholar manqué, thin faced, a little stooping, my meagre hair already thinning. She worked on the cosmetic counter of our High Street store. She was beautiful then, but with a delicate, tentative, unsophisticated loveliness which gave little promise of the polished mature beauty which is hers today. Our story was very ordinary. She returned a book to the library one evening when I was on counter duty. We chatted. She asked my advice about novels for her mother. I spent as long as I dared finding suitable romances for her on the shelves. I tried to interest her in the books I liked. I asked her about herself, her life, her ambitions. She was the only woman I had been able to talk to. I was enchanted by her, totally and completely besotted.

I used to take my lunch early and make surreptitious visits to the store, watching her from the shadow of a neighbouring pillar. There is one picture which even now seems to stop my heart. She had dabbed her wrist with scent and was holding out a bare arm over the counter so that a prospective customer could smell the perfume. She was totally absorbed, her young face gravely preoccupied. I watched her, silently, and felt the tears smarting my eyes.

It was a miracle when she agreed to marry me. Her mother (she had no father) was reconciled if not enthusiastic about the match. She didn't, as she made it abundantly plain, consider me much of a catch. But I had a good job with prospects; I was educated; I was steady and reliable; I spoke with a grammar school accent which, while she affected to deride it, raised my status in her eyes. Besides, any marriage for Elsie was better than none. I was dimly aware when I bothered to think about Elsie in relation to anyone but myself that she and her mother didn't get on.

Mrs Bowman made, as she described it, a splash. There was a full choir and a peal of bells. The church hall was hired and a sit-down meal, ostentatiously unsuitable and badly cooked, was served to eighty guests. Between the pangs of nervousness and indigestion I was conscious of smirking waiters in short white jackets, a couple of giggling bridesmaids from the store, their freckled arms bulging from pink taffeta sleeves, hearty male relatives, red faced and with buttonholes of carnation and waving fern, who made indelicate jokes and clapped me painfully between the shoulders. There were speeches and warm champagne. And, in the middle of it all, Elsie, my Elsie, like a white rose.

I suppose that it was stupid of me to imagine that I could hold her. The mere sight of our morning faces, smiling at each other's reflection in the bedroom mirror, should have warned me that it couldn't last. But, poor deluded fool, I never dreamed that I might lose her except by death.

Her death I dared not contemplate, and I was afraid for the first time of my own. Happiness had made a coward of me. We moved into a new bungalow, chosen by Elsie, sat in new chairs chosen by Elsie, slept in a befrilled bed chosen by Elsie. I was so happy that it was like passing into a new phase of existence, breathing a different air, seeing the most ordinary things as if they were newly created. One isn't necessarily humble when greatly in love. Is it so unreasonable to recognize the value of a love like mine, to believe that the beloved is equally sustained and transformed by it?

She said that she wasn't ready to start a baby and, without her job, she was easily bored. She took a brief training in shorthand and typing at our local Technical College and found herself a position as shorthand typist at the firm of Collingford & Major. That, at least, was how the job started. Shorthand typist, then secretary to Mr Rodney Collingford, then personal secretary, then confidential personal secretary; in my bemused state of uxorious bliss I only half registered her progress from occasionally taking his dictation when his then secretary was absent to flaunting his gifts of jewellery and sharing his bed.

He was everything I wasn't. Rich (his father had made a fortune from plastics shortly after the war and had left the factory to his only son), coarsely handsome in a swarthy fashion, big muscled, confident, attractive to women. He prided himself on taking what he wanted. Elsie must have been one of his easiest pickings.

Why, I still wonder, did he want to marry her? I thought at the time that he couldn't resist depriving a pathetic, under-privileged, unattractive husband of a prize which neither looks nor talent had qualified him to deserve. I've noticed that about the rich and successful. They can't bear to see the undeserving prosper. I thought that half the satisfaction for him was in taking her away from me. That was partly why I knew that I had to kill him. But now I'm not so sure. I may have done him an injustice. It may have been both simpler and more complicated than that. She was, you see – she still is – so very beautiful.

I understand her better now. She was capable of kindness, good humour, generosity even, provided she was getting what she wanted. At the time we married, and perhaps eighteen months afterwards, she wanted me. Neither her egoism nor her curiosity had been able to resist such a flattering, overwhelming love. But for her, marriage wasn't permanency. It was the first and necessary step towards the kind of life she wanted and meant to have. She was kind to me, in bed and out, while I was what she wanted. But when she wanted someone else, then my need of her, my jealousy, my bitterness, she saw as a cruel and wilful denial of her basic right, the right to have what she wanted. After all, I'd had her for nearly three years. It was two years more than I had any right to expect. She thought so. Her darling Rodney thought so. When my acquaintances at the library learnt of the divorce I could see in their eyes that they thought so too. And she couldn't see what I was so bitter about. Rodney was perfectly happy to be the guilty party; they weren't, she pointed out caustically, expecting me to behave like a gentleman. I wouldn't have to pay for the divorce. Rodney would see to that. I wasn't being asked to provide her with alimony. Rodney had more than enough. At one point she came close to bribing me with Rodney's money to let her go without fuss. And yet – was it really as simple as that? She had loved me, or at least needed me, for a time. Had she perhaps seen in me the father that she had lost at five years old?

During the divorce, through which I was, as it were, gently processed by highly paid legal experts as if I were an embarrassing but expendable nuisance to be got rid of with decent speed, I was only able to keep sane by the knowledge that I was going to kill Collingford. I knew that I couldn't go on living in a world where he breathed the same air. My mind fed voraciously on the thought of his death, savoured it, began systematically and with dreadful pleasure to plan it.

A successful murder depends on knowing your victim, his character, his daily routine, his weaknesses, those unalterable and betraying habits which make up the core of personality. I knew quite a lot about Rodney Collingford. I knew facts which Elsie had let fall in her first weeks with the firm, typing pool gossip. I knew the fuller and rather more intimate facts which she had disclosed in those early days of her enchantment with him, when neither prudence nor kindness had been able to conceal her obsessive preoccupation with her new boss. I should have been warned then. I knew, none better, the need to talk about the absent lover.

What did I know about him? I knew the facts that were common knowledge, of course. That he was wealthy; aged thirty; a notable amateur golfer; that he lived in an ostentatious mock Georgian house on the banks of the Thames looked after by over-paid but non-resident staff; that he owned a cabin cruiser; that he was just over six feet tall; that he was a good business man but reputedly close-fisted; that he was methodical in his habits. I knew a miscellaneous and unrelated set of facts about him, some of which would be useful, some important, some of which I couldn't use. I knew – and this was rather surprising – that he was good with his hands and liked making things in metal and wood. He had built an expensively-equipped and large workroom in the grounds of his house and spent every Thursday evening working there alone. He was a man addicted to routine. This creativity, however mundane and trivial, I found intriguing, but I didn't let myself dwell on it. I was interested in him only so far as his personality and habits were relevant to his death. I never thought of him as a human being. He had no existence for me apart from my hate. He was Rodney Collingford, my victim.

First I decided on the weapon. A gun would have been the most certain, I supposed, but I didn't know how to get one and was only too well aware I wouldn't know how to load or use it if I did. Besides, I was reading a number of books about murder at the time and I realized that guns, however cunningly obtained, were easy to trace. And there was another thing. A gun was too impersonal, too remote. I wanted to make physical contact at the moment of death. I wanted to get close enough to see that final look of incredulity and horror as he recognized, simultaneously, me and his death. I wanted to drive a knife into his throat. I bought it two days after the divorce. I was in no hurry to kill Collingford. I knew that I must take my time, must be patient, if I were to act in safety. One day, perhaps when we were old, I might tell Elsie. But I didn't intend to be found out. This was to be the perfect murder. And that meant taking my time. He would be allowed to live for a full year. But I knew that the earlier I bought the knife the more difficult it would be, twelve months later, to trace the purchase. I didn't buy it locally. I went one Saturday morning by train and bus to a north-east suburb and found a busy ironmongers and general store just off the High Street. There was a variety of knives on display. The blade of the one I selected was about six inches long and was made of strong steel screwed into a plain wooden handle. I think it was probably meant for cutting lino. In the shop its razor sharp edge was protected by a strong cardboard sheath. It felt good and right in my hand. I stood in a small queue at the pay desk and the cashier didn't even glance up as he took my notes and pushed the change towards me.

But the most satisfying part of my planning was the second stage. I wanted Collingford to suffer. I wanted him to know that he was going to die. It wasn't enough that he should realize it in a last second before I drove in the knife or in that final second before he ceased to know anything for ever. Two seconds of agony, however horrible, weren't an adequate return for what he had done to me. I wanted him to know that he was a condemned man, to know it with increasing certainty, to wonder every morning whether this might be his last day. What if this knowledge did make him cautious, put him on his guard? In this country, he couldn't go armed. He couldn't carry on his business with a hired protector always at his side. He couldn't bribe the police to watch him every second of the day. Besides, he wouldn't want to be thought a coward. I guessed that he would carry on, ostentatiously normal, as if the threats were unreal or derisory, something to laugh about with his drinking cronies. He was the sort to laugh at danger. But he would never be sure. And, by the end, his nerve and confidence would be broken. Elsie wouldn't know him for the man she had married.

I would have liked to have telephoned him but that, I knew, was impracticable. Calls could be traced; he might refuse to talk to me; I wasn't confident that I could disguise my voice. So the sentence of death would have to be sent by post. Obviously, I couldn't write the notes or the envelopes myself. My studies in murder had shown me how difficult it was to disguise handwriting and the method of cutting out and sticking together letters from a newspaper seemed messy, very time consuming and difficult to manage wearing gloves. I knew, too, that it would be fatal to use my own small portable typewriter or one of the machines at the library. The forensic experts could identify a machine.

And then I hit on my plan. I began to spend my Saturdays and occasional half days journeying round London and visiting shops where they sold secondhand typewriters. I expect you know the kind of shop; a variety of machines of different ages, some practically obsolete, others comparatively new, arranged on tables where the prospective purchaser may try them out. There were new machines too, and the proprietor was usually employed in demonstrating their merits or discussing hire pur- chase terms. The customers wandered desultorily around, inspecting the machines, stopping occasionally to type out an exploratory passage. There were little pads of rough paper stacked ready for use. I didn't, of course, use the scrap paper provided. I came supplied with my own writing materials, a well-known brand sold in every stationers and on every railway bookstall. I bought a small supply of paper and envelopes once every two months and never from the same shop. Always, when handling them, I wore a thin pair of gloves, slipping them on as soon as my typing was complete. If someone were near, I would tap out the usual drivel about the sharp brown fox or all good men coming to the aid of the party. But if I were quite alone I would type something very different.

'This is the first communication, Collingford. You'll be getting them regularly from now on. They're just to let you know that I'm going to kill you.'

'You can't escape me, Collingford. Don't bother to inform the police. They can't help you.'

'I'm getting nearer, Collingford. Have you made your will?'

'Not long now, Collingford. What does it feel like to be under sentence of death?'

The warnings weren't particularly elegant. As a librarian I could think of a number of apt quotations which would have added a touch of individuality or style, perhaps even of sardonic humour, to the bald sentence of death. But I dared not risk originality. The notes had to be ordinary, the kind of threat which any one of his enemies, a worker, a competitor, a cuckolded husband, might have sent.

Sometimes I had a lucky day. The shop would be large, well supplied, nearly empty. I would be able to move from typewriter to typewriter and leave with perhaps a dozen or so notes and addressed envelopes ready to send. I always carried a folded newspaper in which I could conceal my writing pad and envelopes and into which I could quickly slip my little stock of typed messages.

It was quite a job to keep myself supplied with notes and I discovered interesting parts of London and fascinating shops. I particularly enjoyed this part of my plan. I wanted Collingford to get two notes a week, one posted on Sunday and one on Thursday. I wanted him to come to dread Friday and Monday mornings when the familiar typed envelope would drop on his mat. I wanted him to believe the threat was real. And why should he not believe it? How could the force of my hate and resolution not transmit itself through paper and typescript to his gradually comprehending brain?

I wanted to keep an eye on my victim. It shouldn't have been difficult; we lived in the same town. But our lives were worlds apart. He was a hard and sociable drinker. I never went inside a public house, and would have been particularly ill at ease in the kind of public house he frequented. But, from time to time, I would see him in the town. Usually he would be parking his Jaguar, and I would watch his quick, almost furtive, look to left and right before he turned to lock the door. Was it my imagination that he looked older, that some of the confidence had drained out of him?

Once, when walking by the river on a Sunday in early spring, I saw him manoeuvring his boat through Teddington Lock. Ilsa – she had, I knew, changed her name after her marriage – was with him. She was wearing a white trouser suit, her flowing hair was bound by a red scarf. There was a party. I could see two more men and a couple of girls and hear high female squeals of laughter. I turned quickly and slouched away as if I were the guilty one. But not before I had seen Collingford's face. This time I couldn't be mistaken. It wasn't, surely, the tedious job of getting his boat unscratched through the lock that made his face look so grey and strained.

The third phase of my planning meant moving house. I wasn't sorry to go. The bungalow, feminine, chintzy, smelling of fresh paint and the new shoddy furniture which she had chosen, was Elsie's home not mine. Her scent still lingered in cupboards and on pillows. In these inappropriate surroundings I had known greater happiness than I was ever to know again. But now I paced restlessly from room to empty room fretting to be gone.

It took me four months to find the house I wanted. It had to be on or very near to the river within two or three miles upstream of Collingford's house. It had to be small and reasonably cheap. Money wasn't too much of a difficulty. It was a time of rising house prices and the modern bungalow sold at three hundred pounds more than I had paid for it. I could get another mortgage without difficulty if I didn't ask for too much, but I thought it likely that, for what I wanted, I should have to pay cash.

The house agents perfectly understood that a man on his own found a three-bedroom bungalow too large for him and, even if they found me rather vague about my new requirements and irritatingly imprecise about the reasons for rejecting their offerings, they still sent me orders to view. And then, suddenly on an afternoon in April, I found exactly what I was looking for. It actually stood on the river, separated from it only by a narrow tow path. It was a one-bedroom shack-like wooden bungalow with a tiled roof, set in a small neglected plot of sodden grass and overgrown flower beds. There had once been a wooden landing stage but now the two remaining planks, festooned with weeds and tags of rotted rope, were half submerged beneath the slime of the river. The paint on the small veranda had long ago flaked away. The wallpaper of twined roses in the sitting-room was blotched and faded. The previous owner had left two old cane chairs and a ramshackle table. The kitchen was pokey and ill-equipped. Everywhere there hung a damp miasma of depression and decay. In summer, when the neighbouring shacks and bungalows were occupied by holidaymakers and week-enders, it would, no doubt, be cheerful enough. But in October, when I planned to kill Collingford, it would be as deserted and isolated as a disused morgue. I bought it and paid cash. I was even able to knock two hundred pounds off the asking price.

My life that summer was almost happy. I did my job at the library adequately. I lived alone in the shack, looking after myself as I had before my marriage. I spent my evenings watching television. The images flickered in front of my eyes almost unregarded, a monochrome background to my bloody and obsessive thoughts.

I practised with the knife until it was as familiar in my hand as an eating utensil. Collingford was taller than I by six inches. The thrust then would have to be upward. It made a difference to the way I held the knife and I experimented to find the most comfortable and effective grip. I hung a bolster on a hook in the bedroom door and lunged at a marked spot for hours at a time. Of course, I didn't actually insert the knife; nothing must dull the sharpness of its blade. Once a week, a special treat, I sharpened it to an even keener edge.

Two days after moving into the bungalow I bought a dark blue untrimmed track suit and a pair of light running shoes. Throughout the summer I spent an occasional evening running on the tow path. The people who owned the neighbouring chalets, when they were there, which was infrequently, got used to the sound of my television through the closed curtains and the sight of my figure jogging past their windows. I kept apart from them and from everyone and summer passed into autumn. The shutters were put up on all the chalets except mine. The tow path became mushy with falling leaves. Dusk fell early, and the summer sights and sounds died on the river. And it was October.

He was due to die on Thursday October 17th, the anniversary of the final decree of divorce. It had to be a Thursday, the evening which he spent by custom alone in his workshop, but it was a particularly happy augury that the anniversary should fall on a Thursday. I knew that he would be there. Every Thursday for nearly a year I had padded along the two and half miles of the footpath in the evening dusk and had stood briefly watching the squares of light from his windows and the dark bulk of the house behind.

It was a warm evening. There had been a light drizzle for most of the day but, by dusk, the skies had cleared. There was a thin white sliver of moon and it cast a trembling ribbon of light across the river. I left the library at my usual time, said my usual good nights. I knew that I had been my normal self during the day, solitary, occasionally a little sarcastic, conscientious, betraying no hint of the inner tumult.

I wasn't hungry when I got home but I made myself eat an omelette and drink two cups of coffee. I put on my swimming trunks and hung around my neck a plastic toilet bag containing the knife. Over the trunks I put on my track suit, slipping a pair of thin rubber gloves into the pocket. Then, at about quarter past seven, I left the shack and began my customary gentle trot along the tow path.

When I got to the chosen spot opposite to Collingford's house I could see at once that all was well. The house was in darkness but there were the customary lighted windows of his workshop. I saw that the cabin cruiser was moored against the boathouse. I stood very still and listened. There was no sound. Even the light breeze had died and the yellowing leaves on the riverside elms hung motionless. The tow path was completely deserted. I slipped into the shadow of the hedge where the trees grew thickest and found the place I had already selected. I put on the rubber gloves, slipped out of the track suit, and left it folded around my running shoes in the shadow of the hedge. Then, still watching carefully to left and right, I made my way to the river.

I knew just where I must enter and leave the water. I had selected a place where the bank curved gently, where the water was shallow and the bottom was firm and comparatively free of mud. The water struck very cold, but I expected that. Every night during that autumn I had bathed in cold water to accustom my body to the shock. I swam across the river with my methodical but quiet breast stroke, hardly disturbing the dark surface of the water. I tried to keep out of the path of moonlight but, from time to time, I swam into its silver gleam and saw my red gloved hands parting in front of me as if they were already stained with blood.

I used Collingford's landing stage to clamber out the other side. Again I stood still and listened. There was no sound except for the constant moaning of the river and the solitary cry of a night bird. I made my way silently over the grass. Outside the door of his workroom, I paused again. I could hear the noise of some kind of machinery. I wondered whether the door would be locked, but it opened easily when I turned the handle. I moved into a blaze of light.

I knew exactly what I had to do. I was perfectly calm. It was over in about four seconds. I don't think he really had a chance. He was absorbed in what he had been doing, bending over a lathe, and the sight of an almost naked man, walking purposely towards him, left him literally impotent with surprise. But, after that first paralysing second, he knew me. Oh yes, he knew me! Then I drew my right hand from behind my back and struck. The knife went in as sweetly as if the flesh had been butter. He staggered and fell. I had expected that and I let myself go loose and fell on top of him. His eyes were glazed, his mouth opened and there was a gush of dark red blood. I twisted the knife viciously in the wound, relishing the sound of tearing sinews. Then I waited. I counted five deliberately, then raised myself from his prone figure and crouched behind him before withdrawing the knife. When I withdrew it there was a fountain of sweet smelling blood which curved from his throat like an arch. There is one thing I shall never forget. The blood must have been red, what other colour could it have been? But, at the time and for ever afterwards, I saw it as a golden stream.

I checked my body for bloodstains before I left the workshop and rinsed my arms under the cold tap at his sink. My bare feet made no marks on the wooden block flooring. I closed the door quietly after me and, once again, stood listening. Still no sound. The house was dark and empty.

The return journey was more exhausting than I had thought possible. The river seemed to have widened and I thought that I should never reach my home shore. I was glad I had chosen a shallow part of the stream and that the bank was firm. I doubt whether I could have drawn myself up through a welter of mud and slime. I was shivering violently as I zipped up my track suit and it took me precious seconds to get on my running shoes. After I had run about a mile down the tow path I weighted the toilet bag containing the knife with stones from the path and hurled it into the middle of the river. I guessed that they would drag part of the Thames for the weapon but they could hardly search the whole stream. And, even if they did, the toilet bag was one sold at the local chain store which anyone might have bought, and I was confident that the knife could never be traced to me. Half an hour later I was back in my shack. I had left the television on and the news was just ending. I made myself a cup of hot cocoa and sat to watch it. I felt drained of thought and energy as if I had just made love. I was conscious of nothing but my tiredness, my body's coldness gradually returning to life in the warmth of the electric fire, and a great peace.

He must have had quite a lot of enemies. It was nearly a fortnight before the police got round to interviewing me. Two officers came, a Detective Inspector and a Sergeant, both in plain clothes. The Sergeant did most of the talking; the other just sat, looking round at the sitting-room, glancing out at the river, looking at the two of us from time to time from cold grey eyes as if the whole investigation were a necessary bore. The Sergeant said the usual reassuring platitudes about just a few questions. I was nervous, but that didn't worry me. They would expect me to be nervous. I told myself that, whatever I did, I mustn't try to be clever. I mustn't talk too much. I had decided to tell them that I spent the whole evening watching television, confident that no one would be able to refute this. I knew that no friends would have called on me. I doubted whether my colleagues at the library even knew where I lived. And I had no telephone so I need not fear that a caller's ring had gone unanswered during that crucial hour and a half.

On the whole it was easier than I had expected. Only once did I feel myself at risk. That was when the Inspector suddenly intervened. He said in a harsh voice:

'He married your wife didn't he? Took her away from you, some people might say. Nice piece of goods, too, by the look of her. Didn't you feel any grievance? Or was it all nice and friendly? You take her, old chap. No ill feelings. That kind of thing.'

It was hard to accept the contempt in his voice but if he hoped to provoke me he didn't succeed. I had been expecting this question. I was prepared. I looked down at my hands and waited a few seconds before I spoke. I knew exactly what I would say.

'I could have killed Collingford myself when she first told me about him. But I had to come to terms with it. She went for the money you see. And if that's the kind of wife you have, well she's going to leave you sooner or later. Better sooner than when you have a family. You tell yourself "good riddance". I don't mean I felt that at first, of course. But I did feel it in the end. Sooner than I expected, really.'

That was all I said about Elsie then or ever. They came back three times. They asked if they could look round my shack. They looked round it. They took away two of my suits and the track suit for examination. Two weeks later they returned them without comment. I never knew what they suspected, or even if they did suspect. Each time they came I said less, not more. I never varied my story. I never allowed them to provoke me into discussing my marriage or speculating about the crime. I just sat there, telling them the same thing over and over again. I never felt in any real danger. I knew that they had dragged some lengths of the river but that they hadn't found the weapon. In the end they gave up. I always had the feeling that I was pretty low on their list of suspects and that, by the end, their visits were merely a matter of form.

It was three months before Elsie came to me. I was glad that it wasn't earlier. It might have looked suspicious if she had arrived at the shack when the police were with me. After Collingford's death I hadn't seen her. There were pictures of her in the national and local newspapers, fragile in sombre furs and black hat at the inquest, bravely controlled at the crematorium, sitting in her drawing-room in afternoon dress and pearls with her husband's dog at her feet, the personification of loneliness and grief.

'I can't think who could have done it. He must have been a madman. Rodney hadn't an enemy in the world.'

That statement caused some ribald comment at the library. One of the assistants said:

'He's left her a fortune I hear. Lucky for her she had an alibi. She was at a London theatre all the evening, watching *Macbeth*. Otherwise, from what I've heard of our Rodney Collingford, people might have started to get ideas about his fetching little widow.'

Then he gave me a sudden embarrassed glance, remembering who the widow was.

And so one Friday evening, she came. She drove herself and was alone. The dark green Saab drove up at my ramshackle gate. She came into the sitting-room and looked around in a kind of puzzled contempt. After a moment, still not speaking, she sat in one of the fireside chairs and crossed her legs, moving one caressingly against the other. I hadn't seen her sitting like that before. She looked up at me. I was standing stiffly in front of her chair, my lips dry. When I spoke I couldn't recognize my own voice.

'So you've come back?' I said.

She stared at me, incredulous, and then she laughed:

'To you? Back for keeps? Don't be silly, darling! I've just come to pay a visit. Besides, I wouldn't dare to come back, would I? I might be frightened that you'd stick a knife into my throat.'

I couldn't speak. I stared at her, feeling the blood drain from my face. Then I heard her high, rather childish voice. It sounded almost kind.

'Don't worry, I shan't tell. You were right about him, darling, you really were. He wasn't at all nice really. And mean! I didn't care so much about your meanness. After all, you don't earn so very much do you? But he had half a million! Think of it, darling. I've been left half a million! And he was so mean that he expected me to go on working as his secretary even after we were married. I typed all his letters! I really did! All that he sent from home, anyway. And I had to open his post every morning unless the envelopes had a secret little sign on them he'd told his friends about to show that they were private.'

I said through bloodless lips, 'So all my notes –'

'He never saw them darling. Well, I didn't want to worry him did I? And I knew they were from you. I knew when the first one arrived. You never could spell communication could you? I noticed that when you used to write to the house agents and the solicitor before we were married. It made me laugh considering that you're an educated librarian and I was only a shop assistant.'

'So you knew all the time. You knew that it was going to happen.'

'Well, I thought that it might. But he really was horrible, darling. You can't imagine. And now I've got half a million? Isn't it lucky that I have an alibi? I thought you might come on that Thursday. And Rodney never did enjoy a serious play.'

After that brief visit I never saw or spoke to her again. I stayed in the shack, but life became pointless after Collingford's death. Planning his murder had been an interest, after all. Without Elsie and without my victim there seemed little point in living. And, about a year after his death, I began to dream. I still dream, always on a Monday and Friday. I live through it all again; the noiseless run along the tow path over the mush of damp leaves; the quiet swim across the river; the silent opening of his door; the upward thrust of the knife; the vicious turn in the wound; the animal sound of tearing tissues; the curving stream of golden blood. Only the homeward swim is different. In my dream the river is no longer a cleansing stream, luminous under the sickle moon, but a cloying, impenetrable, slow moving bog of viscous blood through which I struggle in impotent panic towards a steadily receding shore.

I know about the significance of the dream. I've read all about the psychology of guilt. Since I lost Elsie I've done all my living through books. But it doesn't help. And I no longer know who I am. I know who I used to be, our local Assistant Librarian, gentle, scholarly, timid, Elsie's husband. But then I killed Collingford. The man I was couldn't have done that. He wasn't that kind of person. So who am I? It isn't really surprising, I suppose, that the Library Committee suggested so tactfully that I ought to look for a less exacting job. A less exacting job than the post of Assistant Librarian? But you can't blame them. No one can be efficient and keep his mind on the job when he doesn't know who he is.

Sometimes, when I'm in a public house – and I seem to spend most of my time there nowadays since I've been out of work – I'll look over someone's shoulder at a newspaper photograph of Elsie and say:

'That's the beautiful Ilsa Mancelli. I was her first husband.'

I've got used to the way people sidle away from me, the ubiquitous pub bore, their eyes averted, their voices suddenly hearty. But sometimes, perhaps because they've been lucky with the horses and feel a spasm of pity for a poor deluded sod, they push a few coins over the counter to the barman before making their way to the door, and buy me a drink.

Q. Patrick

ALL THE WAY
TO THE MOON

The short stories of Q. Patrick, of which 'All the Way to the Moon' is an excellent and characteristic example, are among the very best things done by American crime writers in the past half century. In most of them somebody is deceived and trapped, or appears to be deceived and trapped, into a situation that can be resolved only by violence. Then, very often in an exotic setting, comes the resolution, which is never quite what we have been led to expect. Sometimes the surprise comes in the very last line, as in 'Mother, May I go out to Swim?' Sometimes, as in the story printed here, total innocence destroys an apparently foolproof plan. It is a matter for regret that there have been no new Q. Patrick stories for twenty years now.

Who is Q. Patrick? Why, Patrick Quentin. But who is or was Patrick Quentin? The answer is complicated because both names, and Jonathan Stagge as well, were used by several combinations of writers. However, many of the best Q. Patrick and Patrick Quentin short stories were written by Hugh Callingham Wheeler (1912–). He gave up crime writing for the theatre and cinema in the sixties, and has scripted a number of successful plays and musicals, including *A Little Night Music* and *Sweeney Todd*. In the cinema he worked on scripts for *Cabaret* and *Travels With My Aunt*, among other films. The Patrick Quentin novels, some written in collaboration, some by Wheeler alone, are also recommended.

Unexpectedly, as John Flint carried his wife's breakfast tray into the bedroom, It came back. Came back was not really the right phrase, because now It was never completely out of his mind. But the spring sunshine, which stole through the half-closed drapes, must have had some quality of Mexican sunshine, for suddenly he was in Mexico City again, breathing the exhilarating mountain air and feeling the wonder of its strangeness.

'Had a good night, dear?' With neat automatism he balanced the tray on his wife's knees and hardly hearing Amy's patient, invalid's response, murmured: 'Well, mind you call Dr Jepson if there's any trouble.'

He crossed to the frilly vanity table and opening the little jewel box, brought it over to his wife's bed. Since he had performed this ritual every morning for five years, he knew exactly what she was doing – although he himself was three thousand miles away. First, the diamond-chip bracelet was slipped on to the thin left wrist; then the clasp of the real pearl necklace was snapped beneath the heavy bun of dark hair, streaked with grey. Then came the two solitaire-diamond earrings. Amy had taken to wearing this jewellery, inherited from an aunt, ever since the first heart attack which had made her virtually bedridden. John Flint had never really wondered why – he was not a curious man; perhaps it was her gesture of rebellion against the drabness of invalidism. After her bad nights, she asked him to help with the earrings; but she didn't today.

'Well, goodbye, dear.' He kissed the dry forehead which reminded him dimly of paper. 'Tell Mrs O'Roylan I'll be back for dinner.'

He was always home for dinner, but those were always his parting words. In the kitchen, bright with shelf paper and flowered oilcloth, he prepared his own breakfast. The daily woman didn't come in until nine-thirty. After stacking the dishes, he moved out into the suburban street lined with neat little homes just like his own, and walked the three blocks to the trolley which would take him to the centre of town.

As he jolted through the tame prettiness of the city spring, with children, housewives, and other businessmen seated around him, It was still with him. At times these curious spells puzzled him, although they had been coming with increasing frequency during the last two years. He had been to Mexico City for a month's vacation a long time ago and he had been fascinated by its exotic beauty. But later, through the years of a dull, not unhappy marriage, he had hardly given it a thought. Why should it have returned to him now? – so transformed, so wonderful and shining like a mirage of Paradise.

He knew that he should bring himself down to earth. There was a lot to be done to perfect his new sales-promotion scheme which had already won an unofficial nod of approval from the head office. As the town's sole representative for Bonifoot Shoes, John was a conscientious employee. But his painstaking efforts to concentrate on shoes only brought him visions of huaraches, and then of bare, dust-stained Mexican feet padding over distant sidewalks – the feet of Indian peons from the hills, carrying baskets of rare flowers, strange fruit, exotic pottery to the markets . . .

When he reached the one-room office where he conducted his business modestly, without the aid of a secretary, John Flint still felt the odd sensation of not belonging here. In these periods he wasn't a man of forty-three dutifully wedded to a bedridden wife and a humdrum job in a banal industrial city. He was – what? A boy – that was it – a boy, free as the mountain wind, in a world where Popocateptl's great hump loomed against a translucent sky.

It was the arrival in the office of Harry Shipley which pulled John back to reality. He hadn't seen Harry for a long time – not since Harry had worked for a while as a salesman for Bonifoot Shoes. But he looked exactly the same – the same flashy sports coat; the same violent, hand-painted tie; the same false camaraderie; all designed to counteract the essential insignificance of his face and personality.

'Hi, there, John, you old horse, you. Long time no see.'

'Hello, Harry. Sit down. What can I do for you?'

Harry Shipley sat down opposite the desk where the mail, which John had picked up from under the door, still lay unopened. The moment Harry started to speak, John sensed a touch. And he was correct. *Kind of a tough period, Johnny. Just the right opening's hard to find.* There were marital difficulties too. Harry had never got on with his wife. Now finally he had persuaded her to agree to a divorce. He was desperately eager to get to Reno and then start a new life with a new girl – a fresh start far away – say, on the Coast. He had a little saved up, but not enough. If John, as an old pal, could see his way clear to a loan of five hundred dollars –

It wasn't difficult to plead temporarily strained circumstances himself and get rid of Harry Shipley. But the look of bleak disappointment on the other man's face remained to haunt John. Secretly he had been impressed by Harry – daring to attempt something so bold as a divorce and a new life. For a moment, as an image of Amy's emaciated figure passed across his mind, he thought It was going to come back . . .

Deliberately, he started to open his mail.

There were two letters from the head office. One finally okayed his promotion scheme, which involved a street check and the distribution of coupons for free shoes. The second letter was from the Personnel Manager. As John read it, his heart began to thump violently.

Dear John, – Old Pemberton, our Mexico City representative, is going to retire shortly. He finds the altitude too high on his ticker. Gummet tells me that you are familiar with Mexico and that you have applied for a South of the Border position. So, if you feel like a change of scenery, here's your chance. There's no hurry about this, but let me know as soon as you can.

Yours for bigger Bonifoot sales,
   Sam.

John Flint found himself shivering. This couldn't be true. Life didn't do this for you. Of course, several years ago he had told Gummet, the District Manager, that he would like a South American assignment if one ever came up. And yet . . . and yet . . . Suddenly It was upon him again, as if It had known all along and had been preparing him for this moment. And now It was much more glorious than ever before. For this was real. Those bustling, colourful streets three thousand miles away were no longer a mirage. They were his future – a true, concrete future which nothing could snatch away.

He read the letter again and, as he did so, his glance settled on the sentence: *The altitude's too tough on his ticker.* A chill began to invade him and with it rushed the image of Amy lying, bejewelled, in her dim bedroom; Amy nursing her high blood pressure and her faltering heart. Somehow in all his golden dreams he had never thought of Amy. With a sense of impending disaster he called Dr Jepson and listened in silence to his clipped, relentless reply.

'Take Amy to Mexico City? My dear man, a week in that altitude and she'd be dead. Out of the question. Quite out of the question. It would be murder.'

John put the receiver back. He sat for a long time looking at the letter . . .

*

Late that night John Flint lay awake in his bed. Only a few feet away, his wife's thin figure was stretched, invisible, in the darkness. He had not told her about the Mexican offer. What was the point? It would only make her feel guilty, make her feel more of a drag on him than she felt already. If only she could be cured! He had a little nest egg put away. And then there were her jewels. Wasn't there some specialist – New York? Even London? But he knew this was only idle dreaming. Dr Jepson had made that abundantly clear many times. There was nothing that could be done for her condition.

Against his will he started to think about Harry Shipley. Harry was divorcing his wife, beginning a new life. Divorce . . . But how could he divorce Amy? She had no one in the world but him. And it wasn't her fault that she was sick. What had she ever done to him except try to be as little trouble as possible?

'John.' Her whispering voice came from the other bed. 'Are you awake?'

'Yes, dear.'

'I hate to ask . . . but could you please get me a glass of milk?'

John scrambled out of bed as he had done a thousand times before and turned on the bedside lamp. Amy blinked up at him. She had forgotten to take off the earrings. They glittered with incongruous splendour beneath her untidy hair. Because John had loved her and knew that it was his duty to go on loving her, he had not for years really thought about her or even looked at her. But now he had been jolted from his anaesthetizing habit-pattern and he saw with merciless clarity the rough skin under the defeated eyes, the sharp angles of her cheek bones, the withering neck. She was suddenly a stranger, something infinitely removed from the solemn, fresh, young girl he had married . . .

So it's this, he thought, almost wonderingly, that stands between me and everything that matters. It's this pointless woman who is chaining me forever to this prim little house, this suburb, this awful town.

He went down to the pretty kitchen. As he was pouring milk into a glass, the thought came, sudden, shocking, unlike any other thought he had ever had.

If she would die, he thought . . . *If she would only die* . . .

In his mind, faint guitar music was trailing from behind pale pink adobe walls. What was that song? Oh, yes, he remembered:

> Ya yo me voy
> All puerte donde se alla . . .

It had come back.

*

Next morning John Flint awoke with the thought: What if burglars broke in some afternoon when Amy was alone in the house and killed her for her jewels? It was not impossible. Mrs O'Roylan was a confirmed gossip. Everyone in the neighbourhood must know about Amy's jewels and her odd habit of wearing them in bed. All that day, as he put the last touches on his Bonifoot promotion scheme, he kept the Personnel Manager's letter unanswered on his desk and the thought of burglars in his mind. Now that he had invented them, it seemed somehow certain that they would come. That evening he returned to his house with a fearful expectancy, half dread, half joy, of what he might find. But Amy greeted him with a smile from her bed: it had been one of her good days.

John could never have told exactly when he decided to make the burglars real. But the next day in his office he found himself working out a Plan with the same impersonal efficiency with which he used to tackle one of Bonifoot's problems.

The burglars would come on Thursday afternoon, of course, because Thursday was Mrs O'Roylan's afternoon off and Amy was invariably alone. In his mind's eye he saw burly men, with handkerchiefs tied over their noses and mouths, creeping up the stairs to the bedroom. Amy was lying there in the semi-darkness, behind closed drapes, the jewels gleaming at her throat and ears. She would see the intruders, of course, so they would have to be quick. A pillow pressed on her face – that would stop her cries for help and work swiftly, considering her heart condition, with a minimum of discomfort to her. He could picture the men, after the deed, fumbling the jewels from the limp body and stealing furtively away.

By this time the burglars were so lifelike that it was all he could do to remember that they would, in fact, merely be himself.

And what of him? At the time of the crime, of course, he would have to be far away, in some definite place, where there would be unimpeachable witnesses to his presence.

It seemed obvious that his Bonifoot promotion scheme should somehow provide the alibi. The scheme was a simple publicity stunt which the company had never tried before; but they had been impressed with John's idea and, if his first tests proved successful, they were considering adopting it throughout the nation. Every day for a week, John was going to stand at a busy midtown intersection, taking note of all the wearers of Bonifoot models who passed him on the sidewalk. Every tenth individual who walked by wearing Bonifoot Shoes would be stopped, asked his or her name and address, and then given a coupon entitling the lucky person to a free pair of Bonifoot Shoes at any of the local stores. As a final twist, every hundredth Bonifoot patron who passed by would receive a coupon for five pairs of shoes.

Yes, if the burglars were to kill Amy next Thursday afternoon, John would be standing with his notebook and coupons at the corner of 15th and Market.

But how? That was the kernel of the problem. How could he be at 15th and Market and at his home, three miles away, simultaneously?

It was the thought of Harry Shipley that clinched it. Harry's blank, nondescript face with its typical salesman's grin came into his mind – and suddenly John Flint saw his way.

He called Harry on the phone.

'Hi, Harry. Still interested in that loan?'

'Johnny, old horse!' Harry's voice was thick with eagerness. 'I knew it. I knew old Johnny-boy wouldn't let me down.'

'Fine. How about coming over to the office right now? I've got a little proposition.'

While he was waiting for Harry, John Flint surveyed his own reflection in the mirror behind his desk. He had always disliked his face. It was so depressingly ordinary: a smooth, uneccentric face which could have been worn by any of countless thousands of small businessmen or salesmen; a face, surely, that gave no hint of his own personal uniqueness. But now, for the first time, the colourlessness of the reflection pleased him. He practised a jovial salesman's grin. Yes, that vacuous face might be anyone's face – Harry Shipley's, for example.

He called the railroad station and was told that the Western Express to Reno arrived daily from New York at 6.47 p.m. and left at 6.49 p.m.

When Harry Shipley burst exuberantly into the office, he was wearing grey flannel trousers, and a brand-new, flashy sports jacket, beige with large orange squares. On his necktie, two hand-painted cockers struggled cutely for a bone against a tan background.

'Hi, Harry, how soon are you headed for Reno?'

'Just as soon as I can put my hands on those five hundred smackers.'

'How about holding off until next Thursday?'

'Gee, Johnny, you really mean . . . ?'

'This week I'm up to my neck. Got a promotion project that'll keep me on the streets all day. I need someone to hold down the office. Just to answer the telephone and make a couple of trade calls. That's all it amounts to. If you'll do that for me, I'll write you a cheque right now. You can knock off a hundred bucks for salary and pay me back the rest when you're good and ready.'

As John scribbled the cheque, Harry's gratitude was almost oppressive. Sure, he'd start work tomorrow, sure, he'd do anything for old Johnny. And, boy, come 6.49 p.m. next Thursday this town wasn't going to see him for dust.

When finally Harry got up to leave with the cheque in his pocket, John Flint glanced from his own sober grey lounge suit to the dazzling sports jacket.

'That's a good-looking jacket, Harry. New, isn't it?'

'Sure. Just picked it up the other day at Hunt & Hunt.' Harry fingered the necktie proudly. 'Picked this up too. Sharp, isn't it?'

'Very sharp. Wear them around the office, Harry. I like a snappy dresser. Gives a good impression.'

After Harry had left, John went out to Hunt & Hunt. A sports coat, exactly like Harry's, was on the rack. He bought it. He also bought a tan necktie with gambolling cockers, and a pair of grey flannel trousers. He took the box back to the office and hid it in a closet.

That evening, as he jolted home on the trolley, the lumbering vehicle seemed suddenly to be crammed with Indians. Bunches of Easter lilies, almost sickeningly sweet, seeemed to be jostling against his face. *Bajando*. The air was full of excitable Mexican voices. *Bajando* . . .

It had come back.

Next morning, at nine o'clock sharp, Harry Shipley, in his gaudy sports jacket, all smiles and co-operation, showed up at the office. John explained the routine set-up to him and then sent him off with some new Bonifoot samples to a large department store. Once he had gone, John Flint produced the box from the closet and quite calmly, as if his entire life wasn't changing, slipped into the sports jacket and flannel trousers and knotted the cocker necktie beneath his collar. Putting his own suit back in the box, he returned the box to the closet and studied his reflection in the mirror. His features, actually, were not at all like Harry's. But essential insipidity gave them a kinship. A hearty smile and, for all any casual observer would notice, that might be Harry Shipley beaming back at him from the glass.

With his notebook and his coupons, John Flint took the trolley to 15th and Market. There he spent the day, conscientiously taking down footwear details, giving out the coupons, noting the names and addresses of the recipients. This was his scheme and there was no reason not to make a good job of it. But The Other Thing was always there, excitingly in the back of his mind. It made him take pains to attract the mild attention of the cop on the block and of the cripple who sold newspapers outside the bank building. A casual greeting, a smile, the beige and orange sports coat – they were enough to make him a distinct if unimportant feature of the corner.

During the day he telephoned his office several times to keep a check on any business that had come up. At five o'clock exactly he called for the last time and told Harry he could go home.

Back in the empty office, he typed up his material for the day and changed back into his grey business suit and sober tie, returning his borrowed plumage almost lovingly to the box in the closet.

He repeated this procedure for four days and during those days he behaved at home exactly as he had always behaved. He found it surprisingly easy. Something had happened, something which had made Amy completely unreal to him. Every morning he brought her breakfast tray, every morning he went through the ritual with the jewel box. Every night he slept in the bed next to her. But she wasn't there – especially at night when the Personnel Manager's still unanswered letter glowed in his mind and then slowly, luxuriously, dissolved into a panorama of broad foreign avenues, brilliant with sunshine, lovelier, more desirable than the streets of any earthly city . . .

The fifth day was Thursday. Before John left the house, he unbolted the kitchen door. Later, when Harry, still in the snappy sports jacket, hurried flushed and apologetic into the office a few minutes after nine, John greeted him with a friendly smile.

'Well, Harry, all packed?'

'I'll say I am. Bags all checked at the depot and my ticket bought. Johnny, you old horse thief, if you knew what you'd done for me!'

'Think nothing of it. Look, Harry, something's come up from the head office. I've got to work on it all day and this is the last day of my street survey. Think you could take over the survey for me? You know the Bonifoot models by now.'

'Sure, Johnny, glad to do it.'

It did not take long to brief Harry on the survey. John explained how to make notes of each Bonifoot model that passed, how to handle the free coupons.

'There should be a hundredth coming up today. That person gets the coupon for five pairs of shoes. And always keep a careful time note. That's important. Jot down the exact minute you give out a coupon. I'm using that in my report. And, Harry, no sales talks, no personal conversations with the coupon winners. I want to keep this whole thing dignified.'

'Fine, Johnny. And until five, you say? That's a cinch. Plenty of time to bring my notes back here before I get that train. Boy, that train! Will I be singing hallelujah when I finally see the last of this old town!'

After he had sent Harry off to 15th and Market, John Flint resisted the temptation to write to the Personnel Manager and accept the Mexico City offer. He found an old copy of *Brush up on Your Spanish* in his desk drawer and carried it out with him to lunch. At two-thirty he took the trolley to his home. It was practically empty and, in any case, his ordinary appearance and drab suit were a perfect camouflage against attracting attention.

Now that the moment of climax was approaching, he didn't exactly feel calm. It was a stronger emotion than that. He felt exalted, infinitely capable, as if there was nothing in the world he couldn't carry off. Some kids were playing ball on the corner lot. It was all he could do to keep himself from jumping off the trolley and running to join them. If he hit that ball, it would travel all the way to the moon. That was it – that was where he was going – all the way to the moon . . .

He had to be careful that no one should see him entering the house at this uncharacteristic hour. He dropped off the trolley several stops before his regular one and, choosing a deserted sidestreet, slipped around to the back door of the house. He turned the knob and entered.

It was so long since he had been home on a weekday afternoon that the quiet kitchen seemed oddly unfamiliar. From upstairs, he could hear symphony music playing on Amy's radio. That was odd too. He disliked classical music and he didn't know that Amy ever listened to it. Quietly – although there was no need to be quiet – he went up the stairs and through the open door into the sombre-draped twilight of the bedroom.

Almost before he saw Amy herself, he saw the jewels. They made little glittering areas in the shadowy monotone. Then Amy noticed him and her voice came warm with pleasure, young, the way he remembered it.

'Why, John, what a lovely surprise!'

He crossed to the little alley between the two beds. She was smiling, and in the vague light she looked fragile and girlish. But he had travelled too far into himself to feel any pity for her.

'Oh, John, that music!' She made a move as if to turn off the radio. 'I know you hate it. But lately when I've been lying here alone . . .'

'That's all right, dear. Let me fix your pillows.'

'Thank you, John.'

As he slipped one of the pillows from beneath her head, she patted his sleeve shyly.

'It's wonderful that you've managed a free afternoon on a Thursday, John. Thursdays, without Mrs O'Roylan, always seem to drag so. But then I shan't complain, shall I? I won't spoil this lovely treat. I . . .'

He brought the pillow violently down against her face. The impact of the unexpected blow knocked her head back on to the other pillow. Caught between the two smothering surfaces, she struggled for a little while. Then her body went limp.

John let his pillow drop to the floor. Automatically, as he had acted a thousand times before, he took off the pearl necklace, the diamond earrings, and the diamond-chip bracelet. Only this time, instead of replacing them in the jewel box, he put them in his pocket. He stood for a moment looking at the dimly discerned body which had no reality for him. Then he removed from her dangling wrist the little watch he had given her on their tenth anniversary. He peered at its dial. It said exactly twenty minutes past three. He threw it on the floor repeatedly until it stopped, so that the precise time could be established from it later. Tossing it on the floor by the bed, he tugged drawers open and simulated a hasty search for other valuables. Then, leaving the radio still playing, he walked out of the room.

With a crowbar from the cellar he forced the bolt on the back door to show where the burglars had broken in. Putting the crowbar back where he had found it, he slipped out through the yard and picked up the trolley four blocks away.

He had rather thought, now that he had killed Amy, that It would come back. But no. While he rode into town, he was still John Flint who had just murdered his wife. He did not feel any emotion. But he was still alert, capable, reviewing what he had done, searching painstakingly for flaws. He could find none. All that remained was to get rid of the jewels, to wait in the office for Harry to bring back his notes from the survey, and then to make sure Harry caught that train.

He had already decided the fate of the jewels. He got off the trolley at the stop before the bridge and, carefully choosing his moment as he walked across, dropped them into the grimy river. He saw them go with no pang. The jewels had no part in his future. It hadn't been jewels that he had wanted from Amy.

At exactly five-thirty Harry barged into the office in a state of great excitement and self-satisfaction.

'Here they are, old boy – all the notes. Exactly the way you said. Gave out coupons. Didn't even whistle at a blonde. The real dignified gentleman – that was me.'

He hovered while John studied the pencilled notes. They couldn't have been more desirable. That afternoon, between two and five, two regular coupons had been handed out and at precisely three-fifteen, one special five-shoe coupon had been given to a woman. Her name and address, like that of the other recipients, were neatly marked down with the exact time.

'Fine, Harry. Thanks a lot.'

'You thanking me? That's for laughs. Johnny, old boy, you've saved a life today – that's what you've done.'

Harry's effusive thanks went on for so long that John began to worry about the train. But that was all right too. At ten to six Harry went exuberantly off to the station.

As John studied the notes, he began to feel a deep craftsman's satisfaction. He had pulled it off. He had done what he had set out to do. He had managed to be in two places, three miles away from each other, at one and the same time.

While Amy was being smothered by the burglars in the dimly lit bedroom, he had been at 15th and Market giving a five-shoe coupon to . . . what was the woman's name? He consulted Harry's notes again. Miss Carmen Gonzales, 1374 Pine Street.

Carmen Gonzales. That name, redolent of distant sunshine and soft Mexican laughter, was surely a favourable omen. The two words rang prettily in his ears, as he carefully typed up Harry's notes, added them to the complete file of the survey, and burned the papers which bore Harry's handwriting.

Everything was set now. He changed into the violent sports outfit and packing his grey suit in the box, wrapped it and tucked it under his arm.

At home, he let himself in by the front door as usual. He went straight upstairs. Hardly glancing at the thing on the bed, he unpacked his suit and hung it neatly in the closet. He left the radio still playing and took the empty cardboard box down to the cellar. Then he went to the telephone in the hall. His voice sounded stunned and incredulous even to himself as he called the police.

It was then that a sudden, unrehearsed detail occurred to him. Mrs Roseway next door had often been kind to Amy; she had brought her doughnuts when she baked; and a couple of times she had sat with her at night when John had had to entertain out-of-town salesmen. He ran now to his neighbour's house, beating on the front door with his fists. When Mrs Roseway, plump and amiable, appeared, he gasped:

'Amy! Quick! Something terrible has happened to Amy!'

Mrs Roseway was with him when the police arrived. And while he hunched in apparent apathy in the living-room, Mrs Roseway took them upstairs. Through the long confused interval that followed, when the house seemed to be full of a regiment of plain clothes men and police officers, Mrs Roseway was constantly at John's side, encouraging and comforting him. It was Mrs Roseway who confirmed the fact that Amy had always worn her jewels in bed and that the jewels were missing. And after John had given his own faltering statement, she plunged to the defence of his as yet unchallenged character. John Flint, she said, was a model citizen, the most affectionate, the most admirable husband on the block.

The Police Inspector, like everyone else, treated her with respect and, partly for her sake perhaps, was as tender with John as a godfather. When the investigation was finally over, it was obvious that John would have to go with the police to the precinct headquarters. But the Inspector patted his shoulder.

'This is a clear case of breaking and entering. And we can prove you were miles away at the time. But we'd better drop by your office, pick up the records of that survey, and check with those people you say you've got on the list. That'll establish it once and for all. And you'll feel better when we get that alibi on record for you.'

'Of course,' said John. 'Thanks. I'm ready to go whenever you are.'

They drove to the office. John gave the survey file to the Inspector. At headquarters, policemen were sent to pick up the three people whose names and addresses appeared on the afternoon list and also, at John's suggestion, the cop on the corner and the crippled newsvendor.

The cop and the newsvendor were the first to be brought in. They both glanced at John, sitting by the Inspector's desk.

'Yeah,' said the cop, 'he's been around the block all week doing a survey or something.'

'That's right,' said the newsvendor. 'Seen him every day.'

The first of the coupon recipients was an elderly woman with the slightly harassed air of a solid citizen unused to police stations. On the Inspector's instructions, she studied John carefully and then said:

'Yes, that's the man who gave me the coupon. I wouldn't forget that coat. This – this doesn't mean the coupon's no good, does it? I haven't used it yet but I was planning . . .'

'No, lady. The coupon's fine.' The Inspector consulted John's typewritten list. 'It says here he gave you the coupon at two-ten. That right?'

'Yes, that would have been it. I had just been around to the five-and-dime store to match some wool and . . .'

'Okay, lady, that'll be all. Thank you.'

The second coupon winner was a young man with a jaunty air. He was even more satisfactory than the woman.

'Sure. I remember that tie. Pretty keen. Figured I might buy one just like it. Keen.'

All that was needed now was Carmen Gonzales. Once she arrived and established the key moment of the alibi, this would be over. John Flint, leaning back in the wooden chair, began to feel a strange affection for the stuffy, drab atmosphere of the police station. He had never been in one before and he hadn't expected it to be like this. It was almost cosy. But only his surface was reacting to it. Underneath, holding itself patiently in check, but waiting, waiting to surge up again, was It.

And as he sat there, John Flint began to realize something immensely important was happening inside him. All his life, up till now, he had been haunted by a nagging sense of failure. Even It, if he ever dared to admit it, had been only a day-dream, a compensation for the dreariness of reality, a shimmering mirage of what might have been but never would be. He had never really believed he would get to Mexico. No, even after he had started to plan Amy's death, he had never believed that It could actually be achieved.

But he had done it. Miraculously, by his own unaided efforts, he had forced life to go his way. He, John Flint, had done that, calmly, efficiently, without a faltering step. Who else among his circle of friends and acquaintances could have pulled off so magnificent an enterprise. Harry? The idea was laughable. He felt a growing wonder at himself and a new, burnished pride.

It was half an hour before Miss Carmen Gonzales was brought in by the officer. She was young, dark, pretty as an exotic tropical flower, and at the sight of her It was suddenly released in John and exaltation rose through him. *Señorita*. That was the word that came with her, and magically, once again, the broad paseos, the softly padding Indians, the little boys scurrying around vending lottery tickets – all vibrant in his mind, beckoning . . .

Come, come . . . come to us . . . we are all yours at last . . .

John was hardly paying any attention to what was happening now, but he saw the girl glance quickly at him and then turn nervously to the Inspector. She was obviously ill at ease. That touched him. You couldn't expect an exquisite little girl like that to be calm in a police station.

The Inspector said: 'You are Miss Carmen Gonzales of 1374 Pine Street?'

'Yes, sir. But what's the matter? The officer wouldn't tell me. Why have you brought me here? What have I done?'

Carmen Gonzales was drifting into it now. Hand in hand, John and this lovely girl were walking down leaf-fringed boulevards – to the bull-fights, perhaps . . .

'Now, there's nothing to be frightened of, miss,' said the Inspector paternally. 'We just want you to answer a few questions. This afternoon at the corner of 15th and Market Street did you receive a coupon entitling you to five free pairs of Bonifoot Shoes?'

A flush started to spread under the girl's dusky cheeks. 'I haven't used it yet. I can give it back.'

'That won't be necessary, miss.'

Suddenly the girl spun to John and clutched his arm. 'Oh, Mr Flint – you must be Mr Flint, aren't you? – I'm sorry. You've been so wonderful to Harry. He's told me about the loan and everything. I knew we shouldn't have done it.' Her pretty pleading face was close to his. 'I told Harry it was mean, petty, almost like stealing. But he thought you wouldn't mind. He said that the five-pairs coupon had to go to someone – so why shouldn't I be the hundredth person to walk by? You see, having to get the trousseau and everything to join Harry in Reno . . . Five pairs of shoes, it did seem such a wonderful chance. But we shouldn't have done it. Oh, Mr Flint, you're kind. I know you're kind. Don't make a charge against Harry; don't have him arrested.'

What was happening inside John Flint was terrible. It was as if an atomic bomb had plunged from the air without a sound of warning, raging into his dream city, cracking the tall buildings, splitting the boulevards, smothering the sunlight in a miasma of dust.

'Harry?' barked the Inspector. 'Who's this Harry?'

The girl turned. 'He's my fiancé. And Mr Flint has been wonderful to him, lending him money for the divorce, giving him a job as his assistant when he didn't really need one. Just to be kind. This afternoon he sent Harry on the street survey and – well, Harry shouldn't have done it, but he called me up and told me if I joined him right away on 15th and Market, I would be able to get the free coupon. He . . .'

Carmen Gonzales spun back to John Flint, leaning toward him, pathetically eager to justify herself, to convince him that, even though she and Harry had done a shoddy act, they were genuinely sorry.

'Please, Mr Flint.' Awkwardly she fumbled the coupon from her pocketbook and held it out to him. 'Take it. I couldn't ever use it. Five pairs of shoes! Why, that'd be over fifty dollars! I can't imagine how we could have been so – so despicable.'

Her warm young smile was like the grin of Disaster stalking through the ruins.

'And, Mr Flint, I only hope that one day *you'll* be in trouble. Then Harry and I will really be able to prove our gratitude.'

Edgar Allan Poe

THOU ART
THE MAN

The five stories of crime and detection written by Edgar Allan Poe (1809–49) contain the germ of a great deal that has been written in what is almost a century and a half since 'The Murders in the Rue Morgue' appeared in 1841. This was the first locked room story. 'The Purloined Letter' is the forerunner of many tales in which a clue or a solution is overlooked because it seems too obvious; 'The Gold-Bug' is among the first of all those stories in which a cipher or a code plays a vital part; and 'The Mystery of Marie Rôget' is the original of many crime stories making a documentary approach, as well as of those based on a real-life crime. Such fiction was only a small part of Poe's output, and he sometimes spoke slightingly of it, saying that 'people think them [his crime stories] more ingenious than they are, on account of their method and *air* of method'. Yet he was the father of the detective story, even though he would have disapproved of many of his descendants.

There remains among the five stories 'Thou Art the Man', printed here. This is sometimes called a comic story, and certainly it has comic elements of the jovially brutal kind that Poe occasionally favoured. It is also, however, emphatically a tale of detection, including false clues planted by the villain, and almost the first use of ballistics – of an elementary kind, it is true – in a crime story. The use of ventriloquism was popular with writers in the early nineteenth century who wanted to provide a surprise, although Poe typically used it in a very outrageous form.

I will now play the Oedipus to the Rattleborough enigma. I will expound to you – as I alone can – the secret of the enginery that effected the Rattleborough miracle – the one, the true, the admitted, the undisputed, the indisputable miracle, which put a definite end to infidelity among the Rattleburghers, and converted to the orthodoxy of the grandames all the carnal-minded who had ventured to be sceptical before.

This event – which I should be sorry to discuss in a tone of unsuitable levity – occurred in the summer of 18—. Mr Barnabas Shuttleworthy – one of the wealthiest and most respectable citizens of the borough – had been missing for several days under circumstances which gave rise to suspicion of foul play. Mr Shuttleworthy had set out from Rattleborough very early one Saturday morning, on horseback, with the avowed intention of proceeding to the city of —, about fifteen miles distant, and of returning the night of the same day. Two hours after his departure, however, his horse returned without him, and without the saddle-bags which had been strapped on his back at starting. The animal was wounded, too, and covered with mud. These circumstances naturally gave rise to much alarm among the friends of the missing man; and when it was found, on Sunday morning, that he had not yet made his appearance, the whole borough arose *en masse* to go and look for his body.

The foremost and most energetic in instituting this search, was the bosom friend of Mr Shuttleworthy – a Mr Charles Goodfellow or, as he was universally called, 'Charley Goodfellow', or 'Old Charley Goodfellow'. Now, whether it is a marvellous coincidence, or whether it is that the name itself has an imperceptible effect upon the character, I have never yet been able to ascertain; but the fact is unquestionable, that there never yet was any person named Charles who was not an open, manly, honest, good-natured, and frank-hearted fellow, with a rich, clear voice, that did you good to hear it, and an eye that looked you always straight in the face, as much as to say, 'I have a clear conscience myself; am afraid of no man, and am altogether above doing a mean action.' And thus all the hearty, careless, 'walking gentlemen' of the stage are very certain to be called Charles.

Now, 'Old Charley Goodfellow', although he had been in Rattleborough not longer than six months or thereabouts, and although nobody knew anything about him before he came to settle in the neighborhood, had experienced no difficulty in the world in making the acquaintance of all the respectable people in the borough. Not a man of them but would have taken his bare word for a thousand at any moment; and as for the women, there is no saying what they would not have done to oblige him. And all this came of his having been christened Charles, and of his possessing, in consequence, that ingenuous face which is proverbially the very 'best letter of recommendation'.

I have already said that Mr Shuttleworthy was one of the most respectable, and, undoubtedly, he was the most wealthy man in Rattle-borough, while 'Old Charley Goodfellow' was upon as intimate terms with him as if he had been his own brother. The two old gentlemen were next-door neighbors, and, although Mr Shuttleworthy seldom, if ever, visited 'Old Charley', and never was known to take a meal in his house, still this did not prevent the two friends from being exceedingly intimate, as I have just observed; for 'Old Charley' never let a day pass without stepping in three or four times to see how his neighbor came on, and very often he would stay to breakfast, or tea, and almost always to dinner; and then the amount of wine that was made way with by the two cronies at a sitting, it would really be a difficult thing to ascertain. Old Charley's favorite beverage was Château Margaux, and it appeared to do Mr Shuttleworthy's heart good to see the old fellow swallow it, as he did, quart after quart; so that, one day, when the wine was *in* and the wit, as a natural consequence, somewhat *out*, he said to his crony, as he slapped him upon the back – 'I tell you what it is, Old Charley, you are, by all odds, the heartiest old fellow I ever came across in all my born days; and, since you love to guzzle the wine at that fashion, I'll be darned if I don't have to make thee a present of a big box of the Château Margaux. Od rot me' – (Mr Shuttleworthy had a sad habit of swearing, although he seldom went beyond 'Od rot me', or 'By gosh', or 'By the jolly golly') – 'Od rot me,' says he, 'if I don't send an order to town this very afternoon for a double box of the best that can be got, and I'll make ye a present of it, I will! – ye needn't say a word now – I *will*, I tell ye, and there's an end of it; so look out for it – it will come to hand some of these fine days, precisely when ye are looking for it the least!' I mention this little bit of liberality on the part of Mr Shuttleworthy, just by way of showing you how *very* intimate an understanding existed between the two friends.

Well, on the Sunday morning in question, when it came to be fairly understood that Mr Shuttleworthy had met with foul play, I never saw anyone so profoundly affected as 'Old Charley Goodfellow'. When he first heard that the horse had come home without his master, and without his master's saddle-bags, and all bloody from a pistol-shot, that had gone clean through and through the poor animal's chest without quite killing him – when he heard all this, he turned as pale as if the missing man had been his own dear brother or father, and shivered and shook all over as if he had had a fit of the ague.

At first, he was too much overpowered with grief to be able to do anything at all, or to decide upon any plan of action; so that for a long time he endeavored to dissuade Mr Shuttleworthy's other friends from making a stir about the matter, thinking it best to wait awhile – say for a week or two or a month or two – to see if something wouldn't turn up, or if Mr Shuttleworthy wouldn't come in the natural way, and explain his reasons for sending his horse on before. I dare say you have often observed this disposition to temporize, or to procrastinate, in people who are laboring under any very poignant sorrow. Their powers of mind seem to be rendered torpid, so that they have a horror of anything like action, and like nothing in the world so well as to lie quietly in bed and 'nurse their grief', as the old ladies express it – that is to say, ruminate over their trouble.

The people of Rattleborough had, indeed, so high an opinion of the wisdom and discretion of 'Old Charley' that the greater part of them felt disposed to agree with him, and not make a stir in the business 'until something should turn up', as the honest old gentleman worded it; and I believe that, after all, this would have been the general determination, but for the very suspicious interference of Mr Shuttleworthy's nephew, a young man of very dissipated habits, and otherwise of rather bad character. This nephew, whose name was Pennifeather, would listen to nothing like reason in the matter of 'lying quiet', but insisted upon making immediate search for the 'corpse of the murdered man'. This was the expression he employed; and Mr Goodfellow acutely remarked, at the time, that it was 'a *singular* expression, to say no more'. This remark of Old Charley's, too, had great effect upon the crowd; and one of the party was heard to ask, very impressively, 'how it happened that young Mr Pennifeather was so intimately cognizant of all the circumstances connected with his wealthy uncle's disappearance, as to feel authorized to assert, distinctly and unequivocally, that his uncle *was* "a murdered man".' Hereupon some little squibbing and bickering occurred among various members of the crowd, and especially between 'Old Charley' and Mr Pennifeather –

although this latter occurrence was, indeed, by no means a novelty, for little good will had subsisted between the parties for the last three or four months; and matters had even gone so far that Mr Pennifeather had actually knocked down his uncle's friend for some alleged excess of liberty that the latter had taken in the uncle's house, of which the nephew was an inmate. Upon this occasion, 'Old Charley' is said to have behaved with exemplary moderation and Christian charity. He arose from the blow, adjusted his clothes, and made no attempt at retaliation at all – merely muttering a few words about 'taking summary vengeance at the first convenient opportunity' – a natural and very justifiable ebullition of anger, which meant nothing, however, and, beyond doubt, was no sooner given vent to than forgotten.

However these matters may be (which have no reference to the point now at issue), it is quite certain that the people of Rattleborough, principally through the persuasion of Mr Pennifeather, came at length to the determination of dispersing over the adjacent country in search of the missing Mr Shuttleworthy. I say they came to this determination in the first instance. After it had been fully resolved that a search should be made, it was considered almost a matter of course that the seekers should disperse – that is to say, distribute themselves in parties – for the more thorough examination of the region round about. I forget, however, by what ingenious train of reasoning it was that 'Old Charley' finally convinced the assembly that this was the most injudicious plan that could be pursued. Convince them, however, he did – all except Mr Pennifeather; and, in the end, it was arranged that a search should be instituted, carefully and very thoroughly, by the burghers *en masse*, 'Old Charley' himself leading the way.

As for the matter of that, there could have been no better pioneer than 'Old Charley', whom everybody knew to have the eye of a lynx; but, although he led them into all manner of out-of-the-way holes and corners, by routes that nobody had ever suspected of existing in the neighborhood, and although the search was incessantly kept up day and night for nearly a week, still no trace of Mr Shuttleworthy could be discovered. When I say no trace, however, I must not be understood to speak literally; for trace, to some extent, there certainly was. The poor gentleman had been tracked, by his horse's shoes (which were peculiar), to a spot about three miles to the east of the borough, on the main road leading to the city. Here the track made off into a by-path through a piece of woodland – the path coming out again into the main road, and cutting off about half a mile of the regular distance. Following the shoe-marks down this lane, the party

came at length to a pool of stagnant water, half hidden by the brambles to
the right of the lane, and opposite this pool all vestige of the track was lost
sight of. It appeared, however, that a struggle of some nature had here
taken place, and it seemed as if some large and heavy body, much larger
and heavier than a man, had been drawn from the by-path to the pool.
This latter was carefully dragged twice, but nothing was found; and the
party were upon the point of going away, in despair of coming to any
result, when Providence suggested to Mr Goodfellow the expediency of
draining the water off altogether. This project was received with cheers,
and many high compliments to 'Old Charley' upon his sagacity and
consideration. As many of the burghers had brought spades with them,
supposing that they might possibly be called upon to disinter a corpse, the
drain was easily and speedily effected; and no sooner was the bottom
visible, than right in the middle of the mud that remained was discovered
a black silk velvet waistcoat, which nearly everyone present immediately
recognized as the property of Mr Pennifeather. This waistcoat was much
torn and stained with blood, and there were several persons among the
party who had a distinct remembrance of its having been worn by its
owner on the very morning of Mr Shuttleworthy's departure for the city;
while there were others, again, ready to testify upon oath, if required, that
Mr P. did *not* wear the garment in question at any period during the
remainder of that memorable day; nor could anyone be found to say that he
had seen it upon Mr P.'s person at any period at all subsequent to Mr
Shuttleworthy's disappearance.

Matters now wore a very serious aspect for Mr Pennifeather, and it
was observed, as an indubitable confirmation of the suspicions which
were excited against him, that he grew exceedingly pale, and when asked
what he had to say for himself, was utterly incapable of saying a word.
Hereupon, the few friends his riotous mode of living had left him deserted
him at once to a man, and were even more clamorous than his ancient
and avowed enemies for his instantaneous arrest. But, on the other hand,
the magnanimity of Mr Goodfellow shone forth with only the more
brilliant lustre through contrast. He made a warm and intensely eloquent
defence of Mr Pennifeather, in which he alluded more than once to his
own sincere forgiveness of that wild young gentleman – 'the heir of the
worthy Mr Shuttleworthy' – for the insult which he (the young gentleman) had, no doubt in the heat of passion, thought proper to put upon
him (Mr Goodfellow). 'He forgave him for it,' he said, 'from the very
bottom of his heart; and for himself (Mr Goodfellow), so far from pushing
the suspicious circumstances to extremity, which, he was sorry to say,

really *had* arisen against Mr Pennifeather, he (Mr Goodfellow) would make every exertion in his power, would employ all the little eloquence in his possession to – to – to – soften down, as much as he could conscientiously do so, the worst features of this really exceedingly perplexing piece of business.'

Mr Goodfellow went on for some half hour longer in this strain, very much to the credit both of his head and of his heart; but your warm-hearted people are seldom apposite in their observations – they run into all sorts of blunders, *contre-temps* and *mal apropos-isms*, in the hot-headedness of their zeal to serve a friend – thus, often with the kindest intentions in the world, doing infinitely more to prejudice his cause than to advance it.

So, in the present instance, it turned out with all the eloquence of 'Old Charley'; for, although he labored earnestly in behalf of the suspected, yet it so happened, somehow or other, that every syllable he uttered of which the direct but unwitting tendency was not to exalt the speaker in the good opinion of his audience, had the effect of deepening the suspicion already attached to the individual whose cause he pleaded, and of arousing against him the fury of the mob.

One of the most unaccountable errors committed by the orator was his allusion to the suspected as 'the heir of the worthy old gentleman Mr Shuttleworthy'. The people had really never thought of this before. They had only remembered certain threats of disinheritance uttered a year or two previously by the uncle (who had no living relative except the nephew); and they had, therefore, always looked upon this disinheritance as a matter that was settled – so single-minded a race of beings were the Rattleburghers; but the remark of 'Old Charley' brought them at once to a consideration of this point, and thus gave them to see the possibility of the threat having been nothing *more* than a threat. And straightaway, hereupon, arose the natural question of *cui bono?* – a question that tended even more than the waistcoat to fasten the terrible crime upon the young man. And here, lest I be misunderstood, permit me to digress for one moment merely to observe that the exceedingly brief and simple Latin phrase which I have employed, is invariably mistranslated and misconceived. '*Cui bono*', in all the crack novels and elsewhere – in those of Mrs Gore, for example (the author of 'Cecil'), a lady who quotes all tongues from the Chaldaean to Chickasaw, and is helped to her learning, 'as needed', upon a systematic plan, by Mr Beckford – in *all* the crack novels, I say, from those of Bulwer and Dickens to those of Turnapenny and Ainsworth, the two little Latin words *cui bono* are rendered 'to what purpose', or (as if *quo bono*), 'to what good'. Their true meaning, nevertheless, is 'for whose advantage'. *Cui*, to whom; *bono*, is it for a benefit. It is a purely legal phrase, and applicable precisely in cases such as we have now under consideration, where the probability of the doer of a deed hinges upon the probability of the benefit accruing to this individual or to that from the deed's accomplishment. Now, in the present instance, the question *cui bono* very pointedly implicated Mr Pennifeather. His uncle had threatened him, after making a will in his favor, with disinheritance. But the threat had not been actually kept; the original will, it appeared, had not been altered. *Had* it been altered, the only supposable motive for murder on the part of the suspected would have been the ordinary one of revenge; and even this would have been counteracted by the hope of reinstation into the good graces of the uncle. But the will being unaltered, while the threat to alter remained suspended over the nephew's head, there appears at once the very strongest possible inducement for the atrocity: and so concluded, very sagaciously, the worthy citizens of the borough of Rattle.

Mr Pennifeather was, accordingly, arrested upon the spot, and the crowd, after some farther search, proceeded homewards, having him in custody. On the route, however, another circumstance occurred tending to confirm the suspicion entertained. Mr Goodfellow, whose zeal led him to be always a little in advance of the party, was seen suddenly to run forward a few paces, stoop, and then apparently to pick up some small object from the grass. Having quickly examined it, he was observed, too, to make a sort of half attempt at concealing it in his coat pocket; but this action was noticed, as I say, and consequently prevented, when the object picked up was found to be a Spanish knife which a dozen persons at once recognized as belonging to Mr Pennifeather. Moreover, his initials were engraved upon the handle. The blade of this knife was open and bloody.

No doubt now remained of the guilt of the nephew, and immediately upon reaching Rattleborough he was taken before a magistrate for examination.

Here matters again took a most unfavorable turn. The prisoner, being questioned as to his whereabouts on the morning of Mr Shuttleworth's disappearance, had absolutely the audacity to acknowledge that on that very morning he had been out with his rifle deer-stalking, in the immediate neighborhood of the pool where the bloodstained waistcoat had been discovered through the sagacity of Mr Goodfellow.

This latter now came forward, and, with tears in his eyes, asked permission to be examined. He said that a stern sense of the duty he owed his Maker, not less than his fellow-men, would permit him no longer to remain silent. Hitherto, the sincerest affection for the young man (notwithstanding the latter's ill treatment of himself, Mr Goodfellow), had induced him to make every hypothesis which imagination could suggest, by way of endeavoring to account for what appeared suspicious in the circumstances that told so seriously against Mr Pennifeather; but these circumstances were now altogether *too* convincing – *too* damning; he would hesitate no longer – he would tell all he knew, although his heart (Mr Goodfellow's) should absolutely burst asunder in the effort. He then went on to state that, on the afternoon of the day previous to Mr Shuttleworthy's departure for the city, that worthy old gentleman had mentioned to his nephew, in *his* hearing (Mr Goodfellow's), that his object in going to town on the morrow was to make a deposit of an unusually large sum of money in the 'Farmers' and Mechanics' Bank', and that, then and there, the said Mr Shuttleworthy had distinctly avowed to the said nephew his irrevocable determination of rescinding the will originally made and of cutting him off with a shilling. He (the witness) now solemnly called upon the accused to state whether what he (the witness) had just stated was or was not the truth in every substantial particular. Much to the astonishment of everyone present, Mr Pennifeather frankly admitted that *it was*.

The magistrate now considered it his duty to send a couple of constables to search the chamber of the accused in the house of his uncle. From this search they almost immediately returned with the well-known steel-bound, russet-leather pocket-book which the old gentleman had been in the habit of carrying for years. Its valuable contents, however, had been abstracted, and the magistrate in vain endeavored to extort from the prisoner the use which had been made of them, or the place of their concealment. Indeed, he obstinately denied all knowledge of the matter. The constables also discovered, between the bed and sacking of the unhappy man, a shirt and neck-handkerchief both marked with the initials of his name, and both hideously besmeared with the blood of the victim.

At this juncture, it was announced that the horse of the murdered man had just expired in the stable from the effects of the wound he had received, and it was proposed by Mr Goodfellow that a *post mortem* examination of the beast should be immediately made, with the view, if possible, of discovering the ball. This was accordingly done; and, as if to demonstrate beyond a question the guilt of the accused, Mr Goodfellow, after considerable searching in the cavity of the chest, was enabled to detect and to pull forth a bullet of very extraordinary size, which, upon trial, was found to be exactly adapted to the bore of Mr Pennifeather's rifle, while it was far too large for that of any other person in the borough or its vicinity. To render the matter even surer yet, however, this bullet was discovered to have a flaw or seam at right angles to the usual suture; and upon examination, this seam corresponded precisely with an accidental ridge or elevation in a pair of moulds acknowledged by the accused himself to be his own property. Upon the finding of this bullet, the examining magistrate refused to listen to any farther testimony, and immediately committed the prisoner for trial – declining resolutely to take any bail in the case, although against this severity Mr Goodfellow very warmly remonstrated, and offered to become surety in whatever amount might be required. This generosity on the part of 'Old Charley' was only in accordance with the whole tenor of his amiable and chivalrous conduct during the entire period of his sojourn in the borough of Rattle. In the present instance, the worthy man was so entirely carried away by the excessive warmth of his sympathy, that he seemed to have quite forgotten, when he offered to go bail for his young friend, that he himself (Mr Goodfellow) did not possess a single dollar's worth of property upon the face of the earth.

The result of the committal may be readily foreseen. Mr Pennifeather, amid the loud execrations of all Rattleborough, was brought to trial at the next criminal sessions, when the chain of circumstantial evidence (strengthened as it was by some additional damning facts, which Mr Goodfellow's sensitive conscientiousness forbade him to withhold from the court) was considered so unbroken and so thoroughly conclusive, that the jury, without leaving their seats, returned an immediate verdict of '*Guilty of murder in the first degree*'. Soon afterwards the unhappy wretch received sentence of death, and was remanded to the county jail to await the inexorable vengeance of the law.

In the mean time, the noble behavior of 'Old Charley Goodfellow' had doubly endeared him to the honest citizens of the borough. He became ten times a greater favorite than ever; and, as a natural result of the hospitality with which he was treated, he relaxed, as it were, perforce, the extremely parsimonious habits which his poverty had hitherto impelled him to observe, and very frequently had little *réunions* at his own house, when wit and jollity reigned supreme – dampened a little, *of course*, by the occasional remembrance of the untoward and melancholy fate which impended over the nephew of the late lamented bosom friend of the generous host.

One fine day, this magnanimous old gentleman was agreeably surprised at the receipt of the following letter:

'*Charles Goodfellow, Esquire –*

'*Dear Sir – In conformity with an order transmitted to our firm about two months since, by our esteemed correspondent, Mr Barnabas Shuttleworthy, we have the honor of forwarding this morning, to your address, a double box of Château Margaux, of the antelope brand, violet seal. Box numbered and marked as per margin.*

'*We remain, sir,*

'*Your most ob'nt ser'ts,*

Hoggs, Frogs, Bogs & Co.

'*City of —, June 21st, 18—.*

P.S. – The box will reach you, by wagon, on the day after your receipt of this letter. Our respects to Mr Shuttleworthy.

H.F.B. & Co.'

The fact is, that Mr Goodfellow had, since the death of Mr Shuttleworthy, given over all expectation of ever receiving the promised Château Margaux; and he, therefore, looked upon it *now* as a sort of especial dispensation of Providence in his behalf. He was highly delighted, of course, and in the exuberance of his joy, invited a large party of friends to a *petit souper* on the morrow, for the purpose of broaching the good old Mr Shuttleworthy's present. Not that he *said* anything about 'the good old Mr Shuttleworthy' when he issued the invitations. The fact is, he thought much and concluded to say nothing at all. He did *not* mention to anyone – if I remember aright – that he had received a *present* of Château Margaux. He merely asked his friends to come and help him drink some of a remarkably fine quality and rich flavor, that he had ordered up from the city a couple of months ago, and of which he would be in the receipt upon the morrow. I have often puzzled myself to imagine *why* it was that 'Old Charley' came to the conclusion to say nothing about having received the wine from his old friend, but I could never precisely understand his reason for the silence, although he had *some* excellent and very magnanimous reason, no doubt.

The morrow at length arrived, and with it a very large and highly respectable company at Mr Goodfellow's house. Indeed, half the borough was there – I myself among the number – but, much to the vexation of the host, the Château Margaux did not arrive until a late hour, and when the sumptuous supper supplied by 'Old Charley' had been done very ample justice by the guests. It came at length, however – a monstrously big box of it there was, too – and as the whole party were in excessively good humor, it was decided, *nem. con.*, that it should be lifted upon the table and its contents disemboweled forthwith.

No sooner said than done. I lent a helping hand; and, in a trice, we had the box upon the table, in the midst of all the bottles and glasses, not a few of which were demolished in the scuffle. 'Old Charley', who was pretty much intoxicated, and excessively red in the face, now took a seat, with an air of mock dignity, at the head of the board, and thumped furiously upon it with a decanter, calling upon the company to keep order 'during the ceremony of disinterring the treasure'.

After some vociferation, quiet was at length fully restored, and, as very often happens in similar cases, a profound and remarkable silence ensued. Being then requested to force open the lid, I complied, of course, 'with an infinite deal of pleasure'. I inserted a chisel, and giving it a few slight taps with a hammer, the top of the box flew suddenly and violently off, and, at the same instant, there sprang up into a sitting position, directly facing the host, the bruised, bloody and nearly putrid corpse of the murdered Mr Shuttleworthy himself. It gazed for a few moments, fixed and sorrowfully, with its decaying and lack-lustre eyes, full into the countenance of Mr Goodfellow; uttered slowly, but clearly and impressively, the words – 'Thou art the man!' and then, falling over the side of the chest as if thoroughly satisfied, stretched out its limbs quiveringly upon the table.

The scene that ensued is altogether beyond description. The rush for the doors and windows was terrific, and many of the most robust men in the room fainted outright through sheer horror. But after the first wild, shrieking burst of affright, all eyes were directed to Mr Goodfellow. If I live a thousand years, I can never forget the more than mortal agony which was depicted in that ghastly face of his, so lately rubicund with triumph and wine. For several minutes, he sat rigidly as a statue of marble; his eyes seeming, in the intense vacancy of their gaze, to be turned inwards and absorbed in the contemplation of his own miserable, murderous soul. At length, their expression appeared to flash suddenly out into the external world, when with a quick leap, he sprang from his chair, and falling heavily with his head and shoulders upon the table, and in contact with the corpse, poured out rapidly and vehemently a detailed confession of the hideous crime for which Mr Pennifeather was then imprisoned and doomed to die.

What he recounted was in substance this: He followed his victim to the vicinity of the pool; there shot his horse with a pistol; despatched the rider with its butt end; possessed himself of the pocket-book; and, supposing the horse dead, dragged it with great labor to the brambles by the pond. Upon his own beast he slung the corpse of Mr Shuttleworthy, and thus bore it to a secure place of concealment a long distance off through the woods.

The waistcoat, the knife, the pocket-book and bullet, had been placed by himself where found, with the view of avenging himself upon Mr Pennifeather. He had also contrived the discovery of the stained handkerchief and shirt.

Towards the end of the blood-chilling recital, the words of the guilty wretch faltered and grew hollow. When the record was finally exhausted, he arose, staggered backwards from the table, and fell – *dead*.

The means by which this happily timed confession was extorted, although efficient, were simple indeed. Mr Goodfellow's excess of frankness had disgusted me, and excited my suspicions from the first. I was present when Mr Pennifeather had struck him, and the fiendish expression which then arose upon his countenance, although momentary, assured me that his threat of vengeance would, if possible, be rigidly fulfilled. I was thus prepared to view the manoeuvring of 'Old Charley' in a very different light from that in which it was regarded by the good citizens of Rattleborough. I saw at once that all the criminating discoveries arose, either directly, or indirectly, from himself. But the fact which clearly opened my eyes to the true state of the case, was the affair of the bullet, *found* by Mr G. in the carcass of the horse. *I* had not forgotten, although the Rattleburghers *had*, that there was a hole where the ball had entered the horse, and another where it *went out*. If it were found in the animal then, after having made its exit, I saw clearly that it must have been deposited by the person who found it. The bloody shirt and handkerchief confirmed the idea suggested by the bullet; for the blood upon examination proved to be capital claret, and no more. When I came to think of these things, and also of the late increase of liberality and expenditure on the part of Mr Goodfellow, I entertained a suspicion which was none the less strong because I kept it altogether to myself.

In the mean time, I instituted a rigorous private search for the corpse of Mr Shuttleworthy, and, for good reasons, searched in quarters as divergent as possible from those to which Mr Goodfellow conducted his party. The result was that, after some days, I came across an old dry well, the mouth of which was nearly hidden by brambles; and here, at the bottom, I discovered what I sought.

Now it so happened that I had overheard the colloquy between the two cronies, when Mr Goodfellow had contrived to cajole his host into the promise of a box of Château Margaux. Upon this hint I acted. I procured a stiff piece of whalebone, thrust it down the throat of the corpse, and deposited the latter in an old wine box – taking care so to double the body

THOU ART THE MAN

up as to double the whalebone with it. In this manner I had to press
forcibly upon the lid to keep it down while I secured it with nails; and I
anticipated, of course, that as soon as these latter were removed, the top
would *fly off* and the body *up*.

Having thus arranged the box, I marked, numbered and addressed it as
already told; and then writing a letter in the name of the wine merchants
with whom Mr Shuttleworthy dealt, I gave instructions to my servant to
wheel the box to Mr Goodfellow's door, in a barrow, at a given signal from
myself. For the words which I intended the corpse to speak, I confidently
depended upon my ventriloquial abilities; for their effect, I counted upon
the conscience of the murderous wretch.

I believe there is nothing more to be explained. Mr Pennifeather was
released upon the spot, inherited the fortune of his uncle, profited by the
lessons of experience, turned over a new leaf, and led happily ever
afterwards a new life.

Ellery Queen

THE ADVENTURE OF
THE BEARDED LADY

Ellery Queen was a pseudonym used by two cousins, Frederic Dannay (1905–82), who was born Daniel Nathan, and Manfred Bennington Lee (1905–71), born Manfred Lepofsky. It was also the name they chose for their detective, who appeared in many novels, from *The Roman Hat Mystery* (1929) onwards, and in several collections of short stories.

In the early tales Ellery is an immensely affected figure equipped with cane and monocle, from whose lips classical quotations drop thick as autumn leaves. Judged as exercises in rational deduction, however, the first ten Queen novels are among the best detective stories ever written. The *French Powder, Dutch Shoe, Greek Coffin* and *Chinese Orange* mysteries are particularly recommended. Later Ellery was made more human, and the puzzles became less strictly cerebral. Two of the best among these books are *Calamity Town* and *The Murderer is a Fox*. Later still, after 1950, the quality of the stories declined sharply.

Something similar happened to Queen as a short-story writer. The first two collections, *The Adventures of Ellery Queen* (1934) and *The New Adventures* (1940) contain stories of truly dazzling cleverness. One reads them not for the characters, but for the tricks played on the reader, and puts them down with a sigh of satisfaction at having been so thoroughly and fairly baffled. 'The Bearded Lady' comes from the first collection, in which there is not a single weak or illogical puzzle. The later volumes of short stories, like the later novels, are much less convincing.

Frederic Dannay also deserves remembrance by all who enjoy crime short stories as the founder in 1941 of *Ellery Queen's Mystery Magazine*, which is by far the best magazine ever devoted to the form. He was also a scholar of the field (his bibliography of *The Detective Short Story* was a landmark at the time of its publication in 1942, and remains a valuable work of reference), an enthusiast for all forms of crime story, and a discerning and encouraging nurse of talent.

Mr Phineas Mason, attorney-at-law – of the richly, almost indigestibly respectable firm of Dowling, Mason & Coolidge, 40 Park Row – was a very un-Phineaslike gentleman with a chunky nose and wrinkle-bedded eyes which had seen thirty years of harassing American litigation and looked as if they had seen a hundred. He sat stiffly in the lap of a chauffeur-driven limousine, his mouth making interesting sounds.

'And now,' he said in an angry voice, 'there's actually been murder done. I can't imagine what the world is coming to.'

Mr Ellery Queen, watching the world rush by in a glaring Long Island sunlight, mused that life was like a Spanish wench: full of surprises, none of them delicate and all of them stimulating. Since he was a monastic who led a riotous mental existence, he liked life that way; and since he was also a detective – an appellation he cordially detested – he got life that way. Nevertheless, he did not vocalize his reflections: Mr Phineas Mason did not appear the sort who would appreciate fleshly metaphor.

He drawled: 'The world's all right; the trouble is the people in it. Suppose you tell me what you can about these curious Shaws. After all, you know, I shan't be too heartily received by your local Long Island constabulary; and since I foresee difficulties, I should like to be forearmed as well.'

Mason frowned. 'But McC. assured me –'

'Oh, bother J. J.! He has vicarious delusions of grandeur. Let me warn you now, Mr Mason, that I shall probably be a dismal flop. I don't go about pulling murderers out of my hat. And with your Cossacks trampling the evidence –'

'I warned them,' said Mason fretfully. 'I spoke to Captain Murch myself when he telephoned this morning to inform me of the crime.' He made a sour face. 'They won't even move the body, Mr Queen. I wield – ah – a little local influence, you see.'

'Indeed,' said Ellery, adjusting his *pince-nez*; and he sighed. 'Very well, Mr Mason. Proceed with the dreary details.'

'It was my partner, Coolidge,' began the attorney in a pained voice, 'who originally handled Shaw's affairs. John A. Shaw, the millionaire. Before your time, I dare say. Shaw's first wife died in childbirth in 1895. The child – Agatha; she's a divorcee now, with a son of eight – of course survived her mother; and there was one previous child, named after his father. John's forty-five now . . . At any rate, old John Shaw remarried soon after his first wife's death, and then shortly after his second marriage died himself. This second wife, Maria Paine Shaw, survived her husband by a little more than thirty years. She died only a month ago.'

'A plethora of mortalities,' murmured Ellery, lighting a cigaret. 'So far, Mr Mason, a prosaic tale. And what has the Shaw history to do –'

'Patience,' sighed Mason. 'Now old John Shaw bequeathed his entire fortune to this second wife, Maria. The two children, John and Agatha, got nothing, not even trusts; I suppose old Shaw trusted Maria to take care of them.'

'I scent the usual story,' yawned Ellery. 'She didn't? No go between stepmother and acquired progeny?'

The lawyer wiped his brow. 'It was horrible. They fought for thirty years like – like savages. I will say, in extenuation of Mrs Shaw's conduct, that she had provocation. John's always been a shiftless, unreliable beggar: disrespectful, profligate, quite vicious. Nevertheless she's treated him well in money matters. As I said, he's forty-five now; and he hasn't done a lick of work in his life. He's a drunkard, too.'

'Sounds charming. And Sister Agatha, the divorcee?'

'A feminine edition of her brother. She married a fortune-hunter as worthless as herself; when he found out she was penniless he deserted her and Mrs Shaw managed to get her a quiet divorce. She took Agatha and her boy, Peter, into her house and they've been living there ever since, at daggers' points. Please forgive the – ah – brutality of the characterizations; I want you to know these people as they are.'

'We're almost intimate already,' chuckled Ellery.

'John and Agatha,' continued Mason, biting the head of his cane, 'have been living for only one event – their stepmother's death. So that they might inherit, of course. Until a certain occurrence a few months ago Mrs Shaw's will provided generously for them. But when that happened –'

Mr Ellery Queen narrowed his gray eyes. 'You mean –?'

'It's complicated,' sighed the lawyer. 'Three months ago there was an attempt on the part of someone in the household to poison the old lady!'

'Ah!'

'The attempt was unsuccessful only because Dr Arlen – Dr Terence

Arlen is the full name – had suspected such a possibility for years and had kept his eyes open. The cyanide – it was put in her tea – didn't reach Mrs Shaw, but killed a house-cat. None of us, of course, knew who had made the poisoning attempt. But after that Mrs Shaw changed her will.'

'Now,' muttered Ellery, 'I *am* enthralled. Arlen, eh? That creates a fascinating mess. Tell me about Arlen, please.'

'Rather mysterious old man with two passions: devotion to Mrs Shaw and a hobby of painting. Quite an artist, too, though I know little about such things. He lived in the Shaw house about twenty years. Medico Mrs Shaw picked up somewhere; I think only she knew his story, and he's always been silent about his past. She put him on a generous salary to live in the house and act as the family physician; I suspect it was rather because she anticipated what her stepchildren might attempt. And then too it's always seemed to me that Arlen accepted this unusual arrangement so tractably in order to pass out of – ah – circulation.'

They were silent for some time. The chauffeur swung the car off the main artery into a narrow macadam road. Mason breathed heavily.

'I suppose you're satisfied,' murmured Ellery at last through a fat smoke-ring, 'that Mrs Shaw died a month ago of natural causes?'

'Heavens, yes!' cried Mason. 'Dr Arlen wouldn't trust his own judgment, we were so careful; he had several specialists in, before and after her death. But she died of the last of a series of heart-attacks; she was an old woman, you know. Something-thrombosis, they called it.' Mason looked gloomy. 'Well, you can understand Mrs Shaw's natural reaction to the poisoning episode. "If they're so depraved," she told me shortly after, "that they'd attempt my *life*, they don't deserve any consideration at my *hands*." And she had me draw up a new will, cutting both of them off without a cent.'

'There's an epigram,' chuckled Ellery, 'worthy of a better cause.'

Mason tapped on the glass. 'Faster, Burroughs.' The car jolted ahead. 'In looking about for a beneficiary, Mrs Shaw finally remembered that there was someone to whom she could leave the Shaw fortune without feeling that she was casting it to the winds. Old John Shaw had had an elder brother, Morton, a widower with two grown children. The brothers quarrelled violently and Morton moved to England. He lost most of his money there; his two children, Edith and Percy, were left to shift for themselves when he committed suicide.'

'These Shaws seem to have a penchant for violence.'

'I suppose it's in the blood. Well, Edith and Percy both had talent of a sort, I understand, and they went on the London stage in a brother-and-sister music-hall act, managing well enough. Mrs Shaw decided to leave her money to this Edith, her niece. I made inquiries by correspondence and discovered that Edith Shaw was now Mrs Edythe Royce, a childless widow of many years' standing. On Mrs Shaw's decease I cabled her and she crossed by the next boat. According to Mrs Royce, Percy – her brother – was killed in an automobile accident on the Continent a few months before; so she had no ties whatever.'

'And the will – specifically?'

'It's rather queer,' sighed Mason. 'The Shaw estate was enormous at one time, but the depression whittled it down to about three hundred thousand dollars. Mrs Shaw left her niece two hundred thousand outright. The remainder, to his astonishment,' and Mason paused and eyed his tall young companion with a curious fixity, 'was put in trust for Dr Arlen.'

'Arlen!'

'He was not to touch the principal, but was to receive the income from it for the remainder of his life. Interesting, eh?'

'That's putting it mildly. By the way, Mr Mason, I'm a suspicious bird. This Mrs Royce – you're satisfied she *is* a Shaw?'

The lawyer started; then he shook his head. 'No, no, Queen, that's the wrong tack. There can be absolutely no question about it. In the first place she possesses the marked facial characteristics of the Shaws; you'll see for yourself; although I will say that she's rather – well, rather a character, rather a character! She came armed with intimate possessions of her father, Morton Shaw; and I myself, in company with Coolidge, questioned her closely on her arrival. She convinced us utterly, from her knowledge of *minutiae* about her father's life and Edith Shaw's childhood in America – knowledge impossible for an outsider to have acquired – that she *is* Edith Shaw. We were more than cautious, I assure you; especially since neither John nor Agatha had seen her since childhood.'

'Just a thought.' Ellery leaned forward. 'And what was to be the disposition of Arlen's hundred-thousand-dollar trust on Arlen's death?'

The lawyer gazed grimly at the two rows of prim poplars flanking a manicured driveway on which the limousine was now noiselessly treading. 'It was to be equally divided between John and Agatha,' he said in a careful voice. The car rolled to a stop under a coldly white *porte-cochère*.

'I see,' said Ellery. For it was Dr Terence Arlen who had been murdered.

A county trooper escorted them through high Colonial halls into a remote and silent wing of the ample old house, up a staircase to a dim cool corridor patrolled by a nervous man with a bull neck.

'Oh, Mr Mason,' he said eagerly, coming forward. 'We've been waiting for you. This is Mr Queen?' His tone changed from unguent haste to abrasive suspicion.

'Yes, yes. Murch of the county detectives, Mr Queen. You've left everything intact, Murch?'

The detective grunted and stepped aside. Ellery found himself in the study of what appeared to be a two-room suite; beyond an open door he could see the white counterpane of a bird's-eye-maple four-poster. A hole at some remote period had been hacked through the ceiling and covered with glass, admitting sunlight and converting the room into a sky-light studio. The trivia of a painter's paraphernalia lay in confusion about the room, overpowering the few medical implements. There were easels, paint-boxes, a small dais, carelessly draped smocks, a profusion of daubs in oils and water-colors on the walls.

A little man was kneeling beside the outstretched figure of the dead doctor – a long brittle figure frozen in death, capped with curiously lambent silver hair. The wound was frank and deep: the delicately chased haft of a stiletto protruded from the man's heart. There was very little blood.

Murch snapped: 'Well, Doc, anything else?'

The little man rose and put his instruments away. 'Died instantly from the stab-wound. Frontal blow, as you see. He tried to dodge at the last instant, I should say, but wasn't quick enough.' He nodded and reached for his hat and quietly went out.

Ellery shivered a little. The studio was silent, and the corridor was silent, and the wing was silent; the whole house was crushed under the weight of a terrific silence that was almost uncanny. There was something indescribably evil in the air . . . He shook his shoulders impatiently. 'The stiletto, Captain Murch. Have you identified it?'

'Belonged to Arlen. Always right here on this table.'

'No possibility of suicide, I suppose.'

'Not a chance, Doc said.'

Mr Phineas Mason made a retching sound. 'If you want me, Queen –' He stumbled from the room, awakening dismal echoes.

The corpse was swathed in a paint-smudged smock above pajamas; in the stiff right hand a paint-brush, its hairs stained jet-black, was still clutched. A color-splashed palette had fallen face down on the floor near him . . . Ellery did not raise his eyes from the stiletto. 'Florentine, I suppose. Tell me what you've learned so far, Captain,' he said absently. 'I mean about the crime itself.'

'Damned little,' growled the detective. 'Doc says he was killed about two in the morning – about eight hours ago. His body was found at seven this a.m. by a woman named Krutch, a nurse in the house here for a couple of years. Nice wench, by God! Nobody's got an alibi for the time of the murder, because according to their yarns they were all sleeping, and they all sleep separately. That's about the size of it.'

'Precious little, to be sure,' murmured Ellery. 'By the way, Captain, was it Dr Arlen's custom to paint in the wee hours?'

'Seems so. I thought of that, too. But he was a queer old cuss and when he was hot on something he'd work for twenty-four hours at a clip.'

'Do the others sleep in this wing?'

'Nope. Not even the servants. Seems Arlen liked privacy, and whatever he liked the old dame – Mrs Shaw, who kicked off a month ago – said "jake" to.' Murch went to the doorway and snapped: 'Miss Krutch.'

She came slowly out of Dr Arlen's bedroom – a tall fair young woman who had been weeping. She was in nurse's uniform and there was nothing in common between her name and her appearance. In fact, as Ellery observed with appreciation, she was a distinctly attractive young woman with curves in precisely the right places. Miss Krutch, despite her tears, was the first ray of sunshine he had encountered in the big old house.

'Tell Mr Queen what you told me,' directed Murch curtly.

'But there's so little,' she quavered. 'I was up before seven, as usual. My room's in the main wing, but there's a storeroom here for linen and things . . . As I passed I – I saw Dr Arlen lying on the floor, with the knife sticking up – The door was open and the light was on. I screamed. No one heard me. This is so far away . . . I screamed and screamed and then Mr Shaw came running, and Miss Shaw. Th-that's all.'

'Did any of you touch the body, Miss Krutch?'

'Oh, no, sir!' She shivered.

'I see,' said Ellery, and raised his eyes from the dead man to the easel above, casually, and looked away. And then instantly he looked back, his nerves tingling. Murch watched him with a sneer.

'How,' jeered Murch, 'd'ye like that, *Mr* Queen?'

Ellery sprang forward. A smaller easel near the large one supported a picture. It was a cheap 'processed' oil painting, a commercial copy of Rembrandt's famous self-portrait group, *The Artist and His Wife*. Rembrandt himself sat in the foreground, and his wife stood in the background. The canvas on the large easel was a half-finished replica of this painting. Both figures had been completely sketched in by Dr Arlen and brushwork begun: the lusty smiling mustached artist in his gaily plumed hat, his left arm about the waist of his Dutch-garbed wife.

And on the woman's chin there was painted a beard.

Ellery gaped from the processed picture to Dr Arlen's copy. But the one showed a woman's smooth chin, and the other – the doctor's – a squarish, expertly stroked black beard. And yet it had been daubed in hastily, as if the old painter had been working against time.

'Good heavens!' exclaimed Ellery, glaring. 'That's insane!'

'Think so?' said Murch blandly. 'Me, I don't know. I've got a notion about it.' He growled at Miss Krutch: 'Beat it,' and she fled from the studio, her long legs twinkling.

Ellery shook his head dazedly and sank into a chair, fumbling for a cigaret. 'That's a new wrinkle to me, Captain. First time I've ever encountered in a homicide an example of the beard-and-mustache school of art – you've seen the pencilled hair on the faces of men and women in billboard advertisements? It's –' And then his eyes narrowed as something leaped into them and he said abruptly: 'Is Miss Agatha Shaw's boy – that Peter – in the house?'

Murch, smiling secretly as if he were enjoying a huge jest, went to the hallway door and roared something. Ellery got out of the chair and ran across the room and returned with one of the smocks, which he flung over the dead man's body.

A small boy with frightened yet inquisitive eyes came slowly into the room, followed by one of the most remarkable creatures Ellery had ever seen. This apparition was a large stout woman of perhaps sixty, with lined rugged features – so heavy they were almost wattled – painted, bedaubed, and varnished with an astounding cosmetic technique. Her lips, gross as they were, were shaped by rouge into a perfect and obscene Cupid's-bow; her eyebrows had been tweezed to incredible thinness; round rosy spots punctuated her sagging cheeks; and the whole rough heavy skin was floury with white powder.

But her costume was even more amazing than her face. For she was rigged out in Victorian style – a tight-waisted garment, almost bustle-hipped, full wide skirts that reached to her thick ankles, a deep and shiny bosom, and an elaborate boned lace choker-collar . . . And then Ellery remembered that, since this must be Edythe Shaw Royce, there was at least a partial explanation for her eccentric appearance: she was an old woman, she came from England, and she was no doubt still basking in the vanished glow of her girlhood theatrical days.

'Mrs Royce,' said Murch mockingly, 'and Peter.'

'How d'ye do,' muttered Ellery, tearing his eyes away. 'Uh – Peter.'

The boy, a sharp-featured and skinny little creature, sucked his dirty forefinger and stared.

'Peter!' said Mrs Royce severely. Her voice was quite in tune with her appearance: deep and husky and slightly cracked. Even her hair, Ellery noted with a wince, was nostalgic – a precise deep brown, frankly dyed. Here was one female, at least, who did not mean to yield to old age without a determined struggle, he thought. 'He's frightened. Peter!'

'Ma'am,' mumbled Peter, still staring.

'Peter,' said Ellery, 'look at that picture.' Peter did so, reluctantly. 'Did you put that beard on the face of the lady in the picture, Peter?'

Peter shrank against Mrs Royce's voluminous skirts. 'N-no!'

'Curious, isn't it?' said Mrs Royce cheerfully. 'I was remarking about that to Captain Burch – Murch only this morning. I'm sure Peter wouldn't have drawn the beard on that one. He'd learned his lesson, hadn't you, Peter?' Ellery remarked with alarm that the extraordinary woman kept screwing her right eyebrow up and drawing it deeply down, as if there were something in her eye that bothered her.

'Ah,' said Ellery. 'Lesson?'

'You see,' went on Mrs Royce, continuing her ocular gymnastics with unconscious vigor, 'it was only yesterday that Peter's mother caught him drawing a beard with chalk on one of Dr Arlen's paintings in Peter's bedroom. Dr Arlen gave him a round hiding, I'm afraid, and himself removed the chalk-marks. Dear Agatha was so angry with poor Dr Arlen. So you didn't do it, did you, Peter?'

'Naw,' said Peter, who had become fascinated by the bulging smock on the floor.

'Dr Arlen, eh?' muttered Ellery. 'Thank you,' and he began to pace up and down as Mrs Royce took Peter by the arm and firmly removed him from the studio. A formidable lady, he thought, with her vigorous room-shaking tread. And he recalled that she wore flat-heeled shoes and had, from the ugly swelling of the leather, great bunions.

'Come on,' said Murch suddenly, going to the door.

'Where?'

'Downstairs.' The detective signalled a trooper to guard the studio and led the way. 'I want to show you,' he said as they made for the main part of the house, 'the reason for the beard on that dame-in-the-picture's jaw.'

'Indeed?' murmured Ellery, and said nothing more. Murch paused in the doorway of a pale Colonial living-room and jerked his head.

Ellery looked in. A hollow-chested, cadaverous man in baggy tweeds sat slumped in a Cogswell chair staring at an empty glass in his hand, which was shaking. His eyes were yellow-balled and shot with blood, and his loose skin was a web of red veins.

'That,' said Murch contemptuously and yet with a certain triumph, 'is Mr John Shaw.'

Ellery noted that Shaw possessed the same heavy features, the same fat lips and rock-hewn nose, as the wonderful Mrs Royce, his cousin; and for that matter, as the dour and annoyed-looking old pirate in the portrait over the fireplace who was presumably his father.

And Ellery also noted that on Mr John Shaw's unsteady chin there was a bedraggled, pointed beard.

Mr Mason, a bit greenish about the jowls, was waiting for them in a sombre reception-room. 'Well?' he asked in a whisper, like a supplicant before the Cumaean Sibyl.

'Captain Murch,' murmured Ellery, 'has a theory.'

The detective scowled. 'Plain as day. It's John Shaw. It's my hunch Dr Arlen painted that beard as a clue to his killer. The only one around here with a beard is Shaw. It ain't evidence, I admit, but it's something to work on. And believe you me,' he said with a snap of his brown teeth, 'I'm going to work on it!'

'John,' said Mason slowly. 'He certainly had motive. And yet I find it difficult to . . .' His shrewd eyes flickered. 'Beard? What beard?'

'There's a beard painted on the chin of a female face upstairs,' drawled Ellery, 'the face being on a Rembrandt Arlen was copying at the time he was murdered. That the good doctor painted the beard himself is quite evident. It's expertly stroked, done in black oils, and in his dead hand there's still the brush tipped with black oils. There isn't anyone else in the house who paints, is there?'

'No,' said Mason uncomfortably.

'Voilà.'

'But even if Arlen did such a – a mad thing,' objected the lawyer, 'how do you know it was just before he was attacked?'

'Aw,' growled Murch, 'when the hell else would it be?'

'Now, now, Captain,' murmured Ellery, 'let's be scientific. There's a perfectly good answer to your question, Mr Mason. First, we all agree that Dr Arlen couldn't have painted the beard *after* he was attacked; he died instantly. Therefore he must have painted it before he was attacked. The question is: How long before? Well, why did Arlen paint the beard at all?'

'Murch says as a clue to his murderer,' muttered Mason. 'But such a – a fantastic legacy to the police! It looks deucedly odd.'

'What's odd about it?'

'Well, for heaven's sake,' exploded Mason, 'if he wanted to leave a clue to his murderer, why didn't he write the murderer's name on the canvas? He had the brush in his hand . . .'

'Precisely,' murmured Ellery. 'A very good question, Mr Mason. Well, why didn't he? If he was alone – that is, if he was *anticipating* his murder – he certainly would have left us a written record of his concrete suspicions. The fact that he left no such record shows that he didn't anticipate his murder before the appearance of his murderer. Therefore he painted the beard *while his murderer was present*. But now we find an explanation for the painted beard as a clue. With his murderer present, he *couldn't* paint the name; the murderer would have noticed it and destroyed it. Arlen was forced, then, to adopt a subtle means: leave a clue that would escape his killer's attention. Since he was painting at the time, he used a painter's means. Even if his murderer noticed it, he probably ascribed it to Arlen's nervousness; although the chances are he didn't notice it.'

Murch stirred. 'Say, listen –'

'But a beard on a woman's face,' groaned the lawyer. 'I tell you –'

'Oh,' said Ellery dreamily, 'Dr Arlen had a precedent.'

'Precedent?'

'Yes; we've found, Captain Murch and I, that young Peter in his divine innocence had chalked a beard and mustache on one of Dr Arlen's daubs which hangs in Peter's bedroom. This was only yesterday. Dr Arlen whaled the tar out of him for this horrible crime *vers l'art*, no doubt justifiably. But Peter's beard-scrawl must have stuck in the doctor's mind; threshing about wildly in his mind while his murderer talked to him, or threatened him, the beard business popped out at him. Apparently he felt that it told a story, because he used it. And there, of course, is the rub.'

'I still say it's all perfectly asinine,' grunted Mason.

'Not asinine,' said Ellery. 'Interesting. He painted a beard on the chin of Rembrandt's wife. Why Rembrandt's wife, in the name of all that's wonderful? – a woman dead more than two centuries! These Shaws aren't remote descendants . . .'

'Nuts,' said Murch distinctly.

'Nuts,' said Ellery, 'is a satisfactory word under the circumstances, Captain. Then a grim jest? Hardly. But if it wasn't Dr Arlen's grisly notion of a joke, what under heaven was it? What did Arlen mean to convey?'

'If it wasn't so ridiculous,' muttered the lawyer, 'I'd say he was pointing to – Peter.'

'Nuts and double-nuts,' said Murch, 'begging your pardon, Mr Mason.

The kid's the only one, I guess, that's got a real alibi. It seems his mother's nervous about him and she always keeps his door locked from the outside. I found it that way myself this morning. And he couldn't have got out through the window.'

'Well, well,' sighed Mason, 'I'm sure I'm all at sea. John, eh . . . What do *you* think, Mr Queen?'

'Much as I loathe argument,' said Ellery, 'I can't agree with Brother Murch.'

'Oh, yeah?' jeered Murch. 'I suppose you've got reasons?'

'I suppose,' said Ellery, 'I have; not the least impressive of which is the dissimilar shapes of the real and painted beards.'

The detective glowered. 'Well, if he didn't mean John Shaw by it, what the hell did he mean?'

Ellery shrugged. 'If we knew that, my dear Captain, we should know everything.'

'Well,' snarled Murch, 'I think it's spinach, and I'm going to haul Mr John Shaw down to county headquarters and pump the old bastard till I *find* it's spinach.'

'I shouldn't do that, Murch,' said Ellery quickly. 'If only for –'

'I know my duty,' said the detective with a black look, and he stamped out of the reception-room.

John Shaw, who was quietly drunk, did not even protest when Murch shoved him into the squad car. Followed by the county morgue-truck bearing Dr Arlen's body, Murch vanished with his prey.

Ellery took a hungry turn about the room, frowning. The lawyer sat in a crouch, gnawing his fingernails. And again the room, and the house, and the very air were charged with silence, an ominous silence.

'Look here,' said Ellery sharply, 'there's something in this business you haven't told me yet, Mr Mason.'

The lawyer jumped, and then sank back biting his lips. 'He's such a worrisome creature,' said a cheerful voice from the doorway and they both turned, startled, to find Mrs Royce beaming in at them. She came in with the stride of a grenadier, her bosom joggling. And she sat down by Mason's side and with daintiness lifted her capacious skirts with both hands a bit above each fat knee. 'I know what's troubling you, Mr Mason!'

The lawyer cleared his throat hastily. 'I assure you –'

'Nonsense! I've excellent eyes. Mason, you haven't introduced this nice young man.' Mason mumbled something placative. 'Queen, is it? Charmed, Mr Queen. First sample of reasonably attractive American I've seen since my arrival. I can appreciate a handsome man; I was on the London stage for many years. And really,' she thundered in her formidable baritone, 'I wasn't so ill-looking myself!'

'I'm sure of that,' murmured Ellery. 'But what –'

'Mason's afraid for me,' said Mrs Royce with a girlish simper. 'A most conscientious barrister! He's simply petrified with fear that whoever did for poor Dr Arlen will select me as his next victim. And *I* tell him now, as I told him a few moments ago when you were upstairs with that dreadful Murch person, that for one thing I shan't be such an easy victim –' Ellery could well believe *that* – 'and for another I don't believe either John or Agatha, which is what's in Mason's mind – don't deny it, Mason! – was responsible for Dr Arlen's death.'

'I never –' began the lawyer feebly.

'Hmm,' said Ellery. 'What's *your* theory, Mrs Royce?'

'Someone out of Arlen's past,' boomed the lady with a click of her jaws as a punctuation mark. 'I understand he came here twenty years ago under most mysterious circumstances. He may have murdered somebody, and that somebody's brother or someone has returned to avenge –'

'Ingenious,' grinned Ellery. 'As tenable as Murch's, Mr Mason.'

The lady sniffed. 'He'll release Cousin John soon enough,' she said complacently. 'John's stupid enough under ordinary circumstances, you know, but when he's drunk –! There's no evidence, is there? A cigaret, if you please, Mr Queen.'

Ellery hastened to offer his case. Mrs Royce selected a cigaret with a vast paw, smiled roguishly as Ellery held a match, and then withdrew the cigaret and blew smoke, crossing her legs as she did so. She smoked almost in the Russian fashion, cupping her hand about the cigaret instead of holding it between two fingers. A remarkable woman! 'Why are you so afraid for Mrs Royce?' he drawled.

'Well –' Mason hesitated, torn between discretion and desire. 'There may have been a double motive for killing Dr Arlen, you see. That is,' he added hurriedly, '*if* Agatha or John had anything to do –'

'Double motive?'

'One, of course, is the conversion of the hundred thousand to Mrs Shaw's stepchildren, as I told you. The other . . . Well, there is a proviso in connection with the bequest to Dr Arlen. In return for offering him a home and income for the rest of his life, he was to continue to attend to the medical needs of the family, you see, with *special* attention to Mrs Royce.'

'Poor Aunt Maria,' said Mrs Royce with a tidal sigh. 'She must have been a dear, dear person.'

'I'm afraid I don't quite follow, Mr Mason.'

'I've a copy of the will in my pocket.' The lawyer fished for a crackling document. 'Here it is. "And in particular to conduct monthly medical examinations of my niece, Edith Shaw – or more frequently if Dr Arlen should deem it necessary – to insure her continued good health; a provision" (mark this, Queen!) "*a provision I am sure my stepchildren will appreciate.*" '

'A cynical addendum,' nodded Ellery, blinking a little. 'Mrs Shaw placed on her trusted leech the responsibility for keeping you healthy, Mrs Royce, suspecting that her dearly beloved stepchildren might be tempted to – er – tamper with your life. But why should they?'

For the first time something like terror invaded Mrs Royce's massive face. She set her jaw and said, a trifle tremulously: 'N-nonsense. I can't believe – Do you think it's possible they've already tr –'

'You don't feel ill, Mrs Royce?' cried Mason, alarmed.

Under the heavy coating of powder her coarse skin was muddily pale. 'No, I – Dr Arlen was supposed to examine me for the first time tomorrow. Oh, if it's . . . The food –'

'Poison was tried three months ago,' quavered the lawyer. 'On Mrs Shaw, Queen, as I told you. Good God, Mrs Royce, you'll have to be careful!'

'Come, come,' snapped Ellery. 'What's the point? Why should the Shaws want to poison Mrs Royce, Mason?'

'Because,' said Mason in a trembling voice, 'in the event of Mrs Royce's demise her estate is to revert to the original estate; which would automatically mean to John and Agatha.' He mopped his brow.

Ellery heaved himself out of the chair and took another hungry turn about the sombre room. Mrs Royce's right eyebrow suddenly began to go up and down with nervousness.

'This needs thinking over,' he said abruptly; and there was something queer in his eyes that made both of them stare at him with uneasiness. 'I'll stay the night, Mr Mason, if Mrs Royce has no objection.'

'Do,' whispered Mrs Royce in a tremble; and this time she was afraid, very plainly afraid. And over the room settled an impalpable dust, like a distant sign of approaching villainy. 'Do you think they'll actually *try* . . . ?'

'It is entirely,' said Ellery dryly, 'within the realm of possibility.'

The day passed in a timeless haze. Unaccountably, no one came; the telephone was silent; and there was no word from Murch, so that John Shaw's fate remained obscure. Mason sat in a miserable heap on the front porch, a cigar cold in his mouth, rocking himself like a weazened old doll. Mrs Royce retired, subdued, to her quarters. Peter was off somewhere in the gardens tormenting a dog; occasionally Miss Krutch's tearful voice reprimanded him ineffectually.

To Mr Ellery Queen it was a painful, puzzling, and irritatingly evil time. He prowled the rambling mansion, a lost soul, smoking tasteless cigarets and thinking . . . That a blanket of menace hung over this house his nerves convinced him. It took all his willpower to keep his body from springing about at unheard sounds; moreover, his mind was distracted and he could not think clearly. A murderer was abroad; and this was a house of violent people.

He shivered and darted a look over his shoulder and shrugged and bent his mind fiercely to the problem at hand . . . And after hours his thoughts grew calmer and began to range themselves in orderly rows, until it was evident that there was a beginning and an end. He grew quiet.

He smiled a little as he stopped a tiptoeing maid and inquired the location of Miss Agatha Shaw's room. Miss Shaw had wrapped herself thus far in a mantle of invisibility. It was most curious. A sense of rising drama excited him a little . . .

A tinny female voice responded to his knock, and he opened the door to find a feminine Shaw as bony and unlovely as the masculine edition curled in a hard knot on a *chaise-longue*, staring balefully out the window. Her négligé was adorned with boa feathers and there were varicose veins on her swollen naked legs.

'Well,' she said acidly, without turning. 'What do you want?'

'My name,' murmured Ellery, 'is Queen, and Mr Mason has called me in to help settle your – ah – difficulties.'

She twisted her skinny neck slowly. 'I've heard all about you. What do you want me to do, kiss you? I suppose it was you who instigated John's arrest. You're fools, the pack of you!'

'To the contrary, it was your worthy Captain Murch's exclusive idea to take your brother in custody, Miss Shaw. He's not formally arrested, you know. Even so, I advised strongly against it.'

She sniffed, but she uncoiled the knot and drew her shapeless legs beneath her wrapper in a sudden consciousness of femininity. 'Then sit down, Mr Queen. I'll help all I can.'

'On the other hand,' smiled Ellery, seating himself in a gilt and Gallic atrocity, 'don't blame Murch overly, Miss Shaw. There's a powerful case against your brother, you know.'

'And me!'

'And,' said Ellery regretfully, 'you.'

She raised her thin arms and cried: 'Oh, how I hate this damned, damned house, that damned woman! She's the cause of all our trouble. Some day she's likely to get –'

'I suppose you're referring to Mrs Royce. But aren't you being unfair? From Mason's story it's quite evident that there was no ghost of coercion when your stepmother willed your father's fortune to Mrs Royce. They had never met, never corresponded, and your cousin was three thousand miles away. It's awkward for you, no doubt, but scarcely Mrs Royce's fault.'

'Fair! Who cares about fairness? She's taken our money away from us. And now we've got to stay here and – and be *fed* by her. It's intolerable, I tell you! She'll be here at least two years – trust her for that, the painted old hussy! – and all that time . . .'

'I'm afraid I don't understand. Two years?'

'That *woman's* will,' snarled Miss Shaw, 'provided that this precious cousin of ours come to live here and preside as mistress for a minimum of two years. That was her revenge, the despicable old witch! Whatever father saw in her . . . To "provide a home for John and Agatha," she said in the will, "until they find a permanent solution of their problems." How d'ye like that? I'll never forget those words. Our "problems"! Oh, every time I think –' She bit her lip, eyeing him sideways with a sudden caution.

Ellery sighed and went to the door. 'Indeed? And if something should – er – drive Mrs Royce from the house before the expiration of the required period?'

'We'd get the money, of course,' she flashed with bitter triumph; her thin dark skin was greenish. 'If something should happen –'

'I trust,' said Ellery dryly, 'that nothing will.' He closed the door and stood for a moment gnawing his fingers, and then he smiled rather grimly and went downstairs to a telephone.

John Shaw returned with his escort at ten that night. His chest was hollower, his fingers shakier, his eyes bloodier; and he was sober. Murch looked like a thundercloud. The cadaverous man went into the living-room and made for a full decanter. He drank alone, with steady mechanical determination. No one disturbed him.

'Nothing,' growled Murch to Ellery and Mason.

At twelve the house was asleep.

The first alarm was sounded by Miss Krutch. It was almost one when she ran down the upper corridor screaming at the top of her voice: 'Fire!

Fire! Fire!' Thick smoke was curling about her slender ankles and the moonlight shining through the corridor-window behind her silhouetted her long plump trembling shanks through the thin nightgown.

The corridor erupted, boiled over. Doors crashed open, dishevelled heads protruded, questions were shrieked, dry throats choked over the bitter smoke. Mr Phineas Mason, looking a thousand years old without his teeth, fled in a cotton nightshirt toward the staircase. Murch came pounding up the stairs, followed by a bleary, bewildered John Shaw. Scrawny Agatha in silk pajamas staggered down the hall with Peter, howling at the top of his lusty voice, in her arms. Two servants scuttled downstairs like frantic rats.

But Mr Ellery Queen stood still outside the door of his room and looked quietly about, as if searching for someone.

'Murch,' he said in a calm, penetrating voice.

The detective ran up. 'The fire!' he cried wildly. 'Where the hell's the fire?'

'Have you seen Mrs Royce?'

'Mrs Royce? Hell, no!' He ran back up the hall, and Ellery followed on his heels, thoughtfully. Murch tried the knob of a door; the door was locked. 'God, she may be asleep, or overcome by —'

'Well, then,' said Ellery through his teeth as he stepped back, 'stop yowling and help me break this door down. We don't want her frying in her own lard, you know.'

In the darkness, in the evil smoke, they hurled themselves at the door . . . At the fourth assault it splintered off its hinges and Ellery sprang through. An electric torch in his hand flung its powerful beam about the room, wavered . . . Something struck it from Ellery's hand, and it splintered on the floor. The next moment Ellery was fighting for his life.

His adversary was a brawny, panting demon with muscular fingers that sought his throat. He wriggled about, coolly, seeking an armhold. Behind him Murch was yelling: 'Mrs Royce! It's only us!'

Something sharp and cold flicked over Ellery's cheek and left a burning line. Ellery found a naked arm. He twisted, hard, and there was a clatter as steel fell to the floor. Then Murch came to his senses and jumped in. A county trooper blundered in, fumbling with his electric torch . . . Ellery's fist drove in, hard, to a fat stomach. Fingers relaxed from his throat. The trooper found the electric switch . . .

Mr Royce, trembling violently, lay on the floor beneath the two men. On a chair nearby lay, in a mountain of Victorian clothing, a very odd and solid-looking contraption that might have been a rubber *brassière*. And something was wrong with her hair; she seemed to have been partially scalped.

Ellery cursed softly and yanked. Her scalp came away in a piece, revealing a pink gray-fringed skull.

'She's a man!' screamed Murch.

'Thus,' said Ellery grimly, holding Mrs Royce's throat firmly with one hand and with the other dabbing at his bloody cheek, 'vindicating the powers of thought.'

'I still don't understand,' complained Mason the next morning, as his chauffeur drove him and Ellery back to the city, 'how you guessed, Queen.'

Ellery raised his eyebrows. 'Guessed? My dear Mason, that's considered an insult at the Queen hearth. There was no guesswork whatever involved. Matter of pure reasoning. And a neat job, too,' he added reflectively, touching the thin scar on his cheek.

'Come, come, Queen,' smiled the lawyer, 'I've never really believed McC.'s panegyrics on what he calls your uncanny ability to put two and two together; and though I'm not unintelligent and my legal training gives me a mental advantage over the layman and I've just been treated presumably to a demonstration of your – er – powers, I'll be blessed if I yet believe.'

'A sceptic, eh?' said Ellery, wincing at the pain in his cheek. 'Well, then, let's start where I started – with the beard Dr Arlen painted on the face of Rembrandt's wife just before he was attacked. We've agreed that he deliberately painted in the beard to leave a clue to his murderer. What could he have meant? He was not pointing to a *specific* woman, using the beard just as an attention-getter; for the woman in the painting was the wife of Rembrandt, a historical figure and as far as our *personae* went an utter unknown. Nor could Arlen have meant to point to a woman with a beard *literally*; for this would have meant a freak, and there were no freaks involved. Nor was he pointing to a bearded man, for there was *a man's face* on the painting which he left untouched; had he meant to point to a bearded man as his murderer – that is, to John Shaw – he would have painted the beard on Rembrandt's beardless face. Besides, Shaw's is a vandyke, a pointed beard; and the beard Arlen painted was squarish in shape . . . You see how exhaustive it is possible to be, Mason.'

'Go on,' said the lawyer intently.

'The only possible conclusion, then, all others having been eliminated, was that Arlen meant the beard *merely to indicate masculinity*, since facial hair is one of the few exclusively masculine characteristics left to our sex by dear, dear Woman. In other words, by painting a beard on a woman's face – any woman's face, mark – Dr Arlen was virtually saying: "My murderer is a person who seems to be a woman but is really a man." '

'Well, I'll be damned!' gasped Mason.

'No doubt,' nodded Ellery. 'Now, "a person who seems to be a woman but is really a man" suggests, surely, impersonation. The only actual stranger at the house was Mrs Royce. Neither John nor Agatha could be impersonators, since they were both well-known to Dr Arlen as well as to you; Arlen had examined them periodically, in fact, for years as the personal physician of the household. As for Miss Krutch, aside from her unquestionable femininity – a ravishing young woman, my dear Mason – she could not possibly have had motive to be an impersonator.

'Now, since Mrs Royce seemed the likeliest possibility, I thought over the infinitesimal phenomena I had observed connected with her person – that is, appearance and movements. I was amazed to find a vast number of remarkable confirmations!'

'Confirmations?' echoed Mason, frowning.

'Ah, Mason, that's the trouble with sceptics: they're so easily confounded. Of course! Lips constitute a strong difference between the sexes: Mrs Royce's were shaped meticulously into a perfect Cupid's-bow with lipstick. Suspicious in an old woman. The general overuse of cosmetics, particularly the heavy application of face powder: *very* suspicious, when you consider that overpowdering is not common among genteel old ladies and also that a man's skin, no matter how closely and frequently shaved, is undisguisably coarser.

'Clothes? Really potent confirmation. Why on earth that outlandish Victorian get-up? Here was presumably a woman who had been on the stage, presumably a woman of the world, a sophisticate. And yet she wore those horrible doodads of the '90s. Why? Obviously, to swathe and disguise a padded figure – impossible with women's thin, scanty, and clinging modern garments. And the collar – ah, the collar! That was his inspiration. A choker, you'll recall, concealing the entire neck? But since a prominent Adam's-apple is an inescapable heritage of the male, a choker-collar becomes virtually a necessity in a female impersonation. Then the baritone voice, the vigorous movements, the mannish stride, the flat shoes . . . The shoes were especially illuminating. Not only were they flat, but they showed signs of great bunions – and a man wearing woman's shoes, no matter how large, might well be expected to grow those painful excrescences.'

'Even if I grant all that,' objected Mason, 'still they're generalities at best, might even be coincidences when you're arguing from a conclusion. Is that all?' He seemed disappointed.

'By no means,' drawled Ellery. 'There were, as you say, the generalities. But your cunning Mrs Royce was addicted to three habits which are exclusively masculine, without argument. For one thing, when she sat down on my second sight of her she elevatéd her skirts at the knees with both hands; that is, one to each knee. Now that's precisely what a man does when he sits down: raises his trousers; to prevent, I suppose, their bagging at the knees.'

'But –'

'Wait. Did you notice the way she screwed up her right eyebrow constantly, raising it far up and then drawing it far down? What could this have been motivated by except the lifelong use of a monocle? And a monocle is masculine . . . And finally, her peculiar habit, in removing a cigaret from her lips, of cupping her hand about it rather than withdrawing it between the forefinger and middle finger, as most cigaret-smokers do. But the cupping gesture is precisely the result of *pipe-smoking*, for a man cups his hands about the bowl of a pipe in taking it out of his mouth. Man again. When I balanced these three specific factors on the same side of the scale as those generalities, I felt certain Mrs Royce was a male.

'What male? Well, that was simplest of all. You had told me, for one thing, that when you and your partner Coolidge quizzed her she had shown a minute knowledge of Shaw history and specifically of Edith Shaw's history. On top of that, it took histrionic ability to carry off this female impersonation. Then there was the monocle deduction – England, surely? And the strong family resemblance. So I knew that "Mrs Royce", being a Shaw undoubtedly, and an English Shaw to boot, was the other Shaw of the Morton side of the family – that is, Edith Shaw's brother Percy!'

'But she – he, I mean,' cried Mason, 'had told me Percy Shaw died a few months ago in Europe in an automobile accident!'

'Dear, dear,' said Ellery sadly, 'and a lawyer, too. She lied, that's all! – I mean "he", confound it. Your legal letter was addressed to Edith Shaw, and Percy received it, since they probably shared the same establishment. If he received it, it was rather obvious, wasn't it, that it was Edith Shaw who must have died shortly before; and that Percy had seized the opportunity to gain a fortune for himself by impersonating her?'

'But why,' demanded Mason, puzzled, 'did he kill Dr Arlen? He had nothing to gain – Arlen's money was destined for Shaw's cousins, not for Percy Shaw. Do you mean there was some past connection –'

'Not at all,' murmured Ellery. 'Why look for past connections when the motive's slick and shiny at hand? If Mrs Royce was a man, the motive was at once apparent. Under the terms of Mrs Shaw's will Arlen was periodically to examine the family, with particular attention to Mrs Royce. And Agatha Shaw told me yesterday that Mrs Royce was constrained by will to remain in the house for two years. Obviously, then, the only way Percy Shaw could avert the cataclysm of being examined by Dr Arlen and his disguise penetrated – for a doctor would have seen the truth instantly on examination, of course – was to kill Arlen. Simple, *nein?*'

'But the beard Arlen drew – that meant he *had* seen through it?'

'Not unaided. What probably happened was that the impostor, knowing the first physical examination impended, went to Dr Arlen the other night to strike a bargain, revealing himself as a man. Arlen, an honest man, refused to be bribed. He must have been painting at the time and, thinking fast, unable to rouse the house because he was so far away from the others, unable to paint his assailant's name because "Mrs Royce" would see it and destroy it, thought of Peter's beard, made the lightning connection, and calmly painted it while "Mrs Royce" talked to him. Then he was stabbed.'

'And the previous poisoning attempt on Mrs Shaw?'

'That,' said Ellery, 'undoubtedly lies between John and Agatha.'

Mason was silent, and for some time they rode in peace. Then the lawyer stirred, and sighed, and said: 'Well, all things considered, I suppose you should thank Providence. Without concrete evidence – your reasoning was unsupported by legal evidence, you realize that, of course, Queen – you could scarcely have accused Mrs Royce of being a man, could you? Had you been wrong, what a beautiful suit she could have brought against you! That fire last night was an act of God.'

'I am,' said Ellery calmly, 'above all, my dear Mason, a man of free will. I appreciate acts of God when they occur, but I don't sit around waiting for them. Consequently . . .'

'You mean –' gasped Mason, opening his mouth wide.

'A telephone call, a hurried trip by Sergeant Velie, and smoke-bombs were the *materia* for breaking into Mrs Royce's room in the dead of night,' said Ellery comfortably. 'By the way, you don't by any chance know the permanent address of – ah – Miss Krutch?'

Ruth Rendell

THE CLINGING
WOMAN

The form of the mystery story, Ruth Rendell has said, makes fewer demands than the novel proper, 'so that it's not difficult to get away with sloppy writing and poor characterization, so long as enough excitement, sex and mystery is injected'. But this is emphatically not true of her own books, which show real people in possible situations, pushed to the point of violence.

Ruth Rendell (1930–) writes two kinds of crime story. The first are orthodox mysteries, set in and around the small Sussex town of Kingsmarkham, with ageing, slightly literary Chief Inspector Wexford as central character. These stories always contain a puzzle to be solved. The other kind of Rendell novel offers no mystery, but is based on the psychological springs of violence, sometimes with an aberrant sexual motive. The majority of her readers prefer the Wexford stories; Rendell herself has a warmer feeling for the others.

And there are the short stories, which like the novels vary considerably. Some are straightforward puzzles, a few involving Wexford, although she is less happy with this kind of tale as short story than as novel. The best are those in which psychological pressures cause violence in relationships between friends, lovers, husbands and wives. 'The Clinging Woman' explores such a theme brilliantly.

The girl was hanging by her hands from the railings of a balcony. The balcony was on the twelfth floor of the high-rise block next to his. His flat was on the ninth floor and he had to look up to see her. It was half-past six in the morning. He had been awakened by the sound of an aircraft flying dangerously low overhead, and had got out of bed to look. His sleepy gaze, descending from the blue sky which was empty of clouds, empty of anything but the bright vanishing arrow of the aircraft, alighted – at first with disbelief – on the hanging figure.

He really thought he must be dreaming, for this sunrise time was the hour for dreams. Then, when he knew he wasn't, he decided it must be a stunt. This was to be a scene in a film. There were cameramen down there, a whole film unit, and all the correct safety precautions had been taken. Probably the girl wasn't even a real girl, but a dummy. He opened the window and looked down. The car park, paved courts, grass spaces between the blocks, all were deserted. On the balcony rail one of the dummy's hands moved, clutching its anchorage more tightly, more desperately. He had to believe then what was obviously happening – unbelievable only because melodrama, though a frequent constituent of real life, always is. The girl was trying to kill herself. She had lost her nerve and now was trying to stay alive. All these thoughts and conclusions of his occupied about thirty seconds. Then he acted. He picked up the phone and dialled the emergency number for the police.

The arrival of the police cars and the ultimate rescue of the girl became the focus of gossip and speculation for the tenants of the two blocks. Someone found out that it was he who had alerted the police and he became an unwilling hero. He was a modest, quiet young man, and, disliking this limelight, was relieved when the talk began to die away, when the novelty of it wore off, and he was able to enter and leave his flat without being pointed at as a kind of St George and sometimes even congratulated.

About a fortnight after that morning of melodrama, he was getting ready to go to the theatre, just putting on his overcoat, when the doorbell rang.

He didn't recognize the girl who stood outside. He had never seen her face.

She said, 'I'm Lydia Simpson. You saved my life. I've come to thank you.'

His embarrassment was acute. 'You shouldn't have,' he said with a nervous smile. 'You really shouldn't. That's not necessary. I only did what anyone would have done.'

She was calm and tranquil, not at all his idea of a failed suicide. 'But no one else did,' she said.

'Won't you come in? Have a drink or something?'

'Oh, no, I couldn't think of it. I can see you're just going out. I only wanted to say thank you very, very much.'

'It was nothing.'

'Nothing to save someone's life? I'll always be grateful to you.'

He wished she would either come in or go away. If this went on much longer the people in the other two flats on his floor would hear, would come out, and another of those bravest-deeds-of-the-year committee meetings would be convened. 'Nothing at all,' he said desperately. 'Really, I've almost forgotten it.'

'I shall never forget, never.'

Her manner, calm yet intense, made him feel uncomfortable and he watched her retreat into the lift – smiling pensively – with profound relief. Luckily, they weren't likely to meet again. The curious thing was that they did, the next morning at the bus stop. She didn't refer again to his saving of her life, but talked instead about her new job, the reason for her being at this bus stop, at this hour. It appeared that her employers had offices in the City street next to his own and were clients of his own firm. They travelled to work together. He left her with very different feelings from those of the evening before. It was hard to believe she was thirty – his neighbours had given him this information – for she looked much younger, small and fragile as she was, her skin very white and her hair very fair.

They got into the habit of travelling on that bus together in the mornings, and sometimes she waved to him from her balcony. One evening they met by chance outside her office. She was carrying an armful of files to work on at home and confessed she wouldn't have brought them if she had known how heavy they were. Of course he carried them for her all the way up to her flat and stayed for a drink. She said she was going to cook dinner and would he stay for that too? He stayed. While she was out in the kitchen he took his drink out on to the balcony. It gave him a strange feeling, imagining her coming out here in her despair at dawn, lowering herself from those railings, then losing her nerve, beneath her a great space with death at the bottom of it. When she came back into the room, he noticed afresh how slight and frail she was, how in need of protection.

The flat was neat and spotlessly clean. Most of the girls he knew lived in semi-squalor. Liberated, independent creatures, holding down men's jobs, they scorned womanly skills as debasing. He had been carefully brought up by a houseproud mother and he liked a clean home. Lydia's furniture was beautifully polished. He thought that if he were ever asked again he would remember to bring her flowers to go in those sparkling glass vases.

After dinner, an excellent, even elaborate meal, he said suddenly, the food and drink lowering his inhibitions:

'Why did you do it?'

'Try to kill myself?' She spoke softly and evenly, as serenely as if he had asked why she changed her job. 'I was engaged and he left me for someone else. There didn't seem much to live for.'

'Are you over that now?'

'Oh, yes. I'm glad I didn't succeed. Or – should I say? – that you didn't let me succeed.'

'Don't ever try that again, will you?'

'No, why should I? What a question!'

He felt strangely happy that she had promised never to try that again. 'You must come and have a meal with me,' he said as he was leaving. 'Let's see. Not Monday. How about . . .?'

'We don't have to arrange it now, do we? We'll see each other in the morning.'

She had a very sweet smile. He didn't like aggressive, self-reliant women. Lydia never wore trousers or mini-dresses, but long flowing skirts, flower-patterned. When he put his hand under her elbow to shepherd her across the street, she clutched his arm and kept hold of it.

'You choose for me,' she said when the menu was given to her in the restaurant.

She didn't smoke or drink anything stronger than sweet white wine. She couldn't drive a car. He wondered sometimes how she managed to hold down an exacting job, pay her rent, live alone. She was so exquisitely feminine, clinging and gentle. And he was flattered when because of the firm's business he was unable to see her one night, tears appeared in her large grey eyes. That was the first night they hadn't met for three weeks and he missed her so much he knew he must be in love with her.

She accepted his proposal, made formally and accompanied by a huge bunch of red roses. 'Of course I'll marry you. My life has been yours ever since you saved it. I've always felt I belonged to you.'

They were married very quietly. Lydia didn't like the idea of a big wedding. He and she were ideally suited, they had so many tastes in common: a love of quietness and order, rather old-fashioned ways, steadiness, regular habits. They had the same aims: a house in a north-western suburb, two children. But for the time being she would continue to work.

It amazed and delighted him that she managed to keep the new house so well, to provide him every morning with freshly laundered underwear and shirt, every night with a perfectly cooked meal. He hadn't been so well looked after since he had left his mother's house. That, he thought, was how a woman should be, unobtrusively efficient, gentle yet expert, feminine and sweet, yet accomplished. The house was run as smoothly as if a couple of silent invisible maids were at work in it all day.

To perform these chores, she got up each morning at six. He suggested they get a cleaner but she wouldn't have one, resisting him without defiance but in a way which was bound to appeal to him.

'I couldn't bear to let any other woman look after your things, darling.'

She was quite perfect.

They went to work together, lunched together, came home together, ate together, watched television or listened to music or read in companionable silence together, slept together. At the weekends they were together all the time. Both had decided their home must be fully equipped with washers and driers and freezers and mixers and cleaners and polishers, beautifully furnished with the brand-new or the extreme antique, so on Saturdays they shopped together.

He adored it. This was what marriage should be, this was what the church service meant – one flesh, forsaking all other. He had, in fact, forsaken most of the people he had once known. Lydia wasn't a very sociable woman and had no women friends. He asked her why not.

'Women,' she said, 'only want to know other women to gossip about their men. I haven't any complaints against my man, darling.'

His own friends seemed a little over-awed by the grandeur and pomp with which she entertained them, by the finger bowls and fruit knives. Or perhaps they were put off by her long silences and the way she kept glancing at her watch. It was only natural, of course, that she didn't want people staying half the night. She wanted to be alone with him. They might have understood that and made allowances. His clients and their wives weren't over-awed. They must have been gratified. Where else, in a private house with no help, would they have been given a five-course dinner, exquisitely cooked and served? Naturally, Lydia had to spend all the pre-dinner time in the kitchen and, naturally too, she was exhausted after dinner, a little snappy with the man who spilt coffee on their new carpet, and the other one, a pleasant if tactless stockbroker, who tried to persuade him to go away on a stag, golfing weekend.

'Why did they get married,' she asked, with some reason, 'if all they want to do is get away from their wives?'

By this time, at the age of thirty-four, he ought to have had promotion at work. He'd been with the firm five years and expected to be made director. Neither he nor Lydia could understand why this directorship was so slow in coming.

'I wonder,' he said, 'if it's because I don't hang around in the office drinking after work?'

'Surely they understand a married man wants to be with his wife?'

'God knows. Maybe I ought to have gone on that river-boat party, only wives weren't invited, if you remember. I could tell you were unhappy at the idea of my going alone.'

In any case, he'd probably been quite wrong about the reason for his lack of promotion because, just as he was growing really worried about it, he got his directorship. An increase in salary, an office and a secretary of his own. He was a little concerned about other perquisites of the job, particularly about the possibility of foreign trips. But there was no need to mention these to Lydia yet. Instead he mentioned the secretary he must engage.

'That's marvellous, darling.' They were dining out, tête-à-tête, to celebrate. Lydia hadn't cared for his idea of a party. 'I'll have to give a fortnight's notice, but you can wait a fortnight, can't you? It'll be lovely being together all day long.'

'I don't quite follow,' he said, though he did.

'Darling, you are slow tonight. Where could you find a better secretary than me?'

They had been married for four years. 'You're going to give up work and have a baby.'

She took his hand, smiling into his face. 'That can wait. We don't need children to bring us together. You're my husband and my child and my friend all in one, and that's enough for me.'

He had to tell her why it wouldn't do for her to be his secretary. It was all true, that stuff about office politics and favouritism and the awkwardness of his position if his wife worked for him, but he made a poor show of explaining.

She said in her small, soft voice, 'Please can we go? Could you ask them for the bill? I'd like to leave now.'

As soon as they were in the house she began to cry. He advanced afresh his explanation. She cried. He said she could ask other people. Everyone would tell her the same. A director of a small firm like his couldn't have his wife working for him. She could phone his chairman if she didn't believe him.

She didn't raise her voice. She was never wild or hysterical. 'You don't want me,' she said like a rejected child.

'I do want you. I love you. But – can't you see? – this is for work, this is different.' He knew, before he said it, that he shouldn't have gone on. 'You don't like my friends and I've given them up. I don't have my clients here any more. I'm only away from you about six hours out of every day. Isn't all that enough for you?'

There was no argument. She simply reiterated that he didn't want her. She cried for most of the night and in the morning she was too tired to go to work. During the day he phoned her twice. She sounded tearful but calm, apparently resigned now. The first thing he noticed when he let himself in at his front door at six was the stench of gas.

She was lying on the kitchen floor, a cushion at the edge of the open oven to support her delicate blonde head. Her face was flushed a warm pink.

He flung open the window and carried her to it, holding her head in the fresh air. She was alive, she would be all right. As her pulse steadied and she began to breathe more evenly, he found himself kissing her passionately, begging her aloud not to die, to live for him. When he thought it was safe to leave her for a moment, he laid her on the sofa and dialled the emergency number for an ambulance.

They kept her in hospital for a few days and there was talk of mental treatment. She refused to undergo it.

'I've never done it except when I've known I'm not loved,' she said.

'What do you mean, "never", darling?'

'When I was seventeen I took an overdose of pills because a boy let me down.'

'You never told me,' he said.

'I didn't want to upset you. I'd rather die than make you unhappy. My life belongs to you and I only want to make yours happy.'

Suppose he hadn't got there in time? He shuddered when he thought of that possibility. The house was horrible without her. He missed her painfully, and he resolved to devote more of his time and his attention to her in future.

She didn't like going away on holiday. Because they never took holidays and seldom entertained and had no children, they had been able to save. They sold the house and bought a bigger, newer one. His firm wanted him to go to Canada for three weeks and he didn't hesitate. He refused immediately.

An up-and-coming junior got the Canada trip. It irritated him when he learned of a rumour that was going about the office to the effect that his wife was some sort of invalid, just because she had given up work since they bought the new house. Lydia, an invalid? She was happier than she had ever been, filling the house with new things, redecorating rooms herself, having the garden landscaped. If either of them was sick, it was he. He hadn't been sleeping well lately and he became subject to fits of depression. The doctor gave him pills for the sleeplessness and advised a change of air. Perhaps he was working too hard. Couldn't he manage to do some of his work at home?

'I took it upon myself,' Lydia said gently, 'to phone the doctor and suggest that. You could have two or three days a week at home and I'd do the secretarial work for you.'

His chairman agreed to it. There was a hint of scorn in the man's smile, he thought. But he was allowed to work at home and sometimes, for four or five days at a stretch, although he talked to people on the phone, he saw no one at all but his wife. She was, he found, as perfect a secretary as a wife. There was scarcely anything for him to do. She composed his press releases for him, wrote his letters without his having to dictate them, answered the phone with efficiency and charm, arranged his appointments. And she waited on him unflaggingly when work was done. No meals on trays for them. Every lunchtime and every evening the dining table was exquisitely laid, and if it occurred to him that in the past two years only six other people had handled this glass, this cutlery, these luxurious appointments, he didn't say so.

His depression wouldn't go away, even though he had tranquillizers now as well as sleeping pills. They never spoke of her suicide attempts, but he often thought of them and wondered if he had somehow been infected by this tendency of hers. When, before settling down for the night, he dropped one pill from the bottle into the palm of his hand, the temptation to let them all trickle out, to swallow them all down with a draught of fresh cold water, was sometimes great. He didn't know why, for he had everything a man could want, a perfect marriage, a beautiful house, a good job, excellent physical health and no ties or restrictions.

As Lydia had pointed out, 'Children would have been such a tie, darling,' or, when he suggested they might buy a dog, 'Pets are an awful tie, and they ruin one's home.' He agreed that his home and these comforts were what he had always wanted. Yet, as he approached forty, he began having bad dreams, and the dreams were of prisons.

One day he said to her, 'I can understand now why you tried to kill yourself. I mean, I can understand that anyone might want to.'

'I think we understand each other perfectly in every way,' she said. 'But don't let's talk about it. I'll never attempt it again.'

'And I'm not the suicidal type, am I?'

'*You?*' She wasn't alarmed, she didn't take him seriously, never thought of him at all as a person except in relation to herself. At once he reproached himself. *Lydia?* Lydia, who had given over her whole life to him, who put his every need and wish before her own? 'You wouldn't have any reason to,' she said gaily. 'You know you're loved. Besides, I should rescue you in time, just like you rescued me.'

His company had expanded and they were planning to open an office in Melbourne. After he had denied hotly that his wife was an invalid, that there was 'some little trouble' with his wife, the chairman offered him the chance of going to Australia for three months to get the new branch on its feet. Again he didn't hesitate. He accepted. The firm would, of course, pay for his trip. He was working out, as he entered his house, how much Lydia's air fare to Melbourne, her board in an hotel, her expenses, would amount to. Suicidal thoughts retreated. He could do it, he could just do it. Three months away, he thought, in a new country, meeting new people, and at the end of it, praise for his work and maybe an increase in salary.

She came out into the hall and embraced him. Her embraces at parting and greeting (though these occasions were no longer frequent) were as passionate now as when they first got engaged. He anticipated a small difficulty in that she wouldn't much want to leave her home, but that could be got over. She would go, as she had often said, anywhere with him.

He walked into their huge living-room. It was as immaculate as ever, but something was different, something had undergone a great change. Their red carpet had been replaced by a new one of a delicate creamy velvety pile.

'Do you like it?' she asked, smiling. 'I bought it and had it laid secretly as a surprise for you. Oh, darling, you don't like it?'

'I like it,' he said, and then, 'How much did it cost?'

This was a question he hardly ever asked, but now he had cause to. She named a sum, much about the figure her trip to Australia would have cost.

'We said we were saving it to get something for the house,' she said, putting her arm round him. 'It's not really an extravagance. It'll last for ever. And what else have we got to spend the money on but our own home?'

He kissed her and said it didn't matter. It wasn't really an extravagance and it would last for ever, for ever . . . They dined off Copenhagen china and Georgian silver and Waterford glass. On the table flowers were arranged, wasting their sweetness on the desert air. He must go to Australia, but she couldn't come with him. He was afraid to tell her, gripped by a craven fear.

For weeks he put off telling her, and treacherously the idea came to him – why tell her at all? He longed to go, he must go. Couldn't he simply escape, phone from the aircraft's first stop, somewhere in Europe, and say he had been sent without notice, urgently? He had tried to phone her before but he couldn't get through. She wouldn't attempt suicide, he was sure, if she knew he was too far away to save her. And she'd forgive him, she loved him. But there were too many practical difficulties in the way of that, clothes, for instance, luggage. He must have been losing his mind even to think of it. Do that to *Lydia*? He wouldn't do that to his worst enemy, still less to his beloved wife.

As it turned out, he didn't get the chance. She was his secretary, from whom a man, however many he keeps from his wife, can have no secrets. The airline phoned with a query and she found out.

'How long,' she asked dully, 'will you be gone?'

'Three months.'

She paled. She fell back as if physically ill.

'I'll write every day. I'll phone.'

'Three months,' she said.

'I was scared stiff of telling you. I have to go. Darling, don't you see I have to? It would cost hundreds and hundreds to take you with me, and we don't have the money.'

'No,' she said. 'No, of course not.'

She cried bitterly that night but on the following morning she didn't refer to his departure. They worked together as efficiently and companionably as ever, but her face was paper-white. Work finished, she began to talk of the clothes he would need, the new suitcases to be bought. In a sad, monotonous voice, she said that she would do everything, he mustn't worry his head at all about preparations.

'And you won't worry about *me* on the flight?'

There was something about the way she said she wouldn't, shaking her head and smiling as if his question had been preposterous, unreal, that told him. The dead cannot worry. She intended to be dead. And he understood that he had been absurdly optimistic in reassuring himself she wouldn't attempt suicide when he was far away.

The days went by. Only one more before he was due to leave. But he wouldn't leave. He knew that. He had known it for more than a week, and he was afraid of telling his chairman he wouldn't as he had been afraid of telling her he would. Again he dreamed of prisons. He awoke to see his life as alternating between fear and captivity, fear and imprisonment. . .

The escape route from both was available. It was on the afternoon of the last day that he decided to take it. He had told neither his wife nor his chairman that he wasn't going to Australia, and everything was packed, his luggage arranged in the hall with a precision of which only Lydia was capable. She had told him she was going out to fetch his best lightweight suit from the cleaners, the suit he was to wear on the following day, and he had heard the front door close.

That had been half an hour before. While she was out he was to go upstairs, she had instructed him sadly and tenderly, and check that there was no vital item she had left unpacked. And at last he went, but for another purpose. A lethal, not a vital, item was what he wanted – the bottle of sleeping pills.

The bedroom door was closed. He opened it and saw her lying on their bed. She hadn't gone out. For half an hour she had been lying there, the empty bottle of pills still clutched feebly in her hand. He felt her pulse, and a firm but unsteady flicker passed into his fingers. She was alive. Another quarter of hour, say, and the ambulance would have her in hospital. He reached for the phone extension and put his finger to the slot to dial the emergency number. She'd be saved. Thank God, once again, he wasn't too late.

He looked down at her peaceful, tranquil face. She looked no older than on that day when she had come to him to thank him for saving her life. Gradually, almost involuntarily, he withdrew his finger from the dial. A heavy sob almost choked him and he heard himself give a whimpering cry. He lifted her in his arms, kissing her passionately and speaking her name aloud over and over again.

Then he walked quickly out of that room and out of the house. A bus came. He got on it and bought a ticket to some distant, outlying suburb. There in a park he didn't know and had never visited, he lay on the grass and fell into a deep sleep.

When he awoke it was nearly dark. He looked at his watch and saw that more than enough time had passed. Wiping his eyes, for he had apparently cried in his sleep, he got up and went home.

Dorothy L. Sayers

THE MAN WHO
KNEW HOW

Dorothy L. Sayers (1893–1957) was in her youth one of the editors of *Oxford Poetry* and the author of two volumes of verse, then a writer of crime stories, and in later years was much engaged with religious plays and essays, and translations of Dante. She was formidably knowledgeable about the crime story, and wrote a masterly introduction to the first of the three volumes of *Great Short Stories of Detection, Mystery and Horror* which she edited, an introduction that is in effect a brief history of the genre.

For most admirers her greatest achievement is the creation of Lord Peter Wimsey, and the novels and short stories in which he appears seem to those admirers the peak of twentieth-century detection fiction. There are those, however, like the present writer, who find the Wimsey tales insufferably snobbish, and their hero not a creation of high style as is sometimes claimed, but a schoolgirl's idea of an aristocrat, a figure who seems to have strayed from the green pastures of the romantic novel into the stony field of crime.

It will be no surprise, then, that Lord Peter is absent from the Sayers story chosen for this collection, even though Wimsey in my view appears to more advantage in short stories than in novels. There are Sayers stories of an entirely unWimseyish kind, and 'The Man Who Knew How' is one of them. The theme of the perfect murder committed by the unknown, untraceable poison is an old one, but it has rarely been used more cunningly and deceptively than here. It suggests that many good novels and short stories were lost when Dorothy Leigh Sayers fell in love with Lord Peter Wimsey.

For the twentieth time since the train had left Carlisle, Pender glanced up from *Murder at the Manse* and caught the eye of the man opposite.

He frowned a little. It was irritating to be watched so closely, and always with that faint, sardonic smile. It was still more irritating to allow oneself to be so much disturbed by the smile and the scrutiny. Pender wrenched himself back to his book with a determination to concentrate upon the problem of the minister murdered in the library.

But the story was of the academic kind that crowds all its exciting incidents into the first chapter, and proceeds thereafter by a long series of deductions to a scientific solution in the last. Twice Pender had to turn back to verify points that he had missed in reading. Then he became aware that he was not thinking about the murdered minister at all – he was becoming more and more actively conscious of the other man's face. A queer face, Pender thought.

There was nothing especially remarkable about the features in themselves; it was their expression that daunted Pender. It was a secret face, the face of one who knew a great deal to other people's disadvantage. The mouth was a little crooked and tightly tucked in at the corners, as though savouring a hidden amusement. The eyes, behind a pair of rimless pince-nez, glittered curiously; but that was possibly due to the light reflected in the glasses. Pender wondered what the man's profession might be. He was dressed in a dark lounge suit, a raincoat and a shabby soft hat; his age was perhaps about forty.

Pender coughed unnecessarily and settled back into his corner, raising the detective story high before his face, barrier-fashion. This was worse than useless. He gained the impression that the man saw through the manoeuvre and was secretly entertained by it. He wanted to fidget, but felt obscurely that his doing so would in some way constitute a victory for the other man. In his self-consciousness he held himself so rigid that attention to his book became a sheer physical impossibility.

There was no stop now before Rugby, and it was unlikely that any passenger would enter from the corridor to break up this disagreeable *solitude à deux.* Pender could, of course, go out into the corridor and not return, but that would be an acknowledgement of defeat. Pender lowered *Murder at the Manse* and caught the man's eye again.

'Getting tired of it?' asked the man.

'Night journeys are always a bit tedious,' replied Pender, half relieved and half reluctant. 'Would you like a book?'

He took *The Paper-Clip Clue* from his briefcase and held it out hopefully. The other man glanced at the title and shook his head.

'Thanks very much,' he said, 'but I never read detective stories. They're so – inadequate, don't you think so?'

'They are rather lacking in characterization and human interest, certainly,' said Pender, 'but on a railway journey –'

'I don't mean that,' said the other man. 'I am not concerned with humanity. But all these murderers are so incompetent – they bore me.'

'Oh, I don't know,' replied Pender. 'At any rate they are usually a good deal more imaginative and ingenious than murderers in real life.'

'Than the murderers who are found out in real life, yes,' admitted the other man.

'Even some of those did pretty well before they got pinched,' objected Pender. 'Crippen, for instance; he need never have been caught if he hadn't lost his head and run off to America. George Joseph Smith did away with at least two brides quite successfully before fate and the *News of the World* intervened.'

'Yes,' said the other man, 'but look at the clumsiness of it all; the elaboration, the lies, the paraphernalia. Absolutely unnecessary.'

'Oh come!' said Pender. 'You can't expect committing a murder and getting away with it to be as simple as shelling peas.'

'Ah!' said the other man. 'You think that, do you?'

Pender waited for him to elaborate this remark, but nothing came of it. The man leaned back and smiled in his secret way at the roof of the carriage; he appeared to think the conversation not worth going on with. Pender found himself noticing his companion's hands. They were white and surprisingly long in the fingers. He watched them gently tapping upon their owner's knee – then resolutely turned a page – then put the book down once more and said:

'Well, if it's so easy, how would *you* set about committing a murder?'

'I?' repeated the man. The light on his glasses made his eyes quite blank to Pender, but his voice sounded gently amused. 'That's different; *I* should not have to think twice about it.'

'Why not?'

'Because I happen to know how to do it.'

'Do you indeed?' muttered Pender, rebelliously.

'Oh yes; there's nothing to it.'

'How can you be sure? You haven't tried, I suppose?'

'It isn't a case of trying,' said the man. 'There's nothing uncertain about my method. That's just the beauty of it.'

'It's easy to say that,' retorted Pender, 'but what *is* this wonderful method?'

'You can't expect me to tell you that, can you?' said the other man, bringing his eyes back to rest on Pender's. 'It might not be safe. You look harmless enough, but who could look more harmless than Crippen? Nobody is fit to be trusted with *absolute* control over other people's lives.'

'Bosh!' exclaimed Pender. 'I shouldn't think of murdering anybody.'

'Oh yes you would,' said the other man, 'if you really believed it was safe. So would anybody. Why are all these tremendous artificial barriers built up around murder by the Church and the law? Just because it's everybody's crime and just as natural as breathing.'

'But that's ridiculous!' cried Pender, warmly.

'You think so, do you? That's what most people would say. But I wouldn't trust 'em. Not with sulphate of thanatol to be bought for two pence at any chemist's.'

'Sulphate of what?' asked Pender sharply.

'Ah! you think I'm giving something away. Well, it's a mixture of that and one or two other things – all equally ordinary and cheap. For nine pence you could make up enough to poison the entire Cabinet. Though of course one wouldn't polish off the whole lot at once; it might look funny if they all died simultaneously in their baths.'

'Why in their baths?'

'That's the way it would take them. It's the action of the hot water that brings on the effect of the stuff, you see. Any time from a few hours to a few days after administration. It's quite a simple chemical reaction and it couldn't possibly be detected by analysis. It would just look like heart failure.'

Pender eyed him uneasily. He did not like the smile; it was not only derisive, it was smug, it was almost gloating, triumphant! He could not quite put the right name to it.

'You know,' pursued the man, pulling a pipe from his pocket and beginning to fill it, 'it is very odd how often one seems to read of people being found dead in their baths. It must be a very common accident. Quite temptingly so. After all, there is a fascination about murder. The thing grows upon one – that is, I imagine it would, you know.'

'Very likely,' said Pender.

'I'm sure of it. No, I wouldn't trust anybody with that formula – not even a virtuous young man like yourself.'

The long white fingers tamped the tobacco firmly into the bowl and struck a match.

'But how about you?' said Pender, irritated. (Nobody cares to be called a virtuous young man.) 'If nobody is fit to be trusted –'

'I'm not, eh?' replied the man. 'Well, that's true, but it can't be helped now, can it? I know the thing and I can't unknow it again. It's unfortunate, but there it is. At any rate you have the comfort of knowing that nothing disagreeable is likely to happen to *me*. Dear me! Rugby already. I get out here. I have a little bit of business to do at Rugby.'

He rose and shook himself, buttoned his raincoat about him, and pulled the shabby hat more firmly down about his enigmatic glasses. The train slowed down and stopped. With a brief good night and a crooked smile the man stepped on to the platform. Pender watched him stride quickly away into the drizzle beyond the radius of the gas light.

'Dotty or something,' said Pender, oddly relieved. 'Thank goodness, I seem to be going to have the compartment to myself.'

He returned to *Murder at the Manse*, but his attention still kept wandering from the book he held in his hand.

'What was the name of that stuff the fellow talked about? Sulphate of what?'

For the life of him he could not remember.

It was on the following afternoon that Pender saw the news item. He had bought the *Standard* to read at lunch, and the word 'Bath' caught his eye; otherwise he would probably have missed the paragraph altogether, for it was only a short one.

Wealthy Manufacturer Dies in Bath
wife's tragic discovery

A distressing discovery was made early this morning by Mrs John Brittlesea, wife of the well-known head of Brittlesea's Engineering Works at Rugby. Finding that her husband, whom she had seen alive and well less than an hour previously, did not come down in time for his breakfast, she searched for him in the bathroom, where the engineer was found lying dead in his bath, life having been extinct, according to the medical men, for half an hour. The cause of the death is pronounced to be heart failure. The deceased manufacturer . . .

'That's an odd coincidence,' said Pender. 'At Rugby. I should think my unknown friend would be interested – if he is still there, doing his bit of business. I wonder what his business is, by the way.'

It is a very curious thing how, when once your attention is attracted to any particular set of circumstances, that set of circumstances seems to haunt you. You get appendicitis: immediately the newspapers are filled with paragraphs about statesmen suffering from appendicitis and victims dying of it; you learn that all your acquaintances have had it, or know friends who have had it and either died of it, or recovered from it with more surprising and spectacular rapidity than yourself; you cannot open a popular magazine without seeing its cure mentioned as one of the triumphs of modern surgery, or dip into a scientific treatise without coming across a comparison of the vermiform appendix in men and monkeys. Probably these references to appendicitis are equally frequent at all times, but you only notice them when your mind is attuned to the subject. At any rate, it was in this way that Pender accounted to himself for the extraordinary frequency with which people seemed to die in their baths at this period.

The thing pursued him at every turn. Always the same sequence of events: the hot bath, the discovery of the corpse, the inquest. Always the same medical opinion: heart failure following immersion in too hot water. It began to seem to Pender that it was scarcely safe to enter a hot bath at all. He took to making his own bath cooler and cooler each day, until it almost ceased to be enjoyable.

He skimmed his paper each morning for headlines about baths before settling down to read the news; and was at once relieved and vaguely disappointed if a week passed without a hot-bath tragedy.

One of the sudden deaths that occurred in this way was that of a young and beautiful woman whose husband, an analytical chemist, had tried without success to divorce her a few months previously. The coroner displayed a tendency to suspect foul play, and put the husband through a severe cross-examination. There seemed, however, to be no getting behind the doctor's evidence. Pender, brooding over the improbable possible, wished, as he did every day of the week, that he could remember the name of that drug the man in the train had mentioned.

Then came the excitement in Pender's own neighbourhood. An old Mr

Skimmings, who lived alone with a housekeeper in a street just around the corner, was found dead in his bathroom. His heart had never been strong. The housekeeper told the milkman that she had always expected something of the sort to happen, for the old gentleman would always take his bath so hot. Pender went to the inquest.

The housekeeper gave her evidence. Mr Skimmings had been the kindest of employers, and she was heartbroken at losing him. No, she had not been aware that Mr Skimmings had left her a large sum of money, but it was just like his goodness of heart. The verdict of course was accidental death.

Pender, that evening, went out for his usual stroll with the dog. Some feeling of curiosity moved him to go around past the late Mr Skimmings' house. As he loitered by, glancing up at the blank windows, the garden gate opened and a man came out. In the light of a street lamp, Pender recognized him at once.

'Hullo!' he said.

'Oh, it's you, is it?' said the man. 'Viewing the site of the tragedy, eh? What do *you* think about it all?'

'Oh, nothing very much,' said Pender. 'I didn't know him. Odd, our meeting again like this.'

'Yes, isn't it? You live near here, I suppose.'

'Yes,' said Pender; and then wished he hadn't. 'Do you live in these parts too?'

'Me?' said the man. 'Oh no. I was only here on a little matter of business.'

'Last time we met,' said Pender, 'you had business at Rugby.' They had fallen into step together, and were walking slowly down to the turning Pender had to take in order to reach his house.

'So I had,' agreed the other man. 'My business takes me all over the country. I never know where I may be wanted next, you see.'

'It was while you were at Rugby that old Brittlesea was found dead in his bath, wasn't it?' remarked Pender carelessly.

'Yes. Funny thing, coincidence.' The man glanced up at him sideways through his glittering glasses. 'Left all his money to his wife, didn't he? She's a rich woman now. Good-looking girl – a lot younger than he was.'

They were passing Pender's gate. 'Come in and have a drink,' said Pender, and again immediately regretted the impulse.

The man accepted, and they went into Pender's bachelor study.

'Remarkable lot of these bath deaths lately,' observed Pender as he squirted soda into the tumblers.

'You think it's remarkable?' said the man, with his irritating trick of querying everything that was said to him. 'Well, I don't know. Perhaps it is. But it's always a fairly common accident.'

'I suppose I've been taking more notice on account of that conversation we had in the train.' Pender laughed, a little self-consciously. 'It just makes me wonder – you know how one does – whether anybody else had happened to hit on that drug you mentioned – what was its name?'

The man ignored the question.

'Oh, I shouldn't think so,' he said. 'I fancy I'm the only person who knows about that. I only stumbled on the thing by accident myself when I was looking for something else. I don't imagine it could have been discovered simultaneously in so many parts of the country. But all these verdicts just show, don't they, what a safe way it would be of getting rid of a person.'

'You're a chemist, then?' asked Pender, catching at the one phrase which seemed to promise information.

'Oh, I'm a bit of everything. Sort of general utility man. I do a good bit of studying on my own, too. You've got one or two interesting books here, I see.'

Pender was flattered. For a man in his position – he had been in a bank until he came into that little bit of money – he felt that he had improved his mind to some purpose, and he knew that his collection of modern first editions would be worth money some day. He went over to the glass-fronted bookcase and pulled out a volume or two to show his visitor.

The man displayed intelligence, and presently joined him in front of the shelves.

'These, I take it, represent your personal tastes?' He took down a volume of Henry James and glanced at the fly-leaf. 'That your name? E. Pender?'

Pender admitted that it was. 'You have the advantage of me,' he added.

'Oh! I am one of the great Smith clan,' said the other with a laugh, 'and work for my bread. You seem to be very nicely fixed here.'

Pender explained about the clerkship and the legacy.

'Very nice, isn't it?' said Smith. 'Not married? No. You're one of the lucky ones. Not likely to be needing any sulphate of . . . any useful drugs in the near future. And you never will, if you stick to what you've got and keep off women and speculation.'

He smiled up sideways at Pender. Now that his hat was off, Pender saw that he had a quantity of closely curled grey hair, which made him look older than he had appeared in the railway carriage.

'No, I shan't be coming to you for assistance yet a while,' said Pender, laughing. 'Besides, how should I find you if I wanted you?'

'You wouldn't have to,' said Smith. '*I* should find *you*. There's never any difficulty about that.' He grinned, oddly. 'Well, I'd better be getting on. Thank you for your hospitality. I don't expect we shall meet again – but we may, of course. Things work out so queerly, don't they?'

When he had gone, Pender returned to his own armchair. He took up his glass of whisky, which stood there nearly full.

'Funny!' he said to himself. 'I don't remember pouring that out. I suppose I got interested and did it mechanically.' He emptied his glass slowly, thinking about Smith.

What in the world was Smith doing at Skimmings' house?

An odd business altogether. If Skimmings' housekeeper had known about that money . . . But she had not known, and if she had, how could she have found out about Smith and his sulphate of . . . the word had been on the tip of his tongue, then.

'You would not need to find me. *I* should find *you*.' What had the man meant by that? But this was ridiculous. Smith was not the devil, presumably. But if he really had this secret – if he liked to put a price upon it – nonsense.

'Business at Rugby – a little bit of business at Skimmings' house.' Oh, absurd!

'Nobody is fit to be trusted. *Absolute* power over another man's life . . . it grows on you. That is, I imagine it would.'

Lunacy! And, if there was anything in it, the man was mad to tell Pender about it. If Pender chose to speak he could get the fellow hanged. The very existence of Pender would be dangerous.

That whisky!

More and more, thinking it over, Pender became persuaded that he had never poured it out. Smith must have done it while his back was turned. Why that sudden display of interest in the bookshelves? It had had no connection with anything that had gone before. Now Pender came to think of it, it had been a very stiff whisky. Was it imagination, or had there been something about the flavour of it?

A cold sweat broke out on Pender's forehead.

A quarter of an hour later, after a powerful dose of mustard and water, Pender was downstairs again, very cold and shivering, huddling over the fire. He had had a narrow escape – if he had escaped. He did not know how the stuff worked, but he would not take a hot bath again for some days. One never knew.

Whether the mustard and water had done the trick in time, or whether the hot bath was an essential part of the treatment, at any rate Pender's life was saved for the time being. But he was still uneasy. He kept the front door on the chain and warned his servant to let no strangers into the house.

He ordered two more morning papers and the *News of the World* on Sundays, and kept a careful watch upon their columns. Deaths in baths became an obsession with him. He neglected his first editions and took to attending inquests.

Three weeks later he found himself at Lincoln. A man had died of heart failure in a Turkish bath – a fat man, of sedentary habits. The jury added a rider to their verdict of accidental death to the effect that the management should exercise a stricter supervision over the bathers and should never permit them to be left unattended in the hot room.

As Pender emerged from the hall he saw ahead of him a shabby hat that seemed familiar. He plunged after it, and caught Mr Smith about to step into a taxi.

'Smith,' he cried, gasping a little. He clutched him fiercely by the shoulder.

'What, you again?' said Smith. 'Taking notes of the case, eh? *Can I do anything for you?*'

'You devil!' said Pender. 'You're mixed up in this! You tried to kill me the other day.'

'Did I? Why should I do that?'

'You'll swing for this,' shouted Pender menacingly.

A policeman pushed his way through the gathering crowd.

'Here!' said he. 'What's all this about?'

Smith touched his forehead significantly.

'It's all right, Officer,' said he. 'The gentleman seems to think I'm here for no good. Here's my card. The coroner knows me. But he attacked me. You'd better keep an eye on him.'

'That's right,' said a bystander.

'This man tried to kill me,' said Pender.

The policeman nodded.

'Don't you worry about that, sir,' he said. 'You think better of it. The 'eat in there has upset you a bit. All right, *all* right.'

'But I want to charge him,' said Pender.

'I wouldn't do that if I was you,' said the policeman.

'I tell you,' said Pender, 'that this man Smith has been trying to poison me. He's a murderer. He's poisoned scores of people.'

The policeman winked at Smith.

'Best be off, sir,' he said. 'I'll settle this. Now, my lad' – he held Pender firmly by the arms – 'just you keep cool and take it quiet. That gentleman's name ain't Smith nor nothing like it. You've got a bit mixed up like.'

'Well, what is his name?' demanded Pender.

'Never mind,' replied the constable. 'You leave him alone, or you'll be getting yourself into trouble.'

The taxi had driven away. Pender glanced around at the circle of amused faces and gave in.

'All right, Officer,' he said. 'I won't give you any trouble. I'll come round with you to the police station and tell you about it.'

'What do you think o' that one?' asked the inspector of the sergeant when Pender had stumbled out of the station.

'Up the pole an' 'alfway round the flag, if you ask me,' replied his subordinate. 'Got one o' them ideez fix what they talk about.'

'H'm!' replied the inspector. 'Well, we've got his name and address. Better make a note of 'em. He might turn up again. Poisoning people so as they die in their baths, eh? That's a pretty good 'un. Wonderful how these barmy ones thinks it all out, isn't it?'

The spring that year was a bad one – cold and foggy. It was March when Pender went down to an inquest at Deptford, but a thick blanket of mist was hanging over the river as though it were November. The cold ate into your bones. As he sat in the dingy little court, peering through the yellow twilight of gas and fog, he could scarcely see the witnesses as they came to the table. Everybody in the place seemed to be coughing. Pender was coughing too. His bones ached, and he felt as though he were about due for a bout of influenza.

Straining his eyes, he thought he recognized a face on the other side of the room, but the smarting fog which penetrated every crack stung and blinded him. He felt in his overcoat pocket, and his hand closed comfortably on something thick and heavy. Ever since that day in Lincoln he had gone about armed for protection. Not a revolver – he was no hand with firearms. A sandbag was much better. He had bought one from an old man wheeling a pushcart. It was meant for keeping out draughts from the door – a good, old-fashioned affair.

The inevitable verdict was returned. The spectators began to push their way out. Pender had to hurry now, not to lose sight of his man. He elbowed his way along, muttering apologies. At the door he almost touched the man, but a stout woman intervened. He plunged past her, and she gave a little squeak of indignation. The man in front turned his head, and the light over the door glinted on his glasses.

Pender pulled his hat over his eyes and followed. His shoes had crêpe rubber soles and made no sound on the pavement. The man went on, jogging quietly up one street and down another, and never looking back. The fog was so thick that Pender was forced to keep within a few yards of him. Where was he going? Into the lighted streets? Home by bus or tram? No. He turned off to the left, down a narrow street.

The fog was thicker here. Pender could no longer see his quarry, but he heard the footsteps going on before him at the same even pace. It seemed to him that they were two alone in the world – pursued and pursuer, slayer and avenger. The street began to slope more rapidly. They must be coming out somewhere near the river.

Suddenly the dim shapes of the houses fell away on either side. There was an open space, with a lamp vaguely visible in the middle. The footsteps paused. Pender, silently hurrying after, saw the man standing close beneath the lamp, apparently consulting something in a notebook.

Four steps, and Pender was upon him. He drew the sandbag from his pocket.

The man looked up.

'I've got you this time,' said Pender, and struck with all his force.

Pender was quite right. He did get influenza. It was a week before he was out and about again. The weather had changed, and the air was fresh and sweet. In spite of the weakness left by the malady he felt as though a heavy weight had been lifted from his shoulders. He tottered down to a favourite bookshop of his in the Strand, and picked up a D. H. Lawrence 'first' at a price which he knew to be a bargain. Encouraged by this, he turned into a small chophouse chiefly frequented by newspaper men, and ordered a grilled cutlet and a half-tankard of bitter.

Two journalists were seated by the next table.

'Going to poor old Buckley's funeral?' asked one.

'Yes,' said the other. 'Poor devil! Fancy his getting bashed on the head like that. He must have been on his way down to interview the widow of that fellow who died in a bath. It's a rough district. Probably one of Jimmy the Card's crowd had it in for him. He was a great crime-reporter – they won't get another like Bill Buckley in a hurry.'

'He was a decent sort, too. Great old sport. No end of a practical joker. Remember his great stunt sulphate of thanatol?'

Pender started. *That* was the word that had eluded him for so many months. A curious dizziness came over him.

'. . . looking at you as sober as a judge,' the journalist was saying. 'No such stuff, of course, but he used to work off that wheeze on poor boobs in railway carriages to see how they'd take it. Would you believe that one chap actually offered him –'

'Hullo!' interrupted his friend. 'That bloke over there has fainted. I thought he was looking a bit white.'

Georges Simenon

INSPECTOR
MAIGRET PURSUES

Some seventy of the works of Georges Simenon (1903–   ) have at their centre Inspector, later Superintendent, Jules Maigret. They are notable less as detective stories – most of them avoid clues like foot- or finger-prints, and ignore ballistic and scientific details – than as studies of human beings under pressure, and demonstrations of the ways in which they react to the plodding energy and endless patience of Maigret. Everything is filtered to us through the personality of this ideal French bourgeois, the surroundings, the weather (Maigret is particularly sensitive to weather, and indeed to most kinds of physical experience), the people. The French policeman is one of the most completely realized characters in all modern fiction. This is true even though Simenon has little affection for him, feeling that the Maigret stories have achieved popularity and publicity at the expense of better work. And indeed it is certainly true that the best of what he calls his 'hard' novels have an intensity of feeling and depth of concentration that the Maigret stories lack. 'Inspector Maigret Pursues' is a typical Maigret tale, showing perfectly his bulldog and bloodhound qualities.

The four men were packed in the taxi. It was freezing all over Paris. At half-past seven in the morning the city looked wan; the wind was whipping the powdery frost along the ground. The thinnest of the four men, on one of the flap seats, had a cigaret stuck to his lower lip and handcuffs on his wrists. The most important one, clothed in a thick overcoat, heavy-jawed, a bowler hat on his head, was smoking his pipe and watching the railings of the Bois de Boulogne file past.

'You want me to put on a big dramatic scene?' the handcuffed man suggested politely. 'With struggling, frothing at the mouth, insults, and all?'

Taking the cigaret from between the man's lips and opening the door, for they had arrived at the Porte de Bagatelle, Inspector Maigret growled, 'Don't overdo it.'

The pathways in the Bois were deserted, white as limestone, and as hard. A dozen or so people were standing around at the corner of a bridle path, and a photographer prepared to go into action on the group as it approached.

But, as instructed, P'tit Louis raised his arms in front of his face.

Maigret, looking surly, swung his head from side to side like a bear, taking everything in – the new blocks of flats on the Boulevard Richard-Wallace, their shutters still closed, a few workmen on bikes coming from Puteaux, a lighted tram, two concierges approaching, their hands blue with cold.

'Is this it?' he asked.

The day before he had arranged for the following information to appear in the newspapers:

BAGATELLE MURDER

This time the police will not have been long in clearing up an affair that looked as if it presented insurmountable difficulties. It will be remembered that on Monday morning a park-keeper in the Bois de Boulogne discovered along one of the pathways a hundred yards or so from the Porte de Bagatelle a corpse it was possible to identify on the spot.

It was Ernest Borms, a well-known Viennese doctor who had been in practice in Neuilly for several years. Borms was wearing evening clothes. He must have been attacked during the night of Sunday/Monday, while returning to his flat on the Boulevard Richard-Wallace.

A bullet fired at point-blank range from a small-caliber revolver struck him full in the heart.

Borms, still young and handsome and well turned out, led a fairly social life.

Scarcely forty-eight hours after the murder Police Headquarters have just made an arrest. Tomorrow morning, between seven and eight o'clock, the man concerned will be conducted to the scene for the purpose of a reconstruction of the crime.

As things turned out, this case was to be referred to at Headquarters as the one perhaps most characteristically Maigret; but when they spoke of it in his hearing, he had a curious way of turning his head away with a groan.

To proceed, everything was ready. Hardly any gaping onlookers, as planned. It was not for nothing that Maigret had chosen this early hour of the morning. Moreover, among the ten or twelve people who were hanging about could be spotted some plainclothesmen wearing their most innocent air. One of them, Torrence, who loved disguises, was dressed as a milkman. At the sight of him his chief shrugged eloquently. If only P'tit Louis didn't overact. An old customer of theirs who had been picked up the day before for picking pockets in the Métro . . .

'You give us a hand tomorrow morning and we'll see that we aren't too hard on you this time . . .' They had fetched him up from the cells.

'Now, then,' growled Maigret, 'when you heard the footsteps you were hiding in this corner here, weren't you?'

'As you say, Chief Inspector. I was famished. Stony broke . . . I said to myself, a gent on his way home all dressed up like that must be carrying a walletful. "Your money or your life!" was what I whispered right into his ear. And I swear it wasn't my fault that the thing went off. I'm quite sure it was the cold made me squeeze the trigger.'

11:00 A.M. Maigret was pacing round his office at Headquarters, smoking solidly and constantly fiddling with the phone.

'Is that you, Chief? Lucas here. I followed the old man who seemed so interested in the reconstruction. Nothing doing there – he's just a lunatic who takes a stroll every morning in the Bois.'

'All right, you can come back.'

*

11:15 A.M. 'Hullo, is that you, Chief? Torrence. I shadowed the young man you tipped me the wink on. He always hangs round when the plainclothes boys are called in. He's an assistant in a shop on the Champs Elysées. Shall I come back?'

From Janvier no call till 11:55.

'I've got to be quick, Chief. I'm afraid he'll give me the slip. I'm keeping an eye on him in the mirror of the booth. I'm at the Yellow Dwarf Bar, Boulevard Rochechouart . . . Yes, he spotted me. He's got something on his mind. Crossing the Seine, he threw something in the river. He's tried over and over to shake me off. Will you be coming?'

So began a chase that was to last five days and nights. Among the hurrying crowds, across an unsuspecting Paris, from bar to bar, bistro to bistro, a lone man on the one hand, and on the other Maigret and his detectives, taking it in turn and, in the long run, just as harassed as the man they were following.

Maigret got out of his taxi opposite the Yellow Dwarf at the busy time just before lunch, and found Janvier leaning on the bar. He wasn't troubling to put on any façade of innocence. Quite the opposite.

'Which one is it?'

The detective motioned with his jaw toward a man sitting in the corner at a small table. The man was watching them; his eyes, which were a light blue-gray, gave a foreign cast to his face. Nordic? Slav? More likely a Slav. He was wearing a gray overcoat, a well-cut suit, a soft felt hat. About thirty-five years old, so far as one could judge. He was pale, close-shaven.

'What're you having, Chief? A hot toddy?'

'Toddy let it be. What's *he* drinking?'

'Brandy. It's his fifth this morning. You mustn't mind if I sound slurred, but I've had to follow him round all the bistros. He's tough, you know. Look at him – it's been like that all morning. He wouldn't lower his eyes for all the kingdoms of the earth.'

It was true. And it was strange. You couldn't call it arrogance or defiance. The man was just looking at them. If he felt any anxiety, it was concealed. It was sadness rather that his face expressed, but a calm, reflective sadness.

'At Bagatelle, when he noticed you were watching him, he went off straight away and I fell into step behind him. He hadn't gone a hundred yards before he turned round. Then, instead of leaving the Bois, as he apparently meant to do, he strode off down the first path he came to. He

turned round again. He recognized me. He sat down on a bench, despite
the cold, and I stopped. More than once I had the impression he wanted
to speak to me, but in the end he only shrugged and set off again.

'At the Porte Dauphine I almost lost him. He jumped into a taxi and it
was just luck that I found one almost immediately. He got out at the Place
de l'Opéra, and rushed into the Métro. One behind the other, we changed
trains five times before he began to realize he wouldn't shake me off that
way . . .

'We went up again into the street. We were at Place Clichy. Since then we
have been going from bar to bar. I was waiting for one with a telephone booth
where I could keep him in sight. When he saw me phoning, he gave a bitter
little laugh. Honestly, you'd have sworn after that he was waiting for you.'

'Ring up HQ. Lucas and Torrence are to hold themselves ready to join
me as soon as they're called. And a photographer, too, from the technical
branch, with a miniature camera.'

'Waiter!' the man called out. 'What do I owe you?'

'Three-fifty.'

'I bet he's a Pole,' Maigret breathed to Janvier. 'On our way . . .'

They didn't get far. At Place Blanche they followed the man into a
restaurant, sat down at the next table. It was an Italian place, and they ate
pasta.

At three, Lucas came to take over from Janvier, who was with Maigret
at a *brasserie* opposite the Gare du Nord.

'The photographer?' Maigret asked.

'He's waiting outside to get him as he leaves.'

And sure enough, when the Pole left the place, having finished reading
the papers, a detective hurried up. At less than three feet he took a shot of
him. The man raised his hand quickly to his face, but it was already too
late. Then, proving that he knew what was going on, he cast a reproachful
look at Maigret.

Aha, my little man, Maigret said to himself, you have some good reason
for not revealing where you live. Well, you may be patient, but so am I.

By evening a few snowflakes were fluttering down in the street; the
stranger walked on, hands in pockets, waiting for bedtime.

'I'll take over for the night, Chief?' Lucas suggested.

'No. I'd rather you coped with the photograph. Look at the hotel
registrations first. Then see what you can find out in the foreign quarters.
That fellow knows his Paris. He didn't arrive yesterday. There must be
people who know him.'

'How about putting his picture in the papers?'

Maigret eyed his subordinate with scorn. How could Lucas, who had been working with him for so many years, fail to understand? Had the police one single clue? Nothing. Not one piece of evidence. A man killed during the night in the Bois de Boulogne. No weapon is found. No prints. Dr Borms lives alone, and his only servant doesn't know where he spent the previous evening. 'Do as I say. Get going . . .'

Finally at midnight the man decides to go into a hotel. Maigret follows him in. It is a second- or even third-class hotel.

'I want a room.'

'Will you register here, please?'

He registers hesitantly, his fingers stiff with cold. He looks Maigret up and down as if to say, 'If you think that's any problem – I can write any name that comes.'

And, in fact, he has done so. Nicolas Slaatkovitch, resident of Cracow, arrived the day before in Paris. It is all false, obviously.

Maigret telephones to Headquarters. They hunt through the files of furnished lodgings, the registers of foreigners, they get in touch with the frontier posts. No Nicolas Slaatkovitch.

'And a room for you?' the proprietor asks with distaste, for he senses the presence of a policeman.

'No, thank you. I'll spend the night on the stairs.'

It's safer that way. He sits down on a step in front of the door of Room 7. Twice the door opens. The man peers through the gloom, makes out Maigret's silhouette, and ends up by going to bed. In the morning his face is rough with stubble. He hasn't been able to change his shirt. He hasn't even got a comb, and his hair is rumpled.

Lucas has just arrived. 'I'll do the next shift, Chief?'

Maigret refuses to leave his stranger. He has watched him pay the bill. He has seen him grow pale. He guesses his thoughts . . .

And a little later, in a bar where, almost side by side, they are breakfasting on white coffee and croissants, the man openly counts up his fortune. One hundred-franc note, two twenty-franc pieces, one of ten, and some small change. He makes a bitter grimace.

Well, he won't get far on that. When he arrived at the Bois de Boulogne, he had come straight from home, for he was freshly shaved, not a speck of dust, not a crease in his clothes. He hadn't even looked to see how much money he had on him.

What he threw in the Seine, Maigret guesses, were his identification papers, perhaps visiting cards. At all costs he wants to prevent their finding out his address.

And so the round of the homeless begins again: the loitering in front of shops or round street traders, the bars one has to go into from time to time, even if it's only to sit down, especially when it's cold outside, the papers one reads in the *brasseries* . . .

One hundred and fifty francs. No more lunchtime restaurant. The man makes do with hard-boiled eggs, which he eats, along with his pint, standing up at the bar counter, while Maigret gulps down sandwiches.

For a long time the man has been thinking about going into a movie, his hand fingering the small change in his pocket. Better to stick it out. He walks . . . and walks . . .

There is, incidentally, one detail that strikes Maigret. It is always in the same districts that this exhausting stroll takes place: from the Trinité to Place Clichy, from Place Clichy to Barbès, by way of Rue Caulaincourt . . . from Barbès to the Gare du Nord and Rue Lafayette. Besides, the man's afraid of being recognized, isn't he? Of course he's chosen the districts farthest from his home or hotel, those he didn't usually frequent . . .

Does he, like many foreigners, haunt Montparnasse? The parts around the Panthéon?

His clothes indicate he is reasonably well off. They are comfortable, sober, and well cut. A professional man, no doubt. What's more, he wears a ring, so he's married.

Maigret has had to agree to hand over to Torrence, and has dashed home. Madame Maigret is displeased: her sister has come up from Orléans, she has taken a lot of trouble over the dinner, and her husband, after a shave and a change of clothes, is already off again, and doesn't know when he'll be back.

He drives off to the Quai des Orfèvres. 'Lucas hasn't left anything for me?'

Yes, he has. There's a note from the sergeant. He's been round several of the Polish and Russian quarters showing the photograph. Nobody knows the man. Nothing from the political circles, either. As a last resource he has had a large number of copies made of the photograph, and police are now going from door to door in all the districts of Paris, from concierge to concierge, showing the document to bar owners and waiters.

'Hello, is that Chief Inspector Maigret? This is one of the usherettes at the newsreel theater on the Boulevard de Strasbourg. It's a gentleman — Monsieur Torrence. He's asked me to call you to say he's here, but he didn't want to leave his place in the theater.'

Not so stupid, on the stranger's part. He has worked out that it's the best heated place to pass a few hours cheaply – two francs to get in, and you can see the program several times.

A curious intimacy has sprung up between follower and followed, between the man, whose face is now dark with stubble and whose clothes are crumpled, and Maigret, who never for a moment stops trailing him. There is even one rather comic point: they've both caught colds. Their noses are red; they pull out their handkerchiefs almost in time with one another. Once, in spite of himself, the stranger had to smile as he saw Maigret going off into a series of sneezes.

After five consecutive newsreel programs, a dirty hotel on the Boulevard de la Chapelle. Same name on the register. And again Maigret installs himself on the stairs. But as this is a hotel with a casual trade, he is disturbed every ten minutes by couples going up and down; they stare at him curiously, and the women don't find him a reassuring sight.

When he's at the end of his tether, or at the breaking point, will the man decide to go home? In one of the *brasseries*, where he stays long enough to take off his gray coat, Maigret without more ado seizes the garment and looks inside the collar. The coat comes from Old England, the shop on the Boulevard des Italiens. It is a ready-made coat, and the shop must have sold dozens of others like it. One clue, however: it is last year's model, so the stranger has been in Paris for a year at least. And in a year must have found somewhere to hang out . . .

Maigret has started drinking grog to cure his cold. The other now pays out his money drop by drop. He drinks his coffee straight; he lives on croissants and hard-boiled eggs.

The news from the office is always the same: nothing to report. Nobody recognizes the photograph of the Pole. No one has heard of any missing person.

As to the dead man, nothing there, either. A good practice, he made a lot of money, wasn't interested in politics, went out a lot, and, as he dealt with nervous diseases, most of his patients were women.

There was one experiment Maigret had not yet had the chance of seeing through to the end: how long it would take for a well-bred, well-cared-for, well-dressed man to lose his outward polish.

Four days. As he now knew. To begin with, the unshavenness. The first morning the man looked like a lawyer, or a doctor, or an architect, or a businessman; you could picture him leaving his cosy flat. A four-day growth transformed him to such an extent that if one had now put his picture in the papers and referred to the Bois de Boulogne affair, everyone would have said, 'You can see he's a murderer.'

The bitter weather and lack of sleep had reddened his eyelids, and his cheeks were feverish from his cold. His shoes, which were no longer polished, seemed to have lost their shape. His coat weighed on him, and his trousers were baggy round the knees.

Even his walk was no longer the same. He sidled along the wall, he lowered his eyes when people looked at him. Another thing: he turned his head away when he passed a restaurant where one could see people sitting down to large meals . . .

'Your last twenty francs,' Maigret worked out, 'poor wretch. What now?'

Lucas, Torrence, and Janvier took over from him from time to time, but he left his post as little as possible. He would burst into the Quai des Orfèvres, would see his Chief.

'You'd be well advised to take a rest, Maigret.'

It was a peevish Maigret, touchy as if he were torn between contradictory emotions. 'Am I or am I not supposed to be finding the murderer?'

'Of course.'

'Well then, back to my post.' As if resentfully, he would sigh, 'I wonder where we'll sleep tonight.'

Only twenty francs left. Not even that – when he got back, Torrence said the man had eaten three hard-boiled eggs and drunk two rum coffees in a bar on the corner of the Rue Montmartre.

'Eight francs fifty. That leaves eleven francs fifty.'

Maigret admired him. Far from hiding himself, Maigret now tailed him quite openly, sometimes walking right next to him, and he had some difficulty to refrain from speaking to him. 'Come now, don't you think it's time to have a proper meal? Somewhere there's a warm home where you're expected. A bed, slippers, a razor. Eh? And a good dinner.'

But the man continued to prowl under the arc lamps of Les Halles, like one who no longer knows where to turn. In and out among the heaps of cabbages and carrots, stepping out of the way at the whistle of the train or when the farmers' trucks passed.

'Hasn't even the price of a hotel room.'

That evening the National Meteorological Office registered a temperature of eight degrees below zero. The man treated himself to hot sausages from a stall in the streets. Now he would reek of garlic and fat the whole night through.

Once he tried to slip into a shelter and stretch out in the corner. A policeman, whom Maigret wasn't able to stop in time, moved him on. He was hobbling now. Along the quais. The Pont des Arts. As long as he didn't take it into his head to throw himself into the Seine. Maigret didn't feel he had the courage to jump in after him into the black water that was beginning to fill with drift ice.

The man was walking along the towpath level, where the tramps lay grumbling and, under the bridges, all the good places were taken.

In a small street close to the Place Maubert, through the windows of a strange bistro, old men could be seen sleeping with their heads on the tables. Twenty sous, wine included. The man stared in through the gloom. Then, with a fatalistic shrug, he pushed open the door.

Before it closed behind him, Maigret had time to be sickened by the smelly gust that struck him in the face. He preferred to stay outside. He called a policeman, posted him in his place on the pavement while he went to telephone Lucas to take over for the night.

'I've been trying to get you for the last hour, Chief. We've found him! Thanks to a concierge. The fellow's called Stefan Strevzki, an architect, thirty-four years old, born in Warsaw, been in France for three years. Works for a firm in the Faubourg Saint-Honoré. Married to a Hungarian, a magnificent creature named Dora. Living at Passy, Rue de la Pompe, in a twelve-thousand-franc flat. No political interests. The concierge has never seen the dead man. Stefan left the house earlier than usual on Monday morning. She was surprised not to see him return, but she wasn't worried, having ascertained –'

'What time is it?'

'Half-past three. I'm alone at Headquarters. I've had some beer brought up, but it's too cold.'

'Listen, Lucas, you're going – yes, I know, too late for the morning ones. But the evening ones . . . understand?'

That morning the man's clothing gave off a muffled odor of poverty. His eyes were sunken. The look he cast at Maigret in the pale morning contained the deepest pathos and reproach.

Had he not been driven, little by little, but for all that at a dizzy pace, to the very lowest depths? He turned up the collar of his overcoat. He didn't leave the neighborhood, but he rushed into a bistro that had just opened and downed four quick drinks, as if to rid himself of the appalling aftertaste the night had left in his throat and chest.

So much the worse for him. From now on he no longer had anything. Nothing was left for him but to walk up and down the streets the frost was making slippery. He must be stiff all over. He was limping with his left leg. From time to time he stopped and looked around despairingly.

As soon as he stopped going into cafés where there was a telephone, Maigret could no longer summon a relief. Back again along the quais. Then that mechanical gesture of flipping through the book bargains, turning the pages, pausing to check the authenticity of an engraving or a print.

A freezing wind was sweeping across the Seine. The water tinkled as the barges moved through it, as tiny fragments of ice glittered and jostled against one another. From a distance Maigret caught sight of the windows of his own office. His sister-in-law had gone back to Orléans. As long as Lucas had . . .

He didn't know yet that this dreadful trail was to become a classic, and that for years the older generation of detectives would recount the details to new colleagues. The silliest thing about it all was that it was a ridiculous detail that upset him most: the man had a pimple on his forehead, a pimple that, on close inspection, turned out to be a boil, which was changing from red to purple.

As long as Lucas . . .

At midday the man, who certainly knew his Paris, made for the free soup kitchen that is situated at the end of the Boulevard Saint-Germain. He took his place in the queue of down-and-outers. An old man spoke to him, but he pretended not to understand. Then another, with a pock-marked face, spoke to him in Russian.

Maigret crossed over to the opposite pavement, and paused. When he was driven to have sandwiches in a bistro, he half turned so that the other should not see him eating them through the windows.

The poor wretches moved forward slowly, went in, four or maybe six at a time, to the room where bowls of hot soup were being served. The queue grew longer. From time to time there was a shove from the back, which aroused protests from some of the others.

One o'clock. A newsboy appeared at the far end of the street; he was running, his body sloping forward. '*L'Intransigeant!* Get your *Intran* –' He, too, was in a hurry to get there before the others. He could tell his customers from far off, and he paid no attention to the queue of down-and-outers. 'Get your –'

'Pst!' Timidly, the man raised his hand to attract the boy's attention. The others stared at him. So he had still a few sous left to spend on a paper?

Maigret, too, summoned the boy, unfolded the paper, and, to his relief, found what he was looking for – the photograph of a beautiful young woman smiling out of the front page.

STRANGE DISAPPEARANCE

A young Polish woman, Madame Dora Strevzki, who disappeared four days ago from her home in Passy, 17 Rue de la Pompe, has now been reported missing. Her husband, Monsieur Stefan Strevzki, has also been missing from his home since the previous day – i.e., Monday – and the concierge, who reported the disappearance to the police, states . . .

The man had only five or six yards more to go in the queue before he could claim his bowl of steaming soup, when he left his place in the line and was almost run over by a bus. He reached the opposite pavement just as Maigret drew level.

'I'm ready,' he said simply. 'Take me away. I'll answer all your questions . . .'

They were all standing in the corridor of Headquarters – Lucas, Janvier, Torrence, and others who had not been in on the case but knew about it. As they passed, Lucas made a triumphant signal to Maigret.

A door opened and shut. Beer and sandwiches on the table.

'Take something to eat first.'

Not so easy. Mouthfuls stuck in his throat. Then, at last, 'Now that she's gone and is somewhere safe . . .'

Maigret couldn't face him: he had to turn away and poke the stove.

'When I read the accounts of the murder in the papers I had already suspected Dora of deceiving me with that man. I knew, too, she wasn't his only mistress. Knowing Dora and her impetuous nature . . . You understand? If he wanted to get rid of her, I knew she was capable of . . . And she always carried an ivory-handled gun in her handbag. When the papers reported that an arrest had been made and there was to be a reconstruction of the crime, I wanted to see . . .'

Maigret would have liked to be able to say to him, as the British police do, 'I must warn you that anything you say may be used in evidence against you.'

He had kept his coat on and he was still wearing his hat. 'Now that she's safe . . . For I suppose . . .' He looked about him anxiously. A suspicion crossed his mind.

'She must have understood when I didn't come home. I knew it would end like that – that Borms wasn't the man for her, that she wouldn't accept the role of a mere plaything, and that she'd come back to me. She went out alone that Sunday evening, as she had been doing recently. She must have killed him then.'

Maigret blew his nose. He took a long time over it. A ray of sunlight – the harsh winter sunlight that goes with sharp frost – came in the window. The pimple or boil gleamed on the forehead of the man – as Maigret found he had to go on calling him.

'So your wife killed him. When she found out he had never really cared for her. And you, you realized she had done it. And you didn't want . . .'

He suddenly went up to the Pole. 'I'm sorry, old man,' he grunted, as if he was talking to an old friend. 'I had to find out the truth, hadn't I? It was my duty.'

Then he opened the door. 'Bring in Madame Dora Strevzki. Lucas, you carry on. I –'

And for the next two days nobody saw him again at Headquarters. His chief telephoned him at home. 'Well now, Maigret. You know she's confessed, and – by the way, how's your cold? They tell me –'

'It's nothing, Chief. It's getting better. Another day. How is he?'

'What? Who?'

'He – the man.'

'Oh, I see. He's got hold of the best lawyer in Paris. He has hopes – you know, *crimes passionnels* . . .'

Maigret went back to bed and sank into a grog-and-aspirin stupor. When, later on, he was asked about the investigation, his grumbled 'What investigation?' was enough to discourage further questions.

As for the man, he came to see him once or twice a week, and kept him informed of the hopes the defense were holding out.

It wasn't a straightforward acquittal: one year's imprisonment, with sentence suspended.

And the man – it was he who taught Maigret to play chess.

Roy Vickers

THE MAN
WHO MURDERED
IN PUBLIC

Roy Vickers (1889–1965) was for much of his career a hack writer, working as a journalist and crime reporter in court, and producing sensational or romantic novels of which there is nothing good to be said. In 1935, however, he published a story called 'The Rubber Trumpet' about the fictional Scotland Yard Department of Dead Ends, where obscure or apparently meaningless things are stored. There is nothing particularly novel about this conception, nor about Inspector Rason who is in charge of the Department (he had already appeared in several novels). What is new is the deadpan realism of the writing, which sprang partly from Vickers's experience as a court reporter. The manner which he first used in this tale, and later developed and perfected, remains unique in the crime story in the way in which it emphasizes the humdrum lives of most murderers and victims. The writing has a deliberate lack of colour. The effect might be dull but is not, because the way in which the stories are told includes the element of surprise.

The first Dead End stories proved unacceptably realistic for the magazines of the period, and Vickers gave them up. He revived them only in the late forties when Ellery Queen discovered 'The Rubber Trumpet', and saw to it that the tale received a prize award from *Ellery Queen's Mystery Magazine*. Queen said rightly that the realism of this and other stories was 'shot through with the credible fantasy which occurs repeatedly in real life – the peculiar touch of the unreal which somehow stamps all works of genuine imagination with the very trademark of reality'.

Thus encouraged, Vickers went on writing Dead End stories almost until his death, and although one or two of his later novels also have that 'trademark of reality', it is as a short-story writer that he found the form and manner in which to work freely. There are three collections of Dead End stories, and ten of the best are included in *The Best Detective Stories of Roy Vickers*, published in 1965. 'The Man Who Murdered in Public', which obviously had its origins in the exploits of the 'Brides in the Bath' murderer George Joseph Smith, is one of them.

I

How little do you know about a man if you only know that he has committed four murders! That is all the public of his day knew of George Macartney. The papers handed out the usual thoughtless nonsense about a 'human monster', and reminded the public that he was the son of Henry Macartney, the fraudulent financier – and that he therefore had a tainted heredity.

Now it is impossible to inherit a tendency to falsify balance sheets (not that George ever did anything of the kind). And as to the human monster stuff, with its suggestion of morbid blood-lust, it may be remarked that George netted by his murders a little over twenty-two thousand pounds. Further, it is the essence of anything to do with morbidity that the act should be secret. George Macartney is perhaps unique amongst murderers in that each of his four murders was eye-witnessed by anything from a dozen to several hundred persons, including a policeman or two.

All the same, the fact that Henry Macartney, his father, actually received fourteen years' penal servitude is the key to the queer psychology of George himself. It was, however, not a matter of heredity but of objective circumstance – being the direct cause of young George receiving his first thrashing.

George was a late grower both physically and mentally. Eventually he grew into a hefty man with plenty of pluck and intelligence. But at fifteen he was about the physical size of a boy of eleven, with much the same mental range. And a pretty dreadful little boy, too!

His mother was a very good sort but she had died when he was three. His father in his private life was amiable and undisciplined. There had been two or three schools which he had allowed the boy to leave, and two or three governesses who had been allowed to give up in despair. Unsuspected by his father, George had become a horrid little snob and a bully.

The story of the murders really starts with this boy sitting down to lunch at home in the big dining-room of their Surrey house on the last day of his father's trial. Akehurst, the butler, and the parlourmaid are both in the environs of the Old Bailey waiting for the verdict which is expected at any time. Elsie Natley, the first housemaid, is waiting on George and thoroughly detesting him. In fact, her fingers are itching to get at him – and she is a very muscular girl of twenty.

'You've got to stand behind my chair when you wait on me. If you don't I shan't tell father – I shall jolly well tell Akehurst and he'll make you cry. I've seen him do it.'

'All right, Master George! I'll stand behind your chair when I come back.'

She ran out of the house because she had seen a telegraph-boy coming up the drive.

'*Guilty. Fourteen years. Akehurst.*'

The other servants had not seen the telegraph-boy coming, so they could wait. She put the telegram down on the hall table, and from a little cupboard in an elaborate fitment surmounted by a stag's head she took a clothes-brush.

'*Now*, Master George!' she said. She whipped his coat over his head and dragged him on to the table, smashing the crockery. It is doubtful whether she was consciously avenging the three governesses and all that the butler and a succession of parlourmaids had endured, but there is no doubt that she laid it well in with the back of the clothes-brush.

We may assume that the pain to his person was no more than salutary. Nevertheless, damage was done of a more subtle nature. He knew that she was only twenty. And she was a girl. And he was fifteen and a boy. And for all his budding manhood he had been unable to offer effective resistance.

The girl cannot be blamed. She was behaving naturally, as others ought to have behaved before – with no cruelty and with no more violence than she would have used towards a young brother if she had had one. It was beyond her imagination that she could have inflicted a deep hurt that would take years to heal.

II

After the home was broken up George did not see Elsie again until he was twenty-one and she was twenty-six, when he met her by chance at Ilfracombe.

In the meantime a sister of his mother's had taken him over and sent him to an expensive private school run on public-school lines. He was there until he was nearly nineteen. They gave him a rudimentary education, taught him manners of a kind, but finally expelled him in spite of the fact that he had been instrumental in winning a swimming-cup for the school.

She sent him up to Cambridge but he did not last there a full term. His aunt did not turn him out – he just drifted off and eventually joined a theatrical touring company, where he was quite a useful man provided he were cast to type.

Elsie had kept herself very well and had scarcely changed at all. To George she no longer looked so dreadfully muscular – she looked rather pink-and-white and nice. He took off his hat to her and smiled, but he had to speak before she answered:

'Well, Master George! Oh, do excuse me calling you that when I ought to say 'Mr Macartney'. Who *would* have thought of meeting you like this!'

The conversation followed standard lines. Elsie was having a holiday in a boarding-house selected by her late mistress who had departed for America, after which she intended to look round again for another job. George gave an account of himself, truthful except for a little romantic colour. He presented her with a stall for that night's performance, and the next afternoon hired a boat and took her for a row.

(*'I wasn't thinking about what she did to me all that time ago. Or if I was, I only thought I would wait for a chance to kiss her and sort of get even that way, like any young fellow might, as she was a good-looking girl and full of fun.'*)

A muscular girl, too, and full of physical energy. George, in spite of some philandering experience, was perhaps a bit slow in making the running. For when they were about a mile off shore she became bored and suggested that she should take a turn at rowing.

Anything to please her, thought George, just like any other young man.

'Here, I may knock this. Put it in your pocket for me, George, and don't forget to let me have it afterwards, whatever you do!'

She detached a bracelet, liberally set with big red stones. George affected to think it valuable. He put it in his pocket-case for her and she began to row. She had never rowed a sea-boat before and the inevitable happened. She lost an oar and made a grab for it. He made a grab, too, and the boat capsized.

George, as we have noted, was a crack swimmer, so here was a chance to play the hero in real life to a maiden in distress. But Elsie had not had time to consider George in the role of hero.

'Leggo, you brute, you'll drown me!' she cried, and landed him a useful blow on the nose.

(*'I swear I had no thought except to rescue her, like anyone else would. But when she hit me, somehow it all came back. I let her swim a couple of strokes to the boat, which was between us and the shore, and then before I knew what I was doing I collared her by the head from behind and put her under.'*)

Fifty or sixty holiday-makers had seen the accident from the Capstan Hill. But there were no motor-boats in those days and it was some little time before a boat rowed by two seamen reached them. George was clinging to the upturned boat with one hand and with the other supporting Elsie.

But Elsie was in a vertical position, and her lungs had been full of water for something like a quarter of an hour.

At the inquest George admitted that she had been a housemaid in his father's house and that they had met by chance. He described the incident truthfully and then:

'I came up under the upturned boat and when I got out it was on the other side. I looked round for Elsie and couldn't see her, for she was on the sea side. Then I wriggled round the boat and after a bit I saw her hand come up. And then I caught hold of one of the oars which was floating and splashed up to where I'd seen her and after a bit I got her. I can't remember much about how I got her back to the boat because I'd swallowed a lot of water myself.'

He took the risk of implying that he could hardly swim at all and no one in the theatrical company could deny it. The Coroner gave him a lecture on the folly of standing up in a small boat, opined that he had had a terrible lesson which would stay with him for the rest of his life and then, like everybody else, forgot about him. There are a certain number of boating and bathing fatalities every year, and this was one of them.

The company had moved on to Plymouth before George discovered that he was still in possession of the bracelet which Elsie had asked him to hold. He had not the slightest intention of stealing it but he did not want to stir things up. So he kept the bracelet and a little later gave it to Polly, a small-part girl in the company. When they quarrelled she gave it back to him, when something she said revealed to him that it was worth about eighty pounds. He was delighted, for he intended to pawn it at once.

Then he reflected that if it was worth all that money Elsie had almost certainly stolen it – which might lead to complications. It would be safer to get rid of it or keep it out of sight for a few years. More or less out of inadvertence, he kept it.

III

The theatre held no future for him. At the end of the tour he went back to sponge on his aunt for the few remaining months of her life. She was an annuitant with a negligible capital, but she left him some two thousand pounds with which he established himself as a motor-car agent.

Selling motor-cars in 1903 was a slow and heart-breaking process. It is incredible nowadays, but on the rare occasions when you booked a customer, some eight months would pass before you could redeem the car from the coach-builder's and collect your cheque.

The two thousand did not last very long. Soon a more balanced concern took over the agency and employed George as part clerk, part salesman. His new employer had been one of his father's victims but very generously felt only sympathy for George. He suggested that the name was an unfair handicap and himself paid the expenses of George changing his name by Deed Poll. Between them they constructed the name of 'Carshaw' as a good omen for business.

George was living fairly contentedly in lodgings in Richmond. We have no clue to his inmost thoughts at this time, but we may deduce that at the back of his thoughts was the consciousness that he had committed murder and got away with it. What fools, we imagine him reasoning, are murderers to be caught! To mess about with poison and guns and knives, which always leave clues! Whereas, if you have an accident which lots of people can witness, it does not matter if you contradict yourself a bit. You are expected to be flurried. And unless they can prove that you deliberately upset the boat there is no possibility of their proving anything at all.

His evenings tended to be lonely, for he was not a very sociable young man and had no friends of his own sex. Indeed his earnings did not give him scope for much in the way of social activities, and he was already inclined to believe that the motor-car trade held no prospects.

Spring came with its insistent urge to be up and doing. If he could have Aunt Maud's two thousand over again he would know better what to do. On Sunday afternoons he began to loaf around the more prosperous residential streets of Richmond. The connection between this activity and the thought of two thousand pounds will not be immediately obvious to you. But it is almost certain that it was not immediately obvious to George.

Violet Laystall was a house-parlourmaid, whom he picked up one Sunday afternoon. She was reasonably good-looking and of quiet manners; and George, though he thought of himself as a gentleman, had been cured of snobbery and class-consciousness. On May 5th, he married her, a notable gift from the bridegroom to the bride being the ruby bracelet which had once belonged to Elsie.

He took her to live in his rooms, for his holiday was not yet due. On May 9th, he insured her life for £2,000. He proposed his own life for a similar amount, but the proposal was rejected by the Insurance Company on account of certain medical information he felt obliged to give the doctor about himself. And, of course, they made wills in each other's favour.

Their deferred honeymoon took place in the middle fortnight of August. He took her to Bognor. On the first three days the sea was choppy. On the afternoon of the fourth day he hired a small rowing-boat. When they were about a mile from the shore he suggested that she might like to try her hand at rowing.

She was a docile little woman and obediently took her place on the thwart. She pulled a few strokes while he manipulated the boat broadside to the shore. There were several pleasure boats dotted about, but none of them too close for his purpose and the nearest was that of the attendant on the fringe of the bathers.

He waited for her to lose an oar but, as time was valuable, he leant forward and bumped the sea-side oar out of the row-lock. Then he stood up and capsized the boat.

The little play had already been rehearsed, and he had only to repeat his lines. Even the Coroner made very much the same little speech about its being a lesson to him for the rest of his life. When he was leaving the Court, in a suitable state of collapse, an official handed him the ruby bracelet that had been taken from the dead woman's wrist.

IV

Even with two thousand pounds in the bank, George Carshaw, as he now was, did not lose his head. Go slow and look round, was his motto. The motor trade, it seemed, was improving of its own accord; so without any extra effort George was soon more than equalling his salary in commission. He decided to stay on, a course which presented no embarrassment. His employer did not even know that he had married; and, as George was an unsociable man, he had not confided in any of his colleagues where he had intended to go for his holiday.

There being no immediate opening for capital, George thought a fellow might as well do himself comfortably for a bit. He began to spend his evenings in the West End. Shortly before Christmas he ran across the girl with whom he had had a flirtation in the touring company. She had a one-line part in pantomime, and was now glad to be taken out to supper. Before the pantomime was actually put on she resigned and joined forces with him, without benefit of clergy, in a flat in Baker Street.

She could not be described as mercenary, but she helped to make a very large dent in the two thousand. He grudged her nothing, for she fascinated him. She was known as 'Little Polly Flinders', lived as Miss Flinders and would never tell him her real name. She certainly did not grab, and it was certainly he who tumbled on the original idea of replenishing their dwindling capital on the racecourse. By June she discovered that she was not good for him and left him for his own sake. She may even have meant it, for they remained friends and from time to time renewed their association.

In September he married Madge Turnham, another muscular girl, a quick-witted, suspicious Cockney. But there was nothing very much to be suspicious about. He gave her the ruby bracelet and she promptly sneaked off and had it valued. When she learnt its worth she opened her eyes. When she had assured herself that he really was employed by a respectable motor agency she thanked her stars for a mug and eagerly married him.

At this stage George was undoubtedly planning everything very carefully. He insured her life for £100 only. Again he proposed a similar policy for his own life, and again got it turned down on the 'confession' he made to the doctor.

Life Insurance at best is a troublesome matter; but Accident Insurance is very simple. He took out an Accident policy on both their lives for ten thousand pounds each. The policy covered death by any kind of accident – including, of course, the accident of drowning.

V

Of his three wives Madge, who was the second, was the only really bad one. She was slovenly and quarrelsome. Her ill-nature, indeed, came near to imperilling George's plan. For she soon became known as a termagant – the kind of woman that nearly every kind of man would very soon come to hate. They lived in the upper part of a jerry-built house in Harringay and all the neighbours knew that occasionally they came to blows, after which she would be docile and well-behaved for nearly a week.

It is probable that her detestable temperament made George speed up the programme. They had a scrap on the Thursday before Whitsun 1906. George lost his temper this time and very nearly had to call a doctor for her afterwards. After the thumping she was extra docile, and perhaps George saw his last chance of staging a reconciliation. He took her to Paignton, a growing seaside resort on the south coast of Devon.

She said that the sea made her sick and she wouldn't go on it. But George, of course, was much more intelligent than his wife. He put up a convincing little pantomone with a five-pound note concealed at the back of his pocket-book against a rainy day – teased her and said that she should have the fiver if she could stay in a small rowing-boat with him for an hour without being seasick. And the greedy fool succumbed.

We imagine that George put to sea with a certain confidence. He had found a method of murder that was clue-proof. But on this occasion he was very nearly tripped by the element of time. For artificial respiration was applied in the boat that picked them up, and the heart was actually restarted, though it beat for a few seconds only.

But this was the only little contretemps – except that George caught a very bad cold. The inquest went off without a hitch. For neither the Coroner nor the local police kept indexed news cuttings of other boating and bathing fatalities in other years and other places.

But Dead Ends, which kept a large number of more or less useless records, used to file a cross-index of every death by violence in any form. They found that, within the space of two years, George Carshaw had lost two wives in precisely the same circumstances, detail for detail. In each case the boat had capsized about the same distance from shore. In each case he had prevented the body from sinking but not from drowning.

Then there was the cross-index ('Fatality – Sea – Boat'). In ten minutes a clerk had found that a similar accident, detail for detail, had happened at Ilfracombe in 1903 with Elsie Natley and George Macartney.

Detective-Sergeant Martleplug, an energetic officer attached to Dead Ends, dug out the Deed Poll and identified George Carshaw with George Macartney. He found that the two wives had been insured, that Elsie Natley was not his wife and was not insured – which puzzled him.

He found George arranging for a sale of his furniture and effects in Harringay. This was a fortnight later. George had drawn the insurance, and their few sticks were not worth preserving. The only joint possession of any value was the ruby bracelet, which he had again recovered.

The detective opened in a friendly manner and George responded.

Martleplug revealed his knowledge of Violet, but was keeping Elsie up his sleeve.

'It fairly beats me, Mr Martleplug, and that's a fact!' said George. 'You'd think that when a thing like that's happened once, it couldn't possibly happen again. It used to haunt me – and that's why poor Madge persuaded me to go out again. And that – but why talk about it?'

'I've come here to talk about it,' said Martleplug. 'And I want to ask you a few questions.'

'I am sorry,' said George, who did not make the ignorant mistake of confusing a detective with a judge, 'but the subject is very painful to me and I cannot discuss it. If you don't like that, why don't you arrest me for murder? I'll tell you why you don't – because you haven't got any evidence and can't get it.'

George, as you will know, was quite right. The Public Prosecutor informed Martleplug that he quite agreed with George.

Of course, as far as common sense goes, they were quite sure that George had murdered Madge. But George was saved by a very simple point in legal procedure. The only ground for assuming that he had forcibly drowned Madge was that he had taken part in two exactly similar 'accidents' before. Neither of these two earlier accidents could be put in as evidence in regard to the third accident, since there was no connection between them except the assumed connection in George's mind.

VI

Ten thousand pounds enabled George to throw up his employment and start an independent agency once again himself. This time he could do it in style. He was able to buy two cars for demonstration purposes. He had a decent showroom with a well-equipped workshop in Tottenham Court Road.

One of his first customers was little Polly Flinders who came in on the arm of a prosperous broker from Newcastle. She was astonished to see him and rather pleased. In the course of the trial run he persuaded her to drop the broker. It meant losing a customer, but Polly was worth it, and he had more than half the ten thousand in reserve.

They took a flat on the unfashionable side of Regent's Park, which was conveniently near the office. This time Polly was determined to be good for him. She put her foot very firmly down on horse-racing, and after the first week or two refused to let him give her expensive dresses – except just a few, which, she said, would be economical in the end. He must, she said, learn to be sensible with his money. He must not speculate – he must invest. And if you invested money sensibly you could get as big a return as if you had speculated with it. There was, for example, The Theatre, of which George already had too much practical knowledge to be fooled, as he had been fooled by racing tipsters.

She had, it transpired, heard of a play only the other day which contained great possibilities of profit. By the instrumentality of one of the economical-expensive frocks she obtained the script from the author. When she read the part which she would play if George should decide to go into production as a sideline, he agreed that it sounded fine.

George paid for the play to be put on and, by running a small mortgage on the agency, managed to prop it up for six weeks at one of the minor West End theatres. He had just enough left to send it on tour in the provinces – with Polly in her part. So he lost both his money and his girl – though she continued to write him most affectionate letters from the provinces until the tour collapsed.

George did quite well with the agency. He had a liking for motor cars and put in plenty of work. But he was handling one of the smaller makes that has since perished. There was the slack first quarter of the new year in which the rent and wages of the workshop staff became a problem. He pulled up a bit in the summer but not quite enough. If the agency were to live it must have new capital.

He found May Toler outside a servants' registry office in Piccadilly. She was thirty-two and the only one of his wives who was definitely pretty, with beautiful long hands, which she had been able to preserve; for it was more than ten years since she had been anything but a very good-class parlourmaid.

With her he had to exert all his resources and his rather crude charm. And there were several setbacks. Her family, who lived at Willesden, did not like him at first. But their hostility was killed by his gift of the ruby bracelet which they recognized to be valuable.

She married him, against her better judgment, in February 1908. He had persuaded her to cut out the still querulous family and more or less make an elopement of it. For the ceremony was performed with paid witnesses before the registrar at Camden Town.

Possibly he thought that in this way he was preventing the police from learning of his marriage. On the other hand we can be quite certain that, at this stage, his attitude to the police was one of open defiance. He was aware that they believed him to be a murderer. Well, he had invented the perfect murder that could even, as it were, be performed in public. And here we must reluctantly concede a small point to the fanatics of heredity – for his father had behaved just like this, faking his balance sheet with a system of his own when he knew the police accountants were looking for the fake.

They took out a joint-life assurance for £500. The joint-life element can hardly have been a serious attempt to throw dust into anyone's eyes, for he used it subsequently as a means of raising a small loan for his business. They made wills in each other's favour – and he sent her on her own to take out an Accident Policy with a different company for £10,000 against death by accident.

Their circumstances during the summer were easy enough, but the winter was a bit of a pinch. They had taken a small, noisy flat off Theobald's Road. The very superior parlourmaid proved a very indifferent cook and a hopeless manager. Personally, too, she went to pieces very soon after the wedding. He seems to have been kind enough to her and she herself was not quarrelsome. But she missed her occupation and she would whine a good deal and drop into melancholy and latterly there is evidence that she took to drink.

It became doubtful whether George would have enough capital to take full advantage of next summer's business. So between Easter and Whitsun he took her to Colwyn Bay in North Wales.

This time the only variation in the programme was that he rowed her farther out from shore. There was no question of her being alive when they were picked up.

He got his shock this time in the Coroner's Court. He had just repeated his little speech as to how it had all happened when a barrister got up, representing the police.

Now the Rules of Evidence in a High Court are many and varied. But the rules of evidence in a Coroner's Court are just exactly what the Coroner likes. It may be a legal anomaly that the man who is often an amateur is given more discretion than a judge – but there it is! And George had to make the best of it.

'Was your wife insured, Mr Carshaw?'

'We had a joint policy for five hundred pounds, in mortgage for my business.'

'Any other insurance?'

'I don't know. She may have.'

'You don't know. Was your last wife insured against death by accident for ten thousand pounds?'

'Yes.'

'Did she on June 15th, 1906, meet with an exactly similar accident at Paignton? I mean, had you rowed her out and did the boat capsize in – er – the precise manner in which you have just described in respect of your – er – latest wife?'

Point by point he brought out the details of the drowning of Madge, then of the drowning of Violet and, point by point, matched them with the drowning of May.

Three was good enough. He could not make the insurance point in respect of Elsie, so he left it alone.

It is open to the critic to take the view that this cross-examination was a definite 'wangle' on the part of the police. They could bring the facts out in the Coroner's Court, though not in the High Court. But by the time the Coroner's case was reported, every man in the country who was likely to sit on the jury would have been certain to have read the facts. So the jury would know.

But the Coroner's Court carried them a bit further than they meant to go. The jury brought in a verdict of wilful murder against George Carshaw and he was committed for trial on the Coroner's warrant.

The Crown felt that it must go on with the case. George was brought up for trial in the following June.

In the meantime, Martleplug had traced George back to the private school where he had been instrumental in winning a swimming-cup. They had got against him now that he was a powerful swimmer, and that his thrice-repeated tale of floundering about with an oar was all non-sense.

But even so George got away with it.

VII

It was a rising young lawyer, later well known as Sir Ernest Quilter, K C, who saved George Carshaw from his reasonably certain fate of being hanged as the murderer of his wife, May.

Counsel for the Prosecution opened by describing in minute detail the circumstances in which May had met her death. He then paused and looked at the judge – an action which was very close indeed to being a pre-arranged signal. But as this was done by arrangement with the defence there could be no objection. The judge promptly ordered the jury to retire and then listened to arguments on both sides as to the admissibility of evidence of the two previously drowned wives. Owing to the absence of the money element the Crown had to come to the conclusion that the first drowning, of Elsie Natley, was a genuine accident which had given George the idea for the subsequent murders.

The Prosecution claimed admissibility of the previous accidents and quoted precedent. But Quilter scotched him.

'In all the precedents which my learned friend has quoted, there has invariably been the *prima facie* assumption of guilt. In this case I submit that there is no *prima facie* assumption of guilt whatever. There is the overwhelming assumption of an accident – which can only be upset by consideration of the previous cases.'

A bold line – for it admitted by implication that George was a murderer.

The judge agreed and ruled that the evidence of the previous drownings was inadmissible until the Prosecution had established a reasonably strong *prima facie* assumption of guilt in respect of May. Each counsel seemed extremely pleased with this ruling.

At an early stage the Treasury man called George's old schoolmaster, together with one of the staff and two men who had been pupils with George. These men proved George's swimming prowess. The Prosecution was triumphant.

'My lord, the deceased was drowned admittedly within a dozen or so yards of the upturned boat. Is it to be believed that the prisoner, who was a very able swimmer, was powerless to effect her rescue, as he stated? I submit that a *prima facie* case has been made out of the prisoner's guilt. I shall therefore ask your lordship's leave to introduce – other evidence.'

Mr Quilter had been waiting for this.

'I object, my lord. It is no part of my case to deny that my client *could* have saved his wife from drowning had he wished to do so.'

Daring again! Sailing right into the wind! There was what the newspapers insist upon calling a sensation in Court. And Quilter went on:

'My learned friend has forgotten more law than I ever knew, so he will not object to my reminding him of the principle enshrined in the doggerel:

> *"Thou shalt not kill, but needst not strive*
> *Officiously to keep alive."*

'I admit that Carshaw *did not strive* to keep his wife alive. I am not here to defend his moral character, nor his conscience. I am still waiting for my friend to show that any action of Carshaw's betrays evidence of felonious intent.'

Quilter scored again.

Once those two persons were in the water, the most that could be proved against George was that he had deliberately refrained from rescuing his wife. Again, the law may be at variance with the public conscience, but the law remains. And the law lays it down that you need never rescue anybody from anything if you don't want to.

That limited the Prosecution to proving that the boat had been feloniously capsized by George – which in the nature of things was unprovable. At the judge's direction the jury found George Carshaw 'not guilty'.

After escaping under police escort from the mob around the Court, George showed his gratitude to Mr Quilter by briefing him to recover the ten thousand pounds from the Accident Insurance Company in respect of May's death. And again Quilter won.

Fortunately for George, he had given his agency a fancy name and was able to resume business, equipped now with ample capital. He got in touch with Polly Flinders, but this time she shrieked when he came near her and he had to run for it.

There was, it would be safe to say, no one in the country who doubted George's guilt. He had to take an assumed name, without Deed Poll this time. But whatever inconvenience he may have suffered in this way was compensated for by his egomaniac delight in the fact that the police knew him to be a multiple murderer and could not touch him.

VIII

In the following October there arrived at a West End hotel a Mr and Mrs Huystefan. Mrs Huystefan was an Englishwoman who had married an American. One evening, while she was dressing for dinner, she was assaulted in her bedroom and robbed of her jewellery. She was too shaken to be of much use to the police that night. But her husband, who was a methodical man, gave them an old typewritten list of items of his wife's jewellery.

His name, he contrived to explain, was that of an old Southern family who had arrived before the *Mayflower*, and on all the gold pieces the family crest, a lion couchant, would be found.

The Yard had not very much hope. A hotel job would mean crooks in a good way of business. But they sent out the drag-net and were rather surprised to get a response from a pawnbroker in Holborn, who produced a ruby bracelet with the crest stamped inside the gold mount.

'How long have you had this?'

'Pawned with me last February by a Mrs Carshaw. There's the address – Theobald's Road –'

'Then you're all right, because it's not what we want. But you might leave it with us for a couple of days.'

On account of the name and address, the bracelet went to Dead Ends as a matter of routine. No purely logical detective would have wasted a moment over that bracelet. Mrs Huystefan had been in England a week and this had been pawned in London last February. And it wasn't as though the crest were in any way an unusual design.

But a ruby bracelet was listed amongst the stolen jewellery. So Detective-Inspector Rason requested Mrs Huystefan, now restored to health, to call at the Yard and identify it.

She identified it at once as her bracelet, and then became profusely apologetic.

'I'm so sorry you've had this trouble with the bracelet,' she said. 'I forgot it was on that old list my husband gave you, or I would have notified you at once. I gave it away as a present when I was in England six years ago. I'm very sorry she had to pawn it. If you are in touch with her, I would be so glad if you would give me her address, as I would like to help her again.'

'Help who, Mrs Huystefan?'

'The girl I gave it to. Elsie Natley. She was one of my maids in Town here just after I married Mr Huystefan. We took a bungalow that year at Croyde, near Ilfracombe in North Devon, and she came with us as cook-general, for we were roughing it, you know. You don't want the whole story, but I gave it to her because she saved my life. It wasn't the sort of thing you could give a money tip for, was it? If she's in trouble I would so like to know her address.'

'Do you mind telling me how she saved your life, Mrs Huystefan?'

'It was at bathing – yes, bathing! The currents round there are simply dreadful and I didn't know it. I swam out and couldn't get in again. It was a bit choppy and my strength was going. My husband rushed in after me, but he was a poor swimmer. Elsie spotted my trouble from the bungalow. She came rushing out, whipping off her skirt as she ran, then her shoes. She outstripped my husband and got to me just in time and brought me in. She was a magnificent swimmer – her father used to be a waterman on the River Lee.'

'Thank you, Mrs Huystefan. You don't think of leaving England for a few weeks?'

'No, we're over for six months.'

Rason thanked her again, then looked up the dossier of Elsie Natley.

Elsie had died, as had the other women, of asphyxia resulting from drowning. Not of anything else.

Rason told his tale to the Chief, and soon was telling it again to a junior lawyer from the Public Prosecutor's office.

Rason, of course, was privileged and he received the young man with a smile.

'If you had been able to prove that Carshaw's wife, May, had been a very strong swimmer, you'd have got a conviction, wouldn't you?'

'Of course we would! We could have used it to prove, what everyone knows, that he held her under! Also, it would have established a *prima facie* case and we could have brought in the other cases.'

'Well, there's a Mrs Huystefan to prove that Elsie Natley was a strong swimmer. And you've still got the two other cases left – Madge and Violet. And as they wouldn't let you use them the other day you can use 'em now.'

George was hanged on Dec. 7th, 1909, for the murder of Elsie Natley.

Arthur Williams

BEING
A MURDERER
MYSELF

The cool and clever story that follows seems clearly to have been written by a professional rather than a weekend writer. Yet in the letter to *Ellery Queen's Mystery Magazine* that accompanied submission of the story in 1948 the author wrote:

As this is the first story I have tried to get published, I do not know whether it is necessary or not to state that, should this story be accepted, I would not like my real name divulged. Not that I am ashamed of the story ... but in this particular case I think the effect of the story might be lost should my real name be given. Incidentally, the pen-name will save me from being troubled by people with no sense of humour. Also, I am writing a novel on South African life in which one of the characters is a detective story writer, Arthur Williams, and it would add to my attempt at realism if stories were actually published under that name.

Apart from the information that the story was written in a Native Reserve just alongside the Kruger National Park Game Reserve, the author said nothing about himself. The magazine published the story, and it was awarded a prize. So who was Arthur Williams? Nothing further had been published by the magazine. A letter to his home (which was named Journey's End) in Cape Province brought a reply from his widow. She told me that his name was Peter Barry Way, and that he had been born in Sunderland in 1917. The family emigrated to South Africa when he was eight years old, and Barry Way studied medicine at Cape Town University. He did not become a doctor, however, but worked for a travel agency, 'travelling across the country and studying people', as his widow put it. He married, had four children, and died unexpectedly in 1969. 'Throughout the years he tried his hand at writing, sitting in the loft of his Cape Dutch home overlooking the Franschoek Mountains.' The novel he mentioned, however, if completed, was never submitted to a publisher, and this remarkable tale was the only story ever published by Barry Way, alias Arthur Williams.

Being a murderer myself, I was very interested in the statement recently made by a well-known reviewer of murder stories that 'the best and most stimulating detective stories being written today are those that stress the puzzle of "why" at least co-equally with "who" and "how".'

It is gratifying to see, even if it is only in the field of fiction, that the character of a murderer is at last being considered worthy of more detailed analysis. In the past too much importance has been attached to discovering the identity of a murderer and the means of apprehending him. On the other hand, I do not consider wasted the time spent on the puzzle of 'how', since, after all, the method adopted is an indication of the type of man employing it; furthermore, it often decides whether the killer is to become famous, as a failure – or unknown, as a success.

I would also like to mention that we murderers do not *always* make a mistake. That fallacy has arisen because only those murderers who *have* made mistakes ever come to the notice of the police. On the whole, we are very efficient, and, taking the number of known cases only, it is evident that we have got away with many murders, in spite of the very large organizations directed against us.

But the most common misconception held by most people is that a murderer is different from the ordinary man. Too often he is described in exaggerated terms such as 'an insane monster' or 'a cold-blooded brute'. Such melodramatic ideas are far from the truth. Actually, a murderer is quite normal, merely possessing greater courage to act on the universal conviction that the true golden rule is 'Every man for himself.'

It is for this reason, therefore – to provide authentic data for the detective-story writer – that I have decided to make public my experience of murder. I have been fortunate in being so clever that I am able to relate this experience without fear of unpleasant consequences.

I felt no animosity towards Susan Braithwaite, personally, when I killed her, though some might consider that I had reason to hate her. I had been very fond of her once and would have married her if she had not been so stupid as to choose Stanley Braithwaite for a husband. Still, as I consider myself a civilized man of the world, I had felt that if she wanted to marry money-bags, that was her own funeral.

I suppose it was the feminine in her which had attracted me, that was in turn more attracted to the obvious maleness of Braithwaite – a great lout of a fellow, but with the right sort of brains to make his way in the world. He had inherited a little money, and being a city man he was able to make the best use of it. He had made a fair income by dealing on the Stock Exchange, not by the haphazard methods of a gambler, but with the unspectacular method of the investor. It was typical of him that during the record boom on the Johannesburg Stock Exchange, brought about by the discovery of gold in the Orange Free State, he continued his phlegmatic way of taking a profit as soon as a deal showed any, in spite of the fever of optimism that raged on the Exchange. He was thus able to build up and consolidate a small fortune, and when the inevitable recession came, his funds were mostly liquid. Then, instead of being affected by the pervading depression, he quietly bought shares which had dropped to next to nothing and so almost doubled his already swollen fortune when the equally inevitable recovery took place. A most infuriating man!

When I introduced him to Susan, she became greatly attracted by his masterful manner, and the success which it spelled. In fact, she was carried away to such an extent that she flew to Europe with him – thus terminating our engagement.

I had hoped never to see her again.

Eighteen months later, on answering a knock at the back door of my house, I found Susan on the step, suitcase in hand. When she had comfortably settled herself on the chesterfield couch in my study, she told me her story. I was not surprised at what she revealed. I could well imagine that Braithwaite's self-assured dominant maleness, which she had preferred to my modest intellectual qualities, would develop into a complacent egoism, ruling with efficient tyranny. When she could bear his insensitiveness no longer, she had walked out on him and had come to me, for she felt that I would help her for old times' sake.

She did not notice, however, that I was not enthusiastic at the prospect of helping her. Actually, I was highly displeased. After she had jilted me, I had worked her out of my system, at the same time making extensive improvements on my poultry farm. I had made the whole farm self-supporting, and with labour-saving devices and processes was able to run the whole place single-handed, for I liked fowls and preferred to do all the work among them myself.

But with Susan there it would have been difficult to continue in the same satisfying way. I knew I would have to entertain her, which meant that I would have had to shelve some of the less important, yet essential work. My routine would probably have got interfered with, and the three thousand chickens, which were at the most awkward age, might have caught cold or contracted some other ailment they are susceptible to.

Unfortunately, I could not think of any valid-sounding excuse for refusing to help her. Also, she had timed her arrival well: she would have had to stay the night at least, for there was no place in the village where she could have found accommodation and there were no trains back to Johannesburg till the following morning. I knew that once the ice had been broken by letting her stay the night it would have been even more difficult to send her away the next day. After all, I had once been very fond of her and during the delirium of that time I had told her that no matter what ultimately happened between us, if she was ever in trouble she was to count on my help; and as I pride myself on being a man of my word, I could not bear to think of her telling our common friends that in an emergency I proved to be a broken reed.

All this passed through my mind while she chattered away about the cruel things her husband had done to her; but under the pretence of listening I followed the trend of my own thoughts till I became annoyed at the calm way she took my sympathy for granted. From the bits of her conversation I did listen to, I guessed in what manner she wished me to help her, and my annoyance mounted.

I saw my little bit of money being spent on lawyers; my comfortable and satisfying life being disturbed; my future peace being threatened by complicated emotions; in short, the whole of my nicely settled life being completely upset. I became so enraged that I thought, 'Really, I could wring her neck!'

The actual strangling was more difficult than one would have thought. But the inability to face her, which had led me to go round the back of the couch to get my hands round her throat, turned out to be an advantage. For by crouching behind the back of the couch I was able to press her neck and head firmly against it, and so, by hanging on like grim death, avoid my hands becoming dislodged by her violent kicking, hitting and threshing for air. Also, when she went limp, I was in a comfortable enough position not to need to relax till I was sure she was dead.

Her face – dark blue with grotesquely protruding tongue – was rather shocking when contrasted with the pretty, animated expression it had had a few minutes before; and her once glossy hair seemed to have lost its blue tints and had become a lifeless-looking black. Otherwise, the sight of Susan's body did not affect me much.

After making sure that Susan was dead, I pushed her tongue back into her mouth and proceeded to dispose of the body in the manner I had been stimulated to devise when reading of the difficulties other murderers had experienced in this respect. I started the process that night, for though there was no urgency, as it would be days or even weeks before there would be any serious inquiry as to Susan's whereabouts, I was keen on putting my ideas to the test. The following morning I was up early as usual and busy at my farm routine.

One afternoon, about three weeks later, Sergeant Theron of the local police turned up at my place and wanted to know if I knew anything about a Mrs Braithwaite.

Sergeant John Theron on duty was a different man from the off-duty Johnny Theron who occasionally, when suitably warmed, entertained us in the backyard of Wiggins's pub by giving a demonstration of Wild West six-shooting. He was a crack shot and, crouching slightly, he would fire two guns from the hip with amazing accuracy, at the same time looking from side to side with melodramatic belligerency; then after each salvo he would spit on the muzzles of the revolvers to 'cool' them, giving a thigh-slappingly funny impression of a cowboy hero surrounded by dastardly villains.

But Sergeant John Theron of the South African Police was an alert and intelligent policeman who took his work seriously, and I knew by the way his question was worded that he was sure I *did* know something about Mrs Braithwaite.

I guessed that she had been reported missing and had been traced to my farm. I decided, therefore, to take Theron into my confidence. I told him briefly all about my association with Susan in the past, winding up by telling him that she had been to see me one evening about three weeks before, but that she had left again the same night.

He naturally wanted further particulars and also wanted to know why I had not come forward and reported to the police that I had seen her at a time later than that which the newspaper appeal had stated was the last time she had been seen. I explained that I never read newspapers, but even if I had read the appeal for information, I would not have reported her visit as she had been running away from her husband.

I went on to tell him that she had wanted me to help her, but that I had refused; that we had quarrelled till she had finally got into such a rage that she had walked out of the house leaving her hat, gloves and suitcase behind. In reply to his questions I said that I did not know where she had gone, or how she intended to manage without her suitcase, or whether she had had a handbag with her or not.

After exhausting the subject of Susan's visit, Theron asked to see her suitcase. I gave it to him. He found it unlocked and opened it. On top was a brown handbag, which on being turned out was found to contain some money, a pair of earrings, a pearl necklace, a diamond ring, the usual feminine requirements, and a few loose keys, one of which fitted the suitcase. After carefully examining the rest of the suitcase's contents, Theron then asked me what Mrs Braithwaite had been wearing that night.

That question had come sooner than I had expected, but I gave him the previously thought-out answer which was a genuine-sounding yet worth-lessly vague desciption of the clothes I had carefully packed, together with the handbag, in the suitcase three weeks before. I had opened the case with one of the keys I had found in the handbag. I had had to leave the suitcase unlocked as I did not want the problem of disposing of the key. Incidentally, I had done the packing of the clothes, shoes, etc., while wearing gloves. I had no intention of leaving fingerprints inside the case and so making the traditional mistake.

Theron listened closely to the description, then pulled out the one dress in the suitcase which had obviously been worn, and asked me if that was the dress Mrs Braithwaite had worn that evening. Of course, I replied that it was not, but I knew that if that dress had already been described by anyone who had seen Susan going to my farm, that description would be more or less the same as the one I had given.

After asking a few more unimportant questions, Sergeant Theron left, taking the suitcase, and the hat and gloves with him.

The police did not visit me again for a few days. I went to the village for a drink on the evening of the week that Johnny Theron usually spent at the pub, but he did not put in an appearance that night.

But I knew that it would only be a matter of time before I saw him again, for Susan's trail definitely ended at my place, and the police would concentrate there until they had reason to look elsewhere. When Theron eventually came again, about a week later, he was accompanied by Constable Barry, a prematurely bald young man who had wooed and won the village belle, Renée Otto, by so manoeuvring his courting that she never saw him without his helmet on – so the story went in the village, anyway. In charge of both Theron and Barry, however, was a man from the CID Headquarters in Johannesburg. This time the only words Sergeant Theron spoke throughout the morning were:

'Mr Williams, this is Inspector Ben Liebenberg.'

I acknowledged the introduction and asked the Inspector what I could do for him. He was a tall, handsome man, more like an actor than a detective. Afterwards I learned that he was a very good mixer – of drinks. His hobby was inventing new recipes for cocktails and other mixed drinks. I was told this, and about his variation of a Green Mamba, which is as deadly as the snake, by Theron later, when he was able to have a drink with me again.

Inspector Liebenberg professed himself sorry to trouble me, but would I mind if he had a look around? Mrs Braithwaite had definitely been seen coming to my place, and had equally definitely not been seen anywhere else; so he would like to satisfy himself that she was not hiding somewhere on my farm.

I assured him that I understood and that it would be a pleasure to show him over the farm.

As we examined the homestead, I explained to them that I liked to be independent of any outside assistance, so had made my house and farm as self-contained as possible. I showed them the coal bin in the kitchen, built like a small room and filled at the top from the outside, having a little square outlet flush with the floor, next to the coal-burning stove. Below the kitchen there was a concrete underground tank for storing rain water. It had a hand pump attached, and pipes were laid from it to the bathroom. The rest of my domestic water supply came from a large gravity tank on the roof, filled by a wind pump from a borehole.

I started the tour outside by taking them to the three-hundred-feet-long, subdivided, intensive-type, poultry house where, judging by the sound, the thousands of Leghorn hens were riveting their eggs together. I showed the policemen the incubator room and the brooder house, which I also used for experimental batches of chickens or fowls.

I then took them to the large corrugated-iron barn which housed my machinery – a tractor, a threshing machine, a hammer mill, and various smaller machines such as lucerne cutters, etc.; also my general farm equipment such as ploughs, harrows, steam drying tank, planters, cultivators, etc., and my stocks of food. For round the sides of the barn were rows of large storage tanks, variously containing whole and crushed maize, maize meal, meat meal, peanut meal, bone meal, lucerne meal and the various other poultry and animal feed requirements I used for making up the different balanced rations.

I could see their eyes measuring the tanks, and the jotting down of copious mental notes.

In the open air again, I pointed out my cultivated lands – the lucerne fields green, owing to the water from the dam, but the maize and other lands a yellowy brown. In the distance we could just make out the few cows, oxen and horses grazing on the uncultivated part of my farm.

When they had seen the whole farm, Inspector Liebenberg thanked me for my trouble and departed – rather depressed, I thought. I would like to have suggested that perhaps twenty maids with twenty mops . . . but decided that it was unwise to trade on my security too much.

A week passed without event, though I began to get irritated by being under continuous surveillance. Even Constable Barry had altered his beat so that he was able to pass my gate which, though a fair distance from the homestead, enabled him to have a clear view across the lawns to the house and garage.

I decided to make a move and bring matters to a climax. My best plan, of course, was to make Crippen's mistake, and run away.

I therefore made preparations, and early one morning I departed in my car at high speed. I drove fast for about five miles, then abruptly slowed down, headed the car into the veld and hid it as much as possible in a bushy bit, well away from the road.

I walked the rest of the way to the underground caves not far from the famous Blyvooruitzicht gold mine. These caves, though extensive, are not beautiful and do not attract many visitors. I had decided that the police would have already searched them thoroughly, so the chances were that I would be undisturbed. I had brought a Coleman lamp, a camp Primus, and ample provisions, and soon settled comfortably in one of the smaller caverns.

I knew the fowls on the farm would be all right for a few days, as their food troughs held enough for about three days, and the water troughs with their ball valves would remain full. The eggs would accumulate in the batteries of nests and ultimately make a mess, but one cannot have murder without breaking eggs. The other animals would not starve and there was plenty of water lying about the place. The chickens were then old enough to do without artificial heat for warmth, only requiring a small economical glow from the lamps to collect them in groups at night.

So, with my mind at peace, I was able to relax and enjoy the two detective books which I had brought with me. The stories were very good, though I noticed, with satisfaction, that the various detectives required considerable assistance from their authors.

On the morning of the third day I imagined that things should be about ripe for me to put in an appearance again.

As luck would have it, it was Sergeant Theron who met me first when I stepped out of the car in front of my house. The human face is not designed to express amazement, excitement, satisfaction, curiosity, wonder, relief, official reserve, friendliness, and regret all at once, but Theron's did its best.

When he recovered, he demanded to know where I had been. I told him that I had gone to the caves to see if Mrs Braithwaite had not perhaps gone there and got lost and died there, and that I had become lost myself and found my way out only that morning. He snapped his fingers in exasperation and I guessed that he had spread his net far and wide, but had not thought of looking for me so close at hand.

While he was thinking what he ought to do next, I looked around to get details of the impression of an upturned ant heap which I had received when I drove up.

I had expected to see signs of activity but nothing like what I saw then. Evidently the police had decided to use more than twenty maids, for the place was in a turmoil.

There were men everywhere – on the roof of the house, round the house, half under the house; there were men walking about with heads bent examining the ground, men digging at various places, men around the dam, round the borehole, in the fields and on the lands. I could not see into the barn, but it must have been full of men, for outside the main double doors a collection of agricultural hardware was scattered like the throwback of a burrowing terrier.

But the most joyous sight was the long hen house. The hens had, very unwisely, all been chased outside so that the concrete floor inside could be examined. To lay the floor bare a six-inch layer of manured straw had first to be removed. This considerable task had already been mostly achieved, for the straw lay in large mounds outside, in front of the entrance doors.

Along the outside of the poultry house there were men trying to uncover the foundations, for whoever was in charge of the searching meant to leave no stone unturned. I write 'trying' advisedly, for the diggers were being considerably hampered by the thousands of hens who had no place to go, but who were trying, with hen-like persistence, to go back where they belonged. Hens are very conservative – besides, they had eggs to lay. There was a precarious and continually changing line of them along the narrow ledge between the mesh wire front of the house and the edge of the low front wall on which the wire front rested. And this was one of the walls the foundations of which the men were hoping to examine.

They were almost smothered in hens. When it wasn't hens, it was dust and dirt. A Leghorn is a very highly strung bird, and jumpy at the best of times. With Leghorns you have to keep up a continual chatter, or be for ever silent. While I was watching, one of the men digging had to reply to a call from a distant policeman. His sudden shouted answer resulted in the thousands of hens leaping into the air as one bird, with, literally, a roaring of wings. The men became lost to view in a cloud consisting of a mixture of fine particles of manure, straw, earth, spilled food, and down.

I was not able to see more, for by then Theron had decided that I had better come along with him to the police station to answer some questions. At the station I was left in charge of Constable Hurndal, who received my nod of recognition rigidly. After a short delay Theron started questioning me, trying hard to give the impression that he did not attach much importance to my answers.

I was half-way through my third cigarette when a constable burst into the room and shouted, 'We've found the body!'

I jumped up, and exclaimed, 'How exciting! Where?' – a remark thoroughly in bad taste considering that I had known Mrs Braithwaite well, but one that could not be interpreted as coming from a guilty and apprehensive mind. I turned to Theron, who had been watching me closely, and saw doubt in his eyes.

Not that it mattered whether I betrayed guilt or not. I was perfectly safe and could never give myself away no matter what trick they tried. But if I had shown any signs of a guilty conscience, Theron would have known definitely that I was a murderer. This I wanted to avoid, or there would not have been much future pleasure in visiting the pub. I did not mind his official suspicion, but his private certainty would have been different.

Theron continued the farce and also asked the constable where the body had been found. The latter went on, with less enthusiasm, to describe vaguely some spot in the uncultivated land. They both looked at me with a last hope that I might indicate they were getting warm. I said, 'Fancy, I wouldn't have thought that was a good place to bury a body. This means that she was murdered, doesn't it?'

Of course they never found Susan's body on my farm, or anywhere else. Nor any trace of it. They examined the stove for any signs of human ash, they swept the chimney for the same purpose. They dug up the drains to see if I had possibly dissolved the body in a bath of chemicals. In short, they looked everywhere and tried every box of tricks possessed by the Johannesburg CID. All to no avail.

Finally they had to give up, baffled, and no matter how much they suspected that Susan had been murdered, they had no proof. In spite of a most thorough search of my farm, no body was found, and this fact plus no obvious motive on my part resulted in the cloud of suspicion hanging over my head gradually becoming dispersed.

That Christmas, to show that there was no ill feeling, I sent Sergeant Theron a couple of fine young cockerels.

The months passed in uninterrupted peace. My content was marred only by the news that Sergeant Theron was leaving to join the Rhodesian Police.

We gave him a fine farewell party, Bill Wiggins providing the drinks, while I contributed the poultry. Poor Johnny was not able to give us a last demonstration of six-shooting that night, for when we went out into the yard the fresh air had a bad effect on him, and it took him all his time to stay relatively upright, hanging on to the swaying washing lines.

The building of a new brooder house began to occupy all my thoughts. But doing it by myself took all my time, with the result that I could not keep my house clean and tidy. So after much indecision, I engaged a housekeeper – a blonde, tall, but giving the impression of childlike plumpness. She is most efficient, yet her warm smile suggests that she could be very kind and affectionate.

It is because she runs the house so well that I now have time in the evening to write this record of my experience with homicide.

I am looking forward to having an interesting time should I get this published. I am particularly curious about Theron's reaction should he read this and so learn the make-up and constitution of those plump chickens he so enjoyed.

I suppose he will be disgusted, though he need not be. After all, how was he to know that those chickens had been feeding on the body of Susan Braithwaite?

I do not mean by crudely pecking at it. On the contrary, the fowls ate Susan in well-balanced rations. Every bit of her body, at different times naturally, had been through the hammer mill, to be ground into fine bone meal and meat meal. A separate process made blood meal.

These processes entailed no difficulty as I had learned how to do it from an article in the *Farmers' Magazine*, and had been doing it with animal carcasses long before. And as far as the hammer-mill process is concerned, human bodies, not requiring to be skinned and having smaller bones, are much easier to manage.

I had only to take extra care that every single piece of the body was powdered. The teeth I had to put through the milling process a couple of times till they became indistinguishable from the rest of the bone meal. The hair I burned on the head, making a sort of charcoal.

After I had processed the body, I wiped everything that it had touched with handfuls of green lucerne, which in turn was ground fine. Animal carcasses were then put through the mill, followed by heaps of lucerne and bags of maize, so that all traces of human cells were completely removed from the machine.

The meat meal, bone meal, and blood meal were made into a ration with other foodstuffs and fed to my experimental batch of chicks – and what fine chickens they grew into, as Theron can testify. As a matter of fact, I have established quite a reputation for fine pullets and cockerels, and other poultry farmers have pestered me for the recipe of my balanced ration.

This will surely be brought to the attention of Inspector Liebenberg, who now, knowing where to look, may try to find some proof that there was once a human body on my farm. But I am certain he will not succeed. It would be no use slaughtering fowls wholesale in an attempt to find the ones that have partaken of Susan – with the object of testing them for any traces of human cells in their make-up. I have seen to it that every fowl that shared that human ration has itself been consumed by other humans.

As people do not eat the bones of fowls, I made a point of selling, or giving, the dressed fowls only on condition that I was allowed to collect the bones afterwards. My explanation of this was that I was short of bone meal. These bones then went through the mill with other bones. A nice example of *ad infinitum*. Also, there are a large number of anonymous people, who, in a remoter degree, took part in this deplorable cannibalism. I mean those who ate the eggs that were laid by the hens.

Then Inspector Liebenberg will no doubt think of the manure. I wouldn't bother if I were he. Every bit of it has been spread over my uncultivated land and thoroughly ploughed in. Alas for the Inspector, the plucked feathers, heads, legs, feet, and innards of the dressed fowls sold or given away, after being burned or steam dried, also did not escape a hammering from the relentless mill.

I hope the good Inspector is not driven to trying to make this story of mine have the value of a legal confession. It would be a great pity if an ardent student of detective fiction, desirous of seeing a story of his own published, should be arrested because he invented a feasible explanation to account for the disappearance of a woman he happened to know.

I suppose I must also expect a certain amount of unpleasantness if this is read in our village. Some narrow-minded people will no doubt look upon me with horror and others will fear me. Since the main result of such attitudes will be that I shall no longer be pestered by casual callers, I shall be only too pleased.

A new development has occurred. My housekeeper, Ann Lissen, may turn out to be a disappointment after all. She is evidently falling, or has already fallen, in love with me and is becoming tiresome. Her solicitude on my behalf is overwhelming and I now seem to have no privacy left, for she is always fussing about doing things to add to my comfort.

I would not like to hurt her feelings by telling her to stop doing what she does out of the kindness of her heart. And as she has no technical qualifications, it would be a shame to send her away to battle for a job again.

I have suggested to her that she should go out more, especially in the evenings, but she said it was dull going about alone. She has no friends, or even relations.

Poor thing! She has no one to miss her, and I am most eager to rear especially good stock next season, fed with rich and well-balanced rations. The President of the National Poultry Society has expressed a desire to see my farm and the fine pullets and cockerels for which I am now so famous.

MORE ABOUT PENGUINS, PELICANS
AND PUFFINS

For further information about books available from Penguins please write to Dept EP, Penguin Books Ltd, Harmondsworth, Middlesex UB7 0DA.

In the U.S.A.: For a complete list of books available from Penguins in the United States write to Dept DG, Penguin Books, 299 Murray Hill Parkway, East Rutherford, New Jersey 07073.

In Canada: For a complete list of books available from Penguins in Canada write to Penguin Books Canada Ltd, 2801 John Street, Markham, Ontario L3R 1B4.

In Australia: For a complete list of books available from Penguins in Australia write to the Marketing Department, Penguin Books Australia Ltd, P.O. Box 257, Ringwood, Victoria 3134.

In New Zealand: For a complete list of books available from Penguins in New Zealand write to the Marketing Department, Penguin Books (N.Z.) Ltd, P.O. Box 4019, Auckland 10.

In India: For a complete list of books available from Penguins in India write to Penguin Overseas Ltd, 706 Eros Apartments, 56 Nehru Place, New Delhi 110019.

THE PENGUIN COMPLETE
SHERLOCK HOLMES
Sir Arthur Conan Doyle

Known and loved by generation after generation, this shrewd amateur detective, with Doctor Watson by his side, has earned a place in our national life and social history. Including four novels and fifty-six short stories, this volume sets out the exciting adventures of Baker Street's most famous resident:

A STUDY IN SCARLET

THE SIGN OF FOUR

THE ADVENTURES OF SHERLOCK HOLMES

THE MEMOIRS OF SHERLOCK HOLMES

THE RETURN OF SHERLOCK HOLMES

THE HOUND OF THE BASKERVILLES

THE VALLEY OF FEAR

HIS LAST BOW

THE CASE-BOOK OF SHERLOCK HOLMES

THE PENGUIN COMPLETE FATHER BROWN
G. K. Chesterton

Here are all forty-nine quietly sensational cases investigated by the high-priest of detective fiction, Father Brown. Immortalized in these famous stories, G. K. Chesterton's little Norfolk priest has entertained and endeared himself to countless generations of readers. For, as his admirers know, Father Brown's cherubic face and unworldly simplicity, his glasses and his huge umbrella, disguise a quite uncanny understanding of the criminal mind at work.

THE COMPLETE TALES
AND POEMS OF EDGAR ALLAN POE

The Fall of the House of Usher, The Murders in the Rue Morgue, The Pit and the Pendulum, The Gold-Bug – some of the most famous tales of terror, the most macabre detective stories ever written. Acknowledged master of suspense, Poe was also a poet and – as his stories of mesmerism and time travel prove – a pioneer of science fiction. In this collection, probing to the depths of the human psyche, Poe's haunted genius will chill and enthrall you.

THE PENGUIN KENNETH GRAHAME

Kenneth Grahame's writings have captivated children and adults alike for over eighty years. This volume contains his three major works: *The Golden Age* and *Dream Days*, his remarkable evocations of childhood, and his masterpiece, *The Wind in the Willows*, which was written originally to entertain his son, and has become a literary classic.

THE PENGUIN COMPLETE
NOVELS OF GEORGE ORWELL

George Orwell stands alone in English literature not simply as a gifted novelist but also as a perceptive essayist and writer of documentary books. This volume collects together the six novels which brought him world fame: *Animal Farm*, his brilliant political allegory; *Burmese Days*; *A Clergyman's Daughter*; *Coming Up For Air*; *Keep the Aspidistra Flying* and his remarkable futuristic vision, *Nineteen Eighty-Four*.

THE PENGUIN COMPLETE
STORIES AND PLAYS OF OSCAR WILDE

Widely quoted, razor-tongued craftsman of the *mot juste*, devotee of beauty and wit, parodist of affectation – Wilde was the inventor of Bunburying and a self-declared genius. This volume spans the flamboyant wickedness of *The Picture of Dorian Gray*, the bubbling comedy of *The Importance of Being Earnest*, and the stark prose of *De Profundis*. It also includes *The Ballad of Reading Gaol* and selections from Wilde's essays and letters.

THE PENGUIN BRONTË SISTERS

This volume contains three novels, differing in style, united in their emotional intensity, passionately held beliefs and creative power. In *The Tenant of Wildfell Hall*, Anne Brontë wrote the first fully sustained feminist novel with her story of the wronged wife. One of the most unforgettable love stories ever written, Charlotte Brontë's *Jane Eyre* spoke out – and still speaks out – for women struggling for personal autonomy and sexual fulfilment in a hostile society. In *Wuthering Heights*, Emily Brontë achieved a unique portrayal of the irresistible forces of sexual passion and of nature, straining against the physical confines of the world.

THE PENGUIN COMPLETE
SHORT STORIES OF FRANZ KAFKA

From 'Metamorphosis' to 'In the Penal Colony', Kafka's stories create a paradoxical world where individuals faced with the absurdity of existence continue to search for the truth.

'The author who comes nearest to bearing the same kind of relation-ship to our age as Dante, Shakespeare and Goethe bore to theirs . . . Kafka is important to us because his predicament is the predicament of modern man' – W. H. Auden

THE PENGUIN COMPLETE
LONGER NON-FICTION OF GEORGE ORWELL

All the force of George Orwell's vision, compassion and candour went into the making of these three books. In *Down and Out in Paris and London* he brings the poor of two capitals to life with eerie intensity; in *The Road to Wigan Pier* he exposes, in a series of painfully vivid descriptions, a cruel system; and in *Homage to Catalonia* he memorably describes the bright hopes and cynical betrayals of the Spanish Civil War.

A THREE PIPE PROBLEM

'With *A Three Pipe Problem* Julian Symons provides a stylish spin-off from the Sherlockian revival. It tells of a fading actor playing the Great Detective in a television series who persuades himself that by following in the master's footsteps he can solve a string of apparently unrelated murders: the Karate killings . . . The result is a four-star entertainment, right up to the finale when the inevitable fog swirls' – Matthew Coady in the *Guardian*

THE TIGERS OF SUBTOPIA AND OTHER STORIES

Julian Symons's vision of our world is witty, ironic and savage. All these stories have twists in the tail. In the suburbia of the title story, a respectable businessman helps to organize a small lynching party. A middle-aged man's infatuation with a beautiful girl leads him into a deadly double-cross in 'A Theme for Hyacinth'. How to plan the perfect murder – and dispose of an unwanted wife – is freshly considered in 'The Best Chess Player in the World'.

'Symons is far more than a maker of puzzles: he is a master of moral conundrums' – *Time*

THE PLOT AGAINST ROGER RIDER

Roger Rider and Geoffrey Paradine grew up together. Roger, now a successful businessman, is dashing and self-assured; Geoffrey, his employee, is timid, subservient and rather drab. Why, then, would the beautiful Mrs Rider choose Geoffrey as a lover? And why would Roger invite Geoffrey to join the Riders at their holiday villa in Spain? When Roger disappears, the entanglements increase . . . Just who is plotting against whom?

'Julian Symons is a splendid practitioner. Here he executes for our fascination another of the virtuoso dances for puppet men . . . Symons piles twist on turn, keeping graspingly just within the limits of plausibility' – H. R. F. Keating in *The Times*